# DAVID

# SIEGE

Copyright © 2007 David Humphry

The moral right of the author has been asserted.

Apart from any fair dealing for the purposes of research or private study, or criticism or review, as permitted under the Copyright, Designs and Patents Act 1988, this publication may only be reproduced, stored or transmitted, in any form or by any means, with the prior permission in writing of the publishers, or in the case of reprographic reproduction in accordance with the terms of licences issued by the Copyright Licensing Agency. Enquiries concerning reproduction outside those terms should be sent to the publishers.

Matador
9 De Montfort Mews
Leicester LE1 7FW, UK
Tel: (+44) 116 255 9311 / 9312
Email: books@troubador.co.uk
Web: www.troubador.co.uk/matador

| FIFE COUNCIL LIBRARIES ||
|---|---|
| HJ092287 ||
| HJ | 28/02/2008 |
| F | £7.99 |
| GEN | KY |

ISBN 978 1906221 737

Cover design by Alias DDesigns
aliasddesigns@mac.com

Typeset in 11pt Bembo by Troubador Publishing Ltd, Leicester, UK
Printed in the UK by The Cromwell Press Ltd, Trowbridge, Wilts

**Matador** is an imprint of Troubador Publishing Ltd

Manchester, England
November 1976

It had been a hell of a row. In the bathroom mirror Sally Beckford saw an only vaguely familiar face staring back at her. Her normally healthy complexion now had the look of putty, her short dark hair was standing on end and her amber eyes – which Gerald had always said were her most striking feature – were bloodshot from the tears. Those same tears had run her mascara into deltas of dried black streaks down both cheeks. She pulled off the remaining false eyelash. God knew where the other one was.

Running over in her mind the previous evening's turn of events Sally desperately wanted to feel sorry for herself but she just didn't have the time. This was another Monday morning and her time would soon belong to her editor on the *Echo*. Anyway, she decided, she was made of sterner stuff.

'You look like shit,' she mumbled into the mirror. 'And I feel like shit,' she added.

Her reflection smirked back at her. She hadn't felt like smiling since Gerald's bombshell the night before but self-deprecating humour was one of Sally's trademarks that had helped to make her one of the most popular of the team of reporters on the *Echo*. If nothing else it now served to jumpstart her senses and focus her attention on getting ready for work. She hurriedly ran the bath, turning the stiff brass taps that prompted the pipes to shudder noisily as the water fought to force itself past an air lock.

She was already undressed, having thrown her clothes into a corner when she returned to the flat the night before and ending up sleeping naked. Not that she had slept much at all. She recalled still being wide awake when she had seen the luminous hands of her alarm clock approaching three o'clock before checking again only moments later and seeing that it had turned seven-thirty. Amid the emotional maelstrom of the previous evening she had forgotten to set the alarm. At first she wasn't sure if she had slept at all but as her thoughts began to focus she knew she must have eventually dropped off after replaying in her mind, during several hours of wakefulness, the scenario between Gerald and herself and thinking what a bloody waste of eighteen months he had been.

She patted her stomach. She was in reasonably good shape, she reflected, but so she should be at twenty-two. Then again, she recalled the story she had done nearly twelve months before, not long after joining the *Echo*, on social deprivation in Manchester's inner city suburbs. Amidst a well-meaning regeneration programme that had ultimately created new slums for old she had seen women of her own age with three or four kids harbouring a strange mixture of despair and intransigence. One had proudly – or perversely – shown Sally her stretch marks after announcing that her three children all had different fathers. If this had been a shock tactic then it had worked although Sally was confident that the disquiet she had felt hadn't manifested itself in her expression. She hadn't wanted to give the girl the satisfaction.

Nevertheless, she was always prone to self-criticism about her body. For a start she was too short – or at least *she* felt so. True, she had been one of the smallest children in her class since nursery but had put on a late spurt of growth half way through grammar school which had topped her out at five feet three by the time she had reached the sixth form. She turned her back to the mirror and twisted her head over her shoulder. She had already decided that her bum was too big and her tits were too small to boot. Gerald had an infuriating habit of alternating compliments, and denials of her own less than exalted opinion of her body, with teasing about her height and anything else about her which she felt was less than perfect. He wouldn't be doing it any more though, the bastard.

She sank into the bath, the warm water enveloping her up to the neck, closed her eyes and shook her head in weary acquiescence. She would have to get on with her life.

The editorial office was the usual mixture of sights, sounds and emotions. Some people were busily typing their copy, yelling down the telephone in an attempt to drown out the hubbub around them or generally rushing around in the peculiar kind of ordered chaos that typified the more urgent aspects, sometimes more imagined than real Sally often thought, of newspaper production. Others seemed to be doing nothing in particular. Scanning the morning papers, fumbling in files or, as always on Mondays during the season, bantering with each other on the relative performances of the city's two football clubs on the Saturday. Sally wondered if any of them had endured a bastard of a weekend like she had. She doubted it.

'Hi, Sally. How was your weekend?' Carol Horne was one of Sally's co-reporters with whom she had struck up a particularly good rapport almost immediately after she had joined the *Echo*. Physically she was the antithesis of Sally with her Junoesque figure and long straight blonde hair. She was self-assured without a hint of arrogance and despite not being outwardly what most people would call beautiful she had a certain *je ne sais quoi* that men found attractive. She was never short of admirers but didn't seem to stay in the same relationship for more than a few months. She had often told Sally that she envied her steady relationship with Gerald.

'Don't ask,' replied Sally, her tone manifesting her exasperation while managing to conceal her relief that Carol had done. She needed someone to talk to and Carol would have a sympathetic ear.

'Oh dear,' said Carol. 'Trouble on the home front?'

'You could say that,' replied Sally, perching herself on the edge of Carol's desk. Gerald and I went for a nice quiet dinner at Enzo's last night. At least that's how it started out.'

'Then what?'

'Then he told me he had been offered a promotion.'

'That's great.'

'To manage the bank's operation in Toronto.'

'I see. But surely you were pleased for him?'

'Of course I was. But I did wonder about the upheaval involved and whether we should bring our wedding forward from next spring.'

'And?'

Sally paused and looked at the floor. 'And he said he felt we should give each other some space so that he could progress his career without affecting my life.'

Carol could see where this was leading. 'So he goes to Canada without you and the wedding's postponed?' she offered as the most optimistic scenario that now appeared possible.

'No. He goes to Canada and the wedding's off. He broke off the engagement there and then.' Sally subconsciously rubbed the third finger of her left hand where there had once been a diamond solitaire.

'Do you want to talk about it?' asked Carol, her voice conveying compassion with no hint of prying.

Sally ran through the sequence of events in the restaurant the previous evening. Enzo's was a pleasant enough trattoria. The food was invariably good and it lacked the pretentiousness prevalent at some of the other Italian restaurants in the city. The décor was mock Italian, with empty Ruffino bottles and sea shells entwined in fishing nets, and so was Enzo himself. With mousy hair and pale blue eyes he was not stereotypically Italian but he affected a strong accent peppered with *signore* and *signorina* and the occasional *grazie* as he shuffled about conspicuously, though not intrusively, attending to his diners' needs. He was in fact only half Italian – his mother was from Genoa but his father was of solid Lancastrian stock – and his real name was Lawrence. Nevertheless, his heart was in the right place and he always provided Sally and Gerald with a genuinely warm and effusive welcome so Sally could forgive him this one idiosyncrasy.

Gerald had clearly got something on his mind and at first had attempted small talk which was not at all his style. She had looked into his dark brown eyes and not for the first time had been drawn to his eyelashes. There was nothing at all effeminate about Gerald but there were plenty of women would kill for such long and shapely eyelashes – including herself she had thought. She had pondered how much she loved him despite the age difference. She had rarely been attracted to boys of her own age group and for this reason had neither sought nor found a steady relationship all through university. Gerald was thirty-four and had never married. She had met him while working as a barmaid during her final Easter vacation the year before and had been attracted to him right away. He was sophisticated without being smug and witty without being patronising. He had asked her out the second time she had seen him at the pub and they had never looked back. His jet black hair had the merest flecks of grey at the temples and his finely chiselled features were rounded off with the dimple in his chin which she found both sexy and cute. At a shade over six feet tall he was in Sally's eyes the epitome of tall dark and handsome and he was clearly on the fast track to a successful career in investment banking. And they were to have been married the following May.

Over pasta Gerald had revealed his decision and expanded on the reasons for it but Sally had switched off. She had heard Gerald's words but her brain had ceased to formulate them into any comprehensible sequence. She had felt herself tensing rapidly from her extremities inwards until she had found herself leaning across the table and tipping the best part of a bottle of rather good Barolo into Gerald's lap. That was one thing about Gerald. He didn't drink cheap wine.

Gerald had stopped in mid sentence with a look of mute disbelief on his face. By the time he had been able to react and turn the bottle upright his beige slacks were soaked with a dark red stain that would never come out. He had seen her in a temper before but she normally burnt on a slow fuse and it took sustained provocation before she lost it. This time had been different. He had never seen her so furious and it had become embarrassing as the other diners' attention had been distracted from their own conversations towards the more entertaining drama unfolding at table five. Enzo had become aware of an impending scene and nervously shuffled over towards them in the hope of defusing the situation. Sally and Gerald were valued customers, Gerald especially as he regularly entertained clients there, but equally he had wished to avoid any unpleasantness that might have discouraged any of the other diners from returning.

He had been too late. Before he reached the table Sally had jumped up and her bowl of spaghetti carbonara had followed the wine into Gerald's lap. She had then stormed out tossing her engagement ring at Gerald with a mumbled apology to the distressed Enzo who for a moment had been torn between trying to calm Sally down and attending to Gerald. Sally's impending departure had removed that decision from him and, as discreetly as circumstances allowed, he had called one of the waiters over to help clean Gerald up. Another waiter had had the presence of mind to fetch Sally's coat and, while holding it up for her to slip into, had somewhat incongruously wished her goodnight and hoped to see her again soon.

By then Gerald had lost any hope of retrieving his dignity in the restaurant and he had impatiently waved away the hapless waiter who had removed the bowl and was gamely trying to clean the spaghetti carbonara from his lap. He had followed Sally out of the restaurant and across the road where he had tried to pacify her and hopefully resume a calmer and more mature dialogue. No chance. Sally had let rip with a barrage of expletives which on later reflection had surprised even herself. There had then followed an animated bout of street theatre which had transfixed by the window most of the other diners as well as the waiters and Enzo himself.

'I'm sorry,' said Carol after Sally had finished the story. 'I know it's a pathetic and inadequate thing to say but really, I am sorry.' Sally liked Carol very much. Some people said she was hard but rather she was strong, the same as Sally thought she was strong until the previous evening. After all they were working in an essentially male environment and both were acutely aware that excellence would be a prerequisite for equality and acceptance.

'Hey, Sally! The boss wants to see you!' shouted a voice from across the office. It was assignment time and life would have to go on. Carol nodded in voiceless encouragement and Sally strode across to Harry Wagstaffe's office and knocked on the already open door.

'Come in Sally,' said Wagstaffe. He invited her to take a seat and scowled as he took a mouthful of coffee that had long since gone cold. 'You're late,' he reminded her.

'Sorry Mr. Wagstaffe,' she said. 'A bit of a domestic crisis.' She knew immediately that she had said the wrong thing but a simple apology had seemed insufficient.

'You've been here long enough to know my feelings on such matters,' growled Wagstaffe. 'Keep your working life and your private life separate. Leave your personal problems at home. I'm a newspaper editor, not an agony aunt.' The rebuke was mild enough by Wagstaffe's standards but she would have appreciated a gesture of sympathy. He didn't even ask what the problem was. A close relative might have been taken seriously ill for all he knew.

She apologised once more. 'It won't happen again.'

'Good,' said Wagstaffe. 'See that it doesn't.'

Wagstaffe's office mirrored Wagstaffe the man. It was a shambles of a place. Files scattered on top of the cabinets that were meant to house them, papers strewn all over his desk along with half a dozen paper cups that once held black coffee but were now stuffed with countless cigarette ends and a waste paper basket that had less in it than around it. It was an antiquated office that clearly hadn't changed, and had rarely even seen a lick of paint, since Wagstaffe had joined the *Echo* forty years before. The high ceiling made a mockery of the two bar electric fire's attempts to keep it warm during the winter but

Wagstaffe didn't seem to notice and certainly never seemed to care. On two sides there were windows looking out over the editorial office although the lower halves were thickly frosted denying visibility from either side to the other which was why he almost always kept his door open. He very rarely held confidential meetings in his office and it had never occurred to him to replace the windows with plain glass. The wall on the other side separated his office from that of the sports editor and behind him the plain glass external windows looked out over one of the roads leading to the city centre half a mile away.

Like all new employees on the *Echo*, Sally had been given a potted biography of Wagstaffe on the day she had started. He had joined the *Echo* straight from school at the age of fourteen in the footsteps of his father and grandfather who had both given long and distinguished service to the paper. He had worked continuously for the *Echo* since just before the abdication of King Edward VIII and notwithstanding the cliché had quite literally worked his way up from tea boy to editor. Harry Wagstaffe had seen and done the lot and was highly respected throughout the newspaper business. He had chalked up many achievements over the years but it had been the *Echo's* coverage of the Moors Murders for a readership in the community most tormented and traumatised by those horrific crimes that he had received his greatest plaudits from the rest of the journalistic world.

Wagstaffe's antiquated telephone rang. 'Excuse me a moment, Sally,' he said before picking up the huge black bakelite handle. Sally looked at his belly straining the buttons on his shirt and not for the first time wondered how a grotesquely untidy and dishevelled man like him could be such a highly respected newspaper editor. All of his clothes were of early to mid sixties vintage and it showed. While speaking on the telephone he subconsciously pulled at his frayed shirt cuff and ran his hand through his thinning grey-streaked hair, making it even more unkempt than it already was. He started to pull at the red braces that served no practical purpose as his trousers needed no accessories to combat gravity. To many on the *Echo* they were his trademark but Wagstaffe wore them simply because he had done so all his adult life and saw no reason to stop. His shirt and trousers were creased and the uninitiated might joke that he must have slept in them. It was no joke. He often worked through the night and had once again done so, snatching a few hours' sleep on a camp bed in one of the storerooms. This was evident from the accumulation of cigarette ends already in the paper cups and the fact that he was unshaven. If nothing else he would at least shave in the morning when he went home for the night.

Although some of the younger staff members considered him a scruffy anachronism it was hard to find anyone who actually disliked him or even didn't respect him. He didn't suffer fools gladly and if anyone fell short of his own high journalistic standards he let them know about it in no uncertain terms but equally he was never short of praise for a reporter who came up with a good story. The more senior members of the team held him in high professional regard and were fiercely loyal to him.

Sally reflected that Wagstaffe looked every part the confirmed bachelor he was and that if ever a man needed a woman's touch it was he. That thought was quickly superseded by the more immediate concern over what her next assignment was to be. Right now she needed to put the business with Gerald at the back of her mind and throw herself into her work.

But here was another source of frustration. Sally had been at the *Echo* just over a year, having been taken on by Wagstaffe following a recommendation from a friend who ran a local clothing manufacturing company to target graduate recruitment. 'They're clever, they're keen and they're cheap,' he had been told. Most other newspapers in the region had already been doing precisely this for some years but Wagstaffe was of the old school and had needed to be convinced. Spared a starting assignment as tea girl only because Wagstaffe's friend advised him that while graduates might be cheap they were not stupid and would be gone in no time if they were given too menial a position, Sally began as a junior reporter covering weddings, fetes and such like.

Her time as editor of her university newspaper had stood her in good stead and Wagstaffe had soon realised that she had outgrown her initial role almost immediately and gave her the inner city social deprivation story to cover when the reporter originally assigned to it had been taken ill. He had complimented her on a decent job and had promptly assigned her to cover local human interest stories. These could range from the banal (a woman retiring after thirty-five years running a sub post office) to the ridiculous (a 'talking' dog) and were rarely even moderately interesting to cover. She had in fact only really enjoyed doing the social deprivation story and had become increasingly disillusioned with the human interest assignments. Her frustration had become evident to the rest of the staff and she had to put up with occasional jibes from the office comedians especially after the talking dog story.

'Sorry about that Sally,' he said, replacing the receiver. 'I had a call earlier from the British Legion. They tell me that the last surviving Victoria Cross holder from the Boer War collapsed at yesterday's Remembrance Service in Manchester. It seems he was just cold and tired and wasn't badly hurt but they think it would be nice to run a story on him.' He scratched the stubble on his chin in contemplation. 'Christ, he must be as old as Methuselah.'

'The Boer War?' queried Sally. 'That was well before the First World War, wasn't it?'

'Turn of the century,' said Wagstaffe. 'My grandfather was out there for the *Echo*. Copped a dose of typhoid but eventually came back in one piece.'

'Any background?'

'Not much. They tell me that apart from him the last one died ten years ago so this old boy probably hasn't got long left. Anyhow he's living history and if you pitch it right it might generate enough national interest for us to be able to syndicate the story. He lives at his daughter's house in Didsbury.' Wagstaffe handed Sally a scrap of paper. 'Here's his name and address.' She knew roughly where it was as it wasn't far from her flat in Withington. 'We'll need a couple of pictures as well so I'll get a message to Mike to join you as soon as he finishes his first assignment. Off you go.'

The squally rain that had continuously assailed the city with varying degrees of ferocity since before dawn had finally eased off but the boisterous wind still hounded Sally as she locked her car. She pulled up her coat collar as she approached the gate to double check the number on the front door and once again wondered why so many people had house numbers that were illegible from the road. It was the right place and she walked up the flagstone path bordering the lawn covered with fallen autumn leaves to the front door of the neat semi-detached house. She had found the address without any problem but there was no sign of Mike. She rang the bell and a few seconds later the door was opened by a petite grey-haired woman in her sixties wearing a bright yellow apron over her dark blue dress and matching yellow Marigold gloves.

'Good morning,' said Sally. 'I'm Sally Beckford from the *Echo*. I believe...'

Sally was cut short. 'Ah yes,' said the woman enthusiastically. 'The Legion said someone would be coming from one of the papers. Do come in.' Peeling off her gloves to shake hands she introduced herself as Mrs. Bray and asked Sally to excuse her appearance. 'I was just cleaning out the kitchen cupboards,' she added by way of irrelevant explanation.

'Thank you.' Sally entered the long but narrow hallway with its light green carpet and faintly patterned matching wallpaper leading up the stairs to the right. Sally caught her reflection in a full-length mirror opposite the front door and self-consciously flattened her wind blown hair with her hand.

'My father's just been taking a nap in the lounge but he's awake now,' said Mrs. Bray, taking Sally's coat. 'Yesterday's fall shook him up a bit but fortunately did no lasting damage. I blame myself you know. Normally, I take him to the Remembrance Sunday service but this year my grandson took him. Not that it was the lad's fault though but I'm more used to looking after him.'

Sally wondered why on earth a young boy was entrusted to look after his great-grandfather. 'How old is your grandson?' she asked almost accusingly.

'Twenty-one next month,' replied Mrs. Bray. She shrugged and smiled. 'Not really a lad any more I suppose.'

His great-grandson's nearly as old as I am, thought Sally, reflecting that not only had she never known any of her own great-grandparents but neither of her grandfathers as well. Jesus, how old *is* this man?

'Follow me,' said Mrs. Bray entering the lounge. 'You'll have to speak up when you talk to him. He's a bit hard of hearing you know.' Sally had started to have a bad feeling about this assignment with visions of a senile incontinent drooling constantly while she yelled at him questions he couldn't comprehend let alone answer. 'Dad, there's a young lady from the *Echo* here to see you.'

Sally followed Mrs. Bray and met the gaze of a man who was clearly of a great age but whose bearing and demeanour were far from what she had anticipated. He was sitting erect in an armchair, wearing a blazer with regimental badge, grey flannels, white shirt and regimental tie and his black brogues shone like a guardsman's boots on parade. His face was creased with age, with a small dewlap under his chin, and bore several of the freckles and moles that are so often the companions of advanced years. His grey hair was sparse but immaculately groomed and behind his black rimmed spectacles his rheumy eyes had bags under them. His hearing aid bore testimony to his deafness but the only other sign of physical impairment was the sticking plaster on his forehead that Sally assumed covered a graze from his fall the previous day.

'Hello, love,' he said chirpily. 'What can I do for you?'

Sally found herself in awe and admiration of the sprightly old gentleman in front of her and took several seconds to absorb and appreciate the fact that she was in the company of the last surviving Victoria Cross holder from the last of Queen Victoria's wars. 'I'm Sally Beckford from the *Echo*,' she said finally, taking her pen and notebook from her bag. 'I believe you have a story our readers would be fascinated to hear.'

The Transvaal-Natal Border, South Africa
October 1899

Piet van Oppen hunched in the saddle and adjusted his oilskin cape as the rain lashed into him but he knew he would not be able to keep all of it from blowing into his face or invading his clothing. He pulled the brim of his hat down as far as he could without restricting his line of vision although by now visibility did not extend much further than the horseman in front of him anyway. He considered himself fortunate. Many in the commando had neither oilskins nor greatcoats and were in for an uncomfortable ride. The rain still seeped in everywhere. His shirt was already damp from a combination of rain and perspiration and he could feel the unwelcome wetness inside his boots and running down the crevice of his backside. Trickles of water ran down the side of his face into his short dark beard and down to the end of his nose from where he blew off the droplets only for others to form almost immediately.

Despite his discomfort he felt proud to be part of the host spread out around him. Men of all ages and backgrounds from all parts of the Transvaal Republic had mobilised into their traditional commandos when President Kruger had declared war following the expiration of his impossible ultimatum to the British government. No Burgher seriously believed Britain would withdraw her troops from the border areas, remove those who had arrived less than four months previously, turn back those in transit on the high seas and then agree to arbitration. Natal and the Cape Colony were British territory and neither *Oom* Paul Kruger nor anyone else remotely expected Britain to forego her right to station troops there.

As far as Piet was concerned he and everyone else in the Republic had realised that war had become inevitable long before the ultimatum. Like most Burghers he despised the damned *Uitlanders* who were becoming ever richer on the back of Transvaal gold but were still not satisfied. These speculators, financiers, engineers and mine managers now outnumbered the Burghers in their own land and had started to demand political rights. The vote. If they got it they would take over the government and the Transvaal would become part of the British Empire, one more territory towards the Cape to Cairo obsession of Rhodes, Milner and the other imperialists. They want our country, thought Piet, but they're not going to get it.

When the call to commando had been made Piet van Oppen had

been one of the first to answer it from his farm just north of Vryheid. So had his father, Koos. At the age of sixty-eight Koos looked every bit the patriarch in his black greatcoat, the tobacco stains alone breaking up the grey of his long beard with his equally long grey hair flaring out from the sides and back of his wide-brimmed black hat. He too was bent low over his horse against the rain. Piet knew there would have been no point trying to dissuade his father from joining the commando and in truth was confident that his father's strength, stamina and experience would make him a valuable member of it. He was still very fit and his marksmanship and horseriding skills were as good as any man he knew and better than most.

Piet was, however, beginning to think that Sannie may have been right about Christiaan. At the time he had felt she was just being an overprotective mother who would not let the child become the man but in truth he was still a mere boy.

As Piet and Koos had been making final preparations to leave, Christiaan had appeared complete with rifle and bandolier, his face bearing an expectant smile directed at his father.

'No, Christiaan,' Sannie had said forcefully. 'You cannot go. You're far too young and you're needed on the farm. President Kruger has enough of a contribution from this family with your father and grandfather.'

'Oh, ma,' Christiaan had groaned. 'I'm fourteen – and a quarter. I'm plenty old enough. Kobus Viljoen is going.'

'Kobus Viljoen is nineteen and old enough to take care of himself. Besides he's got two older brothers also on commando. Piet, you tell him.'

Piet had looked sternly at his wife. 'Sannie, these are momentous times. The boy will benefit from the experience and who knows, he may never get the opportunity to go on commando again.' He had reflected that at the age of forty this would be his own first experience on commando. All of his contemporaries in the area, as well as his own father, had ridden with the British against the Zulus in 1879 and against the British themselves in the First War of Independence a mere two years later. It had been his misfortune to miss the first campaign with a broken foot and the second through a near-fatal bout of smallpox as his pitted face testified. 'In any case pa and I can look after Christiaan just as well as the Viljoen boys can look after Kobus.'

Piet recalled how he had looked at his son with pride. His short-cropped mousy hair topped a round face that always seemed to bear a smile. That smile would have faded and no doubt have been replaced by tears if his plea to join his father and *oupa* had been rejected. He hadn't wanted to stay behind on the farm with his mother, sisters and baby brother and miss all the excitement. He had learned to ride at the age of three and could handle a rifle with skill by the time he was eight. Yes, he is old enough, Piet had thought. He can come on commando with us.

Sannie's protestations had gone unheeded as an overjoyed Christiaan had responded to his father's consent with a whoop. Sannie and the three girls would manage on the farm while they were gone. In any case it would only be for a few weeks, a couple of months at most. Just enough to teach the British once and for all to leave us alone, Piet had thought.

As they had prepared to mount up the womenfolk had gathered on the *stoep*, baby Dirk in Sannie's arms. Sannie's sobbing had prompted the twins to join in and even two of the maids had started to cry. Piet had often since recalled the sight of Katrien, his eldest and favourite child, standing impassively as they had been about to depart. It wasn't that she didn't care but there had always been a special bond between Katrien and himself. Words were superfluous. She understood him and supported him unconditionally. Sannie had hugged Christiaan so tightly that he had squirmed to free himself, partly through physical discomfort but mostly due to embarrassment. He loved his mother but didn't want her fussing over him like this. He was a man now and was about to embark on the greatest adventure of his life. Wait until Kobus Viljoen saw him.

Koos had gone back into the house and re-emerged barely a minute later. He had walked over to Christiaan and pinned on the top pocket of his jacket a silver disc with a clasp bearing the year '1879' attached to a golden yellow ribbon with two broad and two thin dark blue stripes. 'What is it *oupa*?' Christiaan had asked, squinting down at his chest.

'It's the badge of a warrior, Christiaan. Now that you are a warrior you must wear it.' Christiaan had been delighted, twisting the disc and reading out loud the engraved name on the rim. 'H. van Oppen, Strydom's Burghers,' he had said but had not comprehended the irony of it. He had become the proud wearer of his grandfather's Zulu War medal awarded by the British government and bearing the portrait of Queen Victoria against whose troops he was about to ride.

"H' for Herculaas,' Koos had said. 'But I never liked that name. I've been called Koos for short ever since I was five years old. Except by my mother. She insisted on calling me Herculaas until the day she died, God rest her soul.' Koos had guffawed loudly but only Katrien had joined Piet and Christiaan in echoing his laughter. It had been a special moment but had passed quickly. Within a matter of seconds they had mounted their horses and ridden off to join the rest of their commando.

Piet looked over towards Christiaan who was similarly hunched up riding on his right. Although his head had been down, instinctively he looked up at his father and grinned. Despite the unrelenting rain tearing at his oilskin and the exposed skin of his face and ears beneath his hat being continuously assaulted by the sharpness of the drops Christiaan would rather be nowhere else right now. Certainly not back on the farm with the women and children.

'How far before we make camp, pa?'

'Not long. It will be dark in a few hours. The commandant will call a halt when we reach a suitable place'. He does look so young, thought Piet.

Piet knew that his son loved him and trusted him implicitly, the same as he had done – and still did – his own father. Yet he could not help feeling a burden of responsibility, not just for Christiaan's physical safety and spiritual well being but also a deeper responsibility, one that gnawed at him with anxiety and not a little fear. He knew that Christiaan's eyes would be on him throughout the forthcoming campaign and he desperately wanted his son to emerge from the experience with his view of him, if not enhanced, then at least intact.

He also wanted to demonstrate to his own father that he was as capable and courageous as any other member of the commando and that, had he been given the chance, he would have acquitted himself well in the Zulu War and the First War of Independence. Koos had never indicated that he thought otherwise but Piet felt that fate had so far denied him the opportunity of gaining his father's unequivocal approval and needed to do so now or he might never get the chance again.

Damn this rain, he thought.

Having eventually called a halt for the night the Burghers made camp on a stretch of rolling grassland close to a small *spruit* now in spate with the unrelenting heavy rain. The tents were in the ox carts following way behind the commandos so everyone had to bivouac as best they could on the wet ground that the hooves of two thousand horses soon churned into mud. 'We'll bed down under here,' said Koos, indicating a small tree. It offered only minimal shelter but even the smallest respite from the remorseless rain was welcome. They unsaddled their horses and tethered them to the tree. 'It's going to be an uncomfortable night,' continued Koos. 'It's far too wet to build a fire.' There would be no hot meal that night and they would be unable to dry out their sodden clothes. Koos fumbled in his saddlebag and brought out several strips of *biltong* which he distributed between the three of them. They chewed listlessly on the dried meat, their hunger as well as their other senses being dulled by the continuing downpour and the cold.

'Where are we now, pa?' asked Christiaan.

'We crossed into Natal this afternoon.'

'Where are the British?'

'Not this far north,' interjected Koos. 'It's too far from any major town and this area has no strategic defensive importance. We'll see them soon enough but we need to make sure they don't see us. They know we're coming but we'll have to hit them hard, then withdraw and regroup and hit them again and so on.' Piet knew his father was right. The *Volk* had always had to fight their battles against numerically superior enemies and the key to their success, which historically had equated to their survival, was an offensive strategy based on mobility and defensively centred on the *laager*. It had served them well at Blood River in 1838 when a party of *Voortrekkers* lashed their sixty-four wagons together in a circle and destroyed Dingane's *impi* with concentrated musket and cannon fire followed by a mounted pursuit. When it was all over three thousand Zulu warriors had lain dead on the field of battle at the cost of just three Burghers wounded. It was there that the seven year old Koos van Oppen and his mother, crouching behind an interior wagon wheel, loaded muskets for his father to fire at wave after wave of Zulu attacks.

Piet was only too aware that his father had had his rite of passage at the age of seven and his son would have his at fourteen. At forty he still awaited his own deliverance.

The three generations of van Oppens huddled together as a cold wind blew down from the Drakensberg to make conditions even more miserable. Within minutes Christiaan had succumbed to a sleep in which exhaustion had overcome discomfort and Koos's snoring confirmed that he too had dropped off. Despite his own tiredness Piet's mind was too cluttered and his body too conscious of the cold and wet that seemed to pervade his every pore for him to drift into sleep. He lay on his groundsheet, his rain sodden blanket around him, in silent contemplation of what might lie in store for them in the days and weeks ahead.

Piet awoke feeling as though he had not slept at all to find that the rain had stopped. Christiaan was still asleep but Koos was already saddling up ready for the day's ride. It was still too wet to light a fire so breakfast would be *biltong* and water. Christiaan had to be roused.

'I thought I could sleep anywhere but you must have been born to ride on commando,' said Koos. Christiaan took this as a huge compliment from such an experienced campaigner. He fingered the cold silver of the medal and grinned at his grandfather.

'I want to be a brave and famous warrior like you, *oupa*.'

'All in good time, boy,' chuckled Koos. ' All in good time.'

The peaks and outcrops of the mountain pass through which they had emerged were thrown into sharp relief against the clearing sky as they rode further southwards into Natal.

'How far are we going, *oupa*?' asked Christiaan.

'All the way to Durban, boy. We'll push the *rooinekke* right back to the sea.' replied Koos enthusiastically. 'You've never seen the sea have you, boy?' Christiaan shook his head as Piet reflected that he too had never seen the sea. 'In Durban there are plenty of bananas,' continued Koos. 'So in Durban we shall all eat bananas.' Koos roared with laughter at the thought of thousands of Burghers riding into Durban and eating bananas by the Indian Ocean and the distress it would cause to the very English population there. Christiaan echoed Koos's laughter but Piet was in more pensive mood. It was an appealing scenario but only the Lord knew what dangers they would have to face and what obstacles they would have to overcome if they were ever to reach the sea.

As they rode on they emerged into a wide plain and began to see the plumes of smoke from a few scattered farms and homesteads among the green valleys in the distance. The body of horsemen crossed the Buffalo River at a point where it was normally little more than a stream, but now running deeper and faster with all the rainwater, and fanned out across the plain. The other two columns of Transvaal Burghers could now be seen far to the left and right of them and they had heard that their cousins from the Orange Free State were starting to make their way over the Drakensberg and would join up with them north of Ladysmith.

The following day they reached Newcastle and as they rode through the main street past the grey sandstone Town Hall a few Afrikaner sympathisers came out to cheer and handed presents to some of the Burghers. Koos was given some tobacco and Christiaan a tin of jam. The pro-British majority merely looked on in silence and Christiaan was unnerved by the look of hatred directed at him by a youth of around eighteen who spat on the floor as he passed. Beyond Newcastle the commando rested until nightfall when they set off again, an operation repeated the following day. During the second night's ride they reached a flat-topped hill overlooking the town of Dundee. 'The forward British army base is beyond this hill – Talana Hill,' said Koos. 'The first battle of the war will be here. It will be unavoidable.'

With rain falling in the pitch darkness as they approached the hill Koos whispered to Christiaan. 'No more talking from here. We want to give the *rooinekke* a nice surprise.' Christiaan nodded. The youngster's excitement was palpable and so far there was no sign that fear had managed to dampen it. However, Piet's stomach was in knots and his head was a tangle of emotions. Yes, he was afraid but not only of British lead and steel. Twenty years late he was finally going to – going to have to – prove himself at least an equal among his peers as well as a worthy father to his son.

At the foot of the hill they dismounted amid rumbles of thunder and handed the horses to one of the Burghers detailed to look after them. They were not alone in nervously adjusting their bandoliers before slinging their Mausers across their backs and starting to climb the steep but even slope of the hill. Christiaan rubbed the medal that had already become a talisman of sorts for him as he began his ascent with his father and grandfather on either side of him. The rain had made the rocks slippery but the increasing frequency of the thunderclaps served to muffle any accidental noise caused by a fall of loosened stones or the occasional Burgher's clumsiness.

Piet could hear his father's breathing on his left but there was no indication that Christiaan was with them. He felt frustrated at not being able to call his name just to make sure that his son was there. Don't be stupid, he thought. Of course he's with us. But, oh for a cough, a muttered curse, anything to show he had not become separated from them. Flashes of lightning exposed in fleeting diorama the sight of Burghers swarming up the hill. Piet caught a glimpse of Koos as he appeared in brief illumination only to vanish back into the blackness a moment later. But no sign of Christiaan! Then in the vividness of one particularly extended flash Piet saw that Christiaan's agility and enthusiasm had combined to propel him up the slope faster than almost everyone else and that he was only a matter of feet from the crest. Piet's heart was pounding at the thought of what might await his son when he topped the crest. The plateau overlooks the British camp so they must have pickets posted there, he thought. My God, they may have heard or even seen in the lightning flashes the Burghers' ascent and right now be waiting for them with rifles raised ready to fire a volley into the first line of Burghers over the crest.

Piet worked his way faster up the slope but slipped on a wet rock and crashed to the ground. Cursing under his breath, he dragged himself to his feet and continued at a half crouch holding his side. Another lightning flash revealed Koos now ahead of him but no sign of Christiaan. He must now be on the plateau, thought Piet, expecting a crash of musketry at any moment. Jesus, why didn't I make him stay at home? He ran on despite the piercing pain of the rib he knew was broken, scrambling, clutching and clawing his way upward until he reached the crest where he paused only to catch his breath before hauling himself over. By now there were many Burghers on the plateau but no sign of a British presence. Luck had been with them. Incredibly, through arrogance or carelessness, the British had neglected to picket the hill that was now in Burgher hands.

Piet got to his feet and pushed forward to the opposite crest overlooking the British camp, anxious to find Christiaan and Koos. If I keep in a straight line I'll surely find them, he thought as he continued wet and sore through the long grass, stumbling over more rocks and working around the thorn trees. Eventually he reached the opposite crest and dropped to the ground exhausted. He was aware of the close presence of others but, apart from the laboured breathing of some, the Burghers maintained their silence as the rain fell still heavier amid the sound and light of the thunderstorm. His reasoning told him that they must be safe as there had been no firing and no sound of distress from any direction but still he wanted to be sure. He lay shivering and wet with his silent companions on the crest feeling completely powerless and vulnerable. He knew that sleep would not come this night.

By daybreak the rain had stopped but the whole area was shrouded in mist and visibility was reduced to less than fifty yards in any direction. The silence was broken only by the raucous cawing of a knot of crows roosting among the blue gum trees that stood concealed in the valley below. Christiaan had hoped to see the British camp but that lay well beyond the limit of vision in the direction of the town. He walked with Koos through the knee-high wet grass close to the crest looking for his father and found him within minutes.

'Pa, you've been wounded!' he cried as he saw Piet sitting on a rock while a pastor tightened a bandage around his ribs.

'No, boy. Just clumsy. A broken rib – nothing serious. Are you and *oupa* all right?'

They assured him that they were and Piet thanked the pastor as he helped him to his feet. Koos offered him a piece of *biltong* which he took and tore in his mouth. He was hungry – they all were – but what he needed more than anything else right now was a mug of hot, strong coffee.

'We'd better take our place in the line,' said Koos. 'The mist is lifting and when the British see us they will throw everything at us. They may be careless but they're not blind.' As the three generations of van Oppens took their positions they looked down at the clearing scene with this side of the hill alternately precipitous and gently sloped. Piet was thankful that they had had the easier ascent and that it would be the British who would have to attempt the much more difficult climb under fire.

They had hardly heard the boom from further along the crest line before they saw a fountain of mud and earth burst forth in the valley below. One of the *Transvaal Staats Artillerie's* three Creusots painstakingly dragged up the hill during the night had announced its presence. The other two guns opened up and a second shell landed just behind the paraded ranks of an infantry battalion while a third exploded in the artillery lines scattering men and horses alike. The Creusots continued to bark their anger at the British and were accompanied by a few Maxim one-pounders. 'The ground's too wet,' said Koos as many of the percussion fused shells failed to explode in the muddy earth. A British field battery prepared to return fire while two more wheeled into position and unlimbered in the valley below.

Christiaan was squinting intently down the barrel of his Mauser. He knew the range was too long but he would be ready when the British started to advance as they must. Koos was calmly smoking his clay pipe while Piet nervously loaded, unloaded and reloaded a five-cartridge clip into the magazine of his Mauser. He knew that his moment was about to arrive and wished to God he didn't have to wait any longer. Not that he was particularly keen to shoot at British soldiers. He just wanted to do his duty and get out in one piece.

Puffs of grey smoke popped above and behind the crest in apparently innocuous concert until the screams of Burghers further along the line testified to the effects of the showers of shrapnel that sought them out among the rocks. This was not what either Piet or Christiaan had envisaged. They had expected firing into massed ranks of British infantry until the time came, as they knew from their Boer heritage that it must, for them to jump on their horses and ride away to fight another day. This was not cowardice. It was the only possible tactic for a small nation that could not afford heavy casualties among its commandos. Mobility and the instinct to know when to stop and fight and when to retire and regroup had long been ingrained in the Burgher psyche.

They did not have to wait long. The artillery exchanges petered out inconclusively as three battalions of infantry formed up in the protective bed of a *spruit* behind a stand of blue gum trees. 'Not long now,' muttered Koos distractedly.

'Not long now pa,' echoed Christiaan enthusiastically, finally looking up from his rifle sight. This is all a game to him, thought Piet. This is war and he's treating it like a buck shoot.

As soon as the infantry emerged from the streambed Christiaan squeezed off his first shot and within seconds the crest line was crackling with Mauser fire. Bullets whistled and tore through the leaves of the gum trees. Several soldiers dropped but the lines moved inexorably on. While Koos, still sucking on his pipe, aimed and fired carefully at individual targets, Piet shot clip after clip into the advancing khaki mass while reciting the Lord's Prayer. The infantry pushed forward. There are still so many of them, thought Piet but he saw their first line take shelter behind a stone wall in a wood on the lower slopes of the hill. The Burghers' concentrated magazine fire had checked their advance. Piet prayed that this would be as far as they advanced. He was discharging his obligations as he discharged every shot. If the British stayed pinned down, or better still retreated, the Burghers could withdraw with duty done and honour satisfied.

There was no sign of movement until an officer, accompanied by a mounted lancer carrying a red pennant, rode up to the gap in the stone wall, dismounted and by his arm movements was clearly exhorting his men to resume their assault on the hill. Suddenly he clutched his stomach and despite the assistance of his aide remounted with difficulty and rode back towards the camp. Christiaan let out a victorious shriek and Koos patted him on the back. 'Well done, boy. You just shot their general.' Other Burghers nearby added their congratulations and word quickly spread along the line that a boy among the Vryheid men had hit the general. Christiaan could see a smiling Kobus Viljoen away on the left waving in acknowledgement and revelled in his newly acquired celebrity.

'Pa, I shot the general.' Piet congratulated his son as enthusiastically as he could. He was proud of the boy but wished it were he being feted by the other Burghers, he whose name would reverberate around the campfires of the other commandos that night, he who would be the hero of the hour.

'Come on man. Give the boy a bit more encouragement,' said one of the Utrecht men next to Piet.

'Yes, yes,' replied Piet uncertainly. Searching for more of a response he added lamely, 'It's just this broken rib of mine. I'm not feeling my best.' He knew instantly it was the wrong thing to say.

'Hey, everybody! This man's son has just shot the general and all he can think of is his poor old broken rib!' the Utrecht man shouted down the line before shaking his head at Piet and resuming his fire. Piet felt humiliated and it was his own stupid fault. Koos continued firing in silence but Christiaan looked at him sympathetically.

'Take no notice, pa. You must have shot more *rooinekke* than me.'

The general's exhortations had had the desired effect, the line of infantry resuming their advance beyond the stone wall. Piet slipped another clip into his Mauser and emptied it into the advancing line but his mind was preoccupied with the twin destructive emotions of guilt and envy. All five shots failed to find a target.

Despite the devastating effects of concentrated rifle fire from the concealed Burghers and the difficulty of the ascent, the khaki soldiers were making progress. Men were dropping at all points but enough were pushing ever upwards to make the Burghers nervous.

Piet was only too aware what they would have to face if the British troops reached the crest. Like every Burgher Piet feared the bayonet, a weapon they never used despite their Mausers being equipped to fit them. Shooting a man from distance was one thing but the bayonet made it personal. Hand to hand fighting had never been a trait of the Burghers. That was how kaffirs fought. Kaffirs and *rooinekke*. Piet took aim at a young officer leading his men. The officer looked over his shoulder to encourage the men forward and as he turned to the front again Piet squeezed the trigger. The officer's head jerked back and Piet saw a fountain of blood spurt from his neck before his body slowly arched back and tumbled down the slope for a few yards before becoming snagged in a thorn tree and lying twisted in a grotesque pose. Piet fired again and again and again, slipped another clip into the magazine and emptied that, each time dropping a man in his tracks or sending him lurching backwards.

As he went to get another clip from his bandolier Piet glanced up to see a rifleman taking aim at Christiaan. God, no! In a split second he realised that neither Koos nor Christiaan had seen the danger and knew that he had no chance of reloading and firing before the rifleman shot his son. The noise of battle seemed to dull and the scene seemed to freeze as he fumbled hopelessly for the clip which his shaking hands spilled to the ground. He could see the rifleman drop his head slightly to perfect his aim and opened his mouth to scream but no sound emerged. A loud crack accompanied a puff of grey smoke in the air in front of their position and allowed Piet's scream to free itself from his throat.

'No! No!'

The rifleman fell like a rag doll. Several of his comrades also dropped as more puffs and cracks filled the air. The British artillery had resumed its shelling but its range was short and it was raining shrapnel on its own troops. The riflemen were thrown into confusion but the fusiliers of the other two battalions were pushing on behind them, forcing them to regroup and continue towards the crest. Word that they were firing into their own troops quickly reached the gunners and the shelling ceased, encouraging the khakis to climb the last and most precipitous section of the hill to the crest. It was time to go. Koos indicated the reverse slope with a movement of his head and Piet nodded. Christiaan was oblivious of the approaching danger and dropped two fusiliers with consecutive shots. Koos shook his grandson's shoulder.

'Come, boy. We've had enough excitement for one day.' Christiaan quickly realised the extent of the imminent danger they were in and knew that such an experienced campaigner as his grandfather would not pull him out of the fight without good reason. The three of them started to run across the plateau towards the opposite slope as the Utrecht man emptied his magazine into a group of fusiliers at close range, dropping five of them, before tossing away his rifle and throwing up his hands. The first fusilier over the crest shouted in a Dublin brogue 'You'll get no fucking mercy from me you Boer bastard!' and bayoneted the Utrecht man in the heart. Christiaan, who had instinctively stopped and turned, witnessed the death of the Utrecht man. He and the Dubliner simultaneously raised their rifles at each other and a single shot rang out. Blood oozed from a neat hole in his forehead as his head jerked back, his knees buckled and the body of the Irishman slumped backwards and hit the ground. By now more riflemen and fusiliers had breached the crest and the Burghers were in full retreat although a few had got caught up in close quarters fighting with the khakis or were trying to surrender.

'Christiaan! Run for the horses!' screamed Piet. 'Now!' Christiaan obeyed and caught up with them as they disappeared over the reverse crest and started down the slope where they passed the Viljoen boy's brothers half carrying and half dragging Kobus's inert body. His face was ashen and his hair matted with blood and Piet gagged at the sight of Kobus's brains oozing from a hole the size of a fist in the back of his skull.

They ran and stumbled down the slope with hundreds of other Burghers, men of Vryheid and Utrecht, Middelburg and Wakkerstroom, all with one aim – to retrieve their horses and ride as hard as they could away from the hill. If they had delayed their retirement any longer their comrades guarding the horses would have taken flight themselves and who could have blamed them? As they mounted their horses they heard a loud cheer. The British had taken the plateau and any Burghers still there would be dead or prisoners. They galloped off and could see dozens of Burghers already far in the distance. They must have left the battle well before they needed to, thought Piet. At least we didn't go until the *rooinekke* were almost upon us. Yes, he thought. We acquitted ourselves well.

Ladysmith and Elandslaagte, Natal
October 1899

Private Charlie Browell dropped his pack on the platform of Ladysmith railway station along with the rest of the half battalion ordered out in full battle gear. It hardly seemed possible. It had been only a few hours earlier that they had been informed, amid resounding cheers, of the victory over the Boers at Talana Hill yet they had been roused from their tents before dawn to prepare for a confrontation with the enemy. Walter had at first thought it was a practical joke and his expletive ridden response to the corporal who had woken them had already landed him on a charge. With his hands gripping his waist Charlie arched his back to stretch the muscles that had been in constant service for the previous two weeks digging defensive positions around Ladysmith.

An engine appeared pulling a seemingly endless procession of open trucks screeching and squealing along the platform until it came to rest, snorting and hissing, at the far end. Charlie sighed. These were the same trucks in which they had been conveyed from Durban and which had marked a new low in transportation discomfort. Even the Highlanders, fresh from India, had complained about having to stand for eight hours in cattle trucks unprotected from the relentless sun.

'The word is that the Boers are only fifteen miles away.' Walter Shawcross could always be relied upon to obtain the latest information circulating in the battalion and he was almost invariably accurate.

The sun was peeking over the eastern horizon with the promise of another hot day and Charlie was already perspiring after the march from camp. He took off his helmet and ran his handkerchief across his brow and through his short fair hair. 'That's less than half the distance from here to Dundee,' he said. 'What's going on?'

'I eavesdropped a conversation between two officers,' said Walter. 'From what I heard another Boer force has captured the railway station and some high ground at Elandslaagte and we're going there to drive them out.' He lit a cigarette and took a drag on it before offering it to Charlie. 'It seems the force at Dundee is preparing to retire on Ladysmith and these other Boers are blocking their route.'

It made tactical sense to Charlie but there was still no obvious explanation why a garrison of four thousand men had to abandon the base at Dundee. Charlie inhaled deeply and slowly released the grey smoke from his mouth and nostrils before handing the cigarette back to his friend. 'Thanks, Walter.'

Walter wasn't universally admired in the battalion. A number of men had felt the sarcastic edge of his tongue, a characteristic of Walter's that had resulted in more than a few fights before and since joining the army. Walter usually came off best and Charlie often thought of him as a born survivor. His wiry frame was in contrast to Charlie's own stockier build but he was deceptively strong and Charlie was glad that they had not had occasion to fight each other since they were at school together in Manchester a decade before. At twenty-two, the same age as himself, Walter was something of a paradox. Although his smooth-skinned features and plastered down dark hair made him less reminiscent of a serving soldier than of the choirboy he had briefly been, he had an old head on his shoulders. There were also those who considered him merely an opportunist who would use any ploy to part them from their pay, tobacco or rations and he was certainly not a man an inexperienced card player should challenge.

Walter wasn't stupid by any means but had plodded through school achieving no more than the average standard for a boy from a working class family but he hadn't cared. He had harboured no educational aspirations and as long as he could read, write and add up that was all he had felt he would need in life. Despite an apparent antipathy towards authority, in reality Walter was generally well disciplined and had proven a most reliable and valuable team worker in the fire brigade, earning three commendations for bravery in less than two years. He had originally started as a loom operator at Cheetham and Betts upon leaving school and had risen to become their youngest ever foreman before leaving for what he had described as something more exciting. Persistent rumours surrounding the pregnancy of one of his unmarried operators, however, led many to believe that Mr. Betts senior had suggested to him that his vocation lay elsewhere.

Charlie, on the other hand, had shown himself to be academically gifted. Mr. Hayes, the headmaster, had spotted Charlie's potential and pleaded with his father to apply for a scholarship which would have allowed him to attend William Hulme's from where he could possibly even have proceeded to university. Charlie's father would have none of it. As far as he was concerned a boy's schooling finished at fourteen after which he worked for the next fifty or so years. Additional education would be a waste of time and money. Who would want to employ a working class upstart who knew more than was good for him? At the time Charlie had not really been disappointed by his father's decision. He too knew that he would find it difficult to fit in with the sons of doctors, lawyers, merchants and the like and he had been content to conform to the natural order of things.

There was the thud of another pack hitting the platform next to Charlie. 'Full set,' said Walter.

'Hello, lads. Any idea what's happening?' Frank Hoyland was the third member of the trio who had been firm friends since their schooldays. Walter repeated what he had told Charlie.

Frank was the smallest of the three yet never seemed troubled by the weight of his pack or the hard physical labour they frequently undertook. He certainly never complained. Economic necessity had curtailed the formal education of all three of them at the age of fourteen but the situation had been most critical for Frank. His father had died in a drunken brawl, leaving him as the man of the house at the age of twelve with responsibilities towards his mother and younger sister. Frank's formal education effectively ceased at that point and although technically truancy, Frank's increasingly frequent absences from school were a result of taking on casual work at a candle maker's, a blacksmith's and anywhere else willing to employ him at a rate rarely above ninepence a day.

After leaving school officially Frank had worked in a succession of manual jobs, each one as badly paid as the one before. There was no doubting his application and capacity for sheer hard physical labour but he had simply been unable to settle in any one job for very long. When he was seventeen his mother had died of peritonitis as a result of a ruptured appendix and his sister had subsequently gone into service in Chester. Frank had become even more restless as there had no longer been any reason to keep him in Manchester or even England. He had contemplated emigrating to America but without any special skills to compensate for his lack of education or the confidence to chance his arm alone in a new land he had abandoned the idea. Petty theft had beckoned as a transient solution for the poverty in which he had found himself. Stealing fruit or pies from the stalls at Ardwick market had been how it had started but as his face had become known he had been forced further afield until he had been compelled to abandon the markets altogether. He had then progressed to stealing bicycles and had established an arrangement with a man on Hyde Road who sold them on or more often broke them down for parts.

Charlie had seen that Frank was on course to get himself into serious trouble in very short order and it was he who suggested they should join the army. In a way he had been in a similar predicament to Frank except that he had stayed in the same job at a firm of bookkeepers since leaving school. He had become increasingly restless and frustrated in a poorly paid position with no apparent prospects for advancement by which time he had started to regret the lost opportunity of furthering his education. He had begun to feel that if he didn't make a break soon he would languish forever in a rut of unfulfilled potential. At least the army offered possibilities for promotion.

Frank had been hesitant at first but the normally cynical Walter had carried him along with a level of enthusiasm that had surprised the other two and the decision was made. They had joined up at the recruiting office the next day, been allocated consecutive regimental numbers and remained as inseparable as they had been since childhood.

'How are you getting on with your book?' Charlie had lent Frank his copy of *Oliver Twist*.

'I'm about halfway through,' replied Frank. 'I'm enjoying it.' Since joining the army the previous year Charlie had been teaching Frank to read and write whenever time permitted. Frank had been as willing a pupil as Charlie was a teacher and had made good progress in reading but still lacked confidence when it came to writing.

'Time to go,' said Charlie as one after the other the side panels of the trucks clanged on the edge of the platform. Walter offered Frank the remains of his cigarette. Frank pinched the tiny stub tightly but delicately between his thumb and forefinger and managed two drags before it became impossible to hold. He ground it out with the heel of his boot and spat out a loose strand of tobacco.

''D' Company, single file into the trucks!' barked Colour-Sergeant Reid. The men clumped up the dropped side panels to enter the trucks and shuffled along inside to make room for as many of their comrades as possible. As the trucks filled up one by one so the railway officials closed and bolted the side panels. In a speedy and efficient operation nearly five hundred men of the battalion as well as another two hundred Natal Volunteers had squeezed into the trucks and were soon slowly chugging their way north out of Ladysmith.

The addition of the volunteers and the much shorter distance meant that the trucks were more crowded than on the journey from Durban and there was no room to shift position. 'If you get any closer we'll have to get married,' quipped a wag to his pal in their truck. The burst of laughter was of sufficient volume for Colour-Sergeant Reid to peer over the end of the truck behind to ascertain the cause. He said nothing. In all probability they would soon be in battle. Let them have a laugh.

Charlie found himself pinned against the right side of the truck facing outwards and as the train left Ladysmith behind one of the Light Horse squadrons rode alongside. 'Rather you than me, Tommy!' The accent was unfamiliar but the Light Horsemen were a mixed bunch of British expatriates and South Africans, mostly of British descent, who had been forced to flee the Transvaal when war had become inevitable. They had left behind most of their possessions and well paid jobs in the mines and other key sectors of the Transvaal economy but had brought with them an abiding hatred of the Boer.

In their new uniforms and slouch hats they look a fine body of men, thought Charlie. They were a recently formed and untried unit but then again, as Charlie reminded himself, he too had not yet been tested in combat. 'Good luck!' was all that he could think of as a response.

'The only ones who will need luck are those damned Boers. We're going to give them no end of a lesson. Then we're going to chase them all the way back to Pretoria.'

'We'll be there with you.'

'What? On foot? I don't think so, Tommy!' said the Light Horseman with a chuckle.

'Quiet in the ranks!' A captain had swivelled in the saddle and met Charlie's eye when turning back. His lean body and easy riding style made him look the part but Charlie had rarely seen such a contemptuous stare. The narrowed eyes, furrowed brow and thin-lipped mouth testified to something more than mere disapproval or lack of humour. Although by any standards a handsome specimen here was a man whose features were full of resentment, a bitter man one might say. Perhaps it was just his hatred of the Boers or nervousness at the thought of the impending scrap. Perhaps it was something more. The Light Horseman simply gave a shrug and faced to the front.

'Great organisation as usual,' said Walter as the battalion stood at ease on the rolling grassland. 'We've been stuck out here for ages.'

'At least the general has realised that there aren't enough of us to take the Boers' position,' said Charlie, indicating a ridge almost two miles away. 'I'd rather wait for reinforcements than risk getting cut up charging that.'

'We still haven't seen a Boer yet,' said Frank. 'Where are they?'

'Hidden out of sight until we advance within their range. No sense in showing themselves until they have to,' replied Charlie. 'We'll see them soon enough, don't you worry.' This would be the first taste of action for all of them but both Charlie and Walter sensed that Frank was becoming particularly edgy.

A drumming of feet on the *veld* and the muffled clatter of their accoutrements announced the arrival at the double of the battalion of Highlanders, sporrans swaying over the green and dark blue tartan of their kilts, while another infantry battalion deployed in front. The field batteries started shelling the Boer defences and prompted a response that overshot the guns and landed shells uncomfortably close to the infantry. Several hasty commands had them dropping their packs and moving off at the double to their right front where they deployed less than a mile from the Boer positions with bayonets already fixed.

'It's a bit late in the day for a battle, lads,' panted Frank. 'Especially as we've been on the go since before dawn. It's all right for those Jocks. They've just got here.'

Frank's right, thought Charlie. It's approaching five o'clock and there won't be much more than an hour's daylight left. Charlie looked towards the storm clouds gathering in their blackness beyond the ridge where the Boers had dug in. If they hasten their approach nightfall may come even sooner, he thought.

They continued forward and the battalion made good progress, soon linking up with the Highlanders on their right with the dismounted Light Horse beyond the Scotsmen. Spurts of dust flew up as bullets from long range rifle fire hit the ground around them. Instinctively they pressed on faster to the temporary but welcoming shelter of a small ridge on their right front where one by one they threw themselves to the ground. They were fit men but by now all three were breathing heavily and perspiring. Walter was the last of the three to crash to the ground where he got a mouthful of the ubiquitous red Natal earth for his pains.

'Jesus,' he complained as he spat out the dirt.

'If you hadn't got that lass into trouble you could have been working your shift at Cheetham and Betts right now instead of being shot at by a bunch of Dutch farmers,' said Frank, laughing.

'Fuck off,' retorted Walter, unamused.

'Advance!' came the cry from their company commander before they had barely had time to catch their breath. Similar commands to the other companies had the battalion rising as one only to run almost immediately into a barbed wire fence on the crest where Frank snagged his tunic. They were still half a mile from the Boer position but the bullets whizzed and whistled in the air around them. Frank was in trouble. The more he tried to free himself the more entangled he became and no one seemed to have any wire cutters. Charlie desperately tried to disentangle Frank while Walter twisted and bent the barbed wire with his bare hands. Not only was Frank in serious danger but while he was stuck on the wire they were all targets for the Boer marksmen. Others to the right and left of them were in a similar predicament and intermittent cries testified to bullets finding their targets. Charlie felt a bullet rip through his sleeve, miraculously without striking flesh, and redoubled his efforts. A man on their right made a choking sound and fell backwards, his comrade whom he was trying free from the wire slumping forward almost immediately afterwards. Walter's strength and determination succeeded in tearing several strands of wire enabling Frank to rush through with a few remnants dangling from his tunic. Immediately Charlie and Walter raced through the gap followed by more of their comrades. Elsewhere further gaps had been forced in the wire enabling a surge of kilt and khaki to press through and forward leaving only their less fortunate comrades on and around the wire.

Rushing forward they could now make out clearly the horseshoe shaped ridge of the Boer position ahead of them and a separate sharp topped *kopje* to the left of it – but still no Boers. The smokeless fire of the Mausers concealed the exact position of the Boer marksmen but their presence was announced by the continuing hail of lead intermingled with the first shower of the approaching storm. Ahead was a boulder strewn hollow that had to be crossed before they could come to grips with the defenders. Faster and faster they ran. Please God let us make it over the hollow, thought Charlie. Reassuring puffs of shrapnel bursts over the Boer lines gave them extra impetus but men were still dropping in the headlong charge. Gasping for breath they dropped flat at intervals and loosed off a few rounds before they hauled themselves up at the call of 'Cease fire! Advance!' and continued their charge.

The rain started to lash down as the first men reached the overhanging ledge of the ridge and clambered up. Charlie, Frank and Walter were in the following group and as they scrambled up to the ledge several of those in front were hit and fell back. One landed on Charlie, spraying him with blood from a head wound and sending him sprawling over the muddy ground. Raising himself on one knee, Charlie looked into the man's staring eyes and knew that he was beyond help.

Frank and Walter had disappeared over the ledge and Charlie resumed his climb amid the frenzied rush around him. Several men trampled over their dead comrade's face and body in their haste to gain the final crest leaving Charlie with a feeling of revulsion in the pit of his stomach. The future memorials will hail the heroes and respect the dead, he thought, but there was no respect for this young man lying dead on an African ridge with his skull shattered by a Boer bullet. Just a mad, undignified scramble to get in there and get it over with.

Charlie had lost sight of Frank and Walter in the headlong dash. He passed more dead and wounded, including Boers – the first he had seen, but thankfully not Frank or Walter. They must be up ahead and be all right, he kept reassuring himself, forgetting about his own vulnerability until a Highlander running alongside him pitched forward and fell to the ground.

The confusion of battle and the concentration of the attack had resulted in the units becoming mixed and Charlie saw a number of the dismounted Light Horsemen as well as Highlanders charging nearby. Men were still dropping but the enemy position was close and he saw a Boer gun captured by an NCO of the Highlanders and another by his company commander accompanied by Walter. The firing intensified from the Boer position as the defenders desperately tried to keep at bay the surge of men from Manchester, Scotland and British South Africa.

Charlie saw a man from his own battalion shot by a bearded Boer wearing a slouch hat. The man went down clutching his side and while lying helpless the Boer took aim again. Charlie screamed an obscenity and charged the Boer but could not reach him before a second shot finished off his comrade. The Boer suddenly became aware of Charlie's imminent presence and threw his hands in the air but Charlie was not to be denied. His momentum carried him forward, his bayonet crashing through the Boer's rib cage whereupon he fired his rifle. He yanked his bayonet clear and fired a few shots at the retreating Boers.

He walked over to the gun where Walter was still standing. 'Have you seen Frank?' Walter asked with concern in his voice.

'I was going to ask you the same question. I haven't passed him so he must be all right.'

'I hope to God he is. We became separated in the charge after we got over the crest but everything became so confused. The daft bugger was still trailing barbed wire from his tunic.'

There was still the occasional crack of rifle fire but the earlier chaos on the ridge had abated with the remaining Boers being rounded up, disarmed and taken to a temporary holding area for prisoners. They walked across the ridge and looked down past the sloping ground at the Boer *laager* in the hollow beyond and the *kopje* to the left. Charlie was still concerned about Frank but Walter was already contemplating the possibilities of plunder from the tents and wagons and began to outpace Charlie in his eagerness to see what lay inside them. As they approached the *laager* a small group of Boers appeared bearing a white flag amid a general order to cease fire. Within seconds all was quiet.

'Another lot for the rear,' said Walter over his shoulder.

'Perhaps we should accept their surrender and lead them back,' said Charlie, hastening to catch up with Walter.

'Don't be daft, Charlie. Leave that to an officer. There are plenty around. Let's have a look in these wagons.' A sudden shot felled an officer, leaving him writhing on the ground, and was immediately followed by the crackling of many more Mausers. Other officers did not have time to issue orders before, emerging from a fold in the ground ahead, dozens of Boers fired into the nearest concentrations of troops. Charlie instinctively dived to the ground and prepared to return fire. Damn! Empty! He groped for a handful of cartridges and used up precious seconds by having to load them singly into the magazine of his Lee Enfield. All around there was disorder as the Boers pushed back the troops who had thought they had already won the day and had been caught off guard. His magazine recharged, Charlie fired into the melee but his aim was hampered by the retirement of troops across his front.

Amid the general confusion he saw Walter waving the claymore of a Highland officer and trying to rally the troops around him. Within seconds Walter was left alone between the charging Boers and the body of troops who had pulled further back. Charlie leapt up, fired off the cartridges remaining in his magazine and charged into the mass of Boers, bayoneting the nearest one. Even in this mayhem, somewhere in his subconscious he realised that he and Walter were alone and about to die. He saw Walter swing the claymore and partially sever the neck of a Boer closing on him, then hack at the head of another. Charlie whipped his rifle barrel round to smash the jaw of one Boer then turned to plunge his bayonet into the chest of another. He knew that he, both of them, would be overwhelmed at any moment.

A rifle shot dropped a Boer bearing down on him and another gasped and gurgled from a bayonet thrust. Charlie was no longer alone. He saw at his side the short, stocky figure of McAdams followed by a slouch hatted Light Horseman and two Highlanders, then a dozen more. The troops who had been pushed back almost to the crest had rallied across the front and Charlie could see that Walter, still waving his claymore, was likewise supported. The Boer charge faltered but Mauser bursts were still being fired into the khaki mass and the Light Horseman fell with a wound to the thigh. The British were not to be denied a second time. The surge soon became irresistible and the Boers surrendered, first a few individuals, then a group or two and finally the whole.

The light was fading when Charlie caught up with Walter who was still carrying the bloodied claymore. 'Not a bad souvenir, eh?' said Walter proudly.

'Where did you get that?' asked Charlie. 'And where's your rifle?'

'A bullet smashed the stock so it was useless. I threw it away and picked this up off a dead officer. It was the nearest weapon I could find.'

'You're a hero and no mistake. You rallied the entire line.'

'That's right enough. You'll probably get a medal, so you will.' It was the distinctive Ulster accent of McAdams. 'When we saw you waving that thing about we thought we'd better counter attack before you got yourself killed.'

Despite being in the same company neither Charlie nor Walter knew McAdams very well. In fact no one seemed to. McAdams was one of the longest serving privates in the battalion and had seen action on the North West Frontier almost a decade before. He was something of a loner and rarely socialised. Charlie had never seen him take a drink although there were stories of a drunken past and a time as a bare knuckle prize fighter. He certainly had the build for it. Being a man of few words and having an outwardly surly manner no one asked him any questions about his past and no information was volunteered. Nevertheless, the officers and NCOs considered him almost a model soldier and it was generally considered that he would be a good man to have with you if you ever got into a scrape. Charlie could now vouch for that.

'Have you seen Frank Hoyland?' Charlie asked McAdams. He hadn't and was himself looking for Colour Sergeant Reid whose last reliable whereabouts was the ledge where Charlie had last seen Frank.

In the left distance they heard the thundering hooves of a body of mounted troops. One squadron each of Lancers and Dragoon Guards had accompanied them out of Ladysmith twelve hours before and had patiently waited in the wings for their call to action. Their time had come. Through the gathering gloom they could make out the British horsemen charging into the fleeing Boers whose mounts were no match for the cavalry horses. They crashed into the retreating flank of the Boers without check or mercy, and wheeled and charged twice more before finally reining in to inspect the damage.

'Poor bastards,' said Walter.

'What?' said McAdams. 'There but for the grace of God go you, my friend. Don't you realise how close you came to meeting your maker? Do you think those Dutchmen would give a damn about you – or your pal Hoyland come to that?'

An officer appeared appealing for volunteers to help locate the dead and wounded. Some men sloped off to look for food and a place to rest but Charlie, Walter and McAdams immediately stepped forward.

'Go and get lanterns and some extra field dressings from the quartermaster,' said the officer. 'Whenever you find a wounded man, call for medical attention if there is an RAMC doctor or orderly nearby. If not, assess the seriousness of the wound, apply a field dressing, make the man as comfortable as possible, and mark the position if you can before going for help. The locations of the dead are to be notified to the NCO in charge of one of the burial parties.'

'Yes, sir,' confirmed all three simultaneously.

'In case you are in any doubt,' added the officer, 'bear in mind that these instructions apply equally to the enemy's casualties.'

McAdams split off from Charlie and Walter as soon as they picked up the lanterns. He was going to search alone for Colour Sergeant Reid just as surely as they were going to concentrate on looking for Frank. If they found anyone else all well and good but locating Frank was their priority. No one they had asked could recall seeing him since just after he cleared the ledge and their concern was etched on their faces.

The rain had stopped but the storm clouds remained to blot out the moon and it was becoming cold. What was miserable enough for a fit man would be an extra agony for the wounded. The area was pitch black apart from the glow of the many swinging lanterns. The cries and groans of the wounded of both sides pierced the still darkness as did the calls of their comrades, Briton and Boer, searching for them.

'Frank! Frank Hoyland!' shouted Charlie and Walter in turn. In the darkness they soon lost the geography of the ridge. The ledge would be the best place to start from but neither was sure where it was. They were going to have to cover the area as well as they could and hope they found Frank alive. Walter called out his name again.

'If we find the bastard drinking tea by the company campfire I'll kill him,' said Walter.

'If we do, I'll thank the Lord. Then I'd let you.' They both laughed nervously but knew deep down that, dead or alive, Frank was somewhere on the ridge.

Charlie stumbled on an inert figure and shone the lantern into the face of a Light Horseman. It was the man who had bantered with him during the train journey that morning. The neat bullet hole in his forehead was a trademark of the Boer marksman and testimony to the accuracy of his shooting. A Boer lay beside him, still gripping the barrel of the colonial's carbine which had killed him, the pair frozen in their death struggle.

'Over here!' they heard a voice shout from the direction of a lantern some forty yards away. 'Over here you bastards! He's still alive!' It was the unmistakable voice of McAdams. He had found Colour Sergeant Reid. Two more flickering lanterns hurried over towards McAdams and bobbed down as their bearers began to treat Reid amid a flood of expletives from McAdams.

The groans that drew them back came from a wounded Boer, his femur shattered by a bullet. Walter applied a field dressing even though it was of little use and called out for medical assistance while Charlie offered the Boer water. He drained what was left in the bottle, the water pouring down the side of his mouth over his long black beard, before pausing for breath and contorting his face in agony. He thanked Charlie as a lantern hurried towards them in response to Walter's call.

*'Kom hier! Drie Burghers en een Engels!'* came a cry to their left. 'Three of ours and one of yours,' said the Boer, wincing with pain. 'A doctor is here for me now. Go and help your man. Good luck – and thanks again.' Charlie and Walter hurried over towards the lanterns from where the cry had come and found two Boers bent over the bodies of their comrades in a small sandbagged emplacement. All three had been bayoneted. A man of their battalion was propped up against the inner wall of sandbags, his legs outstretched and his helmetless head bent forward. They rushed to him with their lanterns and Charlie gently lifted up the soldier's chin. Blood that had poured from a head wound had congealed, obscuring most of his face, but even in the light of their lanterns they could see that it was Frank.

Dundee, Natal
October 1899

The van Oppens picked their way through the detritus of what had only a few days ago been the British Army's forward base in Natal. Four thousand British soldiers had been camped here, had fought a battle against them and supposedly won, thought Piet. And now, apart from the wounded and the medical staff who were left to care for them, they were gone. Burghers were going from tent to tent looking for loot. The Tommies' tents were unlikely to yield much of value but the officers' tents and the medical stores would surely contain something of interest. For some Burghers that would be some compensation for having let the British slip away when they had them trapped. And trapped they had been, on three sides, despite their so-called victory at Talana Hill — until they had sneaked away towards Ladysmith under cover of rain and darkness three nights later.

A Burgher emerged from a tent wearing an officer's red mess jacket and swigging from a bottle of champagne. He slipped on the churned up muddy surface and ended up on his backside, laughing uncontrollably at his ineffectual efforts to regain his footing. He was thoroughly drunk and enjoying every minute of it. Another was marching around banging a regimental band's bass drum. Everywhere there were Burghers dashing in and out of the tents with souvenirs and plunder.

'This is crazy,' said Koos, clenching his fists in frustration. 'The British are marching away unmolested while our generals dither and our Burghers get drunk.' Piet understood the Burghers' exhilaration but knew that their task would be that much more difficult when the Dundee force made it back to Ladysmith and augmented the garrison there. The chance to deal the Britishers a crushing blow had gone for the want of decisive leadership and self-discipline.

Christiaan ducked into a tent and emerged a few minutes later with a bugle. The tortured note it squealed was disproportionate to the effort he put into trying to blow it. His face was red and his ears throbbed. 'Can I keep it, pa?' he asked. Piet was about to voice his disapproval of his son's small part in the looting spree with a blunt refusal when Koos put his hand on Piet's shoulder.

'Let the boy have it, Piet. He did well. We all did. Let him take a souvenir from his first battle. It's only a trivial thing.'

Reluctantly Piet agreed. 'But nothing more. Understand?'

'Yes, pa. Thank you.' Christiaan's eyes caressed the instrument as he read the regimental inscription on it. Another attempt to blow it was no more successful than the first so he fastened a length of cord to it and hung it around his neck. He liked going on commando. Now he had a medal *and* a bugle. Who knew what else he might pick up by the time they reached the sea. 'I promise I'll have learned to play it before we get to Durban.'

'Somehow I don't think we're going that far,' Koos confided to Piet.

'What makes you say that?'

'We lost our chance here. The British were isolated with no chance of reinforcements. They would never have dared to weaken their garrison in Ladysmith by sending more troops up here. We could have destroyed the British in camp with our big guns or smashed their retreating column and sent their whole Natal field force scurrying to the other side of the Tugela River at least. The whole of northern Natal would have been in our hands in days. But now.' Koos paused and sighed. 'Now we will have to take Ladysmith.'

'But surely you believe we can do that.'

'Piet, there will be at least twelve thousand troops in Ladysmith within a few days when the Dundee garrison gets there. We will have to attack it or invest it. Either way we will have problems. If we attack we'll risk a scale of casualties the republics cannot afford. If we lay siege we'll lose time and each day that passes will bring nearer the reinforcements the British are preparing. The one thing we don't have is time.'

What his father said made sense but the mood of the Burghers in the camp was anything but mindful of the situation they would face in the coming weeks. They had driven the *rooinekke* away and were going to push them all the way back to the sea.

They came to the field hospital area with its huge Red Cross flag flying among the tents. There was a commotion inside one of the tents that spilled out of the flapping entrance in front of them. Two Burghers were struggling with a large chest and a bespectacled man with a Red Cross armband on his British sergeant's uniform pulled at the sleeve of one of them. 'For God's sake man we need those medicines for our wounded. Our entire supply of morphine is in that chest.'

'We have wounded too,' replied the Burgher. 'Don't worry. We won't take it all but you'll have to share it.' The sergeant put his hands to his head in despair and ran back into the tent where another Burgher was rifling through a drawer of surgical instruments.

The van Oppens moved further on where the situation was much more tranquil. No drunken Burghers, no looting. Piet entered one of the tents where a surgeon was amputating a soldier's leg. The surgical team were too busy to notice him and he turned to leave just in time to prevent Christiaan from walking in. 'What's in there, pa?' he asked.

'A brave soldier. Let's go.' Piet then looked inside a bell tent adjacent to the operating theatre tent where there were two neat rows each of about twenty cot beds all containing wounded British soldiers. Their wounds were clearly of varying severity but all had been unfit to join the forced march to Ladysmith. Some soldiers were sitting up, some lying down. Some were swathed in bandages while others had lost a limb. A doctor wearing the uniform of a captain in the Royal Army Medical Corps beneath his open white coat was unravelling the bandage of a man with a head wound while an orderly stood by with a large kidney bowl containing fresh dressings, antiseptic and forceps. He looked up at them with scarcely disguised contempt.

'There's no loot for you here, Boers. Only pain and honour.'

'We bleed too, Englishman,' said Koos. 'We too have our wounded, our pain, our honour.'

'Well, I can guarantee that you'll have plenty of pain before this war's over but you'll never have any honour.'

'Why do you say that?' asked Piet.

'Because your guns shelled this hospital the day after the battle and several of the men here were wounded again.'

That can only have been an accident,' said Piet. 'Our people are not like that.'

The doctor stood up and hustled Piet out of the entrance. 'Look,' he said, pointing to the revelling Burghers. 'That is what your people are like. Now get out.'

'Don't take it to heart,' said Koos as they left. 'He knows deep down that our guns didn't deliberately target his field hospital. He's trying to care for his patients and keep as many of them as possible alive. He's been abandoned by his comrades and is effectively our prisoner. He's under enormous pressure.'

'I suppose so,' said Piet.

'And he's right about one thing.'

'What's that?'

'There will be plenty of pain for us, for everybody, before the end of the war.'

They moved on and out of curiosity looked inside some other bell tents, all containing similar scenes of overworked medical staff caring for their wounded, until they came upon a smaller tent outside which several Burghers were gathered. Koos recognised one of the commandant-general's aides, a man in his late fifties with similar weather beaten and grizzled looks as himself. They had been in the same unit together in the Zulu War and ever since had remained on good terms with each other without exactly becoming close friends. They greeted each other warmly and moved to one side for a conversation. After a couple of minutes Koos returned and without saying a word took Christiaan's arm and led him into the tent. Puzzled, Piet followed.

Inside the tent was a single bed where a middle-aged man with thinning black hair and a moustache was laying, attended by two doctors, one a British army major and the other a Burgher. His face was pale and the perspiration dotting his brow was being carefully dabbed by the Burgher while the British doctor pulled back the sheets revealing his heavily bandaged stomach. There was some blood on the bandages and the movement when the doctor started to unravel them caused the patient's face to contort in agony.

'I'm sorry sir,' said the doctor. 'But I need to check your wound and change your dressing.' The patient winced again. 'Bring some morphine,' the doctor snapped at an orderly who ran out in the direction of the medical stores where the van Oppens knew he would not find any.

'There's your general, boy,' said Koos to Christiaan. The youngster looked up at his grandfather with a mixture of shock and surprise.

'You mean....,' he began.

'Yes', said Koos. 'This is the British General Symons. The general you shot during the battle. You remember when all the Burghers around us were cheering you?'

Piet began to feel as uncomfortable as Christiaan looked. He did not understand why his father was doing this to the boy.

'Will he live?' whispered Christiaan with genuine concern.

Koos looked him in the eye. 'He took a gut shot, boy. It may take a couple of days or a couple of weeks but a gut shot is invariably fatal in the end. He'll die all right, your general. My guess is he won't last the night.'

Christiaan bowed his head in silent contemplation. The proximity of the mortally wounded man – he may have ranked a general but essentially he was a man like all the others – had made a mockery, an obscenity even, of his euphoria when his shot struck home. Piet led him out of the tent and flashed a questioning look at his father.

'Now he knows,' said Koos simply. 'Now he knows.'

Ladysmith
October 1899

The recent heavy rain had churned up Murchison Street into a quagmire which both the ladies and gentlemen of the town crossed gingerly to avoid smearing the red brown slime over their shoes and lower clothing. Murchison was the main thoroughfare through Ladysmith, a quiet backwater notable only for its location at the junction of the railway from Durban and Pietermaritzburg to the Transvaal on one line and to the Orange Free State on the other. It had, however, assumed a military and strategic significance two years earlier when the British army had decided to make the town its main supply base and training area in Natal. Nestled in a loop of the Klip River, it was a hot and dusty place susceptible to flooding and disease and was hemmed in on all sides by a series of hills and ridges. What was a convenient location for an army base in peacetime was by no means an ideal place to defend in time of war.

    Within the town itself rose a steep ridge on top of which was the convent that General White had commandeered as his headquarters. The rest of the town was flat with the unpaved streets laid out in a grid pattern although those running across Murchison and the parallel street to its east soon petered out. There were few substantial buildings. Completed only six years previously, the brown sandstone town hall with its portico and clock tower was the centrepiece of Murchison and indeed Ladysmith itself. A little further down on the opposite side of the street was the Royal Hotel with its ornate wrought iron balustrade and first floor balcony. Once a favoured stopover for Natalians making their way to the gold fields of the Rand, it was now the haunt of journalists, war artists and sundry southern African celebrities there to witness and report on the unfolding events of the Natal campaign. Further down was the single storey Crown, an older and less favoured hotel with its gabled frontage and covered entrance jutting out on the pavement but nonetheless also full of newsmen looking for a story. Opposite the Crown were the Dutch Reformed Church and the small stone fort hastily built at the time of the Zulu War twenty years earlier but now serving as Ladysmith's post office. Hardly more then a minute's stroll from the post office and at the edge of habitation was All Saints Church built from locally quarried cut flagstone and the spiritual centre for the town's Anglican population. Add in a few stores and businesses and that was Murchison Street.

The quality of the residences was variable. Some of the stone and clapboard houses were substantial and attractive with gardens where azaleas bloomed around an extensive lawn and a few acacias or blue gum trees were all that was necessary to mark their boundaries. The meaner houses tended to be shabby affairs, often with a tin or corrugated iron roof. What was not in short supply was land and even the poorest residences had a plot attached. A solitary peach or apple tree there was replicated ten or twenty fold in the orchards of the wealthier inhabitants while pigs, ducks and chickens snuffled, shuffled and scratched around in many gardens. Most homes had at least one domestic or maid supplied from the local native population.

Charlie and Walter had walked down from the military camp at Tin Town and across the Oval cricket field towards the back entrance of the Town Hall which was now serving as Number One Stationary Hospital. They entered one of the administration tents and after receiving a desultory response from a disinterested RAMC corporal made their way through a throng of doctors, nurses and orderlies into the Town Hall building and what had formerly been the council chamber but was now ward two.

Charlie clicked the catch of the brass handle and pulled one of the two frosted glass doors. 'Christ, this place stinks,' said Walter. The smell of iodoform and disinfectant hit them immediately they entered the ward and caught uncomfortably in the back of their throats. But there was something else. There was the smell of decay, putrefaction and death. The most careful treatment that circumstances would allow had been defeated by sepsis and gangrene which had nurtured and developed inside the wounds of some of the men. Here were the men wounded at the battle of Elandslaagte and some would not survive.

'Where do you men think you're going?' demanded an authoritative voice that belied its owner's appearance. A slip of a girl, thought Charlie, and very pretty too, especially in that blue uniform with the white apron. The nurse hitched up her skirts and marched towards the pair. 'I said where do you think you're going?'

Charlie became flustered. Walter noted his unease and stifled a laugh. 'I...er, I mean we... have permission from our company commander....' His voice tailed off as he fumbled in his pocket for the pass slip that authorised their absence from camp.

'I'm not interested in military paperwork,' snapped the nurse. 'I'm only interested in hygienic nursing. Don't you think we have enough to contend with without people like you?' she added, lowering her eyes to the floor. Their own eyes followed hers and locked on to their boots. They had kicked off much of the mud on the steps outside but there was still plenty clinging to their uppers. As they followed her disapproving gaze they twisted their necks to see behind a trail of mud that was until very recently adhered to their soles. They understood immediately and even the normally phlegmatic Walter became uncomfortable. They were genuinely embarrassed at their gaffe but were even more so at receiving a dressing down from a young nurse and a very attractive one at that. Their predicament caused much amusement among the less badly wounded patients, including Frank who was sitting up in the last bed on the left row holding his bandaged head as though it would fall off from laughing too much.

Charlie started to mumble an apology but the words would not come out properly. 'I.. er, we.. er.'

'Didn't think,' offered Walter sheepishly.

'No, you didn't. Well, before you get any older you can both get mops and buckets from the ward orderly, clean up that mess and disinfect the floor from here to the doors.' Suitably chastised and amid the jeers and mock encouragement of the patients, both men set about restoring the part of the tiled floor they had adulterated to the pristine cleanliness of that of the rest of the ward.

'And when you've finished,' interjected the nurse, 'you can leave your boots outside the ward and put on these.' She tossed two pairs of cotton overshoes at them and went back to the patient whose dressing she had been changing when Charlie and Walter had entered her realm.

After finishing their unexpected task they shuffled like novice skaters in the loose fitting overshoes down the ward towards Frank, passing every other bed on the way. They looked down all the way, partly through trepidation and partly to avoid the mocking gaze of the other patients. Charlie prayed that they would not add to their humiliation by slipping on the highly polished floor and falling flat on their backsides.

'How are you Frank?' asked Charlie when they had reached Frank's bed and recovered their composure.

'I've got the mother and father of all headaches and a ringing in my ears but otherwise I'm fine,' replied Frank when he had stopped laughing. 'You've already met Nurse Dyson,' he added, nodding towards one of the beds opposite where she was attending to her patient.

'Bit of a tartar,' said Walter in a half whisper.

'She's a Godsend, an angel,' said Frank sincerely. 'I don't know when she rests. She seems to be on duty all the time. She takes very good care of us, particularly the badly wounded and dying.'

It was the first time that Charlie and Walter had seen Frank since they had found him on the field at Elandslaagte. They had thought he was as dead as the three Boers he had bayoneted. Even when the RAMC sergeant had found a pulse they did not raise their hopes as Frank's bloodied head and blood-soaked uniform testified to a frightful wound.

Nurse Dyson finished dressing the other patient's wound and walked over to Frank's bed. 'Your friend Private Hoyland is a very lucky man,' she said, her tone much softer now. 'The bullet tore off a length of scalp exposing his skull in one place but didn't do any serious damage.' Her red-brown hair was piled up underneath a small white cap, accentuating her high cheekbones and her brown eyes contrasted sharply with her pale complexion. Charlie was captivated by her petite figure and the tiny waist pinched by the whalebone corset beneath her uniform. Her efficient authority in the ward belied her age. She could not be much more than twenty-one, twenty-two, thought Charlie.

'Dr. Barlow says he has never seen a wound so close to shattering the skull without doing so,' added Frank enthusiastically. 'An eighth of an inch lower and I would have died.' Charlie looked around the ward where four other men clearly had much more serious head wounds. Three were either sleeping or unconscious while the other was mumbling incoherently under the effects of morphine. After seeing the bodies of the dead lined up as if on parade after they had been collected from the field at Elandslaagte, Charlie and Walter had not been alone in realising that the Boers favoured head shots.

'I'll check your wound and change your dressing when your friends have gone,' said Nurse Dyson.

'How long will he be in here?' asked Charlie.

'That's up to Dr. Barlow. He won't be discharged until Dr. Barlow is satisfied that he has recovered and convalesced sufficiently. Don't underestimate his wound. He lost a lot of blood you know.' Charlie's gaze followed her as she returned to the dressing trolley, moved further up the ward and stopped by another patient. She's lovely, he thought.

Charlie and Walter listened as Frank related the details of his hospitalisation, Nurse Dyson having filled the gaps in his own memory. He had been unconscious for over twenty-four hours after admission and had been sedated with morphine for the following two days. When he finally regained consciousness in the middle of the third night he was disorientated and to the consternation of the medical staff had started to throttle an orderly who had been alerted by his movement and bent over him. It was then that he saw a girl's face in the candlelight. Her mouth was moving but he could hear no sound. While two or three other orderlies flapped ineffectively she soothed him so that he relaxed his grip on the orderly's throat and fell back, an agonising pain searing in his head. While his improvement had been rapid he still had a constant headache and ringing in his ears. Dr. Barlow had stopped his morphine and to ease the pain substituted some other tablets he had brought from England. It was new type of medication not yet in full production, Dr. Barlow had told him, but Frank had been assured that aspirin would soon become a widely used painkiller. It was not as effective as morphine of course but it had no side effects and its use helped to preserve morphine stocks for the more serious cases.

'Dr. Barlow says that I'll have a scar right across the crown of my head for the rest of my life,' said Frank.

'You'll have a centre parting too, whether you like it or not,' chuckled Walter. 'Or didn't Dr. Barlow tell you that your hair won't grow there again?'

Dr. Barlow hadn't told him and Frank hadn't considered it but it was a small price to pay to avoid death or mutilation. 'Listen,' he said, 'I consider I got off lightly in all this. Look at those poor bastards,' he gestured towards the other end of the ward. 'Some of those will be dead sooner or later. Head shots and gut shots. They can't do anything for them. They keep all the worst cases nearest the doors so that they can take them out as quickly and quietly as possible when they die. Another one went last night.'

The other patients in the ward included Highlanders as well as men from their own battalion and a couple from other units not so heavily involved. The Light Horse's wounded were in the volunteer hospital situated among the tents behind the Town Hall. Frank's voice lowered in a conspiratorial whisper. 'Still, it's better here than in ward one.'

'Why? What's in ward one?' asked Charlie.

'Fever.'

Both Charlie and Walter had heard stories of men in some units falling sick but their battalion had so far been spared. 'What kind of fever?' asked Charlie.

'Enteric,' replied Frank. 'Plus a few dysentery cases.'

'It's no wonder in this fly blown hole,' said Walter. 'The water from that poxy river is the colour of shit and probably full of shit as well. If fever takes hold it will go through the place like a dose of salts.'

Frank thought that at least in the surgical ward there was a majority of men like himself who were conscious, rational and would recover. In the fever ward many of the men were delirious especially at night when their cries and screams gave voice to their personal hells. 'They tell me there's no cure for enteric,' said Frank. 'Some survive and some don't.' They all knew that the odds against survival must inevitably lengthen in a place like Ladysmith with its population swollen by the thousands of troops, with their thousands more horses, mules and oxen, stationed there and the heat and rains of the southern summer approaching.

Charlie and Walter were greatly comforted by Frank's progress, Charlie especially so at Frank's request to recommence his literacy lessons on his next visit. They were more disturbed by the news of the enteric fever outbreak and the potential for disaster that it represented.

As they crossed the Oval they met McAdams on his way to visit Colour Sergeant Reid for the first time. 'How is he?' asked McAdams anxiously. They knew he meant Reid and not Frank.

'Not too good,' replied Charlie. They had seen Reid in one of the beds near the door. He had taken four bullets to the body including one in the liver. Frank had reckoned he would probably be spirited away from the ward one night soon but they didn't pass his opinion on to McAdams. 'I think he was sleeping while we were there,' said Walter, knowing full well that he had been unconscious. Frank said he had only briefly regained consciousness a couple of times since his admission and was clearly causing concern to Dr. Barlow and the other medical staff.

McAdams said nothing and walked on. Charlie didn't know what to make of McAdams. At times he seemed almost primeval, as if at any moment he was about to explode into uncontrolled physical violence, yet his devotion to Reid was absolute. Like most of his comrades he had seen McAdams in action for the first time at Elandslaagte and the man had fought bravely with no apparent fear of death or injury. Charlie was convinced that Reid's well being meant more to McAdams than his own.

'Enemy at the gate! Form up in sections! Front rank, prepare for volley fire!'

The imperative shrieks of this sudden and unexpected order awoke men from their deepest slumbers. In the darkness there was a clatter as equipment and accoutrements were sent hurtling around the place and curses as men bumped into each other in the confused rush for weapons and clothing. Never mind the clothing, thought Frank, where's my bloody rifle. No rifle! Jesus, I'll be on a charge if I can't find my rifle! Another crash as he tripped over a pair of crutches.

'Front rank, aim, fire!'

Frank waited for the crash of a rifle volley but there came no sound save the noise of mayhem and confusion in the ward. This can't be right, he thought. What's going on? Holding his head in a forlorn attempt to relieve the pain that had erupted there, he gradually pieced together the parts of the puzzle. There were men shouting, crying, crawling. Frank looked towards a lantern that had appeared at the far end of the ward. He could make out an orderly trying to hold down Colour-Sergeant Reid while Dr. Barlow prepared a syringe to inject him with a sedative and Nurse Dyson holding the lantern.

Dr. Barlow was saying something to Reid but Frank could only hear Reid's response. 'Yes, sir! Yes, sir!' he bellowed. Reid arched his back in an attempt to raise himself from the bed and free himself from the orderly's grip. 'Hold him still, man!' shouted Barlow.

'I'm trying sir, but he has the strength of ten!'

'Nonsense!' retorted Barlow. 'The man's an invalid. Hold him still!' With that Reid launched his upper body at the orderly sending him tumbling backwards into Barlow whose spectacles were dislodged and crushed under the falling orderly's body. Reid thrashed about inflicting further punishment on his ravaged body until a torrent of blood erupted from his throat and gushed on and around his bed. He remained sitting upright for a few seconds before keeling over sideways and hitting the floor.

'Walter's on guard duty, so I've come alone today,' said Charlie taking two books from a leather pouch slung over his shoulder. He had been particularly careful to ensure his boots were clean before entering the ward this time. His eyes met Nurse Dyson's when he glanced surreptitiously at her at the exact moment she chose to turn and look in his direction. He blushed furiously and she turned back to hide the smile creeping across her face at Charlie's self-consciousness and embarrassment.

On his way down the ward he had noticed that Reid's bed had another occupant, similarly prone but bearing no visible indication of a wound.

'Reid went last night,' said Frank in that unnecessary whisper of his. He related the details to Charlie.

'Does McAdams know yet?' said Charlie.

'I doubt it. Who's going to tell him?'

'I will if I see him.'

'Brave man. There's no telling how he'll react.'

'Who's the new man?' asked Charlie, indicating with a movement of the head the other end of the ward.

'Enteric case,' whispered Frank. 'Ward one is full so they've started overflowing them into the other wards. I hear there's nearly a tent full in the volunteers' hospital outside.'

'What? I thought they had to keep fever patients isolated.'

'So did I. There's not much use patching up the wounded for them to die of fever.'

Charlie couldn't think of anything more to say to Frank without exacerbating his friend's own morbid comment. 'Well, let's get started,' he said as cheerily as he could, changing the subject. He opened one of the books at a marked page. 'It's been a while since we did any reading together.' In fact, Charlie thought, with all the events of the last few weeks they hadn't done any since they were en route from Gibraltar to Durban although he had been pleased to note that Frank had continued on his own.

'I'd prefer to read from *Oliver Twist*,' said Frank, picking up the copy he had borrowed from Charlie from the small table by the side of his bed. 'I'm over half way,' he added proudly. Frank found the page and started to read slowly and carefully, exaggerating the syllables of the longer words almost as if he had a stammer until the finished product emerged whole and he took an audible intake of breath at the effort. Charlie was pleased with Frank's progress but more so with his attitude. Frank had not only had the guts to ask him to help him to read and write but had also stuck to the task in spite of the demands of army life and the jibes, by no means all good-natured, of some of their comrades. He would get there, thought Charlie, but how many other Franks, who lacked the courage or the application to become literate, filled the ranks of the British army?

Nurse Dyson was by the ward entrance when Charlie was making his way out and he took the opportunity to enquire about Frank's likely discharge date. He felt a little ashamed. Although he genuinely wanted to know how Frank was progressing, he was really more interested in finding an excuse to talk to Nurse Dyson.

'That will be Dr. Barlow's decision but I dare say it won't be too long now,' said Nurse Dyson vaguely but as honestly as she could.

'Frank speaks very highly of you. He says you're always there when anyone needs anything.' Charlie was wrestling with his shyness for words that would keep her interested in prolonging their conversation. 'Don't you ever get any time off from your duties?'

She was intrigued both by the man and the paradox he presented. His outward shyness must disguise the harder edge of a trained soldier and one who had only recently been in battle at that. Apart from her nursing duties she was a good listener and was happy to spend time with any of her patients who wanted to talk. Frank spoke mostly about his pals Charlie and Walter but particularly Charlie who represented the older brother he had never had and often the dead father he had barely known. Charlie was a good man and the truest friend anyone could ever have, he had told her. He didn't drink to excess and rarely swore, unlike Walter, although he never chastised Walter for doing so. Charlie had always been a regular churchgoer and on many occasions had managed to drag Walter and him along although they had done so out of a desire to be together rather than any evangelical persuasion on Charlie's part. Charlie wasn't one of those people who rammed their religious beliefs down other people's throats. He would live and let live. A good sort. Frank had also told her about the reading and writing lessons Charlie gave him. This had surprised her as such philanthropy did not fit her image of the British Tommy. She had not failed to notice Charlie's patience while Frank, to her mind, had struggled with such a basic offering as *Oliver Twist*.

Charlie seemed to tower over her even taking into account her own height. She could see the uncertainty in his pale blue eyes as he ran his hand nervously through his short fair hair and fiddled with the rim of the helmet under his arm. 'I don't get much time off because of the demands of the hospital but that's what I'm here for.'

Charlie found her accent peculiar but familiar since his arrival in Natal. She was obviously a colonial, he thought. He would have been puzzled to learn that she also found his accent curious as he did not consider he had one. 'May I see you some time?' he blurted out, surprising himself in the process. He screwed up his eyes, wishing he hadn't said that.

'I'm sure you'll see me whenever you visit your friend.' She could not help adding to the discomfort of this gauche young man by teasing him.

'No, I mean... may I...' Involuntarily he screwed up his eyes again and inhaled. 'May I see you when you are off duty?' He exhaled with the effort and felt a flush rise from his neck. He cast his eyes to the floor, in dread of meeting an expression of derision.

'I suppose so. I'm lodging at the Dunkley residence on Poort

Road. Seven o'clock sharp, after dinner. I'm back on duty in the evening Private...'

'Browell. Charlie Browell. Seven o'clock then...'

'Nurse Dyson,' she added unnecessarily. 'Seven o'clock then Private Browell.'

She turned away down the ward leaving Charlie numbed and immobile by her acceptance. Feeling more relieved than elated he left the ward and made his way down the steps at the rear entrance, through the tents of the volunteer hospital and administrative section and across the Oval back to camp. It had not yet occurred to him that he still did not know her first name.

Walter was just coming off guard duty when Charlie arrived back at camp. It was then that he realised that while making such a bold arrangement Charlie had not considered whether he would even be free to meet Nurse whatever-her-name-was Dyson at seven even though his pass was theoretically valid until nine. After giving Walter the latest situation on Frank and the news of Colour-Sergeant Reid's death he checked the sentry roster and found to his immeasurable relief that he was not on duty until ten in the evening.

Walter echoed Frank in not envying the one to break the news of Reid's death to McAdams. Charlie was fully prepared to do so but Walter knew McAdams had gone out with a fatigue party to cut shelters in the riverbank. 'Shelters?' queried Charlie.

'Yes. It seems they're expecting the Boers to start artillery bombardments at any time. The riverbank will probably be one of the safest places to be so they're preparing some shelters, mainly for the civilians by the looks of things.'

Charlie found the Dunkley residence easily enough. It was a substantial property set in the most exclusive area of the town. The two-storey green clapboard house was set on rising ground that elevated gradually as the road looped round towards Convent Ridge. The long porch dominated the front aspect, the gable end of the front upper storey being set back, and a double-storey extension abutted from the left side of the far end giving the house an inverted L-shaped configuration. On the left the garden was loosely enclosed by acacias and sycamores within the hollow of the 'L' while the plot on the right was given over to a dozen peach and apricot trees. The noises from a patch of ground to the rear betrayed the presence of goats, geese and chickens.

Charlie stood nervously at the path to the house, licked the palm of his hand and smoothed his hair down for the umpteenth time, carefully replacing his helmet in a futile attempt not to disturb a single hair. He had made an effort to look as smart as possible which was not easy with only one uniform and the alternating dust and mud of Ladysmith, not to mention the recent battle. He checked his sleeve. He had darned the hole where the bullet had passed through. It wasn't very smart but it would have to do. Even so his efforts had been derided by Walter and his other tent mates. Nobody made an effort to look any smarter than required by the company sergeant-major unless he was trying to impress someone better looking. Walter guessed immediately the object of his attention and made a series of ribald comments, none of which flustered Charlie. Most of the others would have risen to the bait – including Frank – but Charlie always infuriated Walter by turning the other cheek. For his part Walter meant no harm but he considered himself the company wit and loved an audience.

Charlie steeled himself and climbed the steps of the steep path to the front door, almost tripping over a wicker chair on the porch in the process. Although it was a warm evening the perspiration on his brow was more the result of nerves. He wiped his forehead with a handkerchief and straightening himself up he cleared his throat, swallowed and held his clenched fist momentarily over the door before knocking.

'Yes, sir?' said the maid on opening the door. Charlie was unsure whether to ask for Nurse Dyson directly or whether it would be more courteous to announce himself first to the master of the house. His dilemma was solved when tall, gaunt and balding man in a dark suit strode to the door and welcomed him effusively. Mr. Dunkley to the rescue, thought Charlie.

'Ah it's the young man Nurse Dyson is expecting. Do come in my good fellow.' Charlie mumbled his thanks, instinctively wiped his boots perhaps a little too energetically on the thick bristle doormat and entered. Nurse Dyson was in the sitting room. She smiled and made a gesture with her forehead. Charlie gave her a puzzled glance. She repeated the gesture a little more emphatically, raising her eyebrows for good measure, and Charlie pulled off his helmet so rapidly that he nearly lost hold of it. He caught sight of her biting her bottom lip to stifle a smile. He already felt embarrassed and socially inferior. Perhaps this wasn't such a good idea after all, he thought.

'Welcome,' said Mr. Dunkley with genuine warmth. 'It's always a pleasure to have a visit from one of our brave Tommies.' He shook Charlie's hand firmly and introduced himself. 'Dunkley's the name. Zachariah Dunkley. I'm a land agent in these parts and a magistrate for the Klip River District.'

'Browell, sir. Private Browell.'

'A drink, Private Browell?'

Charlie was unsure what to ask for. He could see from the half full decanter on the mahogany sideboard that it was not a teetotal household but couldn't help wondering if in polite society there were specific drinks that should or should not be requested, or even if convention dictated a polite refusal. He swallowed. 'A beer please sir,' he ventured.

'Splendid. A beer it shall be.' Charlie's relief was palpable. Beer was acceptable. He hadn't made a fool of himself in front of either Nurse Dyson or the gracious Mr. Dunkley.

While waiting for the beer Dunkley introduced his wife Ada, a plump woman in her mid-forties, and their seventeen-year-old daughter Grace who was a younger and slimmer version of her mother. Both women had black hair, the mother's flecked with grey, pointed noses and dimples in their chins. Charlie had no difficulty imagining how the daughter would look in thirty years' time. 'My son Ralph is serving with the Carbineers. Most of the regiment are here in Ladysmith but his troop are currently stationed down the line at Estcourt.'

Charlie looked around the drawing room which was rather larger than its average counterpart in England, probably also that in Natal for all he knew, but was just as cluttered. Three chunky leather armchairs, a large sofa and three upholstered chairs were arranged in such a way that they all faced each other, indicating that the Dunkleys were used to having company. One wall was almost obscured by watercolours of various landscapes, so many that Charlie guessed they were the creations of one of the family members. A scattering of silhouettes adorned another wall above the mahogany sideboard while the wall facing the door was dominated by a large unmade hearth adorned with terracotta vases of dried flowers. He wondered who played the upright piano in the corner. Perhaps for an evening's amusement Mrs. Dunkley sang while Mr. Dunkley played, he thought, but he hoped he wouldn't have to suffer such a distraction when he knew he would only have a short time in Nurse Dyson's company.

Another figure entered the room in Charlie's peripheral vision. 'Ah, Captain, do meet Private Browell. Private Browell, this is Captain Turnbull. He's staying with us while he convalesces from his wound.' Charlie instantly recognised the newcomer whose left arm was in a sling with the hand bandaged. It was the Light Horse captain who had rebuked one of his men for bantering with him on the way to Elandslaagte. The Light Horse trooper he and Walter had found dead on the battlefield when they were looking for Frank. Charlie saluted him and Turnbull gave a half-hearted response.

A servant brought in a bottle of beer and a glass on a tray and offered it silently to Charlie. He took them and automatically thanked the servant. 'Thank you? *Thank you?*' sneered Turnbull. 'You don't thank kaffirs, Browell. Kaffirs do as they're told and if they don't you give them a kick until they do.'

Charlie found this as offensive to himself as to the servant who had to stand and listen to Turnbull's outburst. It was even more galling that Turnbull"s accent indicated his English origin. It was one thing for the colonials to have their attitudes and prejudices but there was no excuse for an Englishman to abuse a native or another white man who didn't. 'Where I come from we don't discriminate in our manners, sir,' said Charlie as evenly as he could.

Turnbull went to reply, anger surfacing in his dark eyes. Dunkley interjected to defuse the situation. 'Captain Turnbull was wounded in the hand and arm at Elandslaagte. I assume you also fought in the battle, Private Browell, since Nurse Dyson tells us you have been visiting one of your comrades at the Town Hall hospital.'

'Yes, sir,' replied Charlie. 'I was a little luckier than Captain Turnbull, sir,' he continued, indicating his darned sleeve. 'The bullet went right through without so much as scratching me.'

'Well, go on,' said Dunkley enthusiastically. 'Tell us a bit more about it. Was your unit heavily involved?'

'Yes, sir. We were.'

Turnbull gave a derisive snort. 'It was the Light Horse who took the Boer position and won the day, Browell. Irregular cavalry doing the regular infantry's job.' Charlie bristled at the insult. The Light Horse had fought bravely, making a vital contribution to the victory, and had suffered heavy casualties but so had his battalion and the Highlanders.

'I believe it was a combined effort, sir. Lots of spirit and dash all round,' he replied calmly. 'The Light Horse did themselves proud but we lost a lot of men too, sir,' he added, thinking of Frank, Colour-Sergeant Reid and other comrades who fell in the charge or were riddled with bullets trying to breach the barbed wire fence.

The cheery atmosphere created by Dunkley was rapidly dissipating. Turnbull clearly resented the presence of a common private from a working class English background while Charlie seethed at Turnbull's version of the battle and the deprecating inferences made towards the British infantry's contribution. Turnbull had obviously enjoyed being the centre of attention as the wounded hero – and from a colonial unit at that – in a household with two fussing women plus Nurse Dyson whenever she was off duty, thought Charlie. Heaven only knew what exaggerated tales of personal heroism he had been regaling them with.

This time it was Nurse Dyson who moved to change the subject and suggested they would be more comfortable on the porch on such a beautifully warm evening. 'Splendid idea,' enthused Dunkley. Turnbull declined graciously for the benefit of the ladies, claiming fatigue. He bade the Dunkleys and Nurse Dyson good night but completely ignored Charlie before retiring to his room. Mrs. Dunkley excused herself, saying that she had to discuss the next day's meal arrangements with cook and dragged her not altogether willing daughter with her. Grace was intrigued about what relationship may develop between this good looking, if slightly gauche, Tommy and Nurse Dyson. Mrs. Dunkley, on the other hand, was content to allow them to spend a little time in private conversation but her husband had not taken the hint. He had already whisked Charlie outside with

Nurse Dyson in their wake and was taking him on a tour of the garden.

'Ah, a Manchester chap are you?' he said, having probed Charlie for some details of his background. 'Cottonopolis. The Empire's source of inexpensive cotton clothing.' Dunkley enquired if he had any background in the cotton industry so Charlie told him about his previous occupation as a bookkeeper's assistant. Walter's original job in the textile industry and his own past having been irrevocably intertwined with Walter's and Frank's meant that he had soon given Dunkley a potted history of himself and his two pals.

Dunkley in turn told Charlie that he had been born in Durban two years after his parents had emigrated from Lincolnshire in eighteen fifty as part of the Byrne settlement project to populate Natal. He had set up his land agency in Ladysmith some fifteen years before, his young family joining him the following year once he had become established, and prospered at a time of burgeoning settlement in northern and central Natal.

Having accompanied them around the garden Nurse Dyson now knew pretty well everything about Charlie but he still knew nothing of her background – and still not even her first name. Charlie was frustrated beyond words. Mr. Dunkley was a proper gentleman and no mistake but he had come to see Nurse Dyson and had so far not even managed to speak to her directly.

He knew the opportunity was lost when the time came for him to return to the camp. He thanked Dunkley for his hospitality and turned to bid goodnight to Nurse Dyson. 'That's perfect timing,' she said. 'I'm back on duty myself soon. Private Browell can escort me to the hospital.' Dunkley was about to query why she was returning a good hour before she needed to but stopped himself, realising that he had monopolised almost all of Charlie's time and that she wanted to take the opportunity to talk with him.

'Very well. Splendid!' said Dunkley. 'I'm sure that Private Browell will prove a more than adequate escort.'

As they walked down the hill on Poort Road the gaslights and lanterns from the houses struggled feebly and futilely to illuminate the way. Charlie went to speak. 'Sarah,' she said, sensing the movement of his head.

'How on earth did you know what I was going to ask you?' said Charlie incredulously.

'If I had taken the trouble to call on someone the first thing I would want to know would certainly be their name.'

'May I call you Sarah?'

'Of course. Charles'

'Charlie, please.'

'No. You're a Charles not a Charlie. It sounds better and suits you better.'

'Oh, all right,' he conceded doubtfully. 'If you must. But not in front of Frank, please.'

'In front of Private Hoyland you will be Private Browell and I will be Nurse Dyson. If you think that's too formal you may simply call me 'nurse' if you wish.' The darkness concealed her smirk. Charlie was beginning to realise that although she cut a figure of stern authority on the ward Sarah Dyson had an impish sense of humour.

As they cut through a similarly darkened Keate Street she told him she was from a small town called Howick not far from Pietermaritzburg, or Maritzburg as she referred to it. She had been nursing at Gray's Hospital in Maritzburg before volunteering on the outbreak of war to work in one of the field hospitals, much to her parents' distress. Her mother and Ada Dunkley were second cousins and she had a brother serving with Ada's son Ralph in the ranks of the Carbineers. She told him about the fabulous sight of the falls at Howick, a three hundred foot drop on the Umgeni River, and how he must take the opportunity to see them while he was in Natal, perhaps after the conflict was over which surely would not be much beyond Christmas. Charlie said he would like that very much and hoped that she would be his guide.

Charlie was becoming increasingly relaxed in her company. She was not only very pretty but clever, confident and witty as well, if perhaps a little strong willed and bossy. For her part Sarah was attracted to this shy and occasionally clumsy Englishman who lacked both the coarseness of a number of his fellow soldiers with whom she had come into contact and the brashness of many Natalians of his age. She liked men who intrigued her and this Charles certainly did that. She also thought him rather handsome.

'What do you make of Captain Turnbull?' he asked.

'I'm afraid he's typical of many of the British expatriates, especially those who have come down from the Transvaal. I admit he's rather arrogant but they have had a hard time of it. Many of them have lost everything, their jobs, their homes and most of their possessions. They came to Natal as refugees but the best of them joined the Light Horse when it was raised. They hate the Boers. I believe he was one of those imprisoned after the Jameson Raid in ninety-six. I can't say I either like or dislike him particularly though Grace thinks he's rather dashing.'

Charlie remembered reading in the newspapers back home the furore that the Jameson Raid had caused. It had been an abortive attempt by an irregular and highly unofficial British force led by Dr. Leander Starr Jameson, Cecil Rhodes's right hand man in his Chartered Company's fiefdom of Rhodesia, to make a lightning strike into Johannesburg and foment a rising by the *Uitlanders*. The Transvaal government got to hear of the plot, commandos were raised and the force was crushed four days after it crossed over the border from British Bechuanaland. The tacit support from within Johannesburg, the Cape and Whitehall evaporated to leave Jameson and the other prominent participants to be tried and imprisoned. Charlie had forgotten about the incident until recently when Ladysmith was buzzing with the news that the famous Dr. Jameson had arrived in town and was at that very moment in residence at the Royal Hotel.

'Well it seems he has a rare contempt for anyone with a lower rank or a different colour skin,' said Charlie.

'His first prejudice is one of snobbery and you may well be lucky enough not to encounter it again while you're in South Africa. His second is a way of life in this part of the world and will be unavoidable wherever you go.'

They cut across the Oval past the tents to the rear entrance of the town hall. Sarah thanked Charlie for his company and bid him good night. 'May I...' began Charlie.

'Of course' she said brightly, once again anticipating his question. Whenever it is mutually convenient.' She turned to enter the building and Charlie reciprocated her farewell. No sooner was he making his way back through the tents than he saw a figure ambling towards him out of the gloom.

'Browell,' said McAdams gruffly in simple acknowledgement. He looks exhausted, thought Charlie. Even in the dim light from the tent lanterns he could see McAdams's lined face ingrained with that red-brown dirt and his sunken, tired eyes. He had been on digging fatigues most of the day and, with or without permission, had plainly come straight from the riverbank to see Colour-Sergeant Reid. He didn't know.

'McAdams,' began Charlie.

McAdams stopped. 'What?' he replied with undisguised irritation.

Charlie hesitated slightly. 'This isn't an easy thing to say but...' He took a deep breath. 'I'm sorry McAdams but Colour-Sergeant Reid died earlier today,' he continued with a slight tremor in his voice. There was a pause as McAdams stared straight into Charlie's eyes. He saw the Ulsterman's arms begin to tremble. 'I'm sorry you had to hear it like this,' Charlie gabbled nervously before tailing off. Everyone in the company considered McAdams to be unpredictable. Charlie had half expected a violent reaction from him but not this. Tears coursed down McAdams's cheeks as first his shoulders shook and then his whole body convulsed with unrestrained sobs. Charlie breathed a sigh of relief and put his arms around McAdams's heaving torso. 'I'm sorry,' he said softly. 'I'm so sorry.'

Charlie left the ward with mixed emotions. On the one hand he was delighted that Frank was making good progress but on the other he was disappointed that he had not been able to see Sarah. She was off duty and having worked consecutive nights she would be sleeping in her billet at the Dunkleys. He was tempted to call there on his way back to camp but discretion finally triumphed over impatience and he decided it would not be a good idea. His attention was drawn to the hubbub of a crowd gathering in the street outside so he made towards the front entrance of the town hall, curious as to the reason.

Outside a growing throng of soldiers and civilians lined Murchison Street amid a buzz of excitement. Charlie trotted down the steps to the roadside, craning his neck in the direction they were all looking. Heads bobbed up and down while those at the front, especially the civilians, tried to resist the swell from behind lest they ended up ankle deep in the churned up mud on the road. The object of their attention came into view as it turned into the far end of Murchison Street from the Newcastle Road. On it came, inexorably growing as it progressed ever nearer the crowd. One man cheered, waving his bowler hat in the air, then another, and another until everyone was cheering and waving headgear, handkerchiefs, swagger sticks and anything else that came to hand in praise and welcome. It was the Dundee column, the remnants of the four infantry battalions, three batteries of artillery and the regiment of Hussars that had won the day at Talana.

Amid the jostling crowd a gunner next to Charlie exclaimed excitedly that the brother he hadn't seen in over a year was among the Rifles and squeezed towards the front only to be disgorged back by the unyielding throng, his helmet spinning from his head. Like most of the crowd, Charlie didn't know anyone in the column but took the opportunity to pay tribute to these men who had fought one battle against the Boers and another against the elements. As the leading troops approached the crowd there was a momentary but palpable lull in the clamour. Charlie stopped in mid cheer at the sight of these mud caked and hollow eyed men plodding through the morass of Murchison, unthinkingly dropping one foot in front of the other as they had done almost incessantly for the last four days and nights. The mounted infantry and Hussars passed, one horse after another with drooping neck and swaying gait, foam flecked muzzle and lolling tongue, gamely and loyally hauling themselves and their human cargoes on the last leg of their journey. Charlie noticed several men asleep in the saddle, exhaustion having overtaken any sense of relief at reaching the sanctuary of Ladysmith. Similarly distressed and cajoled by their drivers, the artillery horses dragged and pulled the field guns, additionally burdened by exhausted gunners riding on the limbers.

Charlie didn't fancy becoming entangled with four thousand troops on his way back to camp so he winkled his way out of the crowd. Once more he fleetingly considered calling on Sarah but the risk of inconveniencing her to the point of being unwelcome finally decided him against the idea and he strode purposefully towards the Oval and the road back to camp.

Sarah leaned on the porch rail watching the column trudge by below and in front of the Dunkley residence. She had been in a deep sleep and her dream was interrupted by the sound of people cheering along Poort Road. As she threw a shawl over her nightdress she tried to recall the dream that was at once vivid and impossible to bring to mind. The harder she tried to grasp the remnants that lingered tantalisingly in her waking state, the more quickly they dissipated. It was so frustrating. She was sure it had been something interesting.

There had been no other sound in the house so she had assumed that everyone else was out as she tiptoed barefoot out of the front door to see what the cheering was about. She would not have emerged dressed so flimsily, some might say immodestly, had there been anyone else at home. Seeing the long file of soldiers made her think of Charles. Had she been dreaming of him? Perhaps. He had certainly been on her mind enough for him to enter her sleeping subconscious. She wondered what he was doing now and wished he were here with her. The earlier rain had stopped and the sun emerged from the clouds. The moisture on the grass and foliage beyond the porch and in the garden behind began to evaporate and filled the air with a warm dampness. She closed her eyes and tilted her face to the sun, smiling to herself as its glow served both to relax and refresh her. The brush against her hand interrupted her reverie. She recoiled with a gasp and spun round in one movement. 'Captain Turnbull!' she exclaimed. 'You startled me.'

'So it seems,' he replied with no trace of emotion in his voice. 'However, it's fair to say that you startled me too.' He smiled and ran his eyes up and down her body. She instinctively pulled the shawl tight around her and entwined her feet in a futile attempt to conceal their immodest exposure. She shivered in spite of the warmth of the sun on her back. Turnbull took a step closer so that his face was almost touching hers and put his free hand on hers more forcefully. Her chest tightened as she tried to back away but instead only pinned herself against the rail as Turnbull moved closer again.

'Captain Turnbull. Please don't.'

'I know what kind of woman you are. You're the kind who pretends she doesn't want the attentions of a man but all the time craves them.' Sarah could feel his warm, tobacco scented breath on her face and closed her eyes to shut out the intimidating image in front of her. 'I've met your sort before.'

'No.' She shook her head from side to side as much in fear as denial. Oh, how she wished Charles were here. Turnbull suddenly sprung back. This time it was his turn for a look of alarm to flash across his face. Sarah could hear the voices whose embodiment he had seen a moment before. Ada and Grace Dunkley were chatting animatedly as they climbed the path towards the porch. They had been watching and cheering the column as it wound its way up Poort Road but Ada had a household to run and was already thinking of meals to plan and servants' tasks to check up on as she huffed and puffed her way up the path. She had dragged her reluctant daughter away but Grace was still chattering excitedly. Neither had seen them yet so while Turnbull was composing himself Sarah took the opportunity to flee back inside the house, her bare feet almost skimming across the porch.

Inside her room she closed and locked the door, leaning back against it both in relief and to act as an additional psychological barrier. Her mouth was dry and she could feel the rapid pounding of her heart. Composing herself, she realised that with Ada and Grace back in the house there was no need to have locked the door but she kept it locked all the same. Fear turned to relief and in her relief she slid down the door until in a sitting position and put her head on her knees. She shook her head as the tears streamed down her face, dampening her nightdress and splashing like raindrops on the floor.

'It's not easy to be clever and stupid at the same time but the *rooinekke* have managed it,' said Koos, peering through the telescope that had served him and his father before him since the days of the Great Trek. Daylight was flooding the plain quickly and putting the hills and *kopjes* encircling Ladysmith into stark relief. 'Take a look, boy.' Christiaan grasped the telescope eagerly and put it to his eye.

'What am I looking for, *oupa*?' said Christiaan. 'How can the British be both clever and stupid?'

'Oh, it's a rare gift.' Koos swung the telescope to the right and nudged it slightly higher revealing to Christiaan the outline of Tchrengula, a flat-topped hill covered with scrub and a scattering of thorn trees that overlooked the pass of Nicholson's Nek and the plain below. 'You see that column on the top of that hill?' Christiaan nodded. 'Well, that's where they have been clever. Our Free State cousins are coming from that direction and the British are going to try to stop them from joining hands with us Transvaalers. They won't succeed of course.'

'But why are they stupid as well?' Koos turned the telescope back to the plain in front of them. Christiaan's eye followed.

'The main force has come out of Ladysmith before dawn to attack us and has managed to get split up. Some of the force has lost its way in the dark. Part of the infantry is in front of us but the rest of it has wandered off near their guns over there,' he said, giving the telescope a nudge to the right. 'And where is their cavalry? Only they can know where they are and how they got there.'

The sudden crash of the Creusot gun to their rear startled them. Ten seconds later the ninety-four pound shell exploded among the British infantry, several men being propelled into the air like rag dolls and landing scattered and motionless in the plain below. Koos chuckled as the British artillery opened up vigorously on a nearby hill which the Burghers had evacuated during the night in anticipation of the morning's attack. Piet took a sharp intake of breath as the shells tore into the hillside and the abandoned emplacements where they had been only a matter of hours before. Koos packed away the telescope in his leather shoulder bag, Christiaan slung the bugle round his back and the three of them took aim from behind their sandbagged emplacement. The range is long, thought Piet, but not too long for Burgher marksmen. He aimed and squeezed off five measured rounds as the crackle of Mauser fire provided the chorus to the bass solo of the Creusot and the intermezzo of the six smaller field pieces spread over the top of the hill.

'What the hell's going on out there?' snapped Walter nervously. It was a rhetorical question. No one in the battalion could see what was happening from their support position in the lee of a hill but they could hear the regular explosion of shells and the constant rattle of musketry.

At least it's not directed towards us, thought Charlie, but somebody's copping it out there.

'Why don't our guns go for that bloody Long Tom?' added Walter. Within a minute or two, as if in answer to him, the Creusot was targeted by the British batteries and soon silenced.

They felt powerless as the forward battalions were decimated by Boer fire. More guns had opened up from other hills as the British concentrated on keeping the Creusot out of action. The interminable waiting was even more frustrating by being unable to see what was going on. Walter took off his helmet and mopped his brow. It was another oppressively hot day. The sun had beaten down so strongly over the last few days that the soggy ground had already dried and hardened. 'Frank's well out of it back at the hospital,' said Walter. 'Tucked up in bed with a nice nurse to look after him,' he added mischievously.

Charlie didn't bite. 'He should be out of hospital in the next day or so,' said Charlie. 'It'll be good to have him back.' The unmistakable discharge of the Creusot boomed again followed by the sound of the earth being torn up ahead of them. 'Long Tom wasn't out of action long,' said Charlie.

Yellow-green smoke billowed high into the air and in places the dry grass on the summit of the hill was ablaze. Shrapnel shells burst overhead and sprayed the Burghers' gun positions. The van Oppens huddled together behind their emplacement. The British are aiming for the Creusot so they should be safe enough here, thought Piet. Unless a shrapnel burst fell short and hit them in the back. He heard the pounding of boots, the approaching sound of heavy breathing, and the thud of bodies as several gunners leapt to join them in the protection of the emplacement.

'Anyone hit?' asked Piet.

'One killed by shrapnel at the gun and two hit on the way here,' said one. 'We didn't have time to stop and see if they were still alive. I'm not even sure who they are as we scattered in all directions when we left the gun pit.'

For the first time since they had come on commando Christiaan was scared. He had curled himself up into a ball with his eyes tightly shut and wedged himself between his father and grandfather. Three more whistles and cracks were followed by a scream as shrapnel burst to the rear. Christiaan was holding back tears. He mustn't cry. He bit his lip but the tears came anyway. At least he mustn't let them see him cry. They would think he was a coward and his father would send him home in disgrace, back to the farm with the women and children. For a moment he dreaded the thought of what Kobus Viljoen would say until he remembered that Kobus himself had had his skull shattered by a piece of shrapnel at Talana.

Several shells exploded on and around the crest, the nearest showering them with dirt and small stones. 'That was a close one.' said the artilleryman calmly. 'Don't worry though. That was the first shot from a different battery and it was short. They're aiming for the Creusot so their officer will lengthen their range. The next salvo will land further behind us.'

Piet had been awed by the earlier shellfire concentrated on the hill they had vacated but found it hard to believe that it could have been any worse than this. It was their bad luck that they had been posted on the same hill as the Creusot that had now become the target of every British field gun out on the *veld* in front of them. Piet was beginning to think that luck was everything. Not good leadership or good marksmanship. Not even faith in God. He had seen God-fearing men cut down irrespectively and it must be the same for the British. It was just a question of luck. Who was luckier? The man who emerged unscathed from all the major battles of a war only to be killed in the last one or the man who was pityingly carried to the rear having been wounded in the first battle but survived the war? Piet had thanked God they had all come safely through Talana and, please God, they would survive this one too but who knew what was in store for them in this war? He felt very vulnerable. Vulnerable and scared. He just didn't want Christiaan to see his fear. That would be too much shame.

'There. I told you,' said the artilleryman triumphantly as another salvo crashed into the ground a hundred yards behind them, close to the gun pit. 'They've adjusted their range.'

Koos had seen the effects of artillery on the massed ranks of an *impi* during the Zulu War. Somehow it didn't seem so awful when kaffirs were on the receiving end, he thought, but the mutilating effects of shellfire are a far more devastating prospect than that of a bullet. Give me a clean head shot any day.

The shelling slackened as the British artillery redirected and dispersed its fire away from the Creusot and towards the other Burgher guns scattered among the surrounding hills. The artilleryman hazarded a glance over the emplacement. 'My God!' he exclaimed 'Look at that!' The others' curiosity overcame any remaining fear or caution and they sprung up to see what had elicited such excitement.

'Look, boy,' said Koos. 'There's a sight you don't see every day.'

The first inclination that something was wrong was when the sound of musketry seemed to come from only one direction and the further direction at that. The colonel of the battalion had still received no orders and, with 'D' company being the closest, directed its commanding officer to take three men on a reconnaissance around the hill and report on the situation on the plain. 'McAdams,' called Captain Young.

'I would have bet money on his name being the first one called,' said Walter.

'Shawcross. Browell. Come with me.'

'Shit,' said Walter. 'I was just getting comfortable here.' All three rose and followed Young. Before they rounded the end of the hill they saw a group of a dozen or so troops coming from the direction of the plain. As they approached they saw another group, then another until their eyes met the sight of the entire force of infantry in full retreat across the plain, a huge dust swirl following the thousands of pairs of feet, at first tramping, then hurrying and finally, in many cases, running. The Boer fire intensified as the retreat became ever more disorderly. They could see only the artillery gamely sticking to their task and covering the infantry's retirement.

Young ordered the small party back to the battalion's position. As soon as he reported to the colonel the battalion was ordered to advance on to the plain and stand fast to cover the withdrawal of the main force. 'Hopefully our presence will encourage the troops to effect an orderly retirement,' Charlie heard the colonel say to Young. 'From what you say they're on the verge of panic.'

The battalion deployed on the plain in extended order in four lines, allowing the retiring troops to pass through them. Walter gave the men passing him a look of contempt and insults were spat out along the line to those considered to be in an unseemly haste to leave the field. 'Stand fast, men. Show them how we behave in the face of the enemy,' exhorted the colonel. This was not an idle boast. The battalion was within range of the Boer Mausers and here and there a man dropped in the line. The dust churned and choked among them as the main body of the force passed through. Charlie blinked and sneezed as it blew into his eyes and nose. Walter gagged and coughed from the irritation to his throat. A sergeant in front of them fell wounded in the chest.

The little khaki figures presented too good an opportunity. The gunners ran back to their Creusot and all three van Oppens opened fire along with thousands of their comrades. Christiaan's fear had evaporated as he began to enjoy this war once more. Piet, too, was more assured. This is how it should be, he thought as he loosed off another clip. Only Koos seemed to be distracted, firing a shot or two and then looking around and across the valley to the other Burgher positions. Piet stopped firing. 'What's the matter, pa?' he asked.

Koos shook his head. 'I don't understand it. Almost the entire garrison is in front of us, retreating and demoralised. We have enough horsemen to destroy them now. Why doesn't General Joubert send them out? Ladysmith is there for the taking.' He fired another shot and paused. 'We'll live to regret this.'

Sarah was on her way to the hospital when she joined the crowd lining a dust choked Murchison Street opposite the Royal Hotel as the mass of troops wearily tramped past. There was no noisy welcome such as was given to the Dundee column. Here was a rabble that had failed to defeat or even damage the Boers who were now close to encircling the town. The subdued crowd did not raise a single cheer. The hushed voices only talked of when, and not if, they would be cut off and besieged. Among the spectators were a number of blacks and Indians. People within Sarah's earshot also expressed their concern about the longer term political effects on that normally disregarded section of the community who were witnessing Britain's inability to protect its colony and citizens or defeat a bunch of Dutch farmers. Sarah could see Joseph, the fifteen-year-old grandson of the Dunkleys' gardener who often came round to help, among a group of Zulu youths silently watching the sad procession.

She was again going on duty earlier than she was obliged to. Ada and Grace had been invited to visit friends for afternoon tea and with Mr. Dunkley having gone to Estcourt and Mooi River to sort out some business matters the day before she was nervous at the prospect of being alone in the house with Captain Turnbull. Ada had been distressed in case the Boers would fire on the train but her husband dismissed her fears and was hoping to have the opportunity to see Ralph while he was down there. She was also anxious about Charles and hoped to see him before she went on duty to allay her fears but his battalion was not among the units which had passed by so far. The firing, especially that of the Long Tom, had been clearly audible and more or less continuous since early morning. She kept telling herself that he would be all right but she felt it would be better to keep occupied. She continued on to the hospital trying in vain to push him out of her mind. She would have to check the casualty list which would be pinned up outside the post office in the morning and pray that his name was not on it.

Ladysmith
November 1899

Charlie wiped the perspiration from his brow and surveyed the view from the crest of the plateau over the sweep of the brush and scrub covered valley below. If the Boers attacked Caesar's Camp they would come from this direction, he thought. Ladysmith looked so small and vulnerable from their bivouac area on the opposite crest and it didn't take a military genius to realise that the position the battalion now occupied was the key to the town. The whole ridge was four miles long, with a dip separating Caesar's Camp, the larger part where they were deployed, from the smaller portion called Wagon Hill. A man in the town guard had told him that the Boers' name for the ridge was the Platrand.

'One stripe doesn't mean you can take it easy, you lazy bastard,' said Walter as he dropped another large rock on the pile. Charlie had wondered what misdemeanour he had been guilty of when he had been summoned before Captain Young the previous day only to be congratulated on his appointment as lance-corporal and hurriedly whisked out by the company sergeant-major. Several men had been nudged up a rank to fill the gap caused by Colour Sergeant Reid's death. Even better news was that Frank had been discharged from hospital and had resumed light duties at the main camp in town. Walter winked as Charlie snapped back to the reality of his section's task to build stone and earth sangars as part of the defences against a possible Boer attack.

'Take a breather Walter. We all need a break in this heat,' he said. 'Fifteen minutes, lads. You've got fifteen minutes for a smoke and a brew,' he shouted to the others. All but one of the party promptly dropped the rocks they were carrying and rushed into the partially completed sangar. They sat or squatted and lit up cigarettes immediately, the myriad grey wisps of smoke rising through the shimmering heat haze, while Walter started a fire under the kettle, blackened and encrusted from years of field use. McAdams heaved his rock on to the pile and made his way unhurriedly round the semi-circular construction to join the others.

Since Charlie had broken the news of Reid's death to McAdams the Ulsterman had become unexpectedly communicative towards him. Perhaps it was out of gratitude for the sympathy and comfort he had shown. Perhaps he had replaced Reid as McAdams's link with the rest of the world. He didn't know and McAdams had never indicated his reasons. He had learned that the bond between McAdams and Reid had been forged on the Frontier years before when their small patrol was ambushed in a mountain pass and all the others killed. McAdams was immobilised by wounds to an arm and a leg and was about to be hacked to death by half a dozen Miranzai tribesmen when Reid appeared from behind a rock, dropped two of them with successive shots, and with a blood-curdling scream launched himself at the others. He bayoneted two, smashed the skull of another with his rifle butt while the last one ran off. Knowing that the escapee would soon return with others, Reid dragged McAdams up to a small cave entrance on a ledge and kept a large party of tribesmen at bay through the night with regular and accurate fire until a relief force arrived the following morning and drove them off. That explained the crimson and dark blue ribbon of the Distinguished Conduct Medal on Reid's uniform, Charlie had thought. He felt as though McAdams had bared his soul to him, had entrusted him with an intimate confidence. McAdams never asked him to keep the contents of their conversations confidential but Charlie would not repeat any of McAdams's disclosures, even to Frank and Walter.

Charlie had begun to appreciate McAdams's qualities and was glad he was in his section. Strangely, he felt that they would both look after each other in a way. As a newly promoted NCO he would benefit from the presence of a solid and experienced man like McAdams while McAdams himself seemed to need the focus of an authority figure, even a humble lance-corporal. He would be even happier when Frank was fit enough to resume regular duties and rejoin Walter and himself. It seemed an age since they had charged together over the ridge at Elandslaagte.

McAdams entered the protective cup of the partially finished sangar. Like the others, beneath his braces he wore only an undershirt the front of which was smeared with a red paste, the combination of dust and dirt from the rocks and his own perspiration. Charlie pulled at his own saturated undershirt where it had stuck to his back and drew deeply on his cigarette. Walter handed him an enamel mug of tea and he slurped at the scalding liquid. He had been thinking of Sarah a lot but hadn't seen her since the evening he had called on her at the

Dunkley house and with the battalion now posted on Caesar's Camp he was unsure when he would next have the opportunity. Right now he had sangars to build. He stood up and looked towards the brown eminence of Umbulwana which rose from the plain like a giant upturned tin loaf. The Boers had dragged guns up to its plateau, including another of those damned Creusots which the men had soon nicknamed Puffing Billy, and had already sent a few shells into the town although he had not heard of any casualties. He nipped his cigarette between his fingers and slid the remnant over his ear. 'Back to work, lads.'

Joseph Ncube kicked the stone along the pavement on Murchison Street. He had been kicking it in the stride of his easy paced walk almost all the way from the railway station. One, two, three, kick. The scuffed boots he was wearing were now too small for him so it was just as well they had no laces. They were no longer loose on his sockless feet and his toes had started to pinch. He had considered going barefoot as he had done for most of his life but rejected the thought almost immediately. They had once belonged to Master Ralph and Mrs. Dunkley had given them to him following a clearout of old and unwanted clothing. With boots he was someone. A man, not a boy. No, he would put up with a bit of discomfort. The trousers and shirt he was wearing came from the same source but were recent gifts and a better fit despite the missing buttons on both garments.

Mrs. Dunkley was a kind lady. He was lucky that his grandfather was the gardener at their house. All the Dunkleys were kind, much kinder than most of the white people who lived in the town. His favourite though was Nurse Sarah. She didn't give him gifts like Mrs. Dunkley – being a lodger from outside she probably had nothing to give – but spoke nicely to him, his grandfather and the other servants. Cook thought she might be connected with the church as church people were usually kinder and more tolerant of the blacks but Joseph didn't subscribe to that view. He knew plenty of regular churchgoers who treated him with contempt. Captain Turnbull was one. Joseph didn't like him at all. He had seen straight away those dark, hateful eyes. Turnbull treated them very badly. He made him clean his riding boots until they shone, even though it wasn't his job to do so, and if they were not to his satisfaction he would kick him. He would often kick him and even grandfather if they were within reach and none of the Dunkleys was about. Concealed behind a tree in the garden the other day he had seen Captain Turnbull frighten and upset Nurse Sarah on the porch. He was a bad man. One, two, three, kick.

There had been no word from Mr. Dunkley and an increasingly distraught Mrs. Dunkley had sent him to the station to find out when the next train from Estcourt may be expected. He had no words of comfort for her. The station and the surrounding area were in chaos, thronged with soldiers assembling to leave town amid the arrival of other soldiers of a kind he had not seen before. Many were dressed in blue shirts and baggy blue trousers instead of the usual khaki and wore wide brimmed hats. They had been struggling to unload two huge guns from the train with the help of dozens of native labourers including his father.

He had tried to explain to the stationmaster the reason for his visit and the information he sought. The man had not waited to hear him even when he tried to show him a note written by Mrs. Dunkley. He had snatched it from his hand, screwed it up and thrown it over his shoulder without bothering to read it. 'Can't you see we're busy here?' he had shouted at him. 'I haven't got time to waste listening to you. Get out of here right now, kaffir,' he had added, helping him on his way with a kick. 'And don't come back.'

There were two types of soldiers in town. They all wore khaki and spoke English but he could tell the difference between them. The locals wore soft hats pinned up at the side and called him kaffir while the British wore harder helmets and called him nigger. He wasn't sure whether one term was any better or worse than the other but it didn't really matter. They would call him what they liked and there was nothing he could do about it. One, two, three, kick.

'Twenty-three seconds, sir,' said Frank as a mule disintegrated in an explosion in the town below amid shouts and screams from the native drivers.

'Right. That's Puffing Billy done,' said Lieutenant Watson, allowing his field glasses to drop against his chest and scribbling the information in a notebook. 'Just one more.' From the top of Convent

Hill they had a clear view of the town and the hills to the north-east, east and south beyond it. The lieutenant stuffed the notebook and pencil back into the breast pocket of his tunic and raised the field glasses again, scanning away from Umbulwana to Pepworth Hill whose Long Tom had caused so much havoc on that Mournful Monday just a few days ago.

Frank was enjoying his light duty attachment to the engineers. He had become bored in the hospital and had been glad to be discharged. Besides, his bed had been needed for a new enteric case. Under normal circumstances he would have been happier with his pals but he was still not feeling quite at his best. In all his life he had never shirked from physical labour but he had to admit that this beat digging defence lines and building sangars on Caesar's Camp with the rest of the battalion. It was undemanding work and the young engineer officer was not a hard taskmaster. A wispy blond moustache set against his freckled face gave the impression that he was trying a little too earnestly to look older than he was. With his wide eyes and an occasional facial muscle spasm when he was nervous or excited, he reminded Frank of some kind of timorous woodland creature.

All Frank had to do on this assignment was to verify the time between the lieutenant's call when he saw the puff of smoke from the barrel of a Creusot and the resultant explosion in the town. So far the shells seemed to be doing little damage to life or property although the last blast among the mules had caused some panic. It was pleasant up on Convent Hill, with the heat tempered by a light breeze and a panoramic view of the surrounding area. Frank had seen battalion commanders and red-tabbed staff officers hurrying to and from General White's headquarters in the convent building. The large Red Cross flag flapped lazily over the building, parts of which, like the town hall, had been converted for hospital use although here more specifically for officers. From time to time small knots of Augustinian nuns shuffled busily between their spiritual and nursing duties.

Several minutes passed as the lieutenant gazed fixedly towards Pepworth Hill. 'Now!' he exclaimed. Frank clicked the stopwatch into life. They waited expectantly until earth and debris spewed from the garden at the back of a tin-roofed house beyond Murchison Street.

'Twenty-five seconds, sir.'

The field glasses dangled from the lieutenant's chest as he scribbled the details into his notebook. 'Well, Hoyland, it seems there is no more than three seconds' difference in the trajectory time between the three Creusots,' he said excitedly with a slight twitch in his cheek. Frank had been told that observers would be set up to give warning whenever they saw the telltale puff of smoke from one of the Creusots so that those in their vicinity would have a hurried opportunity to find shelter or at least lie flat on the ground. Frank felt that anyone caught in the open might as well stay put as there was no way of knowing where a shell would land. As Walter never tired of saying about shell or bullet, 'If one's got your name on it there's nowhere to hide.' Nevertheless, with these calculations soldier and civilian alike would at least know how much time they had between the alarm being raised and the shell's impact.

Fiddling Jimmy, the third Creusot, was in the opposite direction on Telegraph Hill and not visible from their vantage point at the convent and Watson had decided to time it first to get it done with. He seemed to find a touching kind of security within the convent grounds as if a combination of divine providence and the Red Cross flag offered sanctuary from the shells. Frank doubted that the Boer gunners could aim with sufficient accuracy to strike or avoid anything in particular but equally this meant that no building or exposed position was safe. They just seemed to lob shells in the general direction of the town where they landed randomly but Frank felt it was only a matter of time before a shell caused serious structural damage or a long list of casualties.

Watson had already been edgy on their way to the point from where Fiddling Jimmy was best observed as he had considered it a very exposed position. Upon arrival at the elevated vantage point behind the convent area he had been mortified at the sight of dozens of sailors from the recently arrived Naval Brigade preparing an emplacement for one of the two 4.7 inch ship's guns they had brought with them. He had been convinced that the gun and the hive of bluejackets surrounding it would make too tempting and distinct a target for the Boer gunners on Telegraph Hill. Surely they would not fail to take advantage of such an opportunity, he had confided to Frank, despite a naval officer's assurance that they had brought khaki uniforms with them and that these would be issued as soon as the initial and urgent defence preparations had been completed. At the same time as being impatient for Fiddling Jimmy's first shell, so that they could make their calculations and get away, he had been fearful of its possible consequences. To Frank's amusement the twitches had come thick and fast while waiting for the Creusot's billowing announcement and especially during the shell's journey. Frank had been so engrossed in watching Watson's taut and twitching face and the apparent suspension of his respiratory function that he had almost missed noting the trajectory time on the stopwatch. The shell had landed well behind them and even cleared Murchison Street. Watson's relief had been palpable as they had made their way to the convent.

'Did you hear that?' asked Watson. Frank cocked his ear in the expectation of hearing a shell burst. 'It's a lark,' he continued without waiting for a reply. 'Do you have larks where you come from, Hoyland?'

'I suppose so, sir,' replied Frank. 'I can't say that I've ever noticed.'

'You've never noticed? If you had ever heard a lark you would never forget it. It's a most gorgeous sound.'

'Look!' he said, pointing enthusiastically beyond the face of the hill to a piece of flatter ground below, 'There it is.' Frank could just make out the tiny bird singing its joyful song as it rose into the air and then dropped sharply back to earth. The lieutenant pulled out his pocket book and feverishly scribbled a note. 'That's twenty-nine species of bird I've seen since I've been in Natal and in less than two months, too. Not bad eh, Hoyland?'

'No, sir. Not bad at all.' Frank could imagine him in deerstalker and cape trudging over some boggy moor, his face twitching with nervous excitement whenever he caught sight or sound of a bird. That's it, thought Frank. He reminded him of a bird. Frank wondered how this timid and nervous man had ever come to join the army at all. He obviously must have some sort of technical or mechanical qualification for him to be in the Royal Engineers, thought Frank, although he looks too young to have had much practical experience. He was certainly harmless, the meekest and most inoffensive officer he had ever known.

Watson once more returned the notebook and pencil to his pocket and then fumbled in his trouser pockets and patted his tunic with a vacantly puzzled expression on his face. 'Sir,' said Frank, handing him the stopwatch.

'Oh, yes,' he responded. 'Thank you, Hoyland. By the way, how are you feeling?'

'Fine, thank you, sir.' Frank's headaches were diminishing in frequency and intensity but his scalp wound was still sore and had to be covered with a dressing. He was temporarily excused from wearing a service helmet and the slouch hat in the style of the colonial units looked slightly at odds with his British infantry uniform.

'Good,' said Watson. He paused. ' You've been very useful, you know. I'll be sorry to see you go when you return to your unit.'

It seemed to Frank that time froze as his response was stifled by a shrill whirr. Lieutenant Watson appeared to be transfixed in open-mouthed anticipation until the unreal perception of stillness was angrily shattered when the shell crashed through the roof of the refectory and exploded fiercely inside. With exclamations and curses from every direction and the incensed accusations of the Boers' disregard of the Red Cross flag from a converging group of officers, Frank instinctively ran into the convent to offer whatever help he could with Watson trailing in his wake. Inside the entrance hall was chaos. Most of the shocked and bewildered crowd were stumbling around in the choking, swirling dust and fumes, instinctively trying to get out of the building but in so doing they were obstructing those attempting to reach the shell ravaged refectory. The disjointed cacophony of human voices assailed Frank's ears; some were shouting, some crying and some calling for assistance while a few officers were attempting to issue orders amid the disorder. As Frank barged his way through the throng a young nun, repeating her Hail Marys, floundered into him and crashed to the floor. He paused for a second but as she seemed unhurt he continued his charge towards the refectory.

Frank's determination soon propelled him beyond the turmoil and he found himself among a small group that had managed to reach the refectory. At the entrance there were two dust and blood covered figures lying groaning on the floor. The force of the explosion had blown out the refectory doors and a doctor and a priest had been hit by flying glass and large wooden splinters. While the others stopped to attend to the injured pair Frank continued alone into the refectory, hardly pausing to vault a fallen rafter which had snapped at a sharp angle. The unmistakable stench of cordite filled the air which was pierced by a large shaft of dusty sunlight from the gaping hole in the roof. He trod more warily over a pile of rubble to reach the central area where a line of tables and chairs had been flattened by falling masonry and the force of the explosion. 'Is anyone there?' he shouted, his voice echoing emptily among the desolation. His call was repeated by others behind him who were clambering less energetically over the fallen rafter.

It occurred to him that if anyone was in the refectory when the shell struck the chances of survival among the debris and destruction around him were non-existent. He shouted again, his voice reverberating off the walls. His call was once again echoed by the rest of the group which now included Lieutenant Watson. There was no response to the calls and looking around the empty room there was no sanctuary. It was clear that the refectory had been mercifully unoccupied when the shell struck. A creaking noise caught Frank's attention. He looked up at the high vaulted ceiling and saw two rafters starting to sag. His thoughts were interrupted by a red tabbed major who was attempting to bring organisation to a situation which no longer demanded it. 'You,' he called to Frank. 'Help those men to clear that rubble away,' he ordered, pointing to the area where the tables and chairs had been crushed. 'There may be survivors underneath.'

This is ridiculous, thought Frank. It might make sense if there was a possibility of finding bodies but there was no one here to rescue. 'But, sir,' he began.

'Get on with it, private or I'll have you on a charge for insubordination,' snapped the major.

'Yes, sir,' he replied and moved over to the pile of rubble where he joined the group energetically removing the stones, slates and lengths of wood under which lay nothing more than broken furniture. It was a pointless exercise but Frank knew it was even more pointless, and asking for trouble, to argue with a superior officer and a staff officer at that. The group worked their way methodically along the line where in quieter times the nuns had taken their frugal meals in tranquil silence. Their efforts released more dust which hung in the air and coated the skin. Frank's eyes and nostrils began to irritate and his mouth was parched. What I wouldn't give for a glass of water, he thought as he looked up and tried to blink the dust from his eyes.

The room seemed to close in on him and for a moment he thought that his exertions and the atmosphere had made him light headed. Two distinct sounds came from different sources and then merged as the splintering of timber was accompanied by the crack of stonework. The two sagging rafters had strained beyond their tensile limits, depriving the shell weakened far wall of adequate support. The rafters yielded with a loud snap and the wall tilted almost in one piece before crashing to the floor and fragmenting into smaller blocks or individual stones. Out of the corner of his eye Frank had caught sight of a figure suddenly inundated by the collapsing wall. Now there *was* a need to clear away rubble.

In the few seconds it took for the shock of events to register with the others Frank had nimbly negotiated the pile of rubble they had been clearing and reached the fallen stonework which was now bathed in the mid morning sunlight. Beyond the massive haemorrhage of masonry lay an uninterrupted view of a stand of acacias rustling gently in the breeze.

He pulled vainly at a large section of stonework under which the unfortunate had appeared to fall. The others joined him and together they heaved and strained but could only coax the slightest of movements from the unyielding masonry. Frank felt across his crown the searing pain he thought he would never have to experience again. 'Sledgehammer,' he said, his eyes squeezed tightly against the agony. 'We need a sledgehammer,' he reiterated with a combination of exasperation and urgency in his voice.' No one moved. 'Now!' he shouted, the pain reverberating excruciatingly inside his head just as his voice echoed around the shattered refectory. The staff major shouted his endorsement towards the refectory door and the demand was repeated down the line. In less than a minute a sapper arrived at the double and stumbled his way towards the group cradling a sledgehammer.

Frank snatched it from his unresisting hands and swung it over his head and down on to the section. A small dent appeared accompanied by a few chips of stone. He swung and struck again and again, each time making bigger dents and cracks and each time feeling the pain race through his head. A larger crack appeared along a mortar line, its fissured tendrils spreading along other lines with each frenzied blow. Perspiration ran down his brow and neck and his shirt quickly became saturated. He coughed and spat as the dust invaded his nose and mouth until finally the section split into several pieces which the others swarmed to lift up and heave aside. The removal of the penultimate piece revealed crushed legs in bloodied khaki trousers. A final effort raised and removed the remaining piece. Frank tossed aside the sledgehammer and knelt by the prone and broken figure huddled in a near foetal position. A doctor pushed through and felt for a pulse. He turned the head slightly, raised an eyelid and shook his head. 'I'm afraid there's nothing I can do for him,' he said, looking up. 'Does anyone know who he is?'

    Frank thought how timid and fragile he looked even in death. 'Yes, sir. Lieutenant Watson, Royal Engineers, sir.'

Ada Dunkley was in no mood to be trifled with. 'Do you know who I am?' she said, prodding the stationmaster with her parasol and waving a podgy finger at him. She was a determined woman who had a habit of getting her own way by one means or another but privately she detested people who used real or imagined positions of influence to obtain preferential treatment or harangue humble and defenceless government employees. Under normal circumstances she would never have addressed anyone like this but the man was clearly both an idiot and a bully and deserved everything she was throwing at him. Besides, there was still no news from her husband and the prospects of any more trains in or out of Ladysmith before the town was completely cut off appeared increasingly remote. 'Well, do you?' she insisted.

    'Yes, Mrs. Dunkley,' said the startled official. He would not normally tolerate being spoken to in this manner by a woman but Mrs. Dunkley was a formidable lady and her husband was known to carry influence in many areas of government and business, no doubt including one or two of the big noises in the Natal Government Railway. 'Mrs. Dunkley, there has been an unfortunate misunderstanding. Please accept my sincere apologies.' It was bad enough having to make a grovelling apology to anyone but it was especially so when it was on behalf of a kaffir. Times were difficult enough without all this.

'When I send someone to make an enquiry on my behalf concerning my husband's arrival time I expect you to show him the same courtesy as if I were making the enquiry in person. And that does not include only white people. Do you understand?'

'Yes, madam,' he replied flinching from another prod from the parasol. The station was quiet now but the commotion had attracted the attention of the booking office clerk, who had to look away to hide his mirth, and a bemused looking army transport officer. Several native children stood giggling by the station entrance.

'And I do not expect any representative of mine to be kicked on his way,' she added with a swipe of the parasol across his shoulder. 'Do I make myself clear?'

'Yes, madam.'

'So if you don't want me to report you to the chairman of the NGR I suggest you tell me exactly when the next train from Estcourt is expected.'

'I'm sorry, madam,' said the stationmaster, not altogether managing to disguise his smugness at being able to give her the bad news. 'The Boers have encircled the town and cut the railway and telegraph lines. I'm afraid there will be no more trains into or out of Ladysmith until further notice.'

Ada's aggressive confidence evaporated instantly. 'Oh no,' she gasped. 'It cannot be. My husband is in Estcourt and must return. For the sake of his family and his business.' She fought back a tear. She was devastated by the news but didn't want to give this dreadful man the satisfaction of seeing how much it had upset her.

The transport officer strode over purposefully with a look of genuine concern on his face. 'I'm afraid it's true ma'am,' he said sympathetically after saluting her. 'The last train out left this morning. It was fired upon by the Boers but got through safely. The last train in was yesterday afternoon.' He paused as if searching vainly for a gentler and less abrupt way of confirming the situation. 'Ladysmith is cut off.'

This time Charlie was sure he had done something wrong. It was the second time in a matter of days that he had been summoned before the company commander. He thought hard. Had his section's work constructing the sangars been unsatisfactory? Was one of his section guilty of some misdemeanour that had escaped his notice? If so, that would surely reflect badly upon him. He couldn't think of any reason why Captain Young would want to see him and in a way that was the most disconcerting thing.

The company sergeant-major ushered him into the cramped company HQ which in reality was nothing more than Captain Young's sleeping quarters. The stone fort on the town side crest of Caesar's Camp had been hastily built from the ubiquitous ironstone boulders that littered the plateau. It was of solid construction and allowed the battalion to feel confident that they would be protected and secure against anything the Boers might throw at them. The walls were nearly three feet above eye level and a good twelve feet thick. The problem as Charlie saw it was that at any one time at least half the battalion would be manning the sangars on the opposite crest where any Boer attack would be directed and where there would be no such feeling of personal security.

The room was dark and dingy, the only source of natural light coming from the entrance over which was tucked a sackcloth cover. This was draped over the entrance whenever Captain Young decided he needed some privacy. Ominously the sergeant-major pulled the cover down over the entrance as soon as they were inside. Apart from a few tiny chinks penetrating the odd hole or gap, the only light was provided by a single large candle on a makeshift table made from two upturned biscuit boxes and another piece of sackcloth. The warmth of the sun did not penetrate this rude shelter and there was an inescapable mustiness that recalled the damp ridden slums of Charlie's childhood. Charlie shivered involuntarily in the coolness of the shelter. Captain Young seemed oblivious of the conditions in which he had to run 'D' Company but Charlie could not help but be reminded of the travelling shows he had visited in his youth where proclaimed freaks of nature could be seen for a penny. These were invariably disappointments and often the dim light and the bowed head that were supposedly meant to heighten the mystery and tension served only to disguise the generally unremarkable features of the alleged freak.

Captain Young used his camp bed as a chair with the improvised table pushed up against his legs. There was barely enough room for Charlie and the sergeant-major to stand and salute. Captain Young yawned and scratched his unshaven chin. Even in this light he looked very tired. He had been out on patrol during the night and had not long awoken. He waved a piece of paper at Charlie. It would have been a struggle to read it in there so Charlie assumed that Young had read it outside but that the contents were so dire that they had to be dealt with in the secretive dimness of his quarters. 'I can do without this, Browell,' said Young. Charlie felt the warm disapproval of the sergeant-major's breath on the back of his neck. 'We need every man we've got at all times especially as the battalion is holding the single most critical area of the town's defences,' Young continued, thrusting the piece of paper towards Charlie despite the impossibility of discerning its contents in this gloom. 'Do you understand?'

'Yes, sir,' replied Charlie instinctively although he didn't understand at all.

'I don't want to know how you made Zachariah Dunkley's acquaintance but it seems he's taken quite a shine to you. I take it you are aware that he left Ladysmith a few days ago and is now stranded outside for the duration of this siege?'

'No, sir. I didn't know that.'

'Well he has. Not only that but he has exerted enough influence to have commandeered the heliograph at Estcourt to send a message to General Sir George White, no less, requesting your services to make thrice weekly checks upon his wife, daughter and property in his absence. Not only that but General White has acceded to his request.' Young gave an exasperated sigh. 'We've got enough to do here with those damned Boers besieging the place without having to nursemaid civilians.' He looked up at Charlie. 'However, irrespective of my own feelings, this order comes from the top. So make arrangements for your visits through the sergeant-major.'

'Yes, sir.'

'Your time there will be kept to a minimum and if an urgent situation develops I want you back here sharp. Understand?'

'Yes, sir.'

'By the way Browell, Hoyland returns to your section tomorrow,' Young added in a more relaxed tone. 'Dismissed.' Charlie was hustled out by the sergeant-major and stood blinking in the strong sunlight. It was going to be another hot day.

'Right , Browell. Before you go calling round for afternoon tea I've got a job for you,' sneered the sergeant-major. Charlie had expected some form of retribution as a result of being singled out for special attention by Dunkley but he didn't care. He now had an opportunity, and an official one sanctioned by the commander-in-chief of the Ladysmith garrison to boot, to see Sarah again. And Frank was to rejoin the section. Things were not so bad after all.

Life was rapidly settling into a routine, giving them the opportunity to rest and take stock of the situation after the last hectic weeks since they had embarked on commando. Christiaan was tending to the horses and Koos was on a visit to a neighbouring commando looking for old comrades from previous wars. Piet slid his thumb into the ungummed corner of the envelope and slit it open in one movement. The Burghers had organised an efficient and reliable postal service and despite the fluidity of the commandos mail passed regularly between them and their loved ones in the two republics.

Sannie had written regularly but, in the manner of one whose daily life continues unchanged, without actually saying much. News of their other children – all were well; the running of the farm – the labourers and servants were doing what was required of them and causing no problems; snippets of information from elsewhere in the district. That was the usual pattern. This time, though, she had some news which affected the whole commando and dwelt for a couple of pages on poor Mrs. Viljoen who had lost her youngest at Talana. It seemed that on receiving the tragic news of Kobus's death she had taken to her bed in a state of nervous collapse and was currently running a fever.

Piet had never been one for letter writing but felt it his duty to maintain the flow of correspondence from the front to home. Sannie and the girls would only become concerned if they did not receive regular reassurances that three of them were all right. Piet was nonetheless unsure whether that was necessarily a good thing as he read that Mrs. Viljoen had received a letter from Kobus telling her he was well and enjoying life on commando a matter of hours before she received notification of his death. She received another similar letter two days later. No wonder she's had a breakdown, thought Piet. Koos displayed no interest in letter writing at all but Piet assumed that this was because he was only partially literate. 'My only requirement is to be able to read the Bible,' Piet recalled him thundering on more than one occasion during his childhood. Christiaan was far too preoccupied with the exciting life on commando to bother telling his mother and sisters all about it. Both were nevertheless always interested to hear news from home and whenever a letter arrived they listened eagerly as Piet read out the mundane details of life back on the farm.

Within the last day or two he had noticed a small but steady influx of wives and even children arriving to give moral support to their men and satisfy their own curiosity as to the conduct and events of the war. He hoped that Sannie wouldn't pitch up one day in her Sunday best like these foolish women. The farm wouldn't run itself and besides she could get hurt. He reassured himself that he had sufficient faith in his wife. She would neither bring baby Dirk and the girls down here nor leave them with others back home while she came alone.

He folded the letter back into the envelope and stuffed it into the back pocket of his corduroy trousers. He would read it out to Koos and Christiaan later. It would help to pass the time during the indolent heat of the afternoon.

Piet always swore that his father could smell coffee brewing and bacon sizzling from miles away and as if on cue Koos rode up with his nostrils in the air. 'It seems I'm just in time,' he said. 'That smell is enough to give anyone an appetite.' Christiaan ran over from the horses at Piet's call.

They slurped the hot, dark coffee between mouthfuls of greasy bacon and chunks of warm bread torn from the loaf Koos had bought from the baker's wagon on his way back. That was another peculiarity Piet had noticed recently. All manner of tradesmen had caught up with the commandos selling mostly food and provisions from their wagons. Coffee, tea, flour, sugar, salt, bacon and so on one could understand but fresh produce was also available – meat, fruit and vegetables – plus sweetmeats and other delicacies. The most surprising thing he noticed was that many of these wagons bore *Uitlander* names and almost invariably English ones at that. Coleman of Johannesburg, Westwood of

Benoni and Melrose of Germiston. They were all there. Men who valued their businesses above political agitation, were grateful for the opportunities living in the Transvaal afforded them and carried on regardless. Some of course might have been second or even third generation immigrants who had been entirely absorbed into Burgher life and culture, as the Huguenots and Germans had done before them, and spoke the *Taal* as their first language. There were plenty of English names scattered among the commandos. Some of these men were idealistic, particularly the Irish, and Piet still found it odd that one set of Irishmen would fight bravely and loyally for Queen Victoria while another would fight equally bravely against her. Talana had already demonstrated that.

'I went over to the Krugersdorp commando to look up a couple of old friends from the First War of Independence,' said Koos wiping his sleeve across his mouth and his right hand on his flowing grey beard.

'Did you find them,' asked Piet.

'No. I must be getting older more quickly than I thought,' he replied with a touch of melancholy in his voice. He packed his pipe with his forefinger and sucked the match's flame into the tobacco. 'Old van Niekerk died two years ago, although his son is with them, and Oosthuizen is at home suffering from rheumatism and can hardly walk.' He pulled the pipe from his mouth and expelled the smoke through the tobacco stained hairs of his moustache. 'It's been a long time,' he said pensively.

Piet pulled Sannie's letter from his pocket, the grease from his fingers smearing the envelope. 'Look what I received this morning,' he said flourishing it in front of them.

'Oh, pa, read it to us please,' pleaded Christiaan excitedly.

Puffing Billy on Umbulwana boomed. Koos belched effusively as if paying homage to the mighty Creusot. 'Yes, let us hear the news from home,' he said, perking up. Piet unfolded the letter and began to read.

'Good afternoon, Private Browell. Do come in,' said Ada, delighted to see Charlie. He had already removed his helmet and crossed the threshold, following the servant who had answered the door and admitted him without referring to her mistress. It felt good to be both expected and welcome and he returned Ada's greeting. It was Sarah who noticed the stripe on his arm.

'It's Lance-Corporal Browell now, I see,' she observed for Ada's benefit. Ada apologised for the oversight, adding her congratulations and hastened Charlie to one of the chunky leather armchairs into which he sank luxuriously.

'I'll have cook make some tea and sandwiches,' she added and bustled out to the kitchen to make the necessary arrangements. Charlie stood up, partly out of politeness to Ada but also because in Ada's haste to seat him Sarah was left standing.

As soon as Ada left the room Charlie and Sarah instinctively looked into each other's eyes. Charlie averted his glance and shyly stared at the floor. He felt awkward. He knew what he wanted to say but was afraid to do so. It had seemed so long since he had walked her back from the Dunkleys' house to the hospital. Perhaps she felt differently about him now. She did say she wanted to see him again. Well, she didn't exactly say it like that but she did indicate that it would be acceptable. He struggled to recall her exact words. Perhaps it was all an illusion and she wasn't really interested in seeing him again at all.

'I've missed you Charles,' she said simply.

'I've missed you too... Sarah.' He looked back into her eyes which were fixed on his.

'You don't have to say that just because I did.'

'No. I didn't. I mean it. I really have missed you. In fact I've thought of little else but you since we last met. It seems ages.'

'I was worried sick during that battle outside the town last week. And afterwards.' She told him about her anxious wait on Murchison Street watching the returning troops. 'It seemed just about every battalion but yours returned before I had to go on duty.'

'We were the last battalion to get back to town,' he said. He explained their role as a protective screen to cover the retirement of all the other infantry units and their subsequent posting to Caesar's Camp. 'That's why I've been unable to contact you since. Then out of the blue I'm ordered – ordered, mind you – to call in here three times a week to check on Mrs. Dunkley and her daughter. I couldn't believe my luck. It seems Mr. Dunkley asked General White personally to allow me to do so.'

'Really?' said Sarah, striving to sound impressed and surprised at the same time. She also strove to keep a straight face. Far from it being Mr. Dunkley's idea it had been she who had precipitated Charles's unorthodox assignment. She had suggested it to Ada who had considered it an excellent proposition and had used her own influence in the town to send a message via the army's heliograph to her husband in Estcourt. Zachariah Dunkley had warmed to the idea instantly and, on the basis that such a request would carry more weight if sent by him from outside, had promptly heliographed back to General White. Sarah had done this primarily because she wanted the opportunity to see Charles, whose path she was increasingly unlikely to cross unless — God forbid — he was badly wounded or seriously ill, but also because it would prevent Captain Turnbull from becoming the sole male presence in the house. She had originally taken a neutral stance over Captain Turnbull but since the incident on the porch she had become increasingly wary of him. He was well mannered and charming to her in front of Ada and Grace but she held no great store by this as she had not since found herself alone in his presence. This may have been just welcome coincidence but she hoped he had shamed himself into keeping a discreet distance. More recently he seemed to be paying closer attention to Grace. In one way this was something of a relief but she had started to become concerned for Grace whose naivety of youth allowed her to relish the attentions of a dashing cavalry officer from a dangerously innocent and uncomplicated perspective.

'You look well,' she said.

'So do you.' He paused. He wanted to tell her how lovely she looked but his shyness stifled the words. 'Frank will be back with us tomorrow,' he said, changing the subject in an attempt to disguise his awkwardness.

'Good. It's always gratifying to see a patient mended and discharged. Let me know how he gets on.'

'Yes, of course.'

'And your other friend.'

'Walter.'

'Yes, the other one who dirtied my ward floor.' She smiled, hoping to put him more at ease and break the artificial atmosphere.

This small talk was killing her. She was sure he liked her but wanted him to tell her in his own words without any prompting. In his own good time, she thought, hoping it would be now.

Mrs. Dunkley returned and over afternoon tea she proceeded to tell Charlie about the shock of learning that her husband was cut off from Ladysmith and the distress she continued to suffer at his continuing absence. She missed him terribly and life would be difficult while the town was besieged although she had every confidence that General Buller's force would sweep the Boers away and relieve them within a matter of three or four weeks at most. 'At least we will be reunited for Christmas,' she proclaimed confidently as she proffered a plate of dainty sandwich triangles.

She expressed her gratitude for his kind and gallant attention to their situation as defenceless women in a besieged town under daily shellfire and no doubt riddled with Boer spies. Nevertheless, she assured him, she would not seek shelter in the funk holes down at the riverbank. She had a household to run and no Boer was going to force her out of her home, Long Tom or no Long Tom. She reflected that Captain Turnbull was at that moment escorting Grace around the shelters cut out of the steep riverbank by the men of the Light Horse but she trusted that her daughter would not be coerced into spending her daylight hours there as so many of the townsfolk did.

Charlie considered her something of a paradox. She was strong willed and stubborn, no doubt with a lively temper if provoked, but this contrasted with the kind, compassionate and hospitable woman he was coming to know. Most notably her superficial self-confidence conflicted with a vulnerability she was unable to disguise. He gave the impression of listening attentively, occasionally sounding a polite assent, but his attention drifted inexorably towards Sarah who was sitting on the sofa beside her. She looked lovely in her blue nurse's uniform, the white frill of the collar and the little white cap almost framing her pale but finely sculptured face. In fact Charlie had never seen her wear anything else. It always seemed that if she wasn't actually working a shift at the hospital she was about to go back on duty. She modestly avoided meeting his eyes in Ada's presence and fiddled nervously with the puffed sleeve of her uniform until she became aware of his glances and clasped her hands on her lap. She looked down as he glanced at her again. She is so attractive, he thought. He was in love with her.

'Don't you think so, Lance-Corporal Browell?' Ada's question sent a flash of panic through him. His attention had been so fixed on Sarah that he hadn't the faintest idea what she had been talking about. He saw Sarah nod almost imperceptibly. 'Yes, of course. No doubt about it,' he replied.

'I'm glad you agree.' Charlie was still none the wiser as the topic of conversation moved on to Ada's concern for her son. 'I'm hoping that Ralph will be among the first troops of the relief force to enter the town. That would make Mr. Dunkley and me very proud.'

'I'm sure he'll do you proud too.'

Mrs. Dunkley tutted that the freshly baked walnut cake had not been brought in and with a hasty apology she bustled off again to the kitchen.

Charlie and Sarah's eyes met again. 'I love you,' he said softly with a boldness that surprised him.

Sarah closed her eyes momentarily in silent gratitude before smiling at him. 'I love you too Charles.'

Life on Caesar's Camp had quickly become dull. The central and peripheral defences had been completed and a battery of field artillery had been dragged up and deployed on the plateau, each of the six guns nestled behind a breastwork of similar but smaller construction to the infantry's sangars. Apart from constant observation of the Boers' positions and nightly picket duty the officers had kept the men busy with drill exercises and fatigues. Boredom was setting in and boredom could lead to reduced vigilance and the resultant hazards that could follow. As Captain Young had told them, this was a defence line. They would make no sorties from their positions. They would have to sit and wait for the Boers to attack them.

Walter had been quick to organise a card school and off duty games of brag attracted men from other sections and platoons and occasionally even from other companies. Charlie, Frank and McAdams would watch silently as agitated men gleefully scooped up the pool of money or, more often, swore and tossed their worthless cards into the middle of the crude table formed by a square of empty ammunition boxes. The atmosphere often became heated although more with the frustration of the losers than through any personal animosity. Charlie nevertheless doubted he was the only one to notice that Walter won more hands than he lost. The bent and greasy cards were well used and Charlie hoped that Walter had not marked them. He didn't want any trouble.

Charlie's salvation lay in his calls at the Dunkley residence although perversely time dragged even more for him between visits than it would have done if he were denied any respite from the continuous life on Caesar's Camp that the others had to endure. Apart from presenting the opportunity to see Sarah it also provided a break from routine and a change of environment. Frank had told him that there had been some resentment expressed within the section and elsewhere in the platoon but that McAdams had had a word with the aggrieved parties and all open criticism had been quickly muted.

Giving his tunic a final quick brush with his hand Charlie noticed that his uniform had started to look a little threadbare. In addition to his darned sleeve both cuffs of his tunic had become slightly ragged and over both knees the material of his trousers was wearing thin. This was not surprising considering that in the last month he had fought a battle, undertaken strenuous physical labour and been out in all weathers in it but there was no chance of a replacement before the relief so he would have to try to preserve it as best as he could until then. He tried to console himself that in this respect he was no different to every other Tommy in the garrison but just hoped Sarah would not find him unattractive in it.

The last forty-eight hours had seemed an eternity yet here on the Dunkleys' porch it seemed only five minutes since he had bid Sarah and Mrs. Dunkley goodnight. He was unable to conceal either his surprise or his delight when Sarah opened the door to his knock.

'Good afternoon, Charles,' said Sarah with a smile. 'I'm so glad you've called round before I go back on duty. I've been looking forward to seeing you again so much.'

The sound of their footsteps resonated down the hallway, the heavy clump of his boots almost overwhelming the dainty clip-clop of hers, as they entered the drawing room. Charlie expected Mrs. Dunkley to come bustling in with such a cheery welcome and an offer of tea and cakes that it would be unthinkable to decline but all was quiet. 'Where is everyone else?' he asked.

'Ada – Mrs. Dunkley – has gone to Mr. Dunkley's office to pick up some documents and tell the staff that their services will not be required for the remainder of the siege.' She paused. 'Well, nobody is going to purchase land they can't see and can't use and which in all probability is right now occupied by Boers,' she added superfluously although Charlie felt sympathy for the employees who would have no source of income while the siege lasted. 'Grace is with Captain Turnbull down at the riverbank shelters, cook has gone to the market for provisions and the other servants are off the premises,' she continued. 'Mrs. Dunkley doesn't allow any of the servants except cook to stay in the house when she's not here,' she added in answer to Charlie's unspoken question.

He was captivated by her and was about to tell her how lovely she looked when a scream overhead and the crash of an explosion in a neighbouring garden announced the arrival of another shell from one of the Creusots. Sarah was startled and in a reflex action threw her arms around Charlie's neck and he responded by cradling his hands protectively around her wasplike waist and on her hips. Her tenseness evaporated and her hold on him relaxed until her hands were stroking his back. She looked at him expectantly. Her lips parted and he pressed his mouth against hers, his tongue probing her delicate mouth. She wanted to immerse herself in his musky, manly odour. She had never had such feelings for a man as she felt for Charles. She loved him. She already knew that. But this was something more – a longing, a craving, a desire to be fulfilled.

His aroused response to her kiss, her touch, the sweet smell of her cologne, made him ache for her. He ran his hand down from her neck and felt the firmness of her breast. Her nipples swelled and her breathing became heavier as his touch excited her in ways she had never experienced. She felt his stiffness against her as his hands pulled up at her skirts. Her lower body was flooded with desire, not with lust but an expressionless yearning for the man she loved. She wanted his hardness inside her moist opening. She wanted him to fill her with his love. She pulled herself from his embrace. 'Not here,' she gasped in an urgent half whisper. We must go to my room. Hurry.' She grabbed his hand and lifted her skirts as they half stumbled out of the drawing room and up the stairs, impatient in their desire for each other.

She threw open the door and locked it behind them. Even then she realised that it was a futile gesture. Having a man in her room when the house was empty would compromise and condemn her anyway if she was discovered. She wanted Charles more than anything, even at the risk of Ada returning to find them together.

She threw her cap and apron on a chair while he discarded his tunic and they pulled off each other's boots. He clumsily started to unbutton her blouse from the top but his shaking hands laboured so much that she undid the buttons from the bottom. He removed her blouse awkwardly, revealing the soft, pale skin of her shoulders and neck above her slip. Together they pulled off her skirts in a series of frantic, clumsy movements until she stood only in her slip and drawers. She undid his trousers and touched his stiffness. For the first time she felt a tinge of shame. If they were discovered she would be branded a slut and would bring shame to her family and embarrassment to the Dunkleys. The Dyson whore abused their hospitality for her own debauched pleasure, they would say, and there would be nowhere to go, nowhere to hide, in a besieged town. It didn't matter. They would never understand how she felt about him. Her desire for Charles submerged all other considerations. She wanted him and not just now. For always.

She lifted off her slip as he rolled her drawers down over ankles, pausing to kiss her inner thigh. She felt a surge of desire even stronger than before. He slipped out of his undershorts revealing for the first time what she had just felt, that stiff prominence she wanted inside her. Her russet hair spilled over her milky white shoulders as he removed the grips. They fell back on the bed, joined in a passionate kiss, their legs and arms entangled. He kissed her neck as she ran her hand over his back and through the matted hairs on his chest. His hand stroked the inside of her thigh and stopped by her divide, already moist and welcoming. His touch sent a shudder through her entire body and she gasped and squirmed as he slipped a finger inside her, exploring her most intimate part. She responded to his movements, thrusting and arching her lower body, always in denial but always wanting more. She felt an unstoppable wave building up inside her, yearning to release it but at the time afraid to do so. She whimpered and then exhaled a long ecstatic sigh as the wave broke and flooded her. She had had no idea that her body was capable of such gratification.

She lay gasping in her intoxication for a few seconds. It was now her turn to satisfy him. She grabbed his swollen part and lay back, guiding him inside her. He gasped as his sensitive flesh slid past her swollen lips and met the warmth and wetness of her intimacy. She felt the tingle and surge of another, different sensation as he squeezed himself snugly into her, his rod gripped by her tight cleft. He pumped and plunged, slowly at first, then ever faster, penetrating deeper inside her. She felt her nipples harden as each thrust gave her another surge of joy until she felt him swell and with a low moan release himself inside her.

They lay entwined on the bed in the exhilarating exhaustion of their sated passion. He kissed her shoulder and arm down to the hand where he kissed each one of her fingers in turn. They articulated the love they felt for each other and he held her close to his chest. Slowly the joy of the moment receded and reality intruded into their private world.

'We need to hurry,' she said. 'Mrs. Dunkley could return at any minute. It's best if you sit in the drawing room as if you've been waiting for her.' He dressed quickly in the urgent but efficient manner of a soldier in the field and went downstairs while she ran a bath. The love he had planted in her was escaping down her leg as she lowered herself into the bath. There was neither the time nor the opportunity to arrange for hot water but that didn't matter. The exertions of their lovemaking had amplified the inescapable torpor of the afternoon and the radiating heat of her body was extinguished by the refreshing coolness of the water. Her limbs seemed strangely dysfunctional as she sponged her leg and cleaned her private area of his residual seed. As she did so a dreadful thought came to mind; not the shame of discovery – that would be bad enough – but the ultimate shame for her, the humiliation of rejection. What if Charles no longer wanted her? What if *he* thought her a slut, a whore – a worthless woman whose only attraction was a fleeting carnal gratification. She had never been with a man before and didn't want any other but him ever again. She loved him but desperately needed the renewed declaration of his love for her. She heard the slam of the front door and the deep rumble of his voice in response to Ada's happy trill. Their time alone was over. She would have to wait.

The eastern sky had quickly mutated from black to indigo and then to bright blue. The sun peeped over the horizon suffusing the surrounding hills with an orange glow. It's going to be yet another clear and hot day, thought Sarah as she stood on the Town Hall steps in weary contemplation at the end of another spell of duty. She buckled her cape around her neck and started to make her way back to the Dunkley residence. Despite a busy night she had been unable to free her mind of Charles and her critical need to hear the reaffirmation of his love for her.

The earth beneath her feet heaved and shuddered and the trees billowed and swayed as she was hurled flat on the ground amid a deafening roar. There was a few seconds' silence before a shower of earth, stones and small shell fragments peppered the pavement behind her in a harmless encore. As she fought to retrieve her senses she heard the sound of hurried footsteps as military and medical personnel scrambled to assess the damage to life and property. Although shaken and winded, she retained sufficient composure to realise that her loss of footing may well have saved her life. As she struggled back on her feet she felt the soreness from a graze on her wrist. Otherwise she was all right.

Two of the four faces of the clock tower had been blown away but Sarah was more concerned about the patients, particularly her own. She had heard that the shell that hit the convent had spared the patients but had killed one poor officer and seriously wounded a doctor and a priest. She dreaded the awfulness of the scene that might greet her but hurried back into the Town Hall nonetheless. Rushing through the front entrance she found that the wards in the main building appeared to be undamaged and that all the attention was focused on the tents of the volunteer hospital and administration at the rear.

She couldn't see what was going on for the crush of people at the rear doorway but she spotted an orderly from her ward emerging from the melee. 'What's happened?' she asked.

'It seems the shell hit the clock tower but it exploded among the tents out there,' he replied. 'They need all the help they can get. I've been ordered to fetch Dr. Barlow from his lodgings but I'll bet he's on his way already. He only lives down Murchison Street and he'd have to be dead to have slept through this.'

'There's a nurse here. Let her through,' shouted a man in civilian clothes next to her. The crowd parted and Sarah squeezed through. Several tents were riddled with holes from shell fragments but most of the attention was concentrated on one of the volunteers' tents. Shredded remains of canvas hung limply from the pole and two sides were completely exposed. The groans and screams from wounded men who had been wounded again pierced the early morning air. As she entered the tent she slipped on the wet grass. She automatically put out a hand to break her fall and winced as the wrist she had just grazed flexed. She went to wipe the dew on her cape when she was alarmed to see the blood that covered her palm and sleeve. For a second or two she stared at her hand incredulously as she tried to equate this substantial smear of blood with what she thought was a trivial graze aggravated by a minor fall. She experienced a sickening feeling in the pit of her stomach as the horror of the situation dawned on her. In a split second this sanctuary of care and healing had been transformed into a bloody slaughterhouse. Surgeons and doctors, nurses and orderlies were giving urgent treatment to the freshly wounded.

'Nurse! Over here!' called a surgeon struggling to treat a patient whose arms were thrashing about. 'Hold his arms down. The man was in state of shock. His head was bandaged from a previous wound but he had now been struck in the groin by a piece of shell. The surgeon and his assistant were trying to clamp off and suture his ruptured femoral artery before he bled to death.

Kneeling by the bed, Sarah held the man's hand and went to whisper in his ear but he fought against her. 'I need you to pin his arms down, girl, not hold hands with him like a courting couple,' shouted the surgeon.

'Sir, please let me do this my way,' she replied calmly. 'Besides, being a mere woman, I lack sufficient strength to pin his arms down.' She caught hold of his hand again and squeezed it.

'Can't you see he's delirious and violent?' snapped the assistant.

Sarah was tempted to ask whether he was referring to the surgeon or the patient but bit her tongue. 'He's neither delirious nor violent, sir, but he *is* frightened and in shock.' She had tempered her reply but felt that they would still consider her to have been insubordinate and impertinent. Right now they had a patient to treat and an uneasy truce prevailed while the surgeon and his assistant continued their efforts to stem the gush of blood while Sarah tried to soothe him.

Among the pathetically small pile of upturned belongings by his bed was a bible. Sarah flipped it open where a spidery hand had inscribed on the flyleaf 'To Jack. God be with you. Your loving mother. October 1899.' She stroked his face and whispered, 'Stay calm, Jack. Everything will be all right.'

He looked at her with wild, panic filled eyes, still agitated but no longer flailing his arms about. 'Am I going to die?'

She hated this. There was only one possible answer she could give and she had given it in the past to desperately sick and injured patients at the hospital in Maritzburg, even to those she knew had no chance. She recalled in particular the paralysed young man who had broken his neck in a fall from a tree. 'If you tell me I'll be all right, I know I will be,' he had said. He had trusted her implicitly. Towards the end he had begun to think she was his mother and just before he had died he had called her an angel and wanted her to come with him to where the other angels were beckoning. She had cried for that boy, not just because his young and unfulfilled life had ended but also because she had lied to him and given him false hope.

'Of course not, Jack. You'll be fine. In any case you have to get better for your mother. She wants to see you again so much.'

'Where's my mother?' He lifted his head from the pillow. 'Is she here?'

'She's at home, Jack.' She could be in Australia for all I know, thought Sarah, but I've just got to give him enough to hold on to. Her soft touch and gentle words soothed him and he lay still, looking at her, while the surgeon continued his work with a calmer urgency.

'Will you stay with me until she gets here?'

'I'll be close by. I'll come to see you from time to time until you get better.'

'Do you promise?'

'Yes,' she affirmed confidently. 'I promise.' He closed his eyes and drifted into sleep, the serene and relaxed sleep of a man at peace with himself.

'Good God,' said the surgeon as he finished suturing the ruptured artery. 'I don't know how you did it young lady but you've saved this man's life. I couldn't even clamp off the artery while he was so agitated.'

'Thank you, sir,' she replied. 'But you and the other doctor saved his life. I merely gave him some comfort.'

'A team effort, then. Well done to us all!' The surgeon's elation and relief at a successful outcome was expressed in his voice. Sarah was pleasantly surprised. She had fully expected a severe reprimand.

Jack was the last of the wounded to finish being treated and the carnage in the remains of the tent was now being cleared up. Three dead and seven wounded – two, including Jack, severely. One patient had taken a direct hit from the shell and had been blown to pieces. They were scraping up his remains into a sack as she left. She shivered in spite of the increasing warmth of the morning. It was that poor man's blood she had slipped on.

Dr. Barlow was in an agitated state as he addressed the nursing staff. The shelling of the Town Hall had precipitated General White's decision to evacuate the patients and staff at the hospitals there and at the convent. A low murmur ran through the room in speculation as to where the hospitals would be relocated.

'Quiet please!' shouted Barlow, clapping his hands in exasperation. He explained that the Boers had agreed to a request to transfer the sick and wounded, the medical staff and such civilians as wished to join them to a neutral site between Ladysmith and the Boer lines at a place called Intombi Spruit. 'At least everyone there will no longer be in the path of shellfire,' he added. 'The Boers have agreed to a twenty-four hour cease fire from noon today and have made it a condition that the removal has to be completed within that period which means...' He paused and lowered his voice. 'Which means we have to prepare to leave immediately.'

This time Barlow did not attempt to silence the buzz around the room, allowing everyone an opportunity for the news to sink in and to articulate their reaction. Sarah had mixed feelings. After the trauma of the previous morning, if it meant that the patients and staff were transferred to a safer area then this could only be welcomed. On the other hand she would probably not see Charles again for some time. Two other nurses next to her were in lively conversation. One asked the question that had immediately surfaced in her own mind.

'How long will we be there, Dr. Barlow?'

She feared the answer but knew it was inevitable. 'At least until the end of the siege,' replied Barlow. 'If the number of wounded and sick increases in the intervening period, probably longer,' he added wearily. The nurses resumed their discussion and her heart sank. She only hoped that General Buller would lead his force to their relief without delay for everyone's sake.

She knew that she could not dwell on her own situation. That would be unprofessional and selfish. The patients' needs came first. She threw herself into the task in hand with renewed vigour and tried unsuccessfully to push Charles to the back of her mind.

Everything would have to be transported the short distance to Intombi by train – patients, beds, tents, provisions, medicines, administrative records and all manner of surgical and medical equipment and accessories. Without the benefit of either advance planning or unrestricted time, arrangements for the move quickly disintegrated into confusion and disorder. Sarah could see that everyone was concentrating on his or her own area of responsibility, no matter how trivial, and there was no co-ordination to establish a practical sequence of evacuation and ensure that nothing was overlooked. This was not the way it should be done but she knew it would be hopeless to try to resist this undisciplined and demeaning clamour.

Orderlies packed dressings, bandages, kidney bowls, scissors, forceps and other ward paraphernalia into boxes while Indian bearers arrived with their *dhoolies* in which they would carry those patients too sick or disabled to walk. Sarah was stripping sheets and blankets from the beds of the ambulatory patients who loitered aimlessly around the ward awaiting orders or organisation.

'*Sawubona, nkosikazi.*' Sarah spun round at the unaccustomed sound of Zulu in the hospital. It was the language of the local natives but somehow seemed so incongruous here in this peculiarly British enclave.

'Good morning to you, too, Joseph,' she replied. 'You can see we're all very busy here. What do you want?' she added, irked by the interruption.

'Mrs. Dunkley and Miss Grace are on their way,' replied Joseph enthusiastically. 'They sent me ahead to help you.'

'Good,' she said, softening her tone. 'All help is gratefully received.' She set Joseph to work folding the sheets and blankets and stacking the mattresses against the wall.

The pathetic exodus snaked towards the station, those who were unable to walk and the equipment conveyed in all manner of carts. As Sarah had expected, Ada had attempted to bring order to the chaos and had done so with some success although at the expense of ruffling a few feathers. Several of the orderlies had felt the sharp edge of her tongue, especially those from other wards who had taken advantage of the general confusion to try to sneak off with the property of Sarah's ward. Ada went about requisitioning several carts from nearby businesses as well as a horse and trap whose driver was pressed into service with a forceful insistence that would brook no refusal. She took particular satisfaction in enlisting the help of a burly gunner to relieve the baker of his cart. The wretched man had had the gall to charge her a shilling for a small loaf of bread the day before. That will teach him not to profit from the siege, she told Sarah who smiled in her admiration of this remarkable woman. Sarah was concerned for her most badly wounded and fevered patients, each of whom was being carried in the large slings of the *dhoolies* slung through a pair of bamboo poles balanced on the shoulders of two bearers. She marvelled at their gentleness as their staccato steps conveyed their fragile human cargoes with neither lurch nor jolt.

The station was once again a hive of activity. Steam hissed from the engine in apparent disapproval of the unseemly scramble to load the carriages. Some patients lay on stretchers on the platform while orderlies, porters and bearers jostled to discharge their burdens. Sarah had managed to secure occupation of the van at the rear of the train where her worst cases could lie flat on the mattresses that Joseph was hauling aboard.

'Squeeze as many in as you can, Joseph,' called Sarah as he

dragged another mattress over the threshold of the drop down door. 'We have eight patients to fit in here.'

'*Yebo, nkosikazi.*' The *dhoolie* bearers stood patiently with their loads as Sarah watched him arrange the mattresses inside the van so as to maximise its capacity. It's like watching someone doing a difficult jigsaw puzzle, she thought as he overlapped three here and repositioned lengthways another two there. She observed the sun creep ever downwards in the western sky and the distant storm clouds approaching from the north. There was precious little twilight in Africa. It would be dark in less than an hour and the evacuation was running late. Joseph reappeared at the entrance to the van. 'Ready, *nkosikazi*,' he beamed triumphantly.

'Well done, Joseph.' Sarah gave a signal to the bearers who carried the patients aboard and tenderly laid them one by one on the mattresses. Eventually all the carriages and vans were loaded. Four of the bearers managed to find room to squat in a huddle in a corner of the van while the others sat cross-legged on the roof. Joseph stood by the entrance as Sarah made a quick check on each of the patients. He noticed his old adversary the stationmaster striding down the platform as two porters came to close and bolt the door of the van.

'Harper! McRae!' he called. He was about to order the porters to eject the kaffir from the van as a prelude to cuffing him round the ear and kicking him up the arse. He would think twice about telling tales to that crazy fat bitch in future. The porters stood motionless waiting for an instruction. As he approached them he heard a familiar voice approaching from behind.

'Joseph! Here, take these for Nurse Dyson.' Joseph took the candles, matches, bottle and string from Ada and smiling broadly held them up to show Sarah before tying the string around the bottle and fixing a candle inside.

'Oh, thank you. I was beginning to wonder how we would manage to offload the patients. It will be nearly dark by the time we get to Intombi and there will be precious few lights or lanterns there.'

'Joseph has volunteered to accompany you and help you until you are settled,' said Ada. 'Good luck.' Many of the townspeople were also evacuating to Intombi but Sarah knew it would be pointless asking Ada if she wanted to join them. She had scorned the opportunity to leave Ladysmith before the siege and derided those who took shelter in the funk holes at the riverbank. She had already expressed her contempt for the civilians who sought sanctuary at Intombi or 'funk camp' as she had started to call it. No Boer would ever make her abandon her home while it still stood, shellfire or no shellfire.

The porters stared expectantly at the stationmaster. 'Well, close the door you idiots,' he snapped and strode straight past them. They gave each other a bewildered look and with a shrug heaved the door to and slid the bolts across. With a wheeze and a whistle the train slowly puffed away from the platform on its short pull down the line to Intombi.

Sarah stared grimly through the mesh grille into the gathering darkness. She could just make out the white shapes of a group of tents some distance from the line. It was difficult to judge how far away they were but whatever the distance it would have to be covered on foot in the dark. Joseph was rattling the door.

'Bad news, Miss Sarah. The door is locked from the outside and there is no platform here. It's too high to reach from the ground.' She could hear the clatter of the carriages being offloaded and the shouts of people struggling down from the train, trying to secure their footing and find their bearings. She banged as hard as she could on the unyielding door. It produced a feeble sound even to her ears.

'Nobody will hear us above the noise around the carriages further up,' she said. Joseph picked his way carefully among the patients towards the bearers in the corner. Following a short exchange one of them shouted in Hindi to his comrades on the roof. There was a patter of footsteps on the roof followed by the reverberation of activity above the door. Within seconds they had managed to unbolt the door from the outside and it dropped open with a crash. In the light of the candle bottle Sarah saw the grinning face of one of the bearers upside down in the doorway.

'I am sorry to startle you, madam. They are holding me by my legs.' He disappeared from sight only to reappear almost immediately, clambering down from the roof. As Sarah thanked him heavy raindrops started to drum on the roof, slowly at first and then ever faster, while the accompanying driving wind performed its malicious dance swirling around and inside the van.

The other bearers on the roof scrambled and jumped down while Joseph and the bearers inside the van gently moved the patients towards the door where they were lifted into the *dhoolies*. Peering inside each *dhoolie* in the faint glow of the candlelight Sarah checked to ensure that each man was as comfortable and secure as possible.

The rain lashed down and around them, whipped up by the ferocity of the wind. She slung the end of her cloak over one shoulder and across the other to give her some protection as the rain pelted into her face. 'Follow me,' she said, holding up her candle bottle with one hand and lifting her skirts with the other. 'We will have to fetch the mattresses in the morning.' Instinctively, she turned round but in the darkness could hear only the rhythmic shuffle of the bearers as they trotted through the knee high grass behind her.

'Joseph, where are you?' she called. 'Joseph!' A faster and more urgent rustle brought Joseph to her side at a crouching run.

'I managed to bring one, Miss Sarah,' he announced triumphantly. She could make out the mattress that almost completely covered his hunched figure and trailed through the grass in his wake.

'Thank you, Joseph.' She was already assessing which of her patients would have the mattress rather than having to spend the rest of the night on rough ground with only the blanket he was wrapped in. A young Highlander called Tom had been shot through the spine and liver at Elandslaagte. He was paralysed and in great pain and had not been expected to survive but had clung on to life for two weeks. She had grown close to him as she nursed him and he had told her all about his mother and his home back in Elgin. Until the last couple of days each time she had gone on duty she had dreaded seeing his bed empty or occupied by another. Now he had a fighting chance and if he did live to return safely home to his mother in Scotland Sarah would regard it as a personal triumph in the midst of so many tragedies. Tom would have it, she decided.

The rain pricked her eyes and her skirts became soaked as she waded through the wet grass. Joseph kept up a steady pace beside her. 'Over there, Miss Sarah.' In the glow she saw his arm point to the right. She struggled to focus her vision in the face of the driving rain but could just make out the scattered dots of the lanterns that marked the camp. They had veered too far to the left and needed to change direction. She said a silent thank you to Ada Dunkley. Joseph was already proving invaluable. She turned round and strained to hear the bearers following behind but could make out no sound other than the howling wind.

'They are coming,' said Joseph quietly. Still Sarah could hear nothing. 'They are coming,' he repeated. Out of the blackness a soft and unhurried patter announced the arrival of a pair of bearers with their load. Then another and another until they had all assembled in front of her. With her head down in the torrential rain and her makeshift lantern held high she lifted her skirts and turned towards the lights of the camp. At her unspoken command the bearers followed with their precious loads.

'Nurse Dyson and eight serious cases,' said Sarah reporting to a Royal Army Medical Corps sergeant sat at a table in a brightly lit administrative tent. It was merciful shelter from the storm outside but the wind still buffeted the sides and flaps of the tent and the flames in the lamps flickered and danced to its tune. She was drenched and shivering. Her cap had blown away in the wind and russet snakes of hair were plastered to her forehead and face. She suddenly realised how hungry she was. It seemed so long since she had snatched a piece of bread and cheese for breakfast as she had finished her night shift. She was also desperately tired. Because of the evacuation she had been on continuous duty for almost twenty-four hours.

'Patients in tent seven,' said the sergeant, scanning his typewritten sheets and stifling a yawn. The men here have had a hectic and trying day as well, thought Sarah. 'The bad news is that the nurses' tent you were assigned to has blown away in the storm. We won't be able to retrieve it until the morning so you'd best bed down with your patients for tonight.' Sarah was past caring. Maybe it was no bad thing for her to be with her patients for the first night anyway in case any of them had been disturbed by the ordeal of their evacuation. She would settle her patients in and look for something to eat before retiring.

The sergeant had anticipated her question. 'The tent next door is serving soup and coffee. You look like you need it.' She straightened herself, nodded an unvoiced appreciation of the sergeant's consideration and went to lead Joseph and the bearers to tent seven.

'Thank you Joseph. Thank you everyone,' she said in weary satisfaction, having ensured that her patients were as comfortable as circumstances would permit. She had taken particular care over Highlander Tom who had fallen into a deep sleep almost as soon as the bearers had tenderly laid him on the mattress. Joseph smiled broadly and the bearers held their hands together in front of their faces and inclined their heads in the traditional Hindu gesture of acknowledgement and deference. Joseph was a Godsend and she admired the steadfast loyalty and quiet dignity of the ever uncomplaining bearers. They had all been soaked to the skin on the way to the camp and were doubtless as hungry as she was. 'You'd better go and get something to eat and drink before it all goes,' said a nurse who arrived to relieve her. Sarah realised that their late arrival and the primary responsibility to see to the patients meant that most of the other arrivals would have already taken some refreshment.

'Come with me,' she said, and led them to the tent where hot soup and coffee awaited.

The tent was much larger than her ward tent and contained a scattering of people, mostly civilians and medical staff but with a few soldiers from the medical and service corps. There were no chairs or tables so everyone had to balance their bowls and mugs in their hands as best as they could. It was cosy and bright inside, with lanterns scattered throughout the tent, although the rain and wind still lashed and tugged at the canvas and the guy ropes. Steam rose from two large aluminium tureens of soup and several jugs of coffee as Sarah joined the queue with Joseph and the bearers lining up behind her. The wonderful aroma of highly seasoned vegetables hit her senses just before it was replaced by the more powerful smell of piping hot coffee. Two soldiers were dispensing this most agreeable fare with pieces of fresh bread. She had certainly had fancier meals before but never one so welcome or gratifying.

She noticed a middle aged civilian couple staring at her, the tall, thin man with a narrow eyed scowl and the snub nosed, thick-set woman with an undisguised glare of contempt. She also became aware of two women ahead of her in the queue looking round at her out of the corners of their eyes and turning back in a conspiratorial whisper. I must look a terrible state, she thought, self consciously brushing back a strand of hair from her forehead as she followed the queue in its gradual shuffle forward. But then again it had been a long and exasperating day and she was too hungry and tired to care.

She reached the head of the queue and one soldier handed her a bowl of soup and a hunk of bread and the other poured a mug of steaming coffee. The soup looked delicious with pieces of potato, carrot, leek and cabbage floating in a rich broth. She tucked the bread into her apron pocket and as she took the mug from the soldier he glanced behind her and then at his companion. Both momentarily looked as if they were waiting for the other to speak and then looked expectantly at Sarah. 'Is there a problem?' she asked, the weariness in her voice more from fatigue than irritation.

The soldiers looked sheepish and flustered as Sarah became aware of a general buzz in the tent. In her exhausted state her mind struggled to comprehend what was going on until the tent flap flew aside, instantly increasing the volume and vigour of the storm. She suddenly, finally, understood.

'What's going on here?' barked the slouch hatted Light Horse officer who had been ushered in by a civilian. It was Captain Turnbull, his arm now out of a sling and his hand covered by only a small dressing. 'Kaffirs and coolies are not allowed in here,' he shouted angrily, striding towards Sarah's group. 'Get out now!' he screamed at Joseph and the bearers, prodding the tip of his riding crop into Joseph's cheek.

'Stay where you are!' Sarah intervened as they all turned to leave the tent. 'Captain Turnbull! Have you no humanity?' she cried. 'Have none of you any humanity?' she demanded of the others, waving her arms expansively. No one answered and most avoided her gaze.

'I might have guessed,' sneered Turnbull, striding towards her. 'Let kaffirs and coolies in here and before we know it people like you will be inviting them round for tea.' He stepped closer and she resisted her first instinct to back away. She tried desperately not to let him see or sense the fear she felt. He pressed his face close to hers. 'I've told you once before,' he hissed. 'I know your sort. In more ways than one.'

'It's all right, madam,' said one of the bearers softly. He was the oldest of them with watery eyes and a stubbly grey beard. Dressed in white rags with a turban swathed around his head, he stood upright in pathetic dignity before her. 'We will find the rest of our people and have something to eat there.'

'No!' cried Sarah, whirling round to address the whole gathering. 'These men have risked their lives on the battlefields caring for our wounded soldiers and daily face the same shells as you do. They have worked tirelessly and with the greatest care to transport our badly wounded soldiers out here. They have had nothing to eat all day. Surely you cannot be so uncharitable.'

'We do not wish to cause a problem,' said the bearer.

'That's a very sound attitude,' crowed Turnbull. 'From someone who knows his place.' He slapped his riding crop against his thigh as if to emphasise that this was not a matter for further discussion.

'And we do not wish to stay where we are not welcome,' added the bearer quietly. He turned towards the tent entrance and the other bearers followed him out amid muted mutters of approval.

'And what about you, kaffir? What are you waiting for?'

Joseph hated Turnbull. He recalled how he had seen him frighten and about to molest Miss Sarah at Mr. Dunkley's house. He had also seen the way he behaved around Miss Grace but she was younger and found his attentions flattering. He stared at Turnbull in expressionless silence but with contempt in his heart. Turnbull's movement was so swift that Joseph felt the blood trickle down his cheek before he felt the pain of the stroke.

'Get out of here and don't come back or you'll get a bigger dose next time,' said Turnbull, waving his riding crop in front of Joseph's face. Joseph stared into Turnbull's eyes with such untamed ferocity that the cavalryman momentarily lost his arrogant confidence.

'Come, Joseph,' said Sarah, seizing the opportunity to spare Joseph any further violence before Turnbull had chance to recover his composure. 'I will not eat here. It would choke me to do so.' As they left Turnbull was tempted to go after them and give Joseph a hiding but an initially restrained ripple of applause grew in intensity and several men hastened to the fore to be the first to congratulate the captain and shake his hand. He felt a glow of satisfaction from the endorsement and appreciation of these good citizens of Ladysmith. The kaffir could wait.

Ladysmith
December 1899

'I'm reducing your visits to the Dunkley household to once a week, Browell,' said Captain Young without looking up from the papers he was signing. 'I can't afford to have you away from your section as often as you have been. Intelligence believes that Boer activity is to be stepped up and if it does it is likely to fall most heavily on our sector. The ladies there seem to be in no greater peril or discomfort than anyone else in this flyblown hole and besides, I hear that a Light Horse officer also makes calls there.' He stacked the papers and finally looked Charlie in the eye. 'Understood?'

'Yes, sir.' In truth Charlie was not unduly perturbed by Young's decision. He liked Mrs. Dunkley and was always made welcome on his visits but the attraction had greatly diminished with Sarah's relocation to Intombi. He had heard that Turnbull continued to call after his return to duty but so far Turnbull's visits had thankfully not coincided with his own.

'Dismissed.' The sergeant-major whisked him out of Young's dark and cramped retreat. In the few minutes he was with Young the first traces of daybreak had pushed back the darkness in the east. The dewy freshness of the dawn would be a fleeting sensation before the scorching heat of another day took hold.

'No more lonely hearts visits for you soon, Browell, I'll be bound.' Charlie did not respond to the sergeant-major's jibe but headed towards his company line some fifty yards forward of the stone fort. He passed through the rest of the company to his platoon's advanced position another fifty yards beyond. At his section's post there was a small huddle around a pile of sticks where Walter was trying to coax some life out of a reluctant fire.

'Just in time for breakfast,' said Walter enthusiastically as he fanned the tiny red glow until a small flame emerged and took hold around a piece of brushwood. 'Bacon for four, then.' Frank and McAdams squatted expectantly by the fire as Walter pulled from a leather bag a wad of bacon wrapped in newspaper and started cutting slices off it. Frank stuck their field scarred kettle on a rusty stand positioned astride the lively, crackling fire while Walter threw the bacon into the frying pan McAdams held over the flames. Charlie sat on a small pile of sandbags nearby and pulled a crumpled envelope from his breast pocket. He had received the letter only two days before but had re-

read it at every opportunity. He and Sarah had exchanged letters frequently since she had moved out to Intombi although it was clear that the constant demands of her own patients and others afforded her fewer occasions to write than he had. Daily life on Caesar's Camp consisted of several hours of picket duty or routine patrol with additional fatigues but there were always opportunities for snatching some time to sit in a corner and write a letter.

There had been no official delivery of mail from outside Ladysmith since the town had been cut off five weeks previously although Charlie had heard that native runners were now being used as couriers to carry despatches to and from the besieged town. He had also heard that small quantities of private mail were being carried but a single sheet letter was being charged at a price equivalent to three weeks wages for a Tommy. Only officers could afford such exorbitant rates. Charlie had last received a letter from his parents nearly a fortnight before that, just after Elandslaagte. He hoped that they had by now received his reply sent the following day assuring them that he was all right and had come through the battle unscathed. He had told them of Walter's bravery that day and of Frank's wound. Walter communicated with his parents regularly if not frequently but it had been a long time since Frank had received a letter. Frank's only living relative was his sister but they had lost touch shortly after she had left service in Chester to try her luck in London. On the rare occasions she had written Charlie would read the letter to Frank and reply on his behalf which was ironic because he was confident that Frank would now be able to do both unaided.

He unfolded the letter which told him of the hard work and privations of life at Intombi but despite the steadily increasing numbers of fever cases the train brought out daily they were managing. She was full of praise for her native assistant called Joseph. This was the young lad who had twice run the four miles from Intombi to the company's post on Caesar's Camp to deliver a letter personally and once even waited patiently while Charlie penned a reply. He read over and over again the part in which she told him how much she missed him and loved him. He so much wanted to see her again but could not imagine when that might be.

'Fancy one of these?' Walter broke Charlie's reverie by producing an egg from the leather bag and holding it triumphantly between his thumb and forefinger in the manner of a magician who has just dazzled his audience with an impressive display of sleight of hand.

'Where did you get that?' asked Charlie incredulously. He hadn't seen an egg in weeks.

'The same place I got these,' he replied, fishing into the bag and emerging with a fistful of apricots. 'You're not the only one who goes into town, you know.' Walter could see the look of alarm on Charlie's face. 'Don't worry. As long as I bring something back for the sergeant-major as well he turns a blind eye. He doesn't like bully beef and biscuits any more than we do.' He cracked the egg in his hand and emptied it with a flourish into the frying pan.

Walter's a survivor all right, thought Charlie as he carefully folded the letter back into the envelope and returned it to his pocket. Charlie was disappointed about the sergeant-major though. He was outwardly such a stickler for military discipline yet he too had his price. It was he who had confiscated Walter's claymore after Elandslaagte on the pretext of returning it to the Highlanders so that it would eventually be presented to the dead officer's next of kin. Walter had been convinced that the sergeant-major had kept it for himself and Charlie was now beginning to think that he had been right.

The sizzling bacon smelled good and his parched throat cried out for a mug of tea. 'This will set us up nicely for a long hot day in the sangars, I suppose,' he said, mindful that in little more than an hour they were due to relieve 'C' Company for a spell of picket duty on the outer crest. Frank and McAdams were already tucking into their bacon and egg as Walter dished up Charlie's portion and cracked another egg into the pan. 'In case you're wondering,' said Walter, aware of Charlie's lingering discomfort, 'I won the bacon in a card game but don't ask me where it came from before that.'

At the first pop the small group froze. At the second they abandoned their breakfasts and joined the rush to grab their rifles from the stacks. There was no individual third shot as the crest beyond exploded in a fierce exchange of rifle fire.

The whole platoon scattered for cover behind the nearest sandbags, bushes, rocks and anthills. 'Most of the firing's coming from 'C' Company's positions about three hundred yards ahead,' said

Charlie to Walter as they lay flat behind a thorn tree. Frank and McAdams were ten yards to the left of them, rifles aimed over a cluster of boulders. Charlie looked around and realised that his small party was further forward than any troops not already engaged in the fighting on the crest.

'What are we waiting for, then?' said Walter rising to his feet. Charlie yanked him back down by the seat of his pants just as a bullet splintered a branch at head height.

'Take it easy, Walter. We can't see them and they can't see us but a stray bullet can kill you just as easily as an aimed one if you're not careful.' They could hear the occasional whistle as bullets passed over them or sputtered into the earth, raising small swirls of red dust. 'Follow me.' Charlie ran forward at a low crouch and dived behind an anthill with Walter crashing next to him a couple of seconds later. Frank and McAdams advanced likewise on their left. They repeated the manoeuvre several times until they all reached a stand of long grass where they could see half a dozen of their comrades firing from a sangar and clearly hear their shouted exclamations and obscenities. Beyond the sanctuary of the long grass there was no cover between them and the sangar. Maybe fifty, sixty yards, thought Charlie. Fifty or sixty yards of killing ground. The bullets continued to hiss thick and fast above and around them.

'We can make it to the sangar if we rush,' suggested Walter.

'I don't think so,' said Charlie. 'The Boers are bound to be able to see us from here and the last thing they want is reinforcements arriving. I'm sure most of the bullets coming our way now are aimed at us.' He pulled out his bayonet. 'Give me your helmet.'

'What's wrong with yours?'

'I want to show you something.'

'Why?'

'You'll see.'

Walter reluctantly gave his helmet to Charlie who placed it on the point of his bayonet and raised it just above the grass. Barely a second later two bullets criss-crossed each other making two pairs of diagonal holes in the helmet. 'That's why,' said Charlie. 'They've got a bead on us. It would be suicide to attempt to run across this open ground. We'd be wiped out before we got ten yards.'

'Shit,' said Walter, fingering the holes on his helmet. 'What am I going to tell the quartermaster?'

'Tell him you had a lucky escape. He'll think you're a hero. Everyone will. Even the sergeant-major.'

'You bastard.'

Charlie warned Frank and McAdams not to advance any further. 'The best assistance we can be to those lads is to fire beyond the sangar to try to make the Boers keep their heads down. At least that will give the Boers something else to think about and distract them from those poor fellows.' From a prone position the four of them fired through the grass towards the crest. Charlie's assessment was accurate. Within seconds a hail of Mauser bullets ripped into the long grass.

'I got one!' cried Christiaan triumphantly.

'So did I,' shouted Piet, barely less excitedly. 'But I think it was the same one,' he added more evenly.

'You're both wrong,' said Koos calmly, continuing to aim and shoot into the long grass. 'That was an old trick. All you got was a helmet and an empty one at that.' Piet felt embarrassed at being taken in by such a simple ruse. A child could be forgiven but it was not a mistake an experienced man would make. 'There are only four of them but there are probably a couple of hundred more not too far behind them.' Koos continued. 'There's no officer among them. An officer would have made a death or glory dash for the sangar and got them all killed.' A burst of fire zipped over their heads. 'While if they were all just privates they would probably lie there doing nothing until they received orders. No, there's an NCO in there and a crafty one at that.' Piet was in awe of his father's battlefield craft. He could be wrong, he thought, but in his heart he knew he wasn't. It all came with experience and Koos van Oppen was one of the best and most experienced warriors in the entire Burgher army.

Koos had been telling Piet and anyone else who would listen that the Burghers' investment of Ladysmith was a waste of time and manpower and that the town should be bypassed with only enough men left behind to prevent the garrison from breaking out in pursuit. That was the only way they could smash Buller's relief force and still reach the coast before more reinforcements disembarked at Durban.

Without a relief force there would be no relief. His views had some currency among the older Burghers, particularly those who knew him or his reputation, but most ignored him. 'And this damned adventure is just as pointless,' he had told Piet the night before. 'To take Ladysmith we need to seize the Platrand but not by attacking with a couple of commandos. We need to strike decisively, in strength and without delay.'

Another helmet appeared over the sangar in front of them. Both Piet and Christiaan ignored it but Koos aimed and fired almost in the same movement. This time the helmet spun off as the head jerked back. 'That wasn't a trick,' he said unnecessarily. 'That was a *rooinek* getting impatient and taking a risk.' And paying for his impatience with his life, added Piet to himself.

To their right the firing slackened off as Burghers started to withdraw down the face of the hill. 'Time to go,' said Koos. 'We aren't going to take this position anyway and reinforcements will be here soon. I told you this would be a useless exercise.' They backed away from the rocks on the crest and ran down the slope, their momentum carrying them swiftly in a controlled retirement to the foot of the hill where their horses were tethered. British soldiers appeared in strength on the crest above and fired into them as they galloped away, one bullet striking Piet's saddle pommel and another tearing the tip off the ear of Christiaan's horse. A Burgher ahead of them slumped in the saddle before slowly keeling over and crashing to the ground, his panic-stricken horse continuing its headlong dash with the rest of the force. There had been no proper objective, no co-ordination and no chance of success, thought Koos. Damned fool commanders.

The Boer sentry yawned and shifted his Mauser from one hand to the other, silhouetted in the light of the full moon. Joseph had lain in a fold of ground in front of him for over three hours waiting for an opportunity to slip past. He would have to be patient. There was no point taking any additional risks. The sentry was tired, bored and approaching the end of his picket duty. It would soon be a good time.

The sentry turned and gazed at the campfire, envying his comrades wrapped in their blankets around its embracing glow. There was no movement. They were all fast asleep. He muttered a tired curse. He would have to rouse his relief or he would be stuck out here all night. After a quick scan around him the sentry ambled back towards the prone figures around the fire. The next time he was due on picket he would not be in such a hurry to relieve any of these selfish bastards. Joseph jumped to his feet and ran swiftly and silently across the open ground, pausing briefly behind a thorn tree to make sure he had not been observed, before running on into the darkness. He was through the Boer lines and now just had to run the last twelve miles to reach the British camp at Frere. This was the easy part.

'A guinea to take a letter through the lines!' an officer had exclaimed incredulously, lighting his cigarette and petulantly blowing the smoke into Joseph's eyes. The prices of everything in Ladysmith were going up all the time. He had probably paid that for the cigarettes in his silver case. How much is your life worth? Joseph had thought. The Boers shot captured mail runners on sight. He had nevertheless paid up but still complained at the brevity of what he was allowed to write. It all depended how badly he needed to get a letter through. His colleague had paid up without complaint.

Once at the British lines the letters would pass through the censor and be transmitted on to Pietermaritzburg, England or wherever they were addressed. He had the officers' single sheet letters tightly rolled up inside one reed and a two sheet letter from Mrs. Dunkley to her husband inside another. He had not charged Mrs. Dunkley and would run the extra twelve miles to Estcourt to deliver her letter personally so that Mr. Dunkley could reply immediately. There would, however, be a limit to his devotion to the Dunkleys. If he was in danger of being captured he would have to discard the reeds and the letters they contained. It might make no difference. The Boers could accuse him of being a spy and kill him anyway but the easily discarded and relatively inconspicuous reeds would provide him with some sort of security. The earlier runners had gone out carrying their letters in a satchel and several had never made it to the British lines. They were not clever like him.

Joseph had dispensed with his precious boots for the time being. They were fine for strolling around town but impossible to run in. He always carried the letters barefoot. He leapt through the scrub and did not flinch whenever his toughened soles trod on one of the ubiquitous thorns or stones.

Starting his mail run in the darkness of the early hours served two purposes. With nervous pickets on the alert for a Boer attack it would be as foolhardy to approach the British positions at night as it would be to try to slip through the Boer lines during daylight. This way he would be in and out of the British lines and back through the Boers to Ladysmith by the following evening.

'What have you got for us this time young fellow?' asked the corporal in the Army Post Office Corps tent, stifling a yawn. Joseph could never understand why some of the British soldiers appreciated that he risked his life carrying their mail and treated him with respect while to others he was just another nigger.

Joseph gave him the reed containing the officers' letters. 'This one is for Mr. Dunkley at Estcourt,' he announced proudly, indicating the other.

'Estcourt, eh? Then you've got a long day ahead of you yet, my lad,' said the corporal poking the letters out with a long needle. 'I bet you're hungry.' Joseph nodded. 'Right,' he continued, putting the letters into a tray and passing them to an officer on the next table. The officer picked them up immediately, scanning them and running thick black ink through certain parts. Joseph smiled to himself. That officer in Ladysmith would be even more irritated if he knew that half of his guinea's worth had just been obliterated by the censor. 'Come with me then,' said the corporal. 'It's my breakfast time as well.'

Joseph followed him around the back of the tent where there was a cookhouse. 'Harry, give our intrepid young mail runner a bowl of porridge and a cup of milk.' Harry glared at Joseph and gave him the porridge and milk without comment or expression. Joseph knew that if the corporal had sent him round on his own he would have been given nothing. 'See you next time, young fellow,' said the corporal taking his breakfast and going to sit with his friends. 'Take care of yourself.' Joseph nodded and thanked him. He devoured the porridge greedily. It didn't taste as good as the mealie meal porridge he had at home but was nevertheless most welcome. He gulped the milk down in one swallow, the white overflow running down the side of his mouth. It was the first fresh milk he had had in weeks and it was delicious. He handed the bowl and cup back to the man called Harry.

'Thank you, sir,' said Joseph. Harry snatched the utensils without word or acknowledgement and went back to his stove. It was clear that Harry didn't like him but that didn't matter. He didn't like Harry either. The corporal was a good man, though, and Joseph hoped that he would be on duty the next time he ran the mail. He wiped his mouth with the back of his hand and set off towards Estcourt.

'This is a wonderful surprise,' enthused Zachariah Dunkley, 'This is the first time that I've had any direct contact with my wife, or anyone else in Ladysmith for that matter, in the seven weeks I've been exiled here.' He was temporarily conducting his business from a small but neatly appointed annex at the office of a local land agent who owed him a favour. He smoothed down the curling pages of his letter and read them again. 'You've done well, Joseph.' He fished into his pocket for a sovereign. 'Very well indeed.'

Joseph shook his head and held up the palms of his hands. 'No, *nkosi*. It is an honour for me to bring this letter to you.'

'Nonsense, Joseph. I know how dangerous these mail runs can be. Take it,' he insisted, extending his hand towards Joseph.

'Sir, it is not necessary.'

'Joseph,' said Dunkley in a more serious but nevertheless benevolent tone, 'You have run the best part of twenty-five miles to bring this letter to me and you will have to run twenty-five miles back again. I shall write a reply to my wife, you shall take it to her and I shall pay you a sovereign for doing so.' Joseph hesitated. 'You would be doing me a great service.' It was clear that Dunkley would not take no for an answer and Joseph nodded his acknowledgement.

When Dunkley finished the letter Joseph rolled the two sheets tightly and inserted them into the reed. Dunkley again offered the sovereign and in the traditional gesture of humble gratitude, with a bow of his head and his left hand gripping his right wrist, Joseph accepted it in the open palm of his right hand. '*Ngiyabonga, nkosi*.'

'It is I who should be thanking you, Joseph. You can't imagine how happy you've made me by bringing me this letter.' Joseph picked up the reed. It was time to go. 'Splendid,' said Dunkley. Joseph inclined his head towards his patron. 'God speed,' said Dunkley as Joseph turned and left.

Grace Dunkley had taken to spending most days down at the riverbank shelters her mother so profoundly disdained. It was not so much through fear of being shelled as to spend time in the company of the debonair Captain Turnbull whose Light Horse detachment was stationed there. She had originally excused her trips to the riverbank by taking her easel and watercolours and was grateful that her mother had been too busy or too distracted to notice the paucity of paintings produced from her visits. She had even given Sarah the watercolour of the Howick falls so as to make room on the drawing room wall for the new creations she had no real intention of producing. Now she didn't even bother with the pretence and took nothing more than a parasol and a light picnic basket. It had meant rising early to join the exodus of townsfolk who went down to the shelters by dawn and did not return home until almost sunset but it wasn't far to go. Moreover, she would be the envy of her friends to be seen chatting to and occasionally escorted by a dapper cavalry officer.

She had told him how poor and uncomfortable the shelters dug by the civilians were compared to those of the Light Horse. He had laughed and reminded her that many of the regiment were experienced mine engineers from the Rand and that such simple constructions as these were child's play for them. The civilian shelters had been hacked out of the high riverbank and most were just big enough for a family to squeeze inside and protect them from almost anything bar a direct hit. The Light Horse's shelters were deeper, shored up with timbers and fitted with lanterns. All manner of furniture and other home comforts were installed. Captain Turnbull even had an upholstered chair and a bookshelf in his shelter and at his invitation Grace had often spent untroubled hours reading his volumes of Jane Austen and Mark Twain and the poetry of Keats and Browning while he was away on some duty or other.

It was on just such a day that he returned from a spell of duty on Wagon Hill shortly before sunset. Grace was engrossed in *Romeo and Juliet* and looked up with a start when he greeted her from the entrance.

'I'm sorry. I didn't mean to alarm you.'

'Not at all,' she replied, trying to disguise her sudden discomfort. Her heart was pounding and she felt her face flush. She had the feeling he had been watching her for a while before he had spoken.

'Ah, the tragic and ill fated romance between Montague and Capulet,' he said as he entered the shelter. He paused and looked her in the eye. 'Are you a romantic, Grace?' She blushed even more and returned the book to the shelf. 'Don't let me stop you. You may borrow it if you wish.'

'No.' She hesitated before adding a thank you. She avoided his gaze in an attempt to conceal her discomfort and embarrassment. 'I've read it before,' she said nervously. 'I was just browsing idly.'

'I think Brother Boer has had enough for today,' said Turnbull. Grace was relieved by the change of subject. 'Why don't you let me escort you back home?'

She recovered her composure quickly. 'That would be most courteous of you, Captain Turnbull.' It was still daylight but the sun would soon be gone and most of the civilians had either left or were packing up to go home, confident there would be no more shells that day. They passed the short stroll with the kind of polite but aimless small talk that Grace imagined refined people in England might do in similar circumstances. The evening was still warm in the fading light as they trudged up the path to the porch. Grace tried the door. It was locked so mama must be out, she told Turnbull. She rummaged in her purse for her key and unlocked the door.

There was a note on the drawing room table. Grace picked it up and read it. 'Mama has gone with cook to Intombi to take some eggs and fresh goat's milk for Nurse Dyson's patients,' she said shortly. 'The fever patients must have milk and there is a shortage at Intombi. It seems to me that our goats don't produce very much but mama makes sure most of it goes to Nurse Dyson. No doubt she's taken some of cook's peach and apricot jam and other treats for the nurses too.' She took off her hat and tossed her head back to shake loose her long, dark hair. She was warm and needed to wash off the accumulation of red dust that she felt had become ingrained in every pore of her face. 'Do take a seat and make yourself comfortable, Captain Turnbull. Please excuse me while I refresh myself and then I shall make some tea.' He remained standing and as she climbed the staircase to her room she observed that he seemed tense and nervous and had not spoken since they entered the house. She hoped that he wasn't disappointed at her mother's absence or that he felt obliged to stay a while and humour her while other duties beckoned. She especially hoped that he didn't think of her as just a frivolous young girl. As she poured water from the decorated porcelain jug into the matching bowl on the dresser she wished she were four or five years older, like Sarah Dyson, so that she might be taken more seriously. She was at an awkward age. Too old to be considered a child but not old enough to be fully accepted into adult society. Grace admired Sarah and wished she could be like her. Sarah had a respected profession and was performing a valuable and effective role in the siege.

She unbuttoned her jacket and the matching sequinned waistcoat her mother always insisted she wore out of the house and hung them carefully over the back of a chair. The weather was far too hot to wear a waistcoat and it was always a matter of wonder to Grace that her mother never seemed uncomfortable in hers. She would leave it off when she went back downstairs. She pulled the bow, loosening the high neck of her blouse and saw in the small oval mirror above the dresser the faint redness of its constriction. There were a few slight patches of perspiration on the blouse so she tossed it into the corner, resolving to freshen her appearance with a clean one. She stared disapprovingly at the thin, almost imperceptible, lines of red dust in the creases around her nose and eyes and in the furrows of her forehead. The dust was inescapable. The only way to escape the dust was to escape Ladysmith. That was not an option for the present of course but when the siege and the war were over she would start a new life – her own life – in Maritzburg, or even Durban. Now there was a thought. What possibilities lay in Durban! Her mother wouldn't like it but there would be no stopping her. Yes, her mind was made up. She would move to Durban. She would marry a successful businessman, have three children and be the toast of society there.

Cupping both hands and closing her eyes she scooped the water up to her face, feeling first the shock and then the refreshing invigoration of its coolness. She let the water drip off her face back into the bowl. With a second scoop she rubbed the water around her forehead, eyes, nose and mouth and with a third she ran her hands around her neck and behind her ears. She took her flannel and a bar of the imported soap her father had brought back from a business trip to

Maritzburg and rubbed its fragrant sweetness around her face and neck. She missed her father. She loved her mother too of course but papa was much less fussy and more tolerant of her ways than her mother.

She was drying her face so vigorously that she didn't hear the door open and was caught completely off guard when she looked up and saw him standing barely three feet in front of her. 'Captain Turnbull!' was all she could exclaim at the shock of seeing him in her bedroom. It was a couple of seconds later when she realised she was wearing nothing more than a revealing slip above the waist and clutched the towel to her breast. She waited for him to say something, anything, to reassure her that only the direst emergency had propelled him up the staircase to trespass into her bedroom.

He stepped forward, grabbing her arm, and roughly pulled her towards him. He pushed his face clumsily into hers and she instinctively recoiled with a squeal that she meant to be a scream. As she struggled to extricate herself his grip tightened. 'Captain Turnbull!' she cried. 'You're hurting me.'

'I won't hurt you,' he said calmly, pushing his mouth to hers with such force that she felt her lip split against her teeth. She shook her head from side to side and clamped her mouth shut as he pressed his lips against hers. At each of her attempts to evade him his hold around her back and waist tightened. 'Please stop,' she gasped when she finally managed to slide her mouth free. She inhaled sharply as she twisted her face away from his. 'For God's sake, please stop.'

'Stop?' he replied, gripping her shoulders and holding her at arm's length. Grace's fear was momentarily supplanted by her surprise at the puzzled expression on his face. 'You don't want me to stop', continued Turnbull, his mouth now contorted into a sneer. 'You've been making it clear to me for weeks that you want me and now for the first time we're alone and have the opportunity. You can't flirt with a man like you've been doing and expect him to back off when he responds.' He had momentarily relaxed his hold and she half pulled free. Her slip tore, exposing a breast, as he grabbed at her and threw her down on to the bed. She sank into the soft eiderdown but before she could move he was on top of her, pinning her arms down and licking her neck. She was creeping with uncontrollable terror as he grabbed her exposed breast and yelped in pain as he bit the nipple.

He held both of her wrists down with one hand while he pulled up her skirts. Her fear turned to panic as she realised what he was going to do. She redoubled her efforts to free herself, kicking out with one leg and then the other but it was no use. He was too big and too heavy. He tugged at her drawers, ripping them as he pulled them down and off. Her intimacy was exposed and at his mercy. She tried to scream but her voice failed her and instead she emitted only a whimper. She tasted the warmth of the blood from her split lip and froze as she saw him unbuckle his belt and lower his trousers. He lay back on top of her and she winced as he roughly jabbed a finger into her part. 'You're dry, you bitch,' he half snarled and half gasped. He slapped her across the face but by now she was so completely overwhelmed by terror that she was unable to give voice to the pain of the blow.

She lay quietly in mute shock, tears welling in her eyes, as he mounted her. Discomfort turned to pain as he forced his way inside her. With each thrust came an agonising, bursting pain as he violated her body but still she could not cry out. She just wanted him to finish so that her agony would end but it seemed an eternity before his breathing quickened, his thrusts became more frenzied and finally with a gasp and a convulsive shudder he released himself inside her.

They lay for long moments, she staring at the ceiling in traumatised silence and he still propped up on his arms with his head bent as mindless lust yielded to reality. A bead of perspiration ran down the side of his face as he looked into her staring but unseeing eyes. He withdrew from her and, sliding from the bed, backed into the dresser in the sudden, awful realisation of the terrible thing he had done. She lay still with her skirts still pulled up over her chest, the crimson evidence of her violated innocence staining the eiderdown and his now flaccid member. He put his hands to his head. Everything was a whirl as he fought to bring order to the chaos in his mind. Must keep calm, he kept telling himself. Must keep a clear head. He buttoned up his trousers, buckled up his belt and sat on the bed.

'Grace,' he said softly. There was no response. There were the tracks of dried tears on her face and her lip was swollen. He leaned forward, extending his left hand, and went to touch her head. 'Grace.' With a barely perceptible frisson she lunged forward, clamping her teeth into the base and knuckle of his index finger and grabbing his hair. He cried out at the shock and pain of her fingernails gouging into his scalp and recoiled backwards. 'Fucking whore!' he shouted. His finger was bleeding profusely from the semicircular lacerations where her teeth had penetrated to the bone and he had blood on the fingers of his other hand where he had touched the growing lump on his head.

His breathing was coming heavy and the pulse in his temple throbbed as he struggled to assess the situation and decide what he should do next. He would hang for this. Hang or be shot. He looked at the cowering remnants of what, barely an hour before, was the vivacious and virginal Grace Dunkley and somewhere deep inside his being he felt a stab of sympathy for her.

He approached the bed slowly, on his guard for her slightest movement, and when he judged he was close enough lunged at her with both hands. She let out a tortured croak as he grabbed her throat and her eyes bulged as he tightened his grip. Ever tighter, ever tighter. His face screwed up both with the effort and with the pain of the pressure exerted on the new and old wounds in his hand. She struggled against his assault but both her strength and her will had been diminished by her ordeal. Her face turned a deeper shade of red and she gave out muted gasps as her mouth gulped in vain for the air her bursting lungs demanded. Her arms flapped limply in a final token gesture of resistance. At last her body stiffened and then sagged. She would no longer be able to accuse him.

He stood up, the magnitude of his crime manifested in Grace's inert form. Her arms were spread wide in a crucifixion-like pose and her pale face and neck were smeared with blood from his hand. He moved to one side to avoid the accusing stare of her lifeless eyes but could not avert his own gaze from her body. This wasn't like the last time. That kaffir bitch back in Johannesburg had got what she deserved and in any case nobody ever asked questions about dead kaffirs. He had even talked about it when he had been drunk but his audiences either hadn't believed him or hadn't cared. This was different. This was a white woman in a small town cut off from the rest of the world. There was no escape. They would know the killer was still in Ladysmith.

He backed away slowly towards the bedroom door as if fearing she might suddenly move or speak, point an accusing finger or scream his name as the rapist and murderer he was. At the doorway he paused to take one last look at Grace Dunkley then turned and ran down the stairs. He paused at the front door and took several deep breaths to compose himself. Peering outside to ensure no one was about, he swung the door open and, resisting the temptation to run, strode purposefully into the night.

No one had seen him, he was sure of that, but he needed a plausible alibi. Turning into Murchison Street, he paused. His hand was hurting like hell. In the darkening street he sniffed and gingerly licked the wound. The bleeding had stopped but the knuckle was swollen and there would be tell tale bloodstains on his hand. He took out his handkerchief and with one end in his teeth fashioned a passable bandage with his free right hand, leaving only the top parts of his fingers exposed. He couldn't go to the M.O. with this but it wasn't serious and would heal in due course. He would obtain a proper dressing from the squadron stores in the morning. He stuck the hand in his pocket and strode towards the sound of revelry emanating from the Royal Hotel. That would do.

Inside the small foyer doors led to a bar on either side. In more peaceful times one had been a lounge where accompanied ladies were permitted to take refreshment and the other a so-called public bar where considerations of gender as well as race substantially restricted the scope of the clientele who were allowed to patronise it. Piano music from both bars was interspersed with frequent bursts of riotous laughter as a ribald joke met with congressional appreciation or someone performed a particularly impressive drinking feat.

On his right the door flew open, disgorging two giggling officers and amplifying the hubbub from within until it swung shut again. 'Hello, Turnbull, old chap,' said one of them. 'Been here long?' It was a Lancer captain he knew vaguely from the hospital but whose name he could not recall. He too had stopped a couple of Boer bullets at Elandslaagte but seemed more the worse for drink than any wound.

'Ever since it started. I've been in there,' he gestured with his head to the bar on the left.

'Ah, the wetting of the baby's head,' said the Lancer expansively, slapping Turnbull's shoulder. 'Wonderful!'

'And you?'

'I've been here since this afternoon,' replied the Lancer. 'Still convalescing, you know,' he added with the double conspiratorial gestures of a wink and two taps on the side of his nose. His companion attempted to straighten himself up against a tall aspidistra but succeeded only in falling backwards into it.

'What's the celebration in your party?'

'Meadows's promotion. He's been made up to major, you know.' Turnbull had no idea who Meadows was but made a mental note of the name. 'It's all a bit dead men's shoes, though,' the Lancer added in hushed tones, switching from jollity to sobriety as swiftly as only a drunk can. 'His squadron commander went down with enteric. Died last week.' He shook his head sombrely in brief contemplation then rediscovered his gaiety as suddenly as he had lost it. 'Why don't you come and join us?' he suggested brightly. 'I'll introduce you to Meadows.'

'I'd like that very much,' replied Turnbull with a beaming smile. Very, very much, he added to himself.

'Come along,' said the Lancer, linking his arm with Turnbull's and guiding him into the fray. They fought their way through the smoke filled room past knots of officers from various regiments.

'Back for more, eh, Pardoe?' said a tall captain of Dragoon Guards. Pardoe. Turnbull would not forget his name this time. Pardoe gave a mock salute with a wide smile and dragged Turnbull through the melee to the bar where more officers and a man in civilian clothes stood talking.

'I'm afraid the champagne and whisky have all gone, old chap' slurred Pardoe apologetically as if it was his fault. 'I don't mean just for tonight,' he added conspiratorially. 'I mean it's *all* gone. Apart from personal stocks of course.' He winked and tapped his nose again. 'The Royal has no more left and the Crown has run out too. They only have Cape wine, Cape brandy or beer.'

'Then I'll take a brandy.'

'Jolly good idea. Me too.' Pardoe tried without success to attract the busy barman's attention. Any notion of waiter service had disappeared with the influx of so many revellers. 'Newspaperman,' he said with an exaggerated flick of his head towards the civilian. 'There are lots of them stuck in Ladysmith and most of them seem to be staying here.' He managed to catch the barman's eye as he shuttled from one end of the bar to the other and ordered two brandies.

'Who is he?'

'Wagstaffe of the Manchester *Echo*. He was sent out here to report on the doings of their local regiment, that lot up on Caesar's Camp, and got shut up for the duration with the rest of us. Still, I'll give him his due. He'll go to any lengths to get his despatches out. He uses the heliograph when he can but if it's not available or the sun isn't shining he uses pigeons or runners.' Pardoe's elbow slipped on the bar and he grabbed the brass rail to steady himself. 'He tends to use that nigger boy who sometimes hangs around the Dunkley place. You'll know the one I mean. Says he's resourceful and reliable.'

Resourceful and reliable? He's an insolent and uppity kaffir, thought Turnbull. 'I'll pay for those,' he said as the barman returned with their brandies. 'And have one yourself,' he added. The barman nodded in acknowledgement. He'll be sure to remember me now, thought Turnbull. He took his time with the brandy and needed no encouragement when Pardoe suggested they have another. Normally he would have avoided socialising with Pardoe and the bores he insisted upon introducing him to but the more people who could vouch for his presence the further he could distance himself from the rape and murder of Grace Dunkley. The only problem was that most of them were very drunk and might not remember anything of the evening by the time their hangovers cleared the following day. On the other hand their perception of time would most likely be muddled and they would not be in a position to contradict any claim he would make as to when he arrived at the Royal and how long he had spent there. 'I've got to get back to the other party,' he told Pardoe and a swaying artillery lieutenant as he drained his glass. He shook hands with them and on his way out waved effusively to several of his recent acquaintances.

He swung the door and paused for breath before entering the other bar. It was equally smoke filled and noisy but the revellers were of a different ilk. Where the other party consisted almost exclusively of British officers, here they were all from colonial units and the volunteers and included a few of his brother officers from the Light Horse.

This bar was smaller and less well appointed, the simple line of bottles contrasting with the great mirror in its ornate gilded frame that formed the backdrop to the lounge bar. As he squeezed between two tables a skinny young officer jumped from his chair. 'Would you care to join us, sir?'

It was Bennett, a second lieutenant from his own squadron. Turnbull nodded and sat down as Bennett surrendered his seat and dragged over another from the next table while its previous occupant was distracted elsewhere. Bennett's two companions, both young subalterns like himself, stood stiffly. Turnbull motioned them to sit down with a weary flap of his hand. 'Would you care for a drink, sir?' asked Bennett, his voice almost drowned out by a burst of raucous laughter from the next table. 'I'm afraid there's ...'

'No more whisky or champagne,' interrupted Turnbull wearily. 'Only wine, brandy or beer. I know. I'll have a brandy.' One of Bennett's companions was nominated to fetch the next round and struggled through the press behind him towards the bar.

Bennett lifted his empty glass. 'Or you can have ginger beer if you prefer, sir,' said Bennett jovially. Turnbull was unmoved. 'You see, sir, I don't drink alcohol,' Bennett explained unnecessarily.

'So I see,' said Turnbull coldly. I should have guessed, he thought. He's far too earnest to enjoy a drink or two.

'I didn't know you were coming here this evening, sir,' said Bennett, changing the subject. Turnbull thought fast. It was lucky he had gone into the other bar first.

'I didn't intend to originally. I was invited to the party in the other bar. Meadows has just been made up to major.'

'Meadows, sir?'

'Yes, Meadows of the Lancers. You probably don't know him.'

'No, sir, I don't. Have you known him long, sir'

Why is he asking so many questions? thought Turnbull. He told himself not to worry. Bennett was only making polite conversation to a superior officer. 'Since shortly after we arrived in Ladysmith,' he replied calmly. 'Thoroughly decent chap.'

'Was he in the squadron that was at Elandslaagte with us, sir?'

'Yes. Yes he was,' replied Turnbull instinctively. He silently cursed this inquisitive little weasel.

'Damn fine charge after the battle, sir. Plenty of good pig sticking, from what I heard. Taught those Johannesburg Boers no end of a lesson.'

'Indeed,' affirmed Turnbull with as much enthusiasm as he could muster. Nobody in Ladysmith detested the Johannesburg commando more than he did but he needed to change the subject quickly. 'So who's the proud new father?'

'Lieutenant Hammond. His wife gave birth to a baby boy yesterday. He got the news by heliograph this morning.' He shook his head and chuckled. 'He says the baby will be called Victor Ladysmith but he hasn't told his wife yet.'

'You must introduce me to him.' Turnbull couldn't have cared less about Hammond or his baby but saw the opportunity to register his presence on the subject of this party as well. Bennett was keen to oblige and brought over a happy if unsteady Hammond and did the honours. Hammond's euphoric momentum had been sustained by copious amounts of wine and brandy and, in the manner of someone who had just been admitted to an exclusive club, he wanted to know all about Turnbull's own progeny. 'I'm afraid I'm not married yet, old chap,' lied Turnbull, anxious to end the conversation now that Hammond had served his purpose. Hammond stood in bemused silence as if discovering that he had just disclosed initiation secrets to one who was not a member of the club. His cheerfulness returned in an instant as one of his colleagues slapped him on the shoulder and motioned him to rejoin his group with the promise of the funniest joke he had ever heard. 'Sorry to drag him away, Bennett old fellow, but he's got to hear this.'

'What have you done to your hand, sir?' asked Bennett, catching sight of the white handkerchief. Damn. He thought he had concealed it under the table and deliberately hadn't stood up when Hammond had been introduced.

'Oh, my wound's playing me up a bit. I'm just keeping it covered for now.'

'I've got a friend in the Mounted Rifles who's a doctor in civilian life, sir. He can take a look at it for you.'

'That won't be necessary,' said Turnbull. 'I don't want to cause any bother,' he added in a mumble.

'Oh, it won't be any bother, sir.'

'I don't want you to go to any trouble.'

'It's no trouble,' insisted Bennett. 'He's only over there.' Turnbull felt a chill run through his body and his chest tighten. 'I'll fetch him over,' said Bennett, rising from his chair.

'You'll do no such thing!' snapped Turnbull. Bennett froze in mid-movement with a look of bewildered hurt on his face and his three companions fell silent in embarrassed astonishment. Keep calm, Turnbull said to himself. Don't overreact. Composing himself, he apologised to Bennett. 'I know you mean well but it's not a problem, really. I'll see the M.O. if I have to but I don't think it will be necessary.' He pulled out his watch. Good. He had spent an hour and a half at the Royal and as far as Bennett and Pardoe were concerned he had been there much longer. Long enough to give him an alibi. 'Well, gentlemen, I must be going.' He bid a now subdued Bennett and his companions farewell and edged his way through the crowd to the door.

The evening was warm and the sky clear as he left the din at the Royal behind and headed down a dark Murchison Street. There were few people on the street and those who were about seemed to be on their way to or from the Royal or the Crown. As he turned up towards Poort Road he could hear the buzz of a crowd of people. Grace's body had been discovered as he knew it must be when Ada returned home. He tried to shut his mind to the fearful scene he had left less than two hours before and the devastation it must have caused. The provost marshal's men would be there now putting together the details of the case and compiling a list of possible suspects. He knew that he would be questioned simply because he was a regular visitor to the house but that would be mere routine. There was no reason to suspect him and in any case he had an alibi verifiable by several people. He quickened his stride and headed towards his squadron's lines.

Joseph had made better time than he had anticipated and cursed himself for his carelessness. There were still over two hours of daylight left when he reached the clump of thorn and scrub just before the Boer lines where he normally rested before embarking on the final and most dangerous stage of the return journey. He would have to hide up here until after dark and hope that the Boer pickets would not be sufficiently inquisitive or vigilant to wander beyond their posts into the scrub. He knew the one thing in his favour was that the Boers' attention was usually concentrated on the Ladysmith side anticipating the possibility of a raid or an intelligence mission from the garrison. Any attack from outside would be in force and both visible and audible even at distance.

He rolled himself into a ball under one of the thorn trees, satisfied he was adequately concealed by its form and shade, and felt physically and mentally comfortable enough to drift into an undulating sleep. He dreamed he was running across the veld carrying letters in a conspicuous and heavy pack slung over his back. The pack got heavier and his legs increasingly leaden with every step as Boers chased him, closing the gap by the second and shouting excitedly. The shouting increased in volume and intensity until he awoke with a start. For a few seconds he lay there, dry mouthed and perspiring, assimilating his surroundings while reality reasserted itself in his consciousness. The shouting continued, several harsh Dutch voices converging in their excitement somewhere to his right. He rolled over slowly and, raising his head slightly, peered through the twisted entanglement of the tree's lower branches.

Two boys, no more than twelve or thirteen years old, were being dragged out of the undergrowth by a small group of Boers some fifty yards away. The Boers were shouting at them in a mixture of Dutch, English and Zulu but the boys were too frightened to respond and one of them started to cry. As they were hauled to the top of the slight rise and thrown to the ground Joseph could see the satchels fall from their shoulders. How could they be so stupid? thought Joseph. They had made the basic errors of carrying the mail, too much mail, in satchels and not travelling alone. His incredulity turned to anger at being compromised before fear took hold. He had a decision to make, a decision on which his life would depend. Either he could sit tight and hope that the Boers didn't start searching for more mail runners or he could make a dash for it. Neither option was appealing but he knew that if he stayed where he was he would be trapped if the picket made a search of the area.

Joseph extricated himself from the cluster of thorn branches and crawled on his belly up the incline to the flat ridge. He hardly dared even to breathe but he slowly twisted his neck until he could see what was happening on his right. Two Boers were going through the mailbags, two more were slapping and kicking the boys while another two stood by shouting questions at them. All of them were distracted and none was facing in his direction. The time was now. He drew himself up in a low crouch and scuttled along the ground, praying that none of the Boers looked his way or could see him in their peripheral vision. The pounding of his heart and his own self-consciousness made him feel that he was making too much noise and was bound to be seen and fired on. And killed. He knew that Boers didn't miss from this range.

It seemed an age before he reached the brief sanctuary of another stand of thorns in a fold in the ground but looking back he had covered no more than two hundred yards. He took a deep breath, inched his way up the slight rise and, lying flat, swung himself over. A quick look around revealed no sign of any Boers on this side but he knew there must be more about. The sudden crack of a rifle shot made his whole body go rigid. He had no time to assess its consequence before the report of a second filled the air. He knew he had made the correct decision when he saw four of the Boer pickets walk away from the boys' bodies and head in the direction of his original hiding place. Slithering down the reverse slope he again sprung into a half crouching run and made for the next clump of thorns tucked into another fold of ground ahead. His breathing came more easily. Once he cleared the next rise he would be safe.

Charlie whistled quietly to himself as he strolled up Poort Road. The week had gone slowly on Caesar's Camp since the excitement of the Boer raid and he was glad to have a change of scenery. He just wished he could see Sarah again. Her letters were a great comfort but he missed her, much more than he had thought he could ever miss a woman. As he climbed the path he saw the house shrouded in darkness and thought it strange that no one was at home at this time, especially as he was expected. He was thinking that he would settle into a chair on the porch until Ada and Grace returned when he noticed the door ajar.

He entered cautiously. 'Hello. Is anyone there?' he called, not expecting an answer even if there was. It was one thing for men like Walter, the type of scrounger found in many platoons, to mysteriously obtain eggs, fruit or the occasional chicken. The instances of housebreaking and looting were quite another. There had so far been only a few but they had put something of a strain on relations between the civilian population and the military authorities. Charlie did not relish the prospect of bumping into a couple of soldiers on their way out. Facing the prospect of a court martial and very probably a death sentence anyone caught in the act would undoubtedly put up a determined resistance, and quite possibly be prepared to kill, to avoid arrest. He wished he had a weapon but had nothing on him more threatening than a pencil.

'Hello,' he called again. There was no response. His heart thumped inside his chest as he held his breath while gingerly edging his way along the hall. He poked his head around the open drawing room door. The shafts of light from the almost full moon partially illuminated the room and there seemed to be nothing amiss. Further along he swung open the double doors of the dining room. Little moonlight penetrated here but there was no evidence of disturbance. Noticing that all the other ground floor doors were also closed, he gripped the banister rail and taking two steps at a time sprang as quietly as he could up to the landing. There were four doors on the landing and a corridor beyond them to the left following the L-shape of the house. The nearest door, on the left, was open while the other three were closed. As he approached the open door he could see the moonlight streaming through the window. He peered round the doorway and saw the distinct figure of Grace on the bed. This was not the usual repose of someone sleeping. She was lying with her arms outstretched and appeared to be partly undressed.

Charlie hesitated. His first instinct was to enter but he felt embarrassed to do so in case she woke up and thought he was a peeping Tom. He tapped lightly on the door and with no response he rapped harder. 'Grace,' he called anxiously. 'Are you all right?'

Satisfied that no one else was in the room he entered and looked down at Grace's inert figure. Thoughts began to race through his mind, faster than he was able to consider and analyse them. Something terrible had happened here. If there had been housebreakers she would have seen or at least heard them and they would have been surprised by her presence. Maybe a frightened shout or scream disturbed them and brought them to her. He touched her neck. Despite the warmth of the evening she was cold. More than that he felt a sticky wetness on his fingers. He rummaged in his pocket for his precious box of matches. They were hard to come by in Ladysmith now and he had conserved them carefully. There were only a few left but he had to use one now. Striking one with a shaking hand he lit the lamp above the dresser and turned the wick up full.

The full horror struck Charlie as he saw Grace's sprawling body without the combined trickery of light and shadow concealing any detail. It was all there in all its obscenity. There was blood on his hand where he had touched her, yet despite one side of her neck being covered with blood she did not seem to be cut there. Her lip was swollen with small spots of blood on the eiderdown where her mouth was resting. There were a few other streaks of blood on the eiderdown around her head and another between her thighs where her private parts were exposed.

Charlie gagged and tears filled his eyes as he sat on the bed and tenderly cradled her head in his arm. 'Oh, Grace,' he wept. 'How could anyone do this?' With the noise of the sobs racking his body as his mind tried to come to terms with the fact that Grace had been murdered he wasn't aware of the voices in the hallway or the noise of footsteps coming up the stairs. The next sounds he heard were Ada Dunkley's scream and the cocking of a revolver.

'I don't care about the niceties of legal procedure, military or otherwise,' thundered the red faced provost marshal. 'I just want a speedy conviction and execution of sentence.'

'I agree with you entirely, old chap,' said the brigadier in a much more relaxed tone. 'That's what we all want but we must ensure that justice is not only done but seen to be done.'

'You're not suggesting Browell is innocent, are you?' boomed the provost marshal incredulously.

The brigadier waved his hand dismissively. 'Of course not. He's as guilty as sin but we don't want there to be the slightest whiff that we've created a scapegoat or even worse, a martyr.'

'The rogue was caught red handed – literally – and there are plenty of witnesses,' continued the provost marshal in the same tone. 'There's poor Mrs. Dunkley, the archdeacon and that Carbineer major. There's even Mrs. Dunkley's cook. If Mrs. Dunkley had returned alone from Intombi that evening heaven only knows what that maniac Browell might have done to her.' He paused and became less agitated. 'In any case,' he resumed more calmly, 'our instructions in this matter come from the very top. There must be a conviction to ensure the civilian population retains its confidence in the military. It's a morale issue, plain and simple.'

The brigadier stroked his chin in contemplation of the provost marshal's words. Davies may be a blustering old fool at times, thought the brigadier, but in essence he had to agree with him. Browell hadn't got a leg to stand on and the question of civilian morale was paramount. The situation was difficult enough without having civilian discontent to contend with as well. Sooner or later the siege and the war would be over at which time everyone wanted to return home with reputations enhanced and a decoration or two thrown in for good measure. No one wanted to carry the legacy of a botched job. One had one's career to think of. He slapped the arms of the chair. 'Very well, Davies,' he said decisively, getting to his feet. 'A conviction it shall be. We'll organise the court martial for Friday.'

'All right, Browell. Let's have your version of events.' Captain Young had serious doubts about taking on this case. No sooner had word of Browell's arrest reached the battalion lines than three men had approached him with a request to defend their section leader. Typically of the ways of the soldier it seemed that every man in the company knew he had some sort of legal background although he couldn't recall ever disclosing this to anyone. He had explained to them that studying law and being a trained lawyer were two entirely different matters and that he had no courtroom experience whatsoever but they were not to be denied. An officer on the provost marshal's staff had originally been appointed to defend Browell but Young had to agree that Browell would have a better chance of a fair hearing if he took on the case. With Browell being in his own company he had also felt he had an obligation to make a decent show of defending him but on the evidence so far accumulated he could not see how he could do so. This would not be a career enhancing exercise.

Charlie went through the sequence of events on that awful evening as Young made some notes. 'The fact remains, Browell, that three witnesses – four if you count the native cook – saw you holding Grace Dunkley's dead body with blood on your hand. There was no one else in the house at the time and you are unable to offer any other explanation.'

Charlie remained adamant. 'I didn't do it, sir. As God is my witness I didn't do it.' Young looked at him, sitting on the opposite side of an old wooden table in the bleak storeroom now converted into a heavily guarded cell. Hands folded neatly on the table, he was alert, lucid and understandably worried without being overtly nervous. He was also desperate for Young to believe him.

Browell had always struck him as a solid man, a good soldier. He had to admit that rape and murder didn't sit comfortably side by side with the character of the man before him but who knew what demons lay in Browell's mind. Every man had his breaking point, especially under the appalling siege conditions, and there had already been a couple of suicides in the garrison. For all he knew this dreadful crime was the result of Browell reaching his. His denials were emphatic but that was understandable when a firing squad, especially one made up of your own comrades, beckoned.

'The immediate problem I have in putting together a case, Browell, is that you are stressing your repeated denials at the expense of a detailed analysis of what you claim happened. The information you have given me is far too superficial and sketchy to offer any sort of defence.' Young paused to let it sink in. 'Let's try it one more time. And tell me every single detail.'

Charlie took a deep breath and started again.

'Are you all right, nurse?' The voice came from a convalescing enteric case propped up in bed near the tent entrance.

Head down, Sarah was holding on to one of the guy ropes by the open flap 'Yes, I'm fine. Thank you.' She appreciated his concern but knew he wouldn't be convinced by her feeble assurance. 'I was just taking some air. The tent is so hot and stuffy. I just felt a little faint.'

She ran her handkerchief across her brow and looked up at the cloudless sky from where a relentless sun beat down. It would be on just such a day as this as a child that her father would lift her brother and herself into the family's cart and with her mother beside him drive off for a family picnic at the falls. It all seemed so long ago, such a distant memory that it was as if it were part of someone else's life and not her own.

They came from all directions, the buzz growing louder until it abruptly stopped as each fly settled on her. She gave a token waft of her hand, temporarily dispersing a few but they merely flew in a tight circle and settled back again. There were millions of them, drawn by this human concentration and its sickness and death. There was no escape on a day like this. Only nightfall and rainstorms afforded relief from the plague of flies but the night brought the scorpions and mosquitoes followed in the wake of the rain.

'Water, nurse,' called an orderly as he and his colleague stopped a bowser in front of the tent. Sarah indicated the empty barrel tucked just inside the tent and they rolled it out on its side, filled it up from the bowser and manoeuvred it back with considerably less ease, jerking it forward and sideways until it was back in the tent. 'That's washing water only, nurse,' said the orderly. 'We'll come back later with the drinking water.'

'Thank you,' said Sarah. Despite herself she had to smile at the insistence of the camp authorities on differentiating between water for drinking and washing. It all came from the sluggish flow of the Klip River on the edge of the camp. When it was drawn it had the colour and consistency of oxtail soup. It was sterilised by boiling and the mud removed in suspension. Even after treatment it was still all the same but the rules on water usage were strict.

At least they could wash the patients now. Another nurse started on the patient who had expressed his concern for her while Sarah started on the opposite row. When she reached Highlander Tom's bed, he gave her a warm smile. 'Hello, Sarah.' He was the only one of her original patients still in hospital, the rest having died or been discharged. By rights he should be dead too but she had never seen such a fighter as this young Scotsman. He was paralysed from the waist down and was making a slow but nonetheless remarkable recovery from his liver wound. He was the only patient who called her by her first name, the others always respectfully calling her Nurse Dyson or more often simply 'nurse'. She didn't object. Tom was her special patient and she had formed a particularly strong bond with him.

'Hello, Tom. How are you feeling?'

'Same as always, Sarah. I was thinking of going for a stroll later and was wondering if you'd care to join me.'

She wasn't sure how to respond. A serious answer ran the risk of sounding patronising while a frivolous one might be inadvertently cruel. It was fine line. 'You know I'd go anywhere with you, Tom.' It was the only neutral reply she could think of.

As she sponged his face he looked directly into her eyes. 'I do believe you would as well.' She felt guilty at stirring his emotions with such an impromptu answer. 'I love you, Sarah,' he said softly. Now she really didn't know how to respond. How did he love her? As his nurse? Like an older sister? As a substitute for his mother so far away in Scotland? Or like Charles. Charles. It came flooding back. The shocking news about Grace was terrible enough but in its wake came the even worse revelation that Charles had been arrested for her rape and murder. It couldn't be. Not Charles. Not the man she loved. The heat and the flies, the spread of fever and the ever dwindling supply of medicines and proper food, the increasing workload and the discomfort, all of this she could deal with if only because it was her job and it was an experience shared by everyone else. But Charles's situation was different. This was a torment she faced alone. She knew almost everyone else assumed he was guilty. He was condemned before his court martial and if he was found guilty she would be condemned to a life without him. It was all too much and she released the feelings could not share with anyone else, the feelings she had buried deep inside her ever since she heard the shattering news. Tears pattered on Tom's bed as, head bowed, she wept silently.

'I'm sorry,' said Tom, both concerned and embarrassed. 'I didn't mean to upset you. I shouldn't have said that.'

She shook her head, unable to utter any words. She looked into his eyes and shook her head again. 'Dear Tom,' she said finally, stroking his hair, 'it's not your fault. It's nothing you've said or done.'

'Then why are you so upset?'

'It's something I can't discuss, even with you.' She dried her eyes. Normally she would have despised herself for becoming upset in front of another person, exposing what she felt was a weakness she would rather conceal, but on this occasion it had had a positive effect. Her outburst had purged herself of the helpless anguish she had allowed to fester inside her. She now knew what she must do.

The door of the improvised cell swung open. 'Visitor,' said the guard, taking a seat in the corner as the door was locked from the outside. Charlie stood up, open-mouthed.

'Sarah.'

'Charles, how are you?' She took a seat opposite him at the table.

'I'm fine.' He hesitated. 'Apart from this pickle I'm in. It's such a lovely surprise to see you. How did you manage to get away from Intombi?' It had been over five weeks since they had last seen each other, an eternity for both of them, but now they were together again, however briefly, the memory of that day seemed so fresh and vital.

'I applied for permission to visit you. Matron refused but was overruled by Dr. Barlow. She said I couldn't be spared but he said I would be more use to them after seeing you and knowing exactly what's happening rather than fretting all the time out at Intombi.' Charlie gave her a quizzical look. 'Don't worry,' she continued. 'They don't know about us. As far as they are concerned you are an acquaintance from the Dunkleys but I've made it clear that I believe you're innocent.'

'I'm glad somebody does.' Charlie breathlessly gabbled out what had happened, anxious to justify and reinforce her faith in his innocence. He told her that Frank, Walter and McAdams had persuaded Captain Young to represent him although he wasn't sure that Young altogether believed he was innocent.

'I know you didn't do it, Charles, but we need to convince others as well.' Like Young she made him repeat the story slowly and without leaving out the slightest detail. Before the brief time allotted for the visit was over she had resolved to meet Captain Young before she returned to Intombi. She would also visit Ada Dunkley.

Sarah walked briskly down to the archdeacon's residence adjacent to All Saints Church at the southern edge of habitation on Murchison

Street, kicking up dust from the unpaved roadway as she went.

'I was expecting the doctor, not a nurse,' said the archdeacon with a puzzled frown when Sarah entered the study. He removed the *pince-nez* from his aquiline nose as if to emphasise his bewilderment at her arrival. She had not considered that her uniform might cause the reason for her visit to be misinterpreted.

'Oh, no sir. I'm not here professionally. I'm a friend of Mrs. Dunkley's and I wanted to take the opportunity to visit her before I return to Intombi. She's related to my mother and I used to lodge at her house.' She paused. 'It's such a terrible tragedy.'

'Well, she's been under sedation. She's awake now but we're expecting the doctor at any moment. I'll have to ask if she will see you.' She gave him her name and he disappeared down the hallway into a room on the right. She heard the mumble of a muted conversation. A dowdy, overweight woman with her grey hair tied up in a bun appeared and glanced inexpressively at her before climbing the stairs. Sarah was unsure if she was the archdeacon's wife or housekeeper. After a minute or so she came back down the stairs, nodded to the archdeacon and motioned Sarah to follow her. 'Only until the doctor arrives, you understand,' said the archdeacon. 'She's tired and of course still very distressed.'

Ada looked a terrible sight, propped up on two huge pillows in a four poster bed with her head peering over a sheet which emphasised her double chin. Her face was drawn and pale and she had dark patches under her reddened eyes. She probably hasn't eaten properly or slept without sedation since the murder, thought Sarah. She greeted Ada warmly and sympathetically. Ada squeezed her hand but her face betrayed neither emotion nor recognition.

Sarah's heart went out to her. 'I'm so sorry,' she said, sitting in a cushioned wicker chair by the bed. She held Ada's hand, allowing her the opportunity to respond but she said nothing. She desperately wanted Ada to say something, anything, which might provide a glimmer of hope for Charles but it would be too cruel to press her into reliving the experience of that awful evening.

They sat for some minutes in silence until Ada turned her head towards Sarah. 'These are such difficult times,' she said in a hoarse whisper. 'And made all the worse by Zachariah and Ralph not being here.' Sarah wondered if the dreadful news had got through to them at Estcourt. They needed to know but she could imagine the unavoidable sense of impotence and despair on top of their grief when they heard. 'The archdeacon and his wife have been so kind,' continued Ada. 'They have invited me to stay with them for as long as I want.' Her face crumpled. 'I couldn't face staying in that house alone. Not after what's happened.' She started to sob gently but with a deep breath she regained her composure. 'I sent cook and the other servants home until further notice. The archdeacon is afraid that the house may be looted with it being unoccupied.'

'I won't now be returning to Intombi today and have not made any arrangements for accommodation,' said Sarah. 'If you're concerned I'd be happy to stay there at least for tonight.'

Ada readily agreed and told Sarah to take her house keys from the top drawer of her bedside cabinet. A discreet cough from the doorway announced the arrival of the doctor accompanied by the archdeacon's wife. Sarah pre-empted her. 'I'd best be going,' she said, getting to her feet. 'I'll call again before I return to Intombi.' She would have to get word that she would not be back until the following day and hoped that Dr. Barlow would retain his sympathy and patience in the face of further protestations from the matron. Ada smiled weakly and thanked her for her kindness and consideration as the doctor entered the room and took control of proceedings.

'That's the first time she has smiled since...since, you know,' said the archdeacon's wife in the hallway, with no trace of her earlier aloofness.

The archdeacon, too, was no longer defensive. 'It's good that you came. Mrs. Dunkley will need all possible care and comfort over the next weeks and months. She will never get over this terrible business but we can all try to alleviate her grief. Our prayers are with her constantly. The funeral was particularly trying for her.' There was already too much death and disease in Ladysmith and Sarah knew that burials in the besieged town were carried out at the earliest opportunity, invariably at night to avoid the unwelcome attention of the Boer Creusots. Grace had been buried the night after her murder with the minimum of ceremony. Without the support of her husband and son Ada had been overwhelmed by the occasion and had fainted by the graveside. She had been confined to bed ever since.

In response to his question Sarah told the archdeacon the background of how she came to know the Dunkleys and the family connection between her mother and Ada. Sarah knew from Charlie's description of events that the archdeacon had been with Ada when she returned home that night and seized the opportunity to ask him about the circumstances of the discovery of Grace's body. It transpired that after Ada and her cook had bid farewell to Sarah at Intombi they had met the archdeacon and a major of the Carbineers on the train taking them the short distance back to Ladysmith. As they were without transport from the railway station the major had gallantly offered her a ride home in his carriage. True to form Ada had insisted that the two gentlemen stay for some refreshment and when the front door was found to be open they had rushed inside and in Grace's bedroom they had found Charles holding her body.

'It was all I could do to prevent the major from blowing the blighter's head off there and then.' The archdeacon shook his head in sad reflection. 'He kept saying he hadn't done it and appeared genuinely distressed but the major reckoned his only anguish was getting caught. The monster will face mortal justice, never fear, but his true punishment will be eternal damnation.'

Sarah had expected to see a man surrounded by files and papers with at least two or three assistants rushing to and fro assembling fresh pieces of evidence with which he would create a robust case for the defence. Captain Young disappointed her. Sitting alone at a desk in a bleak and cramped office temporarily assigned to him by the provost marshal's department, he had the weary and distracted look of a man whose heart was not in it.

'I have to be frank with you Nurse Dyson,' said Young, leaning back in his chair. 'I didn't ask to take on this case and I did so against my better judgement at the request of the men in Lance-Corporal Browell's section. I felt duty bound to represent the interests of a man in my own company but I'm not trained in courtroom procedure and have no experience in preparing or presenting a case.'

Her heart sank. 'What you mean is that he has no chance.' She almost choked on her own words.

'What I mean is that Browell is in an extremely serious situation and I'm not sure if I'm equipped to give him the kind of support he is going to need.'

'Do you think he's guilty?'

'I did at first but his story is so simple that I have to admit it makes me doubt it. Browell's also a good man. He's never been in any kind of trouble and has never let me down.'

Sarah perked up. 'So you do think he has a chance,' she said brightly.

'Well, I don't want to give you false hope. It's the members of the court martial panel who have to be convinced, not me.' He knew that the staff and the provost marshal wanted a conviction to reassure the civilian population that they were on top of the security situation and an execution to discourage the rest of the garrison from any further misdeeds. 'Look at this.' He tossed a black folder tied with a red ribbon across the desk. Sarah didn't pick it up. She knew what he meant. The folder was thin, too thin to contain the documentation and evidence he would need for an acquittal. 'It contains statements from Browell, the archdeacon and a Carbineer officer and a report from the doctor who certified Grace Dunkley dead. Mrs. Dunkley was, and still is, too distressed to make a statement. Browell's proclamations of innocence are unverifiable while the other two corroborate each other and point to guilt.' He paused and looked directly at her. 'Which would you believe?'

'A man's life is at stake. A man who trusts you and follows your orders without question.' She paused. 'We have to make them believe, Captain Young.'

'We?'

'The court martial is tomorrow. I think you'll agree that you could use some help.'

He nodded. 'There's no question of that, Nurse Dyson, but where do you suggest we start?'

She dangled the house keys in front of him. 'The Dunkley residence. With Mrs. Dunkley's blessing I stayed there last night. I slept in the guestroom I used to have as a billet. Otherwise I touched nothing.'

Young sat bolt upright, staring at the keys as if mesmerised by them. The all-embracing control of the military authorities and the rush to bring the case to court martial had caused everyone to overlook the most basic issue of all. There had been no attempt to run the case on the lines of a regular murder investigation. 'We'll need the assistance of a trained policeman to examine the evidence at the house for possible clues,' he said, rising from his chair and pondering the possibilities such an approach could offer as he paced up and down. 'There are seventy or eighty members of the Natal Police holed up in Ladysmith,' he said excitedly. 'They can't all be just mounted troopers or jailers. Surely at least one of them must have some detective experience.'

'You're absolutely right,' said Sarah. 'And I think I know just the man.'

The earthy odour of horses and manure pervaded the hot, still air as Sarah and Young walked down the colonial cavalry lines to the bivouac of the Natal Police detachment. Sarah found the smell strangely appealing, even attractive, evoking memories of the stable back home in Howick where the family's carriage horse was kept. The relentless and inescapable swarms of flies were the real nuisance. There seemed to be nearly as many here as at Intombi. A few of the horses indolently wafted their tails or shook their heads in a futile attempt to disperse the pestilential insects but most seemed to have forsaken the effort.

As they approached the tent to which a trooper had directed them a tall figure in khaki emerged. 'Sarah!' he exclaimed. 'We *are* honoured! What brings you to our humble camp?' Sarah introduced him to Young as Captain Branagan, an old family friend from Howick who had been transferred to the Klip River division of the Natal Police earlier in the year. She had told Young that he had a lot of experience in detective work and a background in the developing science of forensics. She hadn't told him that he had incurred the wrath of his superior by trying to implement his knowledge of forensics on his return from a course in Durban and that his insistence had resulted in being put back into uniform and banished to this backwater. They sat on flimsy canvas backed chairs and Sarah fanned herself with the pitifully slender case file they had brought. It was hot in the open but it would be unbearable inside the tent as she knew only too well from Intombi. 'I'd heard you were in Ladysmith but have never had the opportunity to look you up,' said Branagan. 'And with all due respect I'd prefer not to have to call on you professionally. Hospitals give me the shivers at the best of times.' He laughed heartily and pulled out a silver cigarette case offering its contents to his visitors. Sarah declined but Young accepted and he and Branagan shared a match. 'I'm not sure which we'll run out of first, cigarettes or matches,' said Branagan, 'but my guess is that the barter value will soon be one cigarette for one match.'

Sarah gave him the background to the case and the very limited time Young had to prepare his defence. 'I see,' said Branagan sombrely, drawing deeply on his cigarette and stroking the end of his thin moustache. 'Nasty business. I've met Zachariah Dunkley several times. He's a decent fellow, unlike some other land agents of my acquaintance in the colony, and doesn't deserve any of this.'

'Neither does his wife', said Sarah. 'She's a remarkable woman.'

'Is that all you've got?' asked Branagan, changing the subject and pointing to the file. Sarah nodded and passed it to him. He read through the statements quickly and closed the file. He leaned back and blew a smoke ring into the air. 'Do you believe the accused is innocent?'

'Yes,' answered Sarah and Young as one.

'Why?'

'Because I know him well and he's not capable of such a crime,' said Sarah.

'I agree,' said Young. 'And the more I think about it the more concerned I am at the military authorities' almost indecent haste in their desire to bring a conviction.'

'Forget your personal feelings,' said Branagan. They count for nothing in a court of law, civil or military. There have been any number of murderers given impeccable references in court by family, friends and employers but they were murderers all the same.' He waved the folder at them. 'The fact is that the prosecution case is based solely on circumstantial evidence. Browell was found at the scene of the crime holding the dead girl's body but otherwise there is not a shred of evidence to link him with the murder. There has been no attempt by the military authorities to conduct any kind of investigation into the crime. They've simply assumed Browell is guilty. This would be thrown out of a civilian court through lack of evidence.'

'But this is a court martial,' said Young apprehensively.

'Exactly.' Branagan leapt up and ground his cigarette out with his foot. 'He's guilty until proven innocent. I suggest we set about proving his innocence without delay.'

Somehow Sarah felt the atmosphere was eerier in daylight than at night. She hadn't felt apprehensive about staying there alone and her exhaustion had combined with the unaccustomed comfort of a real bed to afford her a restful and undisturbed sleep. Now, even accompanied by two men, the emptiness of the place was thrown into stark relief. In the drawing room, where the Dunkleys had so often generously entertained their guests, everything was in its place except for the people whose gaiety and conversation gave it life. There was no sound from the kitchen where at another time cook might be heard scolding one of the other servants. It was on the landing where she felt most uneasy as Branagan turned the handle, opening Grace's bedroom door for the first time since the night of the murder.

'Perfect,' said Branagan, looking at the rumpled and blood spotted eiderdown. 'It looks very much as though nothing has been touched.' He moved around the room wordlessly, stopping here and there to peer closely at whatever attracted his interest or attention. He waved an arm at them. 'Please don't touch anything yourself.' He pulled out a notebook and scribbled a few quick notes. He closed the notebook and gave the cover a contented tap with the pencil. 'Good.'

'Well?' said Young after a short pause.

'I also believe that your man Browell is innocent.'

Sarah was overjoyed at Branagan's unexpected statement. 'I'm so pleased to hear you say that,' she enthused. 'But how do you know?' she added more evenly.

'According to the archdeacon's and the major's statements they apprehended Browell at ten minutes past seven in the evening. Browell says he had arrived there only a matter of minutes before, gaining entry through the open front door and found Grace's body when he went upstairs.' Branagan pointed to the spent match on the dresser. 'Browell also stated that he lit this lamp.'

'Correct,' affirmed Young.

'Captain Young, purely hypothetically of course, if you had just committed a murder would you take the trouble to light a lamp?'

'Well, no. I suppose not.'

'Why not?' asked Branagan. 'Again purely hypothetically,' he added as if to reassure Young.

'I wouldn't want to risk attracting attention with the light and...' He hesitated.

'And?' encouraged Branagan.

'And I would want to get away from the scene as quickly as possible.'

'Exactly.' Branagan strode towards them. 'But what if you had committed the murder, say, an hour earlier?'

The answer is obvious, thought Young. 'I would still want to get away from the scene. I certainly wouldn't hang around for an hour.'

'Of course. But that's only part of the answer.'

Sarah was encouraged by Branagan's enthusiasm for the case but still could not see where his reasoning was leading or why he was already so sure Charles was innocent. 'I don't follow,' she said.

'You will,' retorted Branagan brightly. 'But we need to work fast. Right now we need to get hold of the doctor who certified the death and another independent doctor to testify before the court martial tomorrow. I'm sure you can suggest one at Intombi who's prepared to help us.'

Sarah did not hesitate. 'Dr. Barlow would be the best choice.' She was confident of his skill and competence as a doctor but his involvement in the case would also help to resist any pressure for her to return to Intombi until after the court martial.

'Good. Captain Young, if you would kindly write a message to Dr. Barlow requesting his immediate assistance I'll send one of my men to deliver it personally with an instruction not to return without him.' He could see the look of scepticism on Young's face. 'Just because the military authorities haven't given you any support doesn't mean you can't obtain any elsewhere. After all you've got me on your team now. You're perfectly entitled to co-opt any assistance you need, call any witness you choose and present any evidence you find. The only significant factor over which we have no control is time. They have set the court martial for tomorrow and that will never be changed whether we are ready or not. It is up to us to be ready.'

Young started writing a note. 'Can I be of any help?' offered Sarah.

'Yes,' said Branagan. 'Entry was not forced. As we are all agreed that Browell is innocent it follows that Grace Dunkley's murderer was someone else. Someone she knew and trusted. Otherwise she would not have admitted him into the house when she was alone. Kindly make a list of all males over the age of eighteen who fall into that category. Whoever it is he is still at large in Ladysmith.'

Sarah could think of few names and considered Ada to be the best person to ask but she doubted that she would be in any fit state to co-operate. She would try. She would have to.

Oh, yes,' added Branagan almost as an afterthought. 'And we need to have Grace's body exhumed.'

The low rumble of distant artillery since before dawn had created an air of expectation among soldiers and civilians alike in Ladysmith. It came from the south-east and could only mean one thing. General Buller's army was on the move and attacking the Boer positions north of the Tugela River. Surely relief would be only a matter of days away. People were already contemplating a siege free Christmas and New Year.

Under normal circumstances Sarah would have succumbed to the mood of excitement but Charles and his court martial had very firmly become the focus of her attention. She sat on one of two parallel benches outside the double doors of the makeshift courtroom where two soldiers stood guard. The court martial was being held in the local school where classes had been suspended immediately after the first Boer shells had fallen on Ladysmith. She knew she wouldn't be allowed inside but would at least catch a glimpse of him as he arrived and he would know that she was there for him.

Dr. Barlow sat beside her. At first he had been angry at being dragged from his work at Intombi where the increasing number of patients had put a severe strain on the medical staff, especially as some had contracted enteric or dysentery themselves. Branagan had told him that if his job was saving lives there was one here he could help to save. 'You'll only be away a day or two,' Branagan had assured him. 'And when you return you'll be able to take Nurse Dyson back with you.' Young and Branagan had briefed him on the case and he had picked up more details from subsequent discussions between them and Sarah. Never an admirer of rigid, unthinking military procedure and a man with a deep sense of justice, he had gradually warmed to the project and offered his unequivocal support. At Branagan's request he had given Charlie a thorough medical examination the previous evening and his report had been added to the file.

Sitting silently on the opposite bench next to Barlow was Dr. Conway, the physician who had certified Grace's death. A small, weasel-like man whose shirt collar was several sizes too big for him, he was quietly spoken at the best of times but these weren't the best of times. Pressed by the military authorities at the scene of the crime to issue an immediate report he had omitted a crucial fact that Branagan had picked up on. He had also failed to notice and report on vital elements of the condition of Grace's body that had become belatedly apparent when he and Barlow had examined her exhumed body. He hoped to redeem himself on the witness stand but he knew his reputation was at stake. He had no doubt in his own mind that if it was subsequently compromised it would be the military's fault.

The hollow clump of army boots on the floorboards announced the arrival of Frank and Walter who mumbled sombre good mornings and sat on the opposite bench, shuffling nervously and clearing their throats. Sarah was pleased to see them although she knew that they too would not be allowed inside the courtroom. 'We got special permission to be here,' said Frank. 'But the whole platoon, most of the company and even men from other companies in the battalion would have been here if they could. The lads are right behind him.'

Young and Branagan arrived and stood whispering intently at the other end of the entrance hall. Sarah hurried to join them. Young looked nervous but Branagan was cheerful and Sarah hoped his optimism would rub off. 'You're the lawyer,' he told Young. 'I'm only the policeman.' The case folder was looking encouragingly thicker and both Sarah and Young knew that the additional evidence would never have been accumulated in time, if ever, without Branagan's contribution. Young's task would be to present and argue their case as skilfully as he could in front of a hostile presiding panel but he would be reassured by Branagan's presence at his side in the courtroom.

'We're as ready as we'll ever be,' said Branagan. 'We now have a defence backed by solid evidence whereas the prosecution has only the flimsiest of cases.' He patted Young's shoulder. 'All we need is a fair hearing and God's blessing.' He paused. 'But we won't get one without the other.'

'When the trial starts I'll call on Mrs. Dunkley and try to get some more names of men of Grace's acquaintance,' said Sarah. From her time as a lodger there she could only recollect the presence of three men whom Grace was ever likely to admit to the house. A local young man she had seemed quite fond of but who had enlisted in the Carbineers and joined Ralph's squadron at Estcourt before Ladysmith was besieged, another who worked for her father's company and Captain Turnbull. She had tried to keep her prejudices to one side but could not help recalling Turnbull's unwelcome advances towards her. There would probably be other candidates and she would have to keep her counsel, at least until after she had spoken to Ada.

The guards clicked to attention and all those seated on the benches rose as three red tabbed staff officers, two colonels and a brigadier, arrived. They returned Frank's and Walter's salutes and entered the courtroom as the guards swung open the doors. In their wake followed Charlie, manacled at the wrists and surrounded by the protective screen of a two man armed guard led by a sergeant. Sarah rushed forward. 'Good luck,' was all she managed to say before he disappeared inside the courtroom. She was confident he had heard her but also knew that he could not divert his gaze or acknowledge her. Young and Branagan headed towards the courtroom as the prosecuting officer followed the entourage. 'This shouldn't take long, gentlemen,' he sneered at them. 'I'm expecting to fit in a game of polo later.' His assistant following behind smirked at the jibe. Young tensed and Branagan sensed he was about to respond. He gently placed a restraining hand on his arm and they silently entered the courtroom, the door closing with a hollow thud behind them.

Sarah closed her eyes and inhaled deeply. The most critical moment in Charles's life and her own had arrived. When he came out of that courtroom he would either be cleared of all charges or – she could hardly bear to contemplate the notion – condemned to death. There was nothing more she could do here. As she left the building a shiver ran through her body and down her limbs. 'Good morning, Nurse Dyson,' said a smiling Captain Turnbull, touching the rim of his slouch hat with his riding crop. 'Another lovely day.'

Charlie felt there was a timeless and almost unreal atmosphere in the schoolroom-turned-courtroom and despite the grave circumstances in which he found himself could not help feeling like a naughty schoolboy brought before the headmaster for some small misdemeanour. The blackboard still had the arithmetic that was chalked on it during the final lesson and the cloth-covered table at which the red tabs sat was actually three of the pupils' desks pushed together. Young and Branagan sat at a makeshift table made up from two desks facing the triumvirate of judges as did the prosecuting officer and his assistant. Charlie sat on a bench to the rear of the counsels with an armed guard on either side of him and the sergeant behind.

The charges were read out and Charlie entered a plea of not guilty. The brigadier looked towards the prosecuting officer. 'Captain Toseland, you may begin your submission,' he said.

'With the court's permission the prosecution will show that on Monday the eleventh of December eighteen ninety-nine Lance-Corporal Charles Browell did rape and murder Miss Grace Dunkley, a civilian resident of Ladysmith.' He held his hand out behind him to indicate Charlie but continued to address the court. 'The accused was apprehended at the scene of the crime by Major Ranson of the Carbineers in the presence of Archdeacon Williams and Mrs. Dunkley. Although Mrs. Dunkley has unfortunately been too distressed to issue a statement' he continued, holding up his file, 'we have the depositions of the major and the archdeacon as well as Dr. Conway's report confirming the cause of death as strangulation. Any and all of these people may be called as witnesses if necessary but it is my belief that the case is sufficiently indisputable that any further anguish or inconvenience, particularly for Mrs. Dunkley, may be avoided.'

Toseland continued his submission in a tone that suggested there could be no possible verdict other than guilty but failed to offer anything more than the circumstantial evidence contained in his file.

He waved the file again as if it held the undeniable truth of a declaration of faith. As Branagan had predicted he made great play of the fact that there was no forced entry, that the murderer must have been known to Grace Dunkley and that Lance-Corporal Browell fitted the bill perfectly. Charlie was bursting to shout out his denial of guilt in the face of such preposterous and unsubstantiated charges while Young seethed at the charlatan Toseland telling a docile and amenable court what they wanted to hear. Branagan was content to indulge Toseland and await their turn. Toseland concluded his submission with his earnest belief that the court would be unable to bring any other verdict but guilty with the prescribed penalty for the accused.

'Captain Young, you may present your submission now,' said the brigadier in a distracted tone without looking up from his papers.

Young thanked the court. 'With the court's permission,' he began. He saw the brigadier engaged in conversation with one of the colonels. Young coughed. 'With the court's permission,' he repeated more loudly, causing both the brigadier and the colonel to jerk their heads up and glare disapprovingly at him, 'the defence will present fresh evidence and demonstrate that the prosecution's case is based entirely on supposition.' Young duly detailed the circumstantial nature of the prosecution's evidence.

In the belief that the statements of the witnesses who had discovered Charlie holding Grace Dunkley's body would be sufficient to secure a conviction from a sympathetic court Toseland had not anticipated such a submission. He could not conceive that the defence would be able to produce any evidence that could overrule the prosecution's or find it either necessary or worthwhile to call any witnesses of their own. He had briefly wondered why Dr. Conway was waiting outside when he had not requested his attendance but failed to see how Conway might benefit the defence's case.

Young resumed his seat after completing his submission and Toseland was invited to proceed with the case for the prosecution. 'I do not propose to take up any more of the court's valuable time than is absolutely necessary,' he continued. 'However, for the sake of record I would like to call Captain Turnbull as an independent character witness.'

The acting clerk swung open the doors and called Turnbull who avoided Charlie's stare and saluted the panel. Toseland wasted no time in priming him. 'Captain Turnbull, how long have you known the accused?'

'Not very long. About six or seven weeks. We occasionally met socially, although I must add coincidentally, at the Dunkley residence.' Branagan started to scribble some notes.

'And how would you describe the accused's conduct at such gatherings?'

'He was awkward and socially inept.' Turnbull paused. 'Completely out of his class I would say.'

'How was his interaction with the members of the Dunkley household?'

'He was nervous and unsure in front of Mr. and Mrs. Dunkley.' He paused again. 'He seemed to be besotted with Miss Grace Dunkley, staring at her when he thought no one was looking. I caught him doing it on several occasions.'

Charlie could stand no more. 'That's a lie!' he blurted out. 'That's a lie and you know it!'

The brigadier's face flushed. 'If the accused makes one more outburst of this nature he will be gagged,' he blustered. Branagan looked round at Charlie and drew his finger across his lips. Charlie understood what Branagan was telling him. Let them handle this. He remained agitated but he would have to avoid another outburst. The court was hostile towards him to begin with and he could not afford to antagonise it further. Besides, he didn't relish the prospect of having a gag across his mouth for the rest of the proceedings. 'Please continue, Captain Turnbull,' said the brigadier in a calmer tone.

'Thank you, sir,' said Turnbull. 'As I was about to say before the unfortunate interruption, Miss Dunkley had mentioned to me that the accused had on more than one occasion made improper advances to her and she solicited my help.' Charlie seethed as Turnbull continued. 'It had been my intention to approach him in this respect and demand that he cease his disgraceful behaviour immediately.' He hesitated, bowed his head momentarily and resumed in a solemn tone. 'Unfortunately, I did not have the opportunity to do so before the tragic circumstances which bring us here today.'

Young jumped to his feet. 'With respect to the court,' he said as evenly as he could, 'this witness's accusations are completely without foundation and totally uncorroborated.'

'Sit down, Captain Young,' said the brigadier testily. 'Another outburst from you and you will be removed from the case.' Barely able to contain his fury, Young resumed his seat. As he did so Branagan gripped his arm in a gesture both of encouragement and restraint. Young envied Branagan his cool and confident manner but fleetingly wondered if his optimism was well founded or merely a delusion. No, Branagan is right, thought Young. Just as he has been right on everything else so far. Branagan was nevertheless wrestling with a conundrum himself. Turnbull looked familiar to him but he couldn't think from where. In such a small and isolated place he had met or seen many officers and men from other units under some circumstance or other but he couldn't place this man.

'Thank you Captain Turnbull,' said Toseland. 'That will be all.' Turnbull saluted the panel and turned to leave.

'If it please the court,' said Young, rising from his chair, 'the defence requests that Captain Turnbull remain available for further cross examination at a later time.'

'A later time?' queried the brigadier impatiently. 'Why can't you do it now?'

'Sir, the defence has other witnesses who are fundamental to the case. It would be more appropriate for the court to hear their testimony before the defence has an opportunity to respond to the specifics of Captain Turnbull's statement.'

'Very well,' conceded the brigadier reluctantly. 'Captain Turnbull, you will stay in the building until the defence no longer requires your presence.' In his anxiety Turnbull almost challenged the brigadier's order. This wasn't supposed to happen. Toseland had assured him that he would be needed only for the few minutes it would take to assassinate Browell's character. No one would query the word of an officer against a humble lance-corporal accused of rape and murder and caught with a corpse in his arms, Toseland had assured him, especially as the military authorities wanted a speedy resolution to the trial and a guilty verdict. Keep calm, thought Turnbull as he quickly regained his composure.

'Of course, sir,' he said. 'I remain at the court's disposal.'

Sarah had left the school at a brisk pace that soon became a half run in her anxiety to leave behind the unexpected vision of Captain Turnbull and reach the archdeacon's residence with the least delay. She had to try to prompt Ada into giving her the names of any other men whom Grace would have freely admitted into the house. After her own experience of his unwelcome attention she already had Turnbull in mind as the prime suspect. There may be any number of other possibilities but she hoped not. She didn't want the focus of suspicion to broaden. Branagan had made the point that they needed to prove Charlie's innocence and the best way to do that would be to provide the court with the real murderer.

As she approached the church she saw a familiar figure sitting on the wall. 'Joseph,' she cried. 'What are you doing here?' He was dirty, dishevelled and in an agitated state 'I heard about Miss Grace and I wanted to see Mrs. Dunkley.' He pointed to the archdeacon's residence adjacent to the church. 'I heard she is staying here.'

'That's right,' said Sarah. 'I'm sure Mrs. Dunkley will be gratified to hear of your concern.'

'I called to see her but the housemaid chased me away with a broom,' said Joseph sounding affronted at the indignity.

Sarah was surprised at Joseph's attitude. He knew as well as anyone that a native could not simply call unannounced at a white person's house, let alone expect to be received with anything other than suspicion and hostility. He was acting very oddly. 'Joseph, are you all right?' She looked at him closely and answered her own question. 'No, you're not.' His eyes were bloodshot and his lips were cracked. 'Show me your tongue,' she ordered. It was swollen with dehydration and coated yellow. 'Have you been on a mail run?' she asked, puzzled. The run was an exhausting challenge even for a naturally fit native youth like Joseph but it would not normally have left him in this condition.

'Yes, Miss Sarah.' He slid off the wall and tottered unsteadily on his feet. 'The other mail runners were scared because two were killed by the Boers on Monday and none of them wanted to do the run that night. I volunteered but I only got back just before dawn today.'

'Good Lord!' she exclaimed. He had been away for three days and four nights.

He told her he had reached the British camp with no more difficulty than usual but shortly after he had started back there had been a big movement of men and guns from the British camp towards the village of Colenso. Every Boer between there and Ladysmith had gone on full alert and many had moved into defensive positions north of the Tugela. They had increased their pickets and were more vigilant than he had ever known previously. He had been forced to stay in hiding during daylight and most of each night and had spent thirty-six hours in the dry bed of a small *spruit* on the last leg of the journey.

'When the British guns started the Boer pickets were only interested in what was happening towards Colenso,' he said. 'So I was finally able to slip through their lines last night.' He had eaten no food for three days and his only source of water had been from the early morning dew on the grass. He had been to the Dunkleys' house but after finding it deserted had made his way home where his grandfather had told him the terrible news about Miss Grace and that Mrs. Dunkley was staying at the archdeacon's house. He held up a reed. 'I brought Mrs. Dunkley's letter. It is from Mr. Dunkley in Estcourt.'

'Joseph, I'm sure Mrs. Dunkley will be very grateful to you but right now we have two problems,' said Sarah. 'The first is to clean you up and get some nourishment inside you. The second is that a man is fighting for his life and desperately needs all our help. You remember Lance-Corporal Browell who used to call on Mrs Dunkley?' Joseph nodded. 'Well, he has been accused of Miss Grace's murder and is on trial right now – but he didn't do it.'

Joseph gave her a perplexed look. 'I know.'

'With the court's permission the defence calls Dr. Conway as a witness.' Toseland was curious to learn what Young had gleaned from Conway that could possibly help the case for the defence and leaned forward as Conway took his seat and formally identified himself.

Young saw that Conway was uncomfortable as he shifted nervously in his seat. He would try not to be too hard on the doctor. All he wanted was for the truth to emerge. It would not materially assist the defence's case by discrediting the poor wretch just for the sake of it. 'Dr. Conway,' he began, 'please tell the court at what time you arrived at the Dunkley residence on the day of the murder.'

'At seven-thirty in the evening, about ten minutes after I was called out by a messenger sent by Archdeacon Williams.'

'And what did you find there?'

'A small crowd had already gathered outside,' said Conway hoarsely. He cleared his throat and continued. 'I understand Mrs. Dunkley's cook had run hysterically out of the house and into the road when Miss Dunkley's body was discovered. Upstairs the body was on the bed and the accused was lying face down on the floor covered by Major Ranson's revolver. The archdeacon was comforting Mrs. Dunkley downstairs.' He paused and looked around the room. 'The poor lady was terribly distraught as one might imagine.'

'Indeed,' said Young matter-of-factly. 'Tell me, Doctor Conway, was there a lamp lit in the bedroom?'

'Oh yes. It was quite dark when I arrived.'

'Indeed,' repeated Young, this time in a tone that indicated an arousal of interest. 'And what was your verdict on the cause of death?'

'Strangulation. It's in my report.'

'Yes it is, Dr. Conway. But what is not in your report is your estimate of the time of death.'

Conway looked to the floor. 'No,' he agreed, almost in a whisper. The brigadier impatiently ordered him to lift his head and repeat his answer clearly enough for the court to hear. 'No,' Conway confirmed in a stronger voice.

'Surely this information is routinely included in such a report, particularly when a crime is involved?' Although couching it as a question Young left no doubt that it was a statement of fact.

Conway nodded. 'Yes, but when the provost marshal's men came to take away the accused soon after I had examined the body I was pressed into writing my report before they left.' Conway's forehead was beaded with perspiration and he swallowed self-consciously, his prominent Adam's apple twitching behind his voluminous shirt collar. 'They wouldn't leave without it,' he said in a vain appeal for the panel's sympathy. Conway's head dropped slightly but sufficiently to take him out of eye contact with Young. 'I've never had to do a murder report before,' he said feebly.

Young pitied this weak and pathetic man. Conway's professional ineptitude and acquiescence to intimidation by the military would not be easily forgiven in a community as small as Ladysmith. He would almost certainly be forced to relocate his practice to another part of the colony after the war. Young could not release him from his torment just yet though. Conway's testimony constituted a vital part of the defence and if it came to a choice between saving Browell's life or Conway's reputation then there was no choice.

'Could you please confirm to the court now your estimate of the time of death?'

'Miss Dunkley had been dead between one and two hours when I examined her body.'

'Between one and two hours prior to seven thirty in the evening?' Conway nodded. 'Yes.'

Young turned to the panel. 'Which means that the murder was committed before darkness fell. All accounts agree that the lamp in Miss Dunkley's room was lit when Mrs. Dunkley's party returned to the house. I therefore submit to the court that whoever had committed the murder would not have stayed around the scene of the crime for an hour or two and then bother to illuminate it.' One of the colonels whispered in the brigadier's ear while a grim faced Toseland frantically scanned his copy of Conway's report in an urgent search for a riposte.

'Furthermore,' continued Young, striving to maintain a measured delivery, 'the accused reported to me at company headquarters on Caesar's Camp at six o'clock prior to leaving for the Dunkley residence. It is approximately an hour's walk from there into Ladysmith, fifty minutes at best.' He paused for effect but his entire audience had already anticipated his next statement. 'Therefore he could not possibly have been at the Dunkley residence when the murder took place between five thirty and six thirty.'

For the first time since his arrest Charlie felt a surge of optimism. Surely that fact alone would be sufficient to acquit him. As he shuffled to the edge of his chair he caught the disapproving glares of both guards in his peripheral vision.

Young had no further questions but Conway's palpable relief was short lived as Toseland sprung to his feet at the brigadier's invitation to cross-examine the hapless doctor. Toseland tried to profit from

Conway's already tarnished reputation by querying his calculation of the time of death after his original examination. 'I confess to an oversight in my report at the time but my memory over the period of the last four days remains intact,' said Conway with a rare confidence fuelled by his growing hatred of the military prosecutors. Their hectoring had caused him to omit a key fact from his report and instead of supporting him they were now trying to compromise him further.

Toseland tried a different approach. 'In your report,' he said, holding up the document, 'you mention that the victim was blood-stained and that the accused had bloodstains on his hand.' He waited for Conway's affirmation before continuing. 'Does this not indicate that, in addition to death by strangulation, a violent attack took place?'

'Yes, but...'

'No 'buts', Dr. Conway. Was there or was there not a violent attack?'

'Yes.' Conway's slight hesitation was all that Toseland needed to cut him off before he could qualify his confirmation.

'No further questions.'


In the archdeacon's kitchen Joseph hungrily ate the mealie porridge specially prepared for him by the housemaid. She was accustomed to serving white people and was unimpressed by having to wait on one of her own kind, particularly this shabby urchin. Joseph lifted the bowl to his mouth and started to lick the sparse remnants that had eluded the spoon. He reeled from an unsympathetic slap across the head and an admonition not to abuse the archdeacon's hospitality by eating like an animal. He really didn't like this woman. She was the one who had chased him away with a broom when he had knocked on the door earlier. Before he was given any food the archdeacon insisted he clean himself up and before he knew it the maid had dragged him out of the kitchen door, stripped him and pushed him into a tin bath of tepid water in the back garden. To add to his indignity she had scrubbed the dirt and grime off him with a stiff brush. The clothes the archdeacon's wife brought from a trunk under the stairs were not ideal. The shirt was too small and the trousers too big and there were no shoes but he felt better now with some food in his belly and the soreness caused by the scrubbing on his back was gradually receding. He had told his story to Miss Sarah and the archdeacon and they were now in deep conversation in the hallway.

'I think we have no alternative sir,' said Sarah quietly. 'We have to tell Mrs. Dunkley of the latest developments. We owe it to her as well as to Grace.'

'If what you and Joseph say is true – and I don't disbelieve you for a moment – then we must take some action in the interests of justice.' The archdeacon rubbed his chin in contemplation. 'On the other hand I'm reluctant to risk distressing Mrs. Dunkley further by involving her at this stage.'

'But she *is* involved,' insisted Sarah. 'In fact she's more involved in this case than anyone. It's our duty to tell her.'

'Very well,' agreed the archdeacon with a sigh. 'You can tell her but please bear in mind her fragile state. Break it to her gently. In the meanwhile Joseph and I will go straight to the court.'

Sarah trotted up the stairs as the archdeacon called for Joseph. She knocked twice on the bedroom door without response and entered quietly. Against her expectations not only did she find Ada awake but also out of bed distractedly staring out of the window overlooking the back garden. She looked over at Sarah and offered a slight smile that served both as recognition and greeting. Ada Dunkley had been to the edge – her daughter murdered, her husband exiled and her son risking his life on campaign – but she had pulled back from the abyss. A mere matter of weeks earlier the Dunkleys were a united and happy family and now she was alone. The experience would have broken a less resilient woman, thought Sarah.

Ada's face still lacked her usual robust bloom and her pale, unmade face was lined with more than the privations of middle age but her subdued demeanour belied her renewed agility of mind. 'Good morning, Sarah,' she said in a voice sturdier than Sarah had anticipated.

Sarah returned her greeting. 'You're looking much better,' she said genuinely.

Ada smiled and looked out of the window again. 'There was a commotion over a tin bath a little while ago. It was rather amusing.' She looked back at Sarah. 'What is Joseph doing here?'

Sarah crossed the room towards her. 'That's what I've come to tell you.'

Conway's ordeal was not yet over but the worst was behind him. He was considerably more relaxed when Young recalled him to the stand and had determined not to be daunted by Toseland's bullying cross-examination. If he were to be hounded from his practice in Ladysmith he would not go without a fight.

'Dr. Conway,' said Young, 'you stated that both the victim and the accused had bloodstains on them. Can you elaborate on the nature and circumstances of these bloodstains?'

The doctor's timidity had vanished and been replaced by an unexpected resolve. His voice was clear and confident. 'The victim had minor bloodstains around her private parts as a result of the rape and around and inside her mouth where she had a cut consistent with a slight blow.'

'Were there any other bloodstains?'

'Yes. The right side of the victim's neck and face was smeared with blood and the accused had blood on his fingers.'

'This is confirmed in your report,' said Young, 'but how much blood was on the victim's fingers?'

'Only a small amount,' said Conway.

'As if he had simply touched the blood on the victim's neck rather than having been the cause of it,' suggested Young.

Toseland leapt to his feet. 'Begging the court's pardon, the prosecution must object to this line of questioning,' he interjected. 'The defence is leading the witness into speculation and unfounded opinion.'

This was an outrageous objection that would never have been admitted in a civilian court but Young was not surprised when the brigadier upheld it. He caught Branagan's signal before he could enter a futile counter objection and did not respond. This was a vital point for the defence but it would be made via the next witness.

With no further questions from either counsel the discredited but defiant Conway was finally extricated from his torment and replaced on the stand by Dr. Barlow. 'At the request of the defence,' said Young, 'Grace Dunkley's body was exhumed and both you and Dr. Conway undertook a detailed examination of it.'

Toseland again sprang out of his seat. 'With the court's permission I must object to the scandalous conduct of the defence,' he blustered. 'Neither the prosecution nor, I am sure, the military authorities were aware of this action. The prosecution insists that the defence must be held culpable for this illegal exhumation and that any testimony based upon it be withdrawn and disregarded.'

Young knew he had to act quickly before the panel could respond. 'If it please the court I would like to advise the prosecution that the exhumation of a civilian corpse is outside the military authorities' jurisdiction and is entirely a civilian matter.' He held up a piece of paper. 'The defence made the appropriate application to the local magistrate and permission was granted.' The process had nevertheless been somewhat irregular. It had been well into the evening when the application had been made and the magistrate had been unwilling to issue the required documentation at such a late hour until Branagan had pulled a few strings and called in a favour. The prosecution and the court might not like it but there was nothing they could do to block Barlow's testimony.

The red tabs muttered amongst themselves for what seemed to Young like an eternity before the brigadier announced with a marked degree of reluctance in his voice that he may proceed.

'To continue, Dr. Barlow, please tell the court of your findings,' said Young.

'Miss Dunkley's body bore the signs of a violent rape and a cut on the inside of her lip as indicated in Dr. Conway's report. However, there was no sign of any cut to account for the blood which Dr. Conway's report and the two witness statements said covered one side of her neck and part of her face.'

'Which means,' said Young addressing the panel, 'that the blood on her neck and face was not hers.' He turned back to Barlow. 'Is that not so?'

'That is correct,' confirmed Barlow.

'You also performed a thorough medical examination of the accused yesterday evening,' said Young. 'Could you please tell the court of your findings?' Toseland realised that he had lost his grip on what he was assured would be an open and shut case. A game of polo would not be the only thing he would forego as he saw the prospects of an early promotion rapidly evaporating in the bleak surroundings of an African schoolroom.

'The accused is in excellent physical shape, considering the privations of the siege, and bears no sign of any cuts or abrasions consistent with a loss of blood in the recent past,' said Barlow.

'So the blood on Grace Dunkley's neck and face was neither hers nor that of the accused?'

'Correct.'

'What about the bloodstains reported on his fingers at the time of his arrest?'

'Well, they certainly weren't his either,' confirmed Barlow.

'Which means,' said Young triumphantly, 'that if the blood on one side of the victim's neck and face was neither hers nor that of the accused, it follows that it came from someone else.' He paused momentarily and lowered his voice. 'The real murderer.' He turned to Barlow. 'Before I conclude, Dr. Barlow, I believe there is another significant fact you uncovered when you examined the victim's body.'

'Yes,' replied Barlow. 'Under her fingernails were small traces of blood and skin with a few strands of hair.'

Young produced a small tin that had once contained snuff. He removed the lid and extended the tin to Barlow who confirmed that the samples of hair laid on a piece of white cotton gauze inside were the same that he and Conway had recovered from beneath Grace Dunkley's fingernails. He then proffered it to the panel. 'As the court can see, the strands of hair are black. The accused's hair is fair.' The few seconds he gave them to examine the samples also served as a dramatic pause. 'I therefore conclude that not only is the accused clearly innocent of the crime but the real murderer is still at large somewhere in Ladysmith. Moreover, the real murderer has a wound or other blood injury, probably to the left hand or lower arm, has black hair and in all probability still bears scratches on his scalp.'

Charlie's heart was in his mouth. Since his earlier outburst he had sat silently throughout the proceedings, praying for an acquittal and, as Young's evidence had gradually unfolded, hardly daring to believe that it was a real possibility. He prayed again. Surely the court would not cheat him now. He desperately wanted to be free. He desperately wanted to see Sarah.

The red tabs spoke quietly among themselves for a couple of minutes after which the brigadier called both Young and Toseland in front of them. 'I'm calling a brief adjournment,' said the brigadier 'during which time we can discuss this case and its implications with both of you gentlemen. One way or another this is very likely to be a momentous day.' He cocked his head towards the distant rumble. 'It sounds as though General Buller is on his way.'

The Burgher force stretched all along the heights above Colenso, dominating the plain south of the Tugela. The British guns had bombarded them since before dawn but the arriving Burghers had already hacked protective entrenchments out of the scrub covered hillside the previous day. In the man-made cave behind the firing position two Burghers crouched over a small fire and the invigorating smell of the coffee they were preparing stimulated Piet's senses as he walked down the emplacement. The sandbagged line ran above head height, concealing from view the plain below, and a sandbagged frontage twelve feet thick offered protection from almost anything the British could throw at them. Only a direct hit from one of the big naval guns could possibly cause any serious damage or loss of life. It had been hard, backbreaking work to prepare these emplacements but it had been worth it. Piet couldn't imagine feeling any more secure in a fortified position.

He looked down at Christiaan, curled up asleep under the firestep with his head resting on a folded sack. He was inclined to let him sleep on a little longer but it would soon be time for action and the boy would once again be expected to forsake his adolescence and conduct himself like a man. Piet's initial apprehension and anxiety over his son's presence on commando had dissipated over recent weeks. Apart from the recent sharp fight on the Platrand there had been little action and none of them had been in any serious danger since they were caught in the bombardment of the Long Tom position. 'Christiaan.' He shook him gently. Christiaan stirred, rubbed the back of his hand vigorously across his nose and mouth and opened his eyes. In the manner of all Burghers in the field, ingrained since the earliest pioneer days and honed to perfection during their conflicts with the Zulus, he was instantly wide awake and alert.

He rolled out from beneath the firestep and grabbed his rifle. 'What is it, pa?' he said, preparing to mount the firestep to join his grandfather and the other Burghers. 'Are the British coming?'

Piet touched his arm. 'Take it easy. There's time for coffee and breakfast first.'

'That's right, boy,' said Koos from his position overlooking the plain below. 'General Buller wouldn't want to spoil our breakfast now, would he?' He gave one of his hearty laughs, sucked noisily on his pipe and spat over the emplacement.

'I want to go on the firestep with *oupa*,' said Christiaan enthusiastically. He grabbed the protruding corner of one of the sandbags and hauled himself up. Even on tiptoe he was unable to see over the parapet. Piet lifted an ammunition box on to the firestep.

'Stand on that,' he said and climbed up between them. Christiaan could now see the scene before them. The day had dawned brilliantly and the dust swirl in the distance announced the approach of the British field artillery's guns and horses under a cloudless sky.

'Like rats in a trap,' said Koos, shaking his head. 'When will they ever learn?'

Piet could see the folly of the British approach. 'They're going to make a frontal attack,' he said. 'Against these positions and with the river in between,' he added incredulously.

'That's not the best of it. Look over there,' said Koos pointing into the right distance and handing his field glasses to Piet. 'That must be a full brigade moving towards the river. They can't be that stupid so their maps and intelligence reports must be faulty.'

'How do you mean?' asked Piet.

'There's a loop in the river where they're heading. We can see it from here but at ground level with all the trees and bushes around the bank they can't.'

Through the field glasses Piet could clearly see the mass of infantry heading towards the salient created by the loop. Their concealed positions on the opposite bank gave the Burghers a field of fire covering three sides. 'They'll be cut to pieces.'

'Exactly,' said Koos. 'And for nothing. They're looking for a place to cross the river but the only drifts are either side of the loop.'

Piet sent Christiaan for coffee while he pulled three strips of *biltong* from his pouch. Koos rested his pipe on top of a sandbag and took one, tearing the tough dried meat between his teeth. A Burgher walked along the position below and behind them. 'No firing until the general order is given,' he shouted. 'Commandant-general's orders.'

Koos nodded appreciatively. 'He's a clever one this Louis Botha,' he said, his mouth still wrestling with the biltong. 'He's going to wait until they've crossed the river this side of Colenso village, catch them in an ambush and destroy them.' He took his coffee from Christiaan who was endeavouring to balance the three mugs without burning his hands or spilling any. 'We may get to the sea yet, boy,' said Koos cheerily. Piet both admired and envied the new commandant-general. He was around his own age and with his field tunic, slouch hat and bandolier he looked like a soldier. Not like the old guard whose dark suits, frock coats and top hats gave them the appearance of church elders. He had a sound grasp of tactics and didn't allow theological considerations to get in the way of military expediency. Most significantly in Piet's mind was the respect and admiration many of the battle hardened Burghers of his father's generation had for him. Koos slurped the hot coffee noisily, put the mug down next to his pipe and peered through the field glasses towards the loop. 'Our cousins over there won't need to wait for the commandant to tell them when to open fire,' he said. 'The British will do that for him.'

As Piet sipped gingerly from his steaming mug his attention was drawn to activity on the front facing their own position. 'What are they doing now?' he enquired of nobody in particular.

Koos swung his field glasses round to enhance the view that had attracted Piet's attention. 'I don't believe this', he said. 'I just don't believe this.' He handed the glasses to Piet. Two batteries of British field artillery had raced forward and unlimbered in an advanced and exposed position. 'They can't be more than a thousand yards away,' said Koos, his astonishment manifest in his voice. 'This is unheard of.' There was a buzz of anticipation along the parapet and the rest of the Burghers in their section rushed to see what the excitement was all about. Within seconds the firestep was crowded with Burghers pressing and craning to get a better view.

The British artillerymen stood at their positions by the guns as the drivers galloped to the rear with the horses and limbers. They were well within Mauser range and a few Burghers took aim. 'Not yet!' yelled Koos. The Burghers were taken aback by the intensity of this grizzled old man's cry and lowered their rifles but Koos realised his plea would be in vain. Those brave but foolhardy British gunners presented too tempting a target and had unwittingly compromised the new commandant's plan to draw the infantry across the river. They would soon open fire themselves and the Burghers would respond long before the infantry caught up.

A few shots from positions on their left were instantly followed by the crash of repeated volleys and echoed by concentrated rifle fire from their own commando. 'Damned impatient Krugersdorpers,' cursed Koos, but he knew that the first shots could have been fired by anyone and had very nearly come from their own emplacement. Now that the element of surprise had been lost he fired as vigorously as anyone, cartridge after cartridge, clip after clip.

Piet was astonished at the conduct of the artillerymen who stood their ground through a storm of Mauser bullets as if on parade. Here and there a man dropped but their comrades calmly continued to serve the guns. Not one broke and ran. He had heard of the steadfast and often reckless courage of the British gunners but never expected to see men face death and injury so prosaically. 'Is this how their gunners always behave?' he asked his father while loading another clip.

'An infantryman can always run away with his rifle,' replied Koos. 'A gunner cannot run away without his gun.' He paused between shots and turned to face Piet. 'In the British army to lose a gun is the ultimate disgrace.' Koos had always admired the cool discipline of the British artilleryman but even he had never seen such casual bravery. 'They've been sold down the river by their commanding officer,' he said. 'But they'll never hesitate to obey an order.' A shell from one of these guns exploded noisily but harmlessly above them, showering earth in front of the emplacement.

One by one the fire of the twelve guns slackened and ceased. As each ran out of ammunition the remaining men of its crew stood stiffly to attention and marched with a controlled and unhurried dignity to a dried river course half a mile behind the batteries. The Burghers' fire didn't slacken and more gunners fell before they reached the shelter of the *donga*. Koos had had enough. 'I shall no longer shoot at these brave men,' he said to Piet. 'They don't deserve to die.' Piet also stopped firing and put his hand on the barrel of Christiaan's rifle to indicate that he should do likewise. Christiaan looked up uncomprehendingly, first at Piet and then at Koos. 'Hate your enemy by all means, boy,' said Koos, 'but don't dishonour him.'

When the last of the surviving gunners dropped into the sanctuary of the *donga* the Burghers' fire quickly abated along the whole of their sector. They could still hear firing to their immediate right as other commandos maintained their barrage of lead into the ranks of the infantry battalions who had circumvented the artillery's route and advanced towards the river further along the line. Koos scanned the extreme right sector with his field glasses and shook his head in sad reflection at the sight of hundreds of infantrymen trying to retreat from the carnage of the loop.

'It looks like we're finished for the day,' said Piet, relieved that they had come through another battle although in truth he had never felt they were in any real danger. He patted Christiaan's back. 'Well done, son.'

Christiaan grinned at him. 'Well done to us all, pa.' The other Burghers were also busy congratulating each other and debating the relative merits of Mauser and field gun. Nods and murmurs of approval met comments on the astonishing discipline and courage of the *rooinek* gunners.

'We're not quite finished yet,' said Koos, peering through his field glasses in front of their position. Piet and Christiaan looked ahead and the Burghers who had dropped out of the firing line scrambled back on to the firestep. In a flurry of dust and hooves two teams of artillerymen, each with a driver astride the lead mount urging and cajoling his horses to drag the limbers, rode at breakneck pace towards the stranded guns accompanied by a handful of mounted men. The line once again burst into life as the entire commando poured its fire into the teams sent to rescue the guns.

Christiaan hesitated. 'I thought you said we shouldn't fire at them any more, *oupa*.'

Piet continued firing. Koos emptied a clip and then turned towards Christiaan. 'There's a world of difference between shooting unarmed men in the back and shooting men who are trying to retrieve guns to use against us in the future.' Christiaan nodded. *Oupa* knew everything about warfare and riding on commando and Christiaan wanted to become as brave and wise a warrior as him. As Christiaan squinted down the barrel of his rifle Koos looked proudly and lovingly at his grandson. 'Aim at the limber horses and the officers riding separately,' he said. 'The drivers can't retrieve the guns without the horses or be given any orders without the officers.'

Piet snapped another clip into his magazine and fired into the melee of horses, men and limbers charging at full gallop towards the abandoned guns, the wheels bouncing into the air as the limbers veered crazily from side to side or struck a mound or rock. He wished his father had taught and nurtured him when he was a boy like the old warrior had been doing with Christiaan ever since they had left home. He tried to reassure himself that he felt this way because fate had previously denied them the opportunity to go on commando together but failed to block out the persistent notion that his father felt closer to Christiaan than to him.

One officer crashed to the ground, his panic-stricken horse rearing by its fallen rider before galloping away from the torrent of bullets that zipped into the earth around it. Another's horse was shot from under him and, extricating himself from the stricken animal, he crawled over to his fallen comrade. The teams and the last mounted officer arrived at the guns and managed to hook the limbers into two of them. With rifle fire filling the air the drivers remounted their lead horses, wheeled and galloped back to safety with their prizes.

Many of the Burghers were still firing as the dismounted officer struggled back with the limp body of his comrade, assisted by another who had crawled out of the *donga* and into the maelstrom. Christiaan looked at Koos. 'We shouldn't shoot at them, should we, *oupa?*'

'No, boy,' he replied softly. 'At least not in my book. But there are always those who will.' He shook his head. 'Perhaps this is how warfare is to be conducted nowadays,' he sighed. 'Or perhaps I'm getting too old.'

'And too soft,' came the voice to his left. The Burgher ceased firing and turned to laugh at him. His mouth had barely formed into a smile as the butt of Koos's Mauser smashed into it spilling several teeth and launching the Burgher off the firestep on to the dirt floor of the emplacement. As his companion jumped down to assist the spluttering and groaning man into the cave the other Burghers nearby stopped shooting and looked over. They did not resume. Koos van Oppen was an old man but those who knew him and his reputation had no desire to tangle with him.

'This is a different matter, boy,' said Koos, packing his pipe and nodding ahead of them. 'These are fair game.' Three more teams had appeared, riding pell-mell towards the guns in the same fashion as the first two. This time the Burghers were prepared. They knew that the British had to attempt the recovery of more than a mere two guns out of the twelve they had abandoned on the veld. Koos calmly lit his pipe, took a couple of puffs as he looked down the sight of his Mauser and resumed firing, the rest of the line following his lead.

By now the other Burghers had realised what Koos had already understood and fired into the horse teams, hitting more than half of them and rendering the limbers useless. The teams ground to a halt well short of the guns and the men retired to the *donga*. 'The guns will be ours,' said Koos, sucking on his pipe with an air of satisfaction. 'We shall use them to give the British a taste of their own medicine.'

Piet continued to observe events along the front through the field glasses while Koos finished his pipe and savoured the aroma of a mug of freshly brewed coffee before noisily sipping the thick, dark liquid. 'They're going,' said Piet excitedly. 'All across the front.' The surviving gunners and drivers were pulling back from the *donga* and the infantry were withdrawing from the riverfront area on their right, joining the shattered remnants of their comrades who were already in full retreat from the loop.

Koos nodded in a gesture of satisfaction and took another slurp of his coffee. 'The good people of Ladysmith had better prepare for Christmas under siege,' he said with a hearty laugh.

Charlie had become nervous again. Why had Young and Toseland left with the red tabs when the brigadier had announced the adjournment? Nobody had told him anything. Was no news good news? He had thought earlier that if he was to be condemned for a crime he didn't commit he wanted to be spared the agony of waiting and be given the verdict now. But Young's line of questioning and fresh evidence had put a whole new slant on the case and given him renewed hope. Please God let there be good news. Let justice be done.

While the brigadier was reconvening the trial Young opened one of two notes that the archdeacon had thrust into his hand as he made his way back into the courtroom with Toseland and the three members of the panel. He scanned it quickly but its contents made him re-read it carefully. This was exactly what he needed to supplement the evidence he had already accumulated. The second note was from Sarah. Ada could add no further names of any men whom Grace would have admitted into the house but her husband's employee had been on picket duty with a detachment of the town guard all afternoon and evening on the day of the murder. That left only Turnbull.

'Would you care to proceed, Captain Young,' said the brigadier in an altogether more cordial tone than he had managed in the first session.

'I call Captain Turnbull to the stand,' said Young.

Turnbull had expected to be inconvenienced by having to stay in the building rather than by being recalled as a witness. He was starting to feel uncomfortable but knew that he must remain cool and unperturbed. They hadn't got anything on him so why give them any reason to cast suspicion on him?

Young approached him closely. Too closely for his own comfort. Young peered at the top of his head. 'Is that a swelling on your head, Captain Turnbull?'

Turnbull was thrown by this totally unexpected question. His hand automatically shot to the bump on his head. Keep calm, he said to himself. This proves nothing. 'Yes,' he replied, affecting puzzlement. 'I banged my head on a beam in my shelter at the riverbank.' The palms of his hands were damp and he subconsciously wiped them on his trousers.

Young was quietly elated that Turnbull had conveniently confessed to having the bump that he suspected must be there but couldn't actually see. He was even more pleased that Turnbull had inadvertently opened up a new avenue for him. 'Have you hurt your hand Captain Turnbull?' he asked with affected concern.

Turnbull cursed himself. He had managed to keep his dressing hidden or at least inconspicuous until he had inadvertently used his injured left hand when instinctively touching the bump on his head. 'It's a wound I picked up at Elandslaagte,' he replied. 'It's nothing serious. Just a scratch really.'

'Elandslaagte?' queried Young who was starting to get into his stride. 'It's taking along time to heal for just a scratch. Elandslaagte was eight weeks ago.'

Turnbull was about to say that the dressing was just a precaution when Young stunned him by calling for Dr. Barlow to examine his hand. He looked at Toseland, anticipating an objection but none came. Toseland knew the original case was lost and that his only practical option was to co-operate with the defence to find the real murderer. That way he stood a chance of redeeming himself with the military authorities and resurrecting the possibility of a promotion. Turnbull turned towards the panel but instead of displaying hostility the brigadier readily agreed to Young's request.

'The original wound has healed,' said Barlow examining Turnbull's left hand. However, there is a more recent injury.' Turnbull's knuckle was bruised and swollen and scabs had formed over the serrated cuts where Grace Dunkley's teeth had sunk to the bone. 'An injury consistent with a bite.'

Turnbull's resolve broke. 'This is outrageous!' he exclaimed. 'Why am I being interrogated like this? I'm not on trial here.'

Young thought otherwise. During the recess Toseland had conceded defeat and the brigadier had assured him of the panel's indulgence while he attempted to construct a solid case around the still circumstantial evidence that pointed to Turnbull's guilt. 'How did you come by this injury?' he asked.

Turnbull had difficulty marshalling his thoughts. In his flustered state he could think of only one answer. 'I was bitten by...'

'A dog?' Young had anticipated Turnbull's feeble response. 'Well, Captain Turnbull?'

He had to brazen it out. He could think of no other answer. Anyway he still had his alibi. 'As a matter of fact, yes,' he replied with as much confidence as he could muster. 'It was a dog.'

'Dr. Barlow?' said Young, appealing for a professional opinion.

'The bite size and configuration do not match that of any type of dog known to me,' said Barlow. 'They are, however, consistent with a human bite.'

Young gave Barlow the snuff tin containing the hair samples and asked him if they matched Turnbull's hair. To Turnbull's immense relief Barlow could not positively match them. 'It's possible but I cannot say for certain.' That was as far as his professional integrity would allow him to speculate.

Damn, thought Young. Even with the bump on Turnbull's head this vital link was still nothing more than circumstantial evidence. He thanked Dr. Barlow and Toseland declined the opportunity to cross-examine the witness. It was time to act on the contents of the archdeacon's note.

'I call Joseph Ncube to the stand,' said Young. No one had anticipated this development. Charlie's and Branagan's expressions evoked as much surprise as those of Toseland and the panel while Turnbull's initial confusion turned to astonishment as Joseph entered the courtroom.

Young could see that Joseph was extremely nervous. The only time a native was likely to be paraded officially in front of so many white men was if he was in serious trouble. Young reassured him that he had only been called to tell the court what he knew which may help to clarify the particular matter under consideration and that he had nothing to fear.

Joseph was not entirely convinced and felt overawed by the presence of so many important people. The only ones he recognised were the hated Turnbull and the soldier Miss Sarah liked. He knew little of the white man's ways but could see that the shackled soldier was in trouble and that Turnbull's presence could only mean more problems for him. Miss Sarah and the archdeacon had insisted that he must appear in this white man's court and promised him that everything would be all right. He trusted Miss Sarah and when the soldier gave him a slight nod that he took to convey encouragement as well as recognition he was heartened.

Young began gently, trying to put him at ease. 'Joseph, please tell the court what happened on Monday last when you returned to Ladysmith.'

'*Returned* to Ladysmith?' queried one of the colonels whose appreciation of siege life was confined to the activities of military personnel.

'Yes, sir,' said Young patiently. 'The witness is a mail runner. And a very good one I'm told.' The colonel mumbled a gruff acknowledgement.

'Well sir, I was late returning,' began Joseph in an almost inaudible whisper with his head bowed. The brigadier interrupted him with a request to face the court and speak more loudly and distinctly. His voice was not harsh or intimidating. It conveyed patience and tolerance. Calling a native to give evidence at a court martial may have been highly irregular but he was intrigued and keen to hear what this young mail runner had to tell the court.

Charlie had no idea what evidence Joseph had to offer but knew his unexpected presence could only be good news for him. He caught Joseph's eye and gave him another nod of encouragement.

Joseph straightened himself up and continued more confidently. He told the court of the narrow escape he had had during his return on Monday and the deaths of the other two young mail runners at the hands of the Boers. He had returned earlier than anticipated and it was still light when he arrived at the Dunkley residence. There had been no one at home so he had rested in the orchard. 'I was very tired and fell asleep. I woke up when I heard voices on the balcony.'

'Whose voices?' said Young.

'Miss Grace.' He hesitated.

'Yes, Joseph,' said Young encouragingly. 'Miss Dunkley and who else?'

Looking straight into his eyes Joseph pointed at Turnbull. 'Him.'

Fuelled both by necessity and the confidence of an intact alibi Turnbull immediately retaliated. 'Sir, this is scandalous!' he objected. 'How can the court accept the slanderous evidence of a kaffir against an officer of the crown? He's an insolent kaffir who has no respect for authority and doesn't know his place. I had cause to chastise him a few weeks ago and he's simply looking for revenge.'

The brigadier was unmoved. 'If you have quite finished, Captain Turnbull,' he said sternly.

'I am not on trial here. I must protest.'

'You have already registered your protest which has been noted by the court,' said the brigadier. 'The witness will continue and if you interrupt again I shall have you gagged. I am sure you will agree that would be extremely undignified for an officer of the crown.'

Joseph continued, encouraged by the discomfort he saw he was causing to Turnbull. He had waited for only a short while after Miss Grace and Turnbull entered the house. 'Mrs. Dunkley had still not returned and I didn't want to give the letter to Miss Grace while that man,' he said, pointing at Turnbull, 'was there.'

'Why not?' asked Young.

'Because the last time I saw him he did this.' Joseph turned his cheek towards Young. The scar caused by the slash of Turnbull's riding crop was still visible. Joseph told how he had stuck the reed containing the letter in a flowerbed after having decided to return the next day to hand it personally to Mrs. Dunkley. However, increased Boer activity and vigilance had unexpectedly prevented his return from that night's mail run until only a matter of hours ago.

'We have already established that Miss Dunkley was murdered before nightfall,' continued Young. Turnbull felt a chill run through his body. He had not been aware that the time of death had been established in court. 'So Captain Turnbull's arrival at the house with Miss Dunkley was closer to the time of the murder than the apprehension and arrest of the accused.' Young turned to Turnbull. 'Captain Turnbull, why didn't you say that you had returned to the house with Miss Dunkley just prior to her murder?'

Turnbull was not about to admit to anything. 'That's simple,' he replied calmly. 'The kaffir is lying. I was not at the Dunkley house at all that day. In fact at the time this kaffir says I was at the house I was in fact attending a celebration party at the Royal Hotel.'

Branagan jerked upright, studied Turnbull for a few seconds and began to write a note. 'I suppose you have witnesses who can corroborate your story?' continued Young.

Turnbull had been waiting for this moment. 'Of course,' he replied smugly. 'Several, in fact.'

Young was deflated. The time had come for Branagan to intervene and he attracted Young's attention. 'With the court's permission,' began Young but before he could finish the brigadier waved his hand in affirmation to continue. Branagan spoke quickly and quietly to

Young who nodded vigorously and returned to the fray. 'Captain Turnbull, whose party was it and what was the celebration?'

'Actually there were two separate parties, one to celebrate Major Meadows's promotion and the other to wet Lieutenant Hammond's baby's head.'

'And you attended both?'

'Yes,' said Turnbull. 'As I know both men I could hardly refuse either so I attended both parties.'

'How long were you at the Royal?'

Turnbull was ready for this. 'I arrived just before five-thirty and left at seven-thirty.'

Young turned to the panel. 'With the court's permission I would like my colleague, Captain Branagan of the Natal Police, to question this witness.'

One of the colonels whispered to the brigadier. 'I know it's irregular,' whispered the brigadier in reply, 'but we've already broken nearly every convention in the book. I want to conclude this trial with a conviction and the defence's evidence seems to offer the only possibility of doing so.' He nodded to Young. 'Very well, carry on.'

Branagan rose and approached Turnbull. 'How long have you known Lieutenant Hammond?'

Turnbull was immediately on his guard. Why was Branagan asking the questions now and why had he asked that particular question? 'Not that long,' he replied vaguely.

'But long enough for you to be invited to attend his party?'

'I wasn't exactly invited. I'd heard that there was a celebration and I went along.'

Branagan was playing with Turnbull in the way a prize fighter might spar with an opponent before landing a big punch. 'In which unit does Lieutenant Hammond serve?'

Turnbull was as stunned by the unexpected nature of the question as he was incapable of answering it. He had never met Hammond before his brief introduction that night. Nobody had mentioned his unit and he hadn't noticed the insignia on his tunic. He didn't know.

Young picked up on his hesitation. 'It seems strange that you don't know the unit of an officer with whom you are sufficiently acquainted to attend his celebration party,' said Branagan. 'There aren't that many different colonial units in Ladysmith.'

Turnbull tried to think. He definitely wasn't Light Horse but he could be in the Carbineers or one of the two regiments of Mounted Rifles. 'I must admit I tend not to differentiate between the colonial units,' said Turnbull with as much bravado as he could muster. 'I class us all simply as volunteers. Hammond is a volunteer like many others in Ladysmith, myself included, doing our duty for queen and empire.' It was a weak answer but it was the safest he could think of. He couldn't risk guessing incorrectly.

'An interesting stance,' said Branagan. 'However, Lieutenant Hammond isn't a volunteer. He's a full time officer of the Natal Police.' Turnbull felt the colour drain from his face. 'In fact,' continued Branagan, 'he's my second in command here in Ladysmith.' Turnbull's eyelids dropped involuntarily. Branagan paused before continuing. 'Moreover, I was also at Hammond's party but I refrained from drinking any alcohol because we are the only officers in the unit and I have instituted a rule that at least one of us must abstain on any given day.' He paced up and down the courtroom, partly to marshal his thoughts but mainly for effect. He could see that Turnbull had become uncomfortable and he wanted to unnerve him further. 'I know you were there, Captain Turnbull, because I was there too. Actually, I recall that when you entered the bar you took my seat.' He paused again to look directly into Turnbull's eyes. 'I also recall that you did not arrive until the party was in full swing and that you left before the end, enabling me to retrieve my chair. You were there barely a quarter of an hour.'

'That's because I was at Major Meadows's party beforehand.' Turnbull was playing his last card. He prayed it would be a trump.

'Then, according to your statement, you must have spent from five-thirty to seven fifteen at Meadows's party.'

'Yes.' He could not answer otherwise.

'I take it, therefore,' Branagan continued, 'that you know Meadows better than you know Hammond.'

'I know Captain Pardoe better. I was with him. He's a colleague of Meadows in the Lancers.' Turnbull felt droplets of perspiration form on his forehead and at the back of his neck. His alibi was falling apart but he had to concentrate. The court was clearly unsympathetic and one wrong answer could hang him.

Branagan hadn't expected this response. Don't jump in yet, he thought. Keep to the original line of questioning. 'You will no doubt be able to tell the court what gift Major Meadows received from his colleagues when his presentation took place at six-thirty.'

Turnbull was at a loss for words. 'I don't recall exactly what the gift was,' was all that he could manage.

'But you were there for the presentation?' queried Branagan.

'Yes. Of course.'

'Do you recall the content of his speech?'

Even as Turnbull felt himself being sucked inexorably into an increasingly nightmarish situation he could not help being aware of the irony of it all. This was Browell's court martial yet he was now the prime suspect and struggling to fend off suspicion and accusation. This was more than highly irregular, it was unheard of, but this was a military court convened at a time of war in a town besieged by the enemy. There was no place for the legal niceties of a civilian court. He had originally offered Toseland his assistance with the sole intention of expediting a guilty verdict and Browell's execution. Case closed. But the case was far from closed and his vague and evasive answers to simple questions would serve only to strengthen the court's suspicion of his own guilt.

'Not exactly,' said Turnbull in a subdued voice, his cocksure arrogance now displaced by doubt and fear.

'Not exactly? How do you mean 'not exactly'?'

'I don't recall his exact words, only that he thanked his colleagues for the gift.' answered Turnbull. 'We'd all had a lot to drink,' he added lamely.

'So much to drink that you suffered hallucinations?' said Branagan enigmatically. Turnbull threw him a perplexed look. Branagan approached so closely that Turnbull could feel his breath, like the breath of a predator that had pinned down its prey and was going for the kill. 'There was no presentation, Captain Turnbull. Nor was there any speech.' Branagan started to walk away in triumph but turned abruptly as though suddenly remembering something. 'And by the way, your acquaintance Pardoe may be in the Lancers but Meadows is in the Hussars.'

As Turnbull stared at him dumbly Young took up the cudgel. 'With the court's permission the defence would like to sum up. The innocence of the accused has already been established. On the other hand, Captain Turnbull was seen accompanying Miss Dunkley into her home within the period of her time of death, has concealed a wound to his hand consistent with a human bite, has a lump on his head caused by an abrasion, hair not dissimilar to the samples found under the victim's fingernails and an alibi that has been totally discredited.' He faced the panel and pointed to Turnbull. 'I therefore accuse Captain Turnbull of the rape and murder of Grace Dunkley.'

A whole range of emotions ran through the courtroom. A pat on the back from one of his guards and a wink from the other were the catalyst that triggered the euphoric relief that swept through Charlie's body in the certain knowledge that he would be freed. Young felt the adrenaline rush at having successfully acquitted one of his own men, righted a wrong and effectively convicted the real murderer. His standing in the battalion would be elevated and he would be a hero to the men of his own company. Branagan was quietly satisfied with his detective work and contemplating the possibility of it helping to resurrect a career thwarted by a jealous and reactionary superior. The brigadier was content that he could report to the General Officer Commanding that the court would still obtain an imminent conviction to placate and reassure the civilian population. Toseland reflected that the outcome had partially saved his face and was mentally preparing for an immediate, and surely brief, official prosecution of Turnbull.

Turnbull was trapped both literally and figuratively. His all-consuming desire for sexual gratification had generated an animalistic instinct for survival that had impelled him to kill the girl. Once his bodily urges had quelled and his unruffled mind had taken over he had covered his tracks with care and cunning. Fortune had even provided another to take the blame. This couldn't be happening. His eyes flitted around the courtroom trying to comprehend this kaleidoscopic blur, rendered eerily remote as the volume of the accompanying sounds ebbed and flowed meaninglessly in his ears. He felt strangely light-headed. Browell was smiling with his guards, Young and Branagan were congratulating each other and Toseland had a smirk on his face as he slipped the papers back into his file. The brigadier was banging his silent gavel while barking soundless orders to the two guards who were approaching him with stern determination on their faces. Closer, closer.

'No!' Turnbull's cry pierced the air, refocusing his sight and equalising his hearing. As the first guard reached him Turnbull lunged forward, yanked the rifle from his loose one-handed grip and kicked him agonisingly in the groin. As he crashed gasping to the floor Turnbull swiftly swung the rifle two-handed and smashed the butt into the jaw of the startled second guard who spun sideways and collapsed motionless on the floor. Turnbull looked wildly around the courtroom and backed against the side wall. No one else was armed. He had got their attention.

The options open to him raced through his mind. He could shoot any of them. The incompetent Toseland, the smug Young, the devious Branagan, the treacherous brigadier and his colonels. Even the ill-bred Browell, whose execution was meant to be his own salvation. As he jerked the bolt of the rifle up and back, slipping a cartridge into the chamber, the door flew open. The commotion had attracted the attention of those in the waiting area and beyond. Four more armed guards rushed in and Turnbull knew his moment had arrived. In the few seconds it took for the newcomers to assess the situation and raise their weapons he swivelled the rifle and closed his lips over the barrel. The shocked and startled looks on the faces of his audience gave him a perverse sense of satisfaction as he hooked his thumb over the trigger. His ephemeral moment passed as the back of his head exploded, a crimson stain tracing his descent as he slid slowly down the wall and crumpled lifeless to the floor.

Ladysmith
January 1900

'Of course it's the twentieth century,' insisted Frank, sitting on a boulder in their bivouac on Caesar's Camp. 'The eighteen hundreds were the nineteenth century so the nineteen hundreds are the twentieth century. It stands to reason.' The debate had started before Christmas and the New Year and had continued beyond it, creating a trivial and harmless diversion for soldier and civilian alike.

'I'm sorry but you're wrong,' said Charlie. 'The twentieth century doesn't start until next year.'

Frank gave an exasperated sigh and shook his head. 'I suppose you'll be telling us next that the world's flat.'

'Look,' said Charlie, with the same, apparently unlimited, patience he had afforded Frank when he had started teaching him to read and write. 'A century is a hundred, right?' Frank raised his eyes and tutted. 'The first century started with the year one and ended with the year one hundred. Agreed?' Frank grunted his affirmation. 'The second century started with the year one hundred and one and ended with the year two hundred and so on. The nineteenth century started with the year eighteen hundred and one and ends with the year nineteen hundred. The twentieth century starts next year.'

Frank stood up and absently scanned the horizon. It had shimmered in a heat haze for most of the day but curtains of rain now trailed from a cluster of black nimbus cloud in the distance. 'What do you think, Walter?'

Walter was sitting cross-legged in front of a small fire in the shade of a canvas canopy stretched from a thorn tree waiting for the kettle to boil. He looked like one of the mysterious Himalayan gurus McAdams had described from his service in India. He drew deeply on a tiny fragment of cigarette impaled on a pin and exhaled tendrils of grey smoke from his mouth and nostrils. 'I don't give a fuck,' he said in his typically matter-of-fact way. He took one last drag from his stub and crushed it into the earth. 'It doesn't matter a damn what day it is, never mind what century it is. We're here today, we were here yesterday and we'll be here tomorrow. God knows how long we'll be here but that's the only thing that matters to me right now.'

McAdams offered no opinion and none was sought. He always gave the impression of being a man with no views on any subject. He had attached himself even more closely to Charlie since the court martial and had begun to include Frank and Walter in his conversations with him. McAdams remained a man of few words but occasionally felt relaxed enough in their company to reminisce about past times with the battalion. He still never mentioned anything about his life before joining up and none of them asked.

'It still seems strange, though,' said Frank, steering the discussion in a different direction. 'I mean, being in nineteen hundred and using it with the date. It's like entering a whole new era except nothing's changed.'

'Of course nothing's changed,' said Walter. 'Like I said, we're still here in this stinking hole.' He rummaged in his satchel and produced a fist-sized piece of goat's cheese wrapped in muslin. He flicked away the flies whose unwelcome attention had been instantly attracted, cut four slices off with his bayonet and handed them round. Raids on civilian orchards and hen houses had abated in the wake of the Dunkley business but Walter had organised some form of barter system that extended well beyond the battalion's lines and was still able to furnish a few luxuries.

Frank blew a speck of dirt off his piece and picked off a spot of mould before biting into it. 'The whole of the century is before us,' he said, smacking his lips as he chewed on the cheese. 'Not just nineteen hundred but nineteen twenty, nineteen fifty, nineteen eighty. Right up to nineteen ninety-nine.'

'What's after that?' said Walter.

'Well, twenty hundred I suppose,' said Frank uncertainly. 'I wonder what life will be like in twenty hundred?' he mused.

'We won't be around so I wouldn't waste your time worrying about it,' said Walter.

'What do you think, Charlie?' asked Frank in the hope of eliciting a more constructive comment.

'Communications,' said Charlie. 'There'll be a world wide communications structure and a faster and more efficient transport system.' He reeled off the inventions of recent years. 'The telephone will be used daily by everybody, even over long distances. The motor car, like the one we saw in Durban, will be improved and efficient production will enable everybody to have one.'

'Where will they put them all?' asked Frank doubtfully.

'Existing roads will be improved and new ones built to take them.'

'What happens when the roads and the towns are full of motor cars?' asked Walter. 'Put wings on them so they can fly people where they want to go?' Walter and Frank burst out laughing and even McAdams managed a smirk.

'Don't laugh,' said Charlie. 'Travel by air is not impossible.'

'What?' said Walter incredulously. 'You mean flying machines?'

'You ought to read some of Mr. Wells's recent works. He certainly thinks so,' said Charlie.

'I suppose these flying machines will take people there,' he said, pointing to the three quarter moon that had risen in the blue afternoon sky.

'Why not?' said Charlie. 'A hundred years is a long time.' The other three roared with laughter. Charlie hadn't even got round to suggesting advances in medicine and the eradication of disease but his dismay at being mildly ridiculed by his friends was exceeded by his astonishment at seeing McAdams's open display of mirth. Apart from the time he broke the news of Reid's death he had never seen him show any emotion.

'You're fucking mad,' said Walter between snorts of laughter. 'Those stripes must have gone to your head.' His promotion to full corporal had been an unexpected Christmas present and Charlie felt that it had been a gesture intended to compensate him in some minor way for his wrongful arrest and court martial. Captain Young had more or less indicated as much but Charlie had accepted the promotion in good grace in recognition of Young's contribution to his acquittal.

The laughter eventually subsided and Walter passed round the mugs of tea. Rationing had diminished the strength and sweetness of the brews as it had also reduced their intake of food. Fresh meat and vegetables had become scarce and whatever luxuries reached the ordinary soldier were generally procured by men like Walter. Bully beef and army biscuits had become the standard fare and their uniforms had begun to hang more loosely on them. 'Mind you,' continued Frank, still intrigued by what the new century might hold, 'in nineteen fifty I'll still only be seventy-three. The world will be a much different place even then.'

'The chances are you'll still be on picket duty up here,' said Walter. He took a mouthful of the weak and lightly sugared tea. 'This is piss,' he grimaced. 'I'll have to see about getting some decent stuff. There's a quartermaster sergeant of the Rifles I know who usually has a good supply. Maybe he's partial to a bit of goat's cheese.'

'You'll have to leave it until tomorrow, though,' said Charlie. They would be spending the night in the forward sangars, the least popular time and place for picket duty. 'Let's get ready. We have to relieve 'B' company in an hour.'

Koos slapped Piet and Christiaan on the back. He had just returned from the commandant's quarters and was in jovial mood. 'At last,' he said, placing his lantern on the floor. 'At last we have some decisive action from our leaders.' He squatted by the fire opposite Piet and Christiaan whose faces were illuminated in its golden glow. Sparks erupted, danced in the air and died as Piet threw another branch into the crackling flames.

'What's the news?' asked Piet.

'Two things,' he said in an almost conspiratorial whisper. 'First, we go tonight. A full scale attack on the Platrand. The Free Staters will assault the western end of the Platrand, the part the r*ooinekke* call Wagon Hill, while we Transvaalers go for the eastern end that they call Caesar's Camp. There will be diversionary attacks on other parts of the defensive line by the Pretoria commando and some other Burghers.'

Piet had heard persistent rumours of a major attack on the Platrand since Christmas but nothing had materialised. He remembered well his father's fury at the futility of the earlier half-hearted and uncoordinated attack in which they had participated. Now it seemed there was a plan that met with Koos's approval.

'What's the second thing, *oupa*?' Christiaan was eager to hear more of this exciting news.

'Well, boy,' beamed Koos, 'the commandant has appointed your *oupa* as a field cornet.'

Christiaan jumped up and ran over to hug his grandfather. 'That's wonderful news, *oupa*!' he cried. 'Just in time for the new battle.'

Piet also congratulated his father. 'That's one in the eye for the young bucks,' he said. Field cornets were usually appointed from the ranks of ambitious and resolute Burghers in their thirties. It was an unorthodox promotion but nonetheless fully deserved. Military discipline ran contrary to the Burghers' ethos of personal freedom and it was quite common for them to ignore orders or take a unilateral decision to go on home leave. The position of field cornet required a man with a rare combination of determination and charisma and Koos certainly had those qualities in abundance. He was widely respected for his military experience, tactical astuteness and personal courage. It would be a popular appointment throughout the commando – with the possible exception of the Burgher who left half of his teeth on the floor of the emplacement above Colenso. Piet was happy for his father but at the same time only too aware that his own name had not even been considered. He thrust a stick into the rabbit that Christiaan had trapped, skinned and gutted and balanced the skewer over the fire in the 'Y' of two other branches stuck into the ground. The flames immediately began to sear the flesh and quickly filled their nostrils with the mouthwatering aroma of the *braaivleis*.

'Ah!' exclaimed Koos enthusiastically. 'Just in time for supper. I'm starving.'

A moth danced around the lantern hooked on the central pole of the tent as Sarah reached the last bed in the line. 'Hello, Sarah,' said Tom cheerily.

She returned his greeting and propped him up against his pillows. 'Here's your beef tea.' The convalescent patients' rations were pitifully meagre but the needs of the fever patients were greater. The problem was the growing number of fever patients. Tom was one of only two wounded men left in the tent and the other was due to be discharged within a matter of days.

'Ah, just what I've been waiting for,' said Tom as he brought the cup to his lips. Despite his lighthearted tone she knew he meant it. Each day must be an endless drudge for him, she thought. A man with a shattered body but an intact mind stuck inside a fly ridden canvas oven surrounded by fevered and delirious patients. She wished she could spend more time with him but the workload resulting from the increasing number of admissions and staff sickness made it impossible. She was now responsible for two tents and one of the other nurses had gone down with fever. She was sure he understood.

The beef tea was only lukewarm but he still sipped sparingly to make it last, savouring each swallow. 'I hear a rumour that they're running out of beef extract and that cavalry horses are going to be slaughtered to make an alternative supply.'

Sarah had heard the same story. 'Well, I can assure you what you are drinking is made from beef extract,' said Sarah 'but if that changes you'll be the first to know.' She knew there was really nothing more they could do for Tom here. He needed specialist care and rehabilitation, perhaps in Maritzburg at first but eventually back home in Scotland, but this would be denied him until after the siege. She wondered what the future held in store for her poor broken Highlander.

She looked over to the other row of beds where Ada Dunkley was cradling the head of a young Carbineer and feeding him milk from a spouted cup. They had started at the top of their respective rows at the same time but by now Ada was three patients behind Sarah. It would have been easy to attribute this to inexperience but ever since Ada had started at Intombi Sarah had noticed that she devoted the same particular tender care to each patient. She had a son of her own in the Carbineers and she treated each young man with the same care as if he were her own.

Ada had been unable to bear the thought of living alone in the house and understandably had no enthusiasm to celebrate Christmas. She had offered her services at Intombi immediately after the court martial and Dr. Barlow had accepted not only out of compassion but also because he desperately needed as much help as he could get. Sarah couldn't help contemplating the irony of Ada's situation. She had consistently and steadfastly refused to evacuate her home since the beginning of the siege but ultimately it was the actions of an officer of the British crown that had done what the Boers had failed to do and driven her out. She pitied this tragic woman and it was for people like Ada and Tom that she prayed for the early relief of the town. She also prayed for the safe deliverance of Ada's husband and son. Ada was stronger than most but another loss would break her.

Sarah went over to Ada. 'This one's on the mend,' she said quietly.

Ada looked up excitedly. 'Do you really think so?' she whispered. She stroked the Carbineer's head.

Sarah knew that Ada treated each patient very much as an individual and liked to give her good news whenever she could. All of the patients in this row were suffering from enteric and Sarah hadn't told her that two of them were unlikely to last more than another night or two. Because of the sheer influx of fever patients and the mounting death rate many of the hospital staff now spoke in terms of numbers of fatalities rather than individual names but Ada took every loss to heart. On the other hand she treated each discharge to convalescence as a personal triumph. Sarah reflected that she was not too dissimilar to Ada herself except that her personal involvement was restricted to Tom rather than dispensed to every patient admitted. Tom was her prop, a kind of talisman, who provided the stability and continuity she needed to cope with the ever changing, ever worsening situation at the hospital camp.

'I'll help you finish off the row,' said Sarah. Ada opened her mouth to insist that she could manage but stopped herself. It wasn't pride or stubbornness that motivated her to complete the round unassisted but a desire to give each of these men a mother's care. The care she hoped Ralph would receive if, God forbid, he ever had cause to be admitted to a field hospital. She conceded to herself that the welfare of the patients would be best served by hastening their supper. She nodded and continued to dribble milk into the Carbineer's mouth.

The sun had disappeared over the western horizon and the last embers of daylight glowed briefly in the camp. Nightfall would give blessed relief from the flies and heat but would also bring death. Despite the easier conditions more fever patients died during the night and not a morning went by without the team of native and Indian gravediggers preparing for more burials at the little cemetery mushrooming beneath a stand of blue gum trees beyond the hospital lines. Sarah and the other nurses had become accustomed to this daily routine, even when it involved one of their own patients, but Ada wept each time. Sarah hoped she wasn't becoming hardened to the deaths of these young men. No, she reassured herself, it was just that she could no longer do anything for the dead. She just had to concentrate her mind and energy on caring for those left behind. She recalled the previous day when she had put a comforting arm around Ada's shoulder as one of these sad processions passed her tent on its way to the cemetery. 'I understand,' she had said sympathetically in the belief that the memory of Grace's funeral and reburial was still too recent and too distressing for her.

Ada had dabbed away the tears with her handkerchief. 'No you don't,' she had replied. 'This isn't about Grace. These are all young men who are dying here. It's Ralph I'm crying for. Each one of these boys could be Ralph.' Sarah realised what she meant. It was the agony of not knowing. Grace was dead and despite the pain she was coming to terms with that but at any given moment she didn't know whether or not Ralph was alive. He could be riding jauntily on patrol with his comrades or just as easily be lying dead on the veld or in a field hospital, wounded or fevered. She just didn't know.

A rustle at the tent flap preceded a cheery wave and a broad grin. Joseph had become something of a celebrity in Ladysmith since the court martial, not only as a result of his evidence against Turnbull but also because his prowess and courage as a mail runner had reached a wider audience. '*Sanibona*,' he called to Sarah and Ada and offered an envelope to Sarah.

They returned his greeting and Sarah thanked him for the letter. It was from Charles. She resisted the gnawing urge to tear the envelope open and instead folded it into her pocket. She would read it later when she had a few moments alone. 'How are things on Caesar's Camp?' she said as she mashed an army biscuit with milk for the next patient.

'Very good, Miss Sarah.' If Joseph was feted in Ladysmith he had become a hero in the battalion lines and warmly welcomed whenever he delivered one of Sarah's letters. 'Corporal Browell and his friends are on picket duty tonight.'

'What have you got in your hand?' asked Ada, straining to see.

He held up a sackcloth bag with what looked like a rock inside. 'It's a present for both of you,' he said, handing it to Ada. She peered inside and caught the pungent aroma.

'This is very welcome,' she enthused. Look,' she said, turning to Sarah. 'This will be a nice treat for some of the convalescents as well.'

Sarah also peered into the bag and thanked him for his kindness. '*Ngiyabonga*, Joseph.'

Joseph was happy that they liked his gift and beamed in delight. He asked for nothing to carry the letters between Miss Sarah and Corporal Browell but the soldiers always gave him something for his trouble. They had little money but he had never left Caesar's Camp empty handed since the court martial. It was usually food provided by Corporal Browell's friend who made the tea and swore a lot. This time the soldier had produced a huge piece of goat's cheese and given him most of it. He had eaten a small piece on his way back to Intombi but was honoured to give the rest of it to Mrs. Dunkley and Miss Sarah.

Their faces were concealed by the darkness as Koos addressed the men under his command on the scrub-covered hillside beyond their bivouac area. 'After the signal to move out we must maintain absolute silence all the way across the plain. When we reach the foot of the Platrand remove your boots and climb barefoot.' He noticed the glow of a pipe. 'And no smoking.' The smoker removed the pipe from his mouth, tapped it against the heel of his boot and ground the smouldering tobacco into the earth. Piet regarded this as a good sign. No one was going to challenge any of his father's orders. 'Any questions?' asked Koos in a tone that suggested he expected none. With no response the party set off silently down the hill and across the valley towards the imposing eminence of Caesar's Camp silhouetted in the pale moonlight. Beyond it lay Ladysmith and occupation of the Platrand would place the town at the Burghers' mercy.

Fanned out to the left of them were men of their own and other Transvaal commandos and still further to the left the Free State commandos had started their approach towards Wagon Hill. While some of the Burghers headed directly for the centre of the ridge most of their own commando veered towards the corner on the extreme right. Koos had explained that the plan was for their commando to attack the defence lines from the flank once they had reached the crest while other commandos undertook a frontal assault. Piet had tried to imbue himself with the confidence and optimism of his father but each step increased his feeling of unease. He was nervous. No, it was more than that. If he were truthful to himself he was afraid but he could never, must never, let his father or his son suspect it. He envied his son's naïve enthusiasm, born of an implicit faith in his grandfather. Christiaan had prepared himself for this battle with his now familiar ritual of hooking his bugle around his neck and rubbing with his handkerchief the medal pinned on his chest, the insignia of war of a fourteen year old child.

Koos had already formed a bond with Christiaan that Piet had never been able to achieve, a bond born out of respect for the brave and wily warrior that he was not and never would be. He had not failed to notice that Christiaan referred to Koos rather than himself on any tactical or battlefield matter. Equally, Koos had forged a relationship with Christiaan that fate had denied him from adolescence. Piet could see that his father treated Christiaan as his protégé, a boy to whom he could pass on his values and the benefit of his experience to stand him in good stead in manhood whenever he would be required to ride on commando. Piet's inexperience had also left him with much to learn but he was far too old to act as his father's apprentice. Men of his age and younger were not just field cornets. Some of them led commandos.

The looming mass of Caesar's Camp grew closer and still there was no sign that the British were aware of their approach. Piet didn't like assaults. He felt safer and more comfortable fighting from defensive strongholds like they had done at Colenso. Even at Talana they were able to run for their horses as the British closed on their position on the crest. They had no horses here. If they did not succeed they would have to run for their lives.

At a small *spruit* the Burghers took off their boots, rolled up their trousers and waded across. From there it was only a few minutes to the foot of the ridge where a few of the Burghers hid their boots by a lone thorn tree or between two prominent boulders to be collected after the battle. Piet and Christiaan followed Koos's example and tied their boots around their necks. Piet could see his father's reasoning. They would be hampered by the boots on the ascent but if they reached the top undiscovered they would be able to put them back on. The climb would be difficult enough in bare or stockinged feet without having to face the descent without boots as well.

The first part of the ascent was easily negotiated but the slope quickly grew steeper. Koos slung his Mauser over his back to free both hands and Piet and Christiaan were among many Burghers to follow suit. They grabbed at small bushes and the larger ironstone boulders for support and leverage as they climbed the ever more precipitous ridge and they had to stifle a cry whenever they trod on a thorn or sharp stone. The hoot of an owl further over on the hillside punctuated the steady breathing of the Burghers around them as they approached the crest. Piet welcomed the respite as the leading Burghers paused just below the crest to put on their boots. As they crawled over the top the remaining Burghers shuffled upwards as each group did likewise, a number of Burghers now regretting leaving their boots behind.

Piet's hands were shaking as he untied the knot holding his laces together and both Koos and Christiaan finished before him and clambered over the crest. Other Burghers passed him and disappeared over the top and the thought flashed across his mind that he could stay hidden in the comfort and security of this sheltered hollow until it was all over. He screwed up his eyes. Of course he couldn't do that. He would have to join his father and his son, his neighbours and countrymen, those who made up the commando. He finished tying up his bootlaces, unslung his rifle and taking a deep breath crawled over the crest and on to the plateau.

Walter snapped shut the case of his gold pocket watch with a flourish. He liked doing that. It was what all the officers and toffs did and gave him a sense of style. The novelty had yet to wear off and he had been annoying the others ever since he had acquired it by constantly producing it, checking the time and clicking it shut. It had been a profitable session especially as that quartermaster sergeant from the nearby field battery didn't know how to play brag with the big boys and, more significantly, didn't know when to quit. Charlie had asked him the time and he had been delighted to check his watch. 'I can't see,' he said, impassively. It was too dark in the recess he occupied and he didn't feel like leaving the sangar's shelter to squint at his watch in the pale moonlight. He remembered that he had a full box of matches in his tunic pocket but he wasn't about to waste one just to let Charlie know the time. Walter had finished his stint on sentinel and, having made himself reasonably comfortable, he was quite content to stay put until the next relief arrived. It won't be long now, he thought as he blew into his cupped hands to fend off the pre-dawn chill.

'It's probably close to three o'clock,' said Charlie. Another half an hour or so and we'll be relieved by 'A' company, he thought. 'I'm gasping for a cup of char. Walter, your first job when we get back to company H.Q. is to make a brew and I won't care how weak it is.'

'No problem,' said Walter, rubbing his hands together and blowing into them again.

Charlie peered around the sangar. It was well constructed with rocks and sandbags and gave them cover on three sides. It was one built by his own section and he had cause to be satisfied that the lads had done a particularly sound job. The shadowy figures standing on ammunition boxes peering over the front layer of sandbags were Frank and McAdams on sentinel. Although he couldn't see their faces they were silhouetted in the moonlight. Walter was squatting by his side while the rest of his section and another section, minus its corporal who had reported sick that afternoon, were standing or sitting within the sangar's concave embrace. 'Doyle, Murray, take over from Hoyland and McAdams.' Doyle and Murray shuffled forward and took their places on the ammunition boxes when Frank and McAdams stepped down.

A sharp burst of rifle fire to their left sent Charlie scurrying over to that side of the sangar and on to an ammunition box from where he squinted into the darkness. Repeated flashes momentarily illuminated the night as the cracks of rifles and the urgent voices testified to fierce close combat at a distance Charlie estimated to coincide with the sangar on the extreme left. Support fire from the sangar in between was being poured into the area from where the attack was coming. 'Quick!' shouted Charlie. 'Everyone to their stations. The Boers are on the hill!' There was a scraping of boots and a clatter of rifles as the occupants of the sangar scrambled into position, some at the front, others at the sides. Charlie was about to ask the men on sentinel if they could see anything in front when a burst of Mauser fire answered his unspoken question and Doyle and Murray were flung backwards on to the floor of the sangar.

Bullets zipped overhead, thudded into the sandbags and ricocheted off the stones as concentrated fire was poured towards their sangar.

'They're attacking right along the line,' shouted Walter as Charlie checked on the two fallen men. Murray was dead with a clean shot through his right eye and a secondary wound to his cheek. Doyle was rolling around the floor clutching his throat and gasping. Charlie touched the side of his face to steady him and Doyle jerked and croaked in pain. His jaw was shattered but the primary wound was in his throat. 'Let me take a look,' he shouted, but Doyle wouldn't release his hands. 'Get a field dressing ready,' he ordered a man next to him. 'I'll try to pull his hands away and then you apply it.' He gripped his wrists and pulled but Doyle resisted and continued to thrash about. Another man who had taken Doyle's position and ventured to take aim over the top of the sandbag layer twisted and fell backwards over Charlie before managing to fire a shot. Charlie was winded but managed to roll the dead weight of the inert body aside before catching his breath.

'Keep your heads down!' he shouted over the noise of the rifle fire. He took another deep breath. 'And watch the left flank. If they take the sangars on our left they could hit us from behind.' Doyle's struggles abated enough for Charlie to pull his hands from his throat, releasing a jet of blood from a severed artery that spurted over the side of his face and shoulder. The man next to him tried to slap on the field dressing but succeeded only in spraying blood in all directions before the dressing was rendered useless by becoming saturated. Doyle convulsed and with a low moan lay still. Bullets were still flying over the sangar but at least only from the front so far, thought Charlie. Grabbing his rifle, he jumped up and rushed over to the left side of the emplacement where he peeked carefully around the corner just above ground level. Oh, hell, he thought.

Piet had tried to catch up with Koos and Christiaan but with so many Burghers pushing forward in the darkness he hadn't been able to locate them. The forward momentum of the surge of Burghers ground to a halt when an alert sentinel in the first sangar heard a noise in the brush and issued a challenge. 'Who goes there?'

The Burghers ducked down. 'We're Carbineers returning from foot patrol,' responded one of them in perfect English. There was a moment or two of silence when Piet felt his heart thump in his chest before several rifle shots whistled over their heads.

The game's up, thought Piet as the Burghers returned fire and moved forward to attack the sangar. Its occupants were now on full alert and had found their range. A volley tore into the ranks of the advancing Burghers felling several amid cries and exclamations. Piet was concerned for Koos and Christiaan. The moonlight illuminated the faces of the casualties just sufficiently for him to check quickly as he passed their prone or writhing bodies. They weren't among them. They must be all right.

Another volley was fired but this time from the crest into the front of the sangar. There were screams and shouts from the stone and sandbag emplacement as Mauser bullets hit home and distracted the defenders. The Burghers rushed forward and looped round to hit the defenders from their unprotected rear. From a kneeling position Piet fired cartridge after cartridge, clip after clip as the sangar became a shooting gallery. The soldiers fought back bravely and their return fire was steady and accurate. Bullets whistled past and when a Burgher kneeling close to Piet slumped backwards he threw himself to the ground and lay flat. Gradually the return fire slackened as one by one the soldiers were hit by the Burghers' remorseless fire until there was no sound from the sangar save the cries and groans of the wounded.

Piet joined a rush to occupy the sangar and fell to the ground as he reached its shelter. Regaining his feet he called out for Koos and Christiaan amid the heaving mass jostling at the right wall to take up firing positions against the next sangar. There was no response. The sound of rifle fire further to their right revealed that many of the Burghers had continued in a wider arc and encountered a party of reinforcements or a chance patrol. They must be in that group, thought Piet. His first instinct was to run over and join them but he realised immediately that this would be a dangerous manoeuvre in the midst of a vicious firefight between two sets of nervous adversaries in the dark. He could end up being shot by either side. Besides, he felt safer in the protective embrace of the sangar.

The right side of the emplacement was congested with Burghers concentrating their fire into the next sangar. Piet leaned against the inner front wall. 'Don't shoot, you stupid bastards!' came an angry shout from beside him after several shots from Burghers on the crest line had hissed overhead. 'We've taken this one. Move up to the next!' It was Koos.

'I thought I'd lost you,' said Piet. With a surge of relief he heard Christiaan's voice.

'Pa! We didn't know where you'd got to,' he said. '*Oupa* gave orders to the other group to pin down and wipe out the reinforcements and we came over here.' They had passed over the stretch of ground that Piet had been afraid to cross.

'It's our bad luck that we reached the top just as fresh parties had set out to relieve the pickets,' said Koos. 'Fifteen minutes earlier and we could have taken these sangars without any distractions.' He stepped over a soldier's body towards the right wall with Christiaan behind him. 'Anyway,' he continued sternly, 'there's no time for family reunions. We've got a job to do.' He pushed his way into the firing line and immediately emptied a clip in the direction of the next sangar. He motioned Christiaan to stay back. 'You won't be able to see over the top, boy,' he said. 'Take a rest. You've earned it.' Piet was still leaning against the wall, his mind a tangle of emotions but predominantly relief. 'What are you waiting for?' snapped Koos. 'Get up here.'

Piet levered himself up and teetered on one of the ammunition boxes already occupied by another Burgher. He had difficulty in raising his rifle because of the squash of bodies in the line but eventually brought it into position and took aim. Before he could manage a single shot, with consecutive dull thuds two bullets pierced the sandbag on which he was leaning while a third hit the Burgher next to him, hurling him backwards. Piet lost his footing on the ammunition box and cursed loudly as he toppled over before hitting his head on the ground.

Christiaan rushed to him. 'Pa! Are you hit?'

Piet propped himself up on one elbow but felt groggy and his head was spinning. He tried to stand but a wave of nausea came over him and he sank to his knees and vomited violently. He knew Christiaan was with him and could vaguely discern rifle fire and his father's voice barking orders but everything else was a confused blur.

Koos jumped down. 'It's only concussion,' he said to Christiaan. 'Another relief party is sheltering in the long grass parallel to the next sangar. We won't be able to move forward until we deal with it so I'm taking a party out.' He patted Christiaan's shoulder. 'Stay here with your father.' He moved out quickly with a group of Burghers following behind. Piet was still on his knees, head bent and a string of drool dangling from his beard. Christiaan touched Piet's head gently, hesitated for a few seconds and ran off to catch up with his grandfather.

The first faint gleam of light filtered over the horizon to the left of their position as Charlie took stock of their situation. Four dead and two wounded, neither of whom was going to make it. Each one had been shot in the head or neck with at least the two wounded men also having been hit in the arms. Any exposed part of the body was vulnerable to Boer marksmanship at this range, especially with daylight approaching, and Charlie had ordered the men to minimise their exposure to the marksmen on the crest.

Nine fit men left plus himself. 'We need to keep a look out on three sides,' he said to Walter. 'They might rush the sangars from the crest but they would take a lot of casualties and they don't need to do that, at least for the time being.' Charlie recalled from their previous encounters that the Boers preferred to retreat rather than risk heavy casualties. 'Our immediate problem will come from the left and rear especially if they take both of the other sangars. They can only attack one sangar at a time without being outflanked themselves so there'll be no danger from the right.'

The early morning sunlight quickly flooded the plateau and brought a sense of perspective to the scene. One of the wounded men was breathing in short gasps from a throat wound with his left arm hanging limply, broken by a bullet just above the elbow. Charlie winced as he saw the blood soaked face of the other man who was lying quietly, half propped up against the wall of the sangar. The man had been hit by at least five bullets, one in the mouth smashing his teeth and jaw, another two taking off his nose and part of an ear, and one in each arm. Despite the hideous nature of his wounds he probably stood a better chance of making it as far as the field hospital than the first but infection would probably kill him eventually even if he received prompt treatment. And right now that was very unlikely.

Charlie heard a movement in the long grass to the rear. He

levelled his rifle and McAdams joined him as he issued a challenge. A voice called out from within the grass. 'Relief picket from 'A' company.'

'It could be a trick,' said McAdams. Charlie had also considered the possibility. Whoever they were they wouldn't show themselves. Boers would never reveal their true identity and their own men wouldn't expose themselves to Boer fire. Charlie felt frustrated at this unnecessary complication. Why hadn't anyone had the foresight to order the brush and grass cleared from the plateau? That would have given them a clear field of fire from the base camp at the inner crest and left no hiding place for the Boers. There's one way to verify their identity, thought Charlie.

'What's the name of your company commander?'

'Captain Little,' came the reply. Charlie gave a sigh of relief and he and McAdams relaxed. They were the relief picket after all. He was about to warn them to lay flat or approach at a crawl when a dozen heads popped up and charged towards the sangar.

'Shit,' said McAdams coldly. No sooner had they exposed themselves than a blast of rifle fire from the captured sangar and the brush behind it hit them, hurling men back into the long grass. Only two made it out of the grass and all the Boer fire was concentrated on them as they rushed to the sanctuary of the sangar. One man dropped to the ground but miraculously the other made it, stumbling into the emplacement and panting breathlessly on all fours.

'You stupid bastards,' said McAdams.

'We'd been out there for nearly three hours,' he gasped. 'We couldn't stay forever. Our corporal told us to make a run for it after he answered your challenge.' As he stood up he strolled towards the four dead bodies and the two grievously wounded men. 'You've not had an easy time of it either,' he said, attempting to brush the patches of red earth and dust off his tunic and trousers. As Charlie was assessing the volume and direction of the volleys that had annihilated this small party he heard Walter's urgent voice.

'Get down you daft bastard!'

Charlie turned to the front to see the man who had miraculously survived the suicidal dash for the sangar take the briefest of glimpses over the sandbags before his neck snapped back and his lifeless body thudded to the emplacement floor. It had all been so instantaneous that it almost seemed as though the man had hit the ground before Charlie had heard the crack of the rifle.

'Talk about curiosity killed the cat,' said Frank, looking down at the body and scratching the back of his head under his helmet.

'Now there's a man who was fated to die,' said Walter philosophically. 'The sort of man I'd like to play at brag.' He walked away shaking his head.

What an unnecessary waste of life, thought Charlie, contemplating how long he and his nine remaining fit men could hold out against a three sided Boer onslaught. A resumption of heavy fire from the direction of the second sangar gave him an inkling. If the Boers took that position they would be next.

It was already fully light and Christiaan could see Koos ahead with his group of Burghers. They had moved off to flush out the relief picket that had gone to ground while making its way to the second sangar but there was some sort of activity beyond that had attracted their attention. He ran at a crouch through the long grass to reach them, his bugle swinging against his chest, being careful not to attract the British soldiers' attention or make himself an easy target. He kneeled down close to his grandfather but Koos was preoccupied with events ahead and unaware of his presence.

The soldiers suddenly broke cover from the long grass ahead but the Burghers were prepared and poured a lethal fire into them. Christiaan hadn't been quite ready and all but two had fallen back into the grass by the time he aimed at the first survivor running for the sangar. The man dropped and he aimed at the second. He pulled the trigger but nothing happened. The clip was empty and by the time he had slipped another one into the magazine the soldier had made it to safety. Lucky man, thought Christiaan.

'I told you to stay with your father,' said Koos irritably, finally noticing him.

'But, *oupa*, he's all right,' said Christiaan. 'He's safe there and I can be of more value here.'

'Don't contradict me, boy,' barked Koos. Christiaan was taken aback at first by his grandfather's testiness. Christiaan had often heard the old man being brusque to the point of discourtesy with others but had rarely been reprimanded like this, especially in front of others. Christiaan felt not so much affronted as ashamed for letting his *oupa* down by disobeying an order. He could not be seen to ignore his field cornet's commands just because he was his grandfather. It would be detrimental to morale among the rest of the Burghers as well as an insult to his beloved *oupa*. He rose to a squat and was about to run at a crouch back to his father in the sangar but felt a restraining hand on the tail of his jacket. 'Stay here, boy,' said Koos more calmly. 'You took an unnecessary risk getting here. There's no point taking another going back.' He gave him a pat of encouragement on the arm. 'Your pa will be fine.'

Koos spread the group out and led it in a still wider loop away from the second sangar to try to locate the relief picket hiding in the long grass. They needed to deal with these soldiers before assaulting the sangar, otherwise they could easily be attacked from behind themselves. The Burghers crept or crouched quietly with only the occasional anthill to negotiate. They're here somewhere, thought Koos, but their NCO isn't going to make the same mistake as the last one.

Christiaan was reminded of the guinea fowl hunts he had been on with his grandfather and father. He had so much enjoyed those little expeditions from an early age, creeping closer and closer in the long grass until the fowl broke cover and were shot down. He raised his crouch so as to catch up with Koos and saw a movement out of the corner of his eye. Now he was the guinea fowl but instead of breaking cover he instinctively threw himself flat, the hiss of the bullet reverberating in his ear before he hit the ground. His bugle dug into his chest on impact, winding him, and in the few seconds it took to regain his breath and composure a deadly crossfire had erupted with bullets from both sides finding their mark. He raised his head carefully above the grass and saw a kneeling soldier aiming at a Burgher half concealed in the grass. It was *oupa*! He raised his rifle and with no time to take precise aim fired. To his immense relief, the soldier dropped his rifle and clutched his arm.

The Burghers outnumbered the relief picket and despite being taken by surprise for the first time they quickly overwhelmed the gallant little party. Koos stopped the firing when all the soldiers were down. 'If you surrender we will send the wounded for medical attention,' he shouted. There was continued silence and one impatient Burgher urged Koos to finish them off. 'Don't be so hasty, Nel,' he said. 'There are only a few left alive and they're all wounded. Warfare is about achieving objectives, not killing. We'll gain no further advantage by wiping them out.' Nel had proven his worth and courage on commando but was also hot headed and impetuous. He had ambitions for high rank both in the Burgher army and the post war government of the Transvaal and was keen to get himself noticed. It was no secret that he had been disappointed not to receive the field cornet promotion that Koos had been given. Koos was reminded of that *rooinek* opportunist Winston Churchill who was at that moment attached to Buller's relief column, no doubt revelling in his celebrity after escaping from the prisoner of war camp in Pretoria. God help us all if those two ever become leaders of their countries, thought Koos.

Shortly there was a movement in the grass ahead of them as a large white handkerchief attached to the barrel of a rifle was waved back and forth. 'Your surrender is accepted,' shouted Koos. 'Put down your weapons and we will arrange to escort the wounded to our lines for treatment.' The rifle disappeared from view and Koos detailed four Burghers to seize the weapons and arrange for the wounded to be evacuated. He turned to Nel. 'That wasn't so difficult, was it?'

The next objective was to take the second sangar. Despite already having sustained some casualties most of its occupants remained unwounded and would prove dangerous adversaries. Koos motioned his men to regroup and Christiaan scuttled forward to join him. 'There's plenty of cover between here and the emplacement,' he said, pointing towards the scattering of thorn trees and clumps of mimosa bushes ahead. 'The long grass continues to within twenty or thirty yards of the position,' he added, marvelling that the defenders hadn't bothered to clear the whole area. 'Spread out as much as you can and take up a secure position. Our brothers on the crest should keep the *rooinekke* pinned down from the front while we attack their exposed rear.'

The Burghers fanned forward and crouched behind the trees, bushes and boulders little more than a hundred yards from the sangar.

The defenders detected the movement but were unable to fix their sights on any clear targets among the cover and fired harmlessly into the trees. Koos had taken cover behind a thorn tree while Christiaan was by his side firing from the shelter of a large boulder. Bullets flew into the sangar as the defenders frantically pulled sandbags off the side walls and dragged over ammunition boxes in a desperate attempt to construct a protective barrier. As he pulled another clip from his bandolier Koos singled out a figure pointing and waving his arms. 'That's the NCO issuing orders', he said to Christiaan without further explanation. The boy needed none. He diverted his aim and fired, hurling the NCO backwards. He learns quickly, thought Koos proudly, as he slipped another clip into his magazine.

More soldiers fell before the handful of survivors managed to lay flat behind the makeshift barricade and return fire. 'Take care,' shouted Koos. 'There aren't many left but they can still put a bullet in you.' The skirmish was proceeding well and they could pick off at their leisure anyone who revealed himself above the little barricade. He noticed the stocky figure of Nel creeping to the right and talking intently to each of the Burghers in turn. Some nodded their heads while a few gave him a puzzled look and glanced over towards Koos. 'What the hell is he up to now?' muttered Koos, loudly enough for Christiaan to hear and be momentarily distracted. He didn't have to wait long for the answer.

With a cry of 'Charge!' Nel emerged from behind a thorn tree and rushed towards the sangar with twenty or so Burghers in his wake followed a few seconds later by another dozen who thought this was a general order. Koos, Christiaan and the rest of the Burghers watched in open mouthed silence as rifle fire from behind the pathetic little barricade ripped into the attacking Burghers.

'He's brave,' said Christiaan laconically, unable to express the peculiar mixture of admiration and disbelief he felt.

He's brave all right, thought Koos. But Nel's bravery was blind and unfeeling, a cold courage of the most dangerous kind. It was a selfish heroism motivated not by patriotism or necessity but by his own ambition. He would take unnecessary risks for his own purposes and he didn't care whoever else got hurt in the process. 'He's crazy,' said Koos. 'He's going to get himself and the rest of them killed.'

It seemed to take them an age to cross the open ground and Burgher after Burgher tumbled and fell under the onslaught of fire. Miraculously Nel was still at the head of his dwindling band when they finally reached the sangar where their superior numbers enabled them to finish off the defenders in a sharp but brief fight at close quarters. 'He must have *rooinek* blood in him,' said Koos to Christiaan who was still distracted by the events he had just witnessed. This was the kind of reckless courage required of British officers, thought Koos. But they made suicidal charges at the head of their men for queen and country. Nel did it only for himself.

A cheer went up and hats were being waved in the sangar. Christiaan joined the other Burghers rushing towards the captured position and Koos followed behind. Inside the emplacement a jubilant Nel was revelling in the accolades of the Burghers. Those who had attacked with him were basking in his reflected glory and savouring the adrenaline rush of having survived the charge. Those who hadn't were grateful that his action had shortened this localised conflict and perhaps even saved their lives. Nel saw the admiring gaze in Christiaan's eyes. 'Well, my lad,' he said expansively, putting his arm around Christiaan's shoulder, 'one day you can tell your grandchildren about the day you saw Danie Nel lead the famous charge into the British defences on the Platrand.'

'That will be a long time from now, *Meneer* Nel,' said Christiaan with a smile.

'About nineteen fifty, I would say.' Nel laughed and most of the other Burghers joined in. Koos was incensed.

'You're a damned lunatic,' he hissed angrily, staring directly into Nel's eyes. 'You didn't even use the cover of the long grass before you charged.'

'They don't seem to think so,' said Nel smugly, indicating the other Burghers around them.

'I'm sure *they* do, though,' responded Koos, pointing back to where the bodies of more than a dozen Burghers lay.

Nel dismissed Koos's objections. 'Casualties of war, van Oppen. It happens all the time.'

Koos tried to control his fury. 'Casualties of war? Try telling that to Venter's widow or Engelbrecht's or du Preez's.'

'Just like you might have had to tell it to *his* widow or his or his,' said Nel angrily, pointing randomly at three of the Burghers with them. 'The problem with you, van Oppen, is that you're too old fashioned. Battles are won by the strong and the daring, not by the weak and the timid.'

Those Burghers who had witnessed Koos's response to the man who had called him soft at Colenso expected a similar or even more violent reaction now but Koos kept calm. Despite the humiliation he couldn't afford to lose his temper now. This wasn't Colenso. They were in an advanced position and still had plenty of hard fighting ahead. He couldn't afford internal bickering to jeopardise their mission or the lives of the others. His first instinct was to retrieve the wounded from the long grass but that would be too risky for the present as the occupants of the third sangar would have been alerted by all the commotion and anyone venturing out now would be a target.

Nel turned to look back at the ground he had crossed. 'A good fifty yards I would say, men.' He was about to congratulate those who had charged with him when a crack was followed by a crimson splash as the side of his skull opened up and he crumpled lifeless to the floor. Koos and the nearest Burghers ducked down in a futile attempt to revive Nel while Christiaan and the others flung themselves against the intact front wall. The bullet had passed over the gap where the defenders had removed the sandbags and where Nel's head had protruded.

This is one political career that's over before it's started, thought Koos as he looked at the frozen countenance of Nel's wide eyed and open mouthed face. He wondered if Winston Churchill would have better luck.

'Got the bastard!' exclaimed Walter triumphantly. 'That'll teach him to keep his head down.'

Charlie was more concerned about their exposed position. Their sangar was next in line and their relief picket had been wiped out. The sun was already high in the sky and the unrelenting heat added to their discomfort. They were tired and hungry. He looked at Frank whose hollow eyes stared out from his dirt lined face. It wasn't just Frank. They all looked like that, he observed, no doubt including himself.

Walter dropped to his side. 'I'm starving. Has anyone got any food on them.' The others mumbled in the negative or didn't reply. Walter flipped open his pocket watch and gave a shrug of resignation. He showed Charlie the time. They hadn't eaten for fourteen hours.

'Trust you to think of your stomach at a time like this,' said Charlie as Walter snapped shut his watch case. It was only now, during a brief respite in the battle, that he realised how hungry he was himself. At least they shouldn't be driven to surrender by thirst. They still had water in their bottles and they could use those of the dead. Here's an irony, thought Charlie. The more of us who get killed the longer the survivors might hold out. He unscrewed the top of his water bottle and took a miserly swig, closing his eyes as he allowed the warm liquid to trickle slowly down his throat. It was neither pleasant nor refreshing but it gave welcome relief from the stale dryness in his mouth.

'Not like that.' It was McAdams. He took a mouthful from his own water bottle, swilled it round and spat it back. 'Our water supply might not be critical right now but we don't know how long we'll be stuck here. Only swallow every third or fourth time. That way your water will last longer but your mouth won't dry up.'

Another old soldier's tip from India, thought Charlie. 'Good idea. Tell the others.'

The sun had edged its way along the sangar and Frank and Walter went to move their two wounded comrades back into the dwindling shade. They had positioned both men upright to prevent them from choking on their own blood. 'This one's gone,' said Frank with no trace of emotion in his voice. It was the man with the throat wound. On this scorched South African hill he had given his life for queen and country and no one had noticed. Charlie went over. The other was still conscious but growing weaker. Charlie flicked the flies away from the blood soaked field dressings that covered the hole where his nose used to be but they returned immediately, feasting on the seepage. Frank gently rested the grievously wounded soldier's head against his shoulder and with his bottle top dribbled some water into his broken mouth. Death would not be far away, thought Charlie and it would be a merciful release.

An unrelenting fire from the crest continued to beat against the sangar and with a low grunt one of the men crouched against the front wall slumped sideways, a bullet in his heart. Walter cursed loudly and flung himself flat, gripping his left arm above the elbow. Boer marksmanship was legendary but this was something else. The uneven dry wall construction had left a number of small gaps and at least one Boer had started shooting through them. Charlie ordered everyone away from any gaps but a man peering through one of them failed to react quickly enough and took a bullet in the eye. Frank scuttled over to Walter and ripped a bigger opening where the bullet had perforated his sleeve. 'It's only a slight flesh wound,' he said. 'The bullet's nicked your arm and passed on.' He pressed a field dressing on Walter's arm. 'You're a lucky man.' Charlie looked around. A fresh trail of blood on the side of the wounded man's head revealed where the bullet that caught Walter had finally struck home. His torment was finally over.

The fire from the crest abruptly changed direction. The sangar was no longer its target and the Boers were firing into the scrub and brush beyond. 'About bloody time,' said Walter, as he and Frank took the opportunity to fire a shot each over the front wall before ducking down again to avoid the instantaneous response. Charlie estimated the reinforcements to be at least three or four companies strong and probably a mixture of their own battalion and the Rifles. They had thankfully diverted the Boers' attention but were pinned down by the concentration of fire from the crest and managing only a sporadic response.

Firing came from the captured sangar to their left. 'Return their fire,' shouted Charlie while ordering two men to cover the front. 'Let's give them something to think about.' The other five clambered on to the boxes and poured fire towards the captured sangar, Walter seemingly unhampered by his wound. Charlie knew this was risky but with the partially dismantled side wall of the other sangar lower than theirs they had a slight advantage and they could not simply wait to be picked off.

Charlie hauled himself up into the firing line and joined in. The firefight was intense with men on both sides hit. The man next to Charlie fell back clutching his head but was dead before he hit the ground and a bullet clipped the top of Frank's helmet. Five Boers had fallen back from their positions before a determined volley ripped into the layer of sandbags and sent McAdams and another man tumbling to the sangar floor. We can't keep sustaining casualties at this rate, thought Charlie. 'Cease fire!' he shouted. 'Take cover!' They dropped down and went over to the two men who had just fallen. The other man was dead but McAdams was clutching his face and spitting out blood and fragments of teeth. He must be in agony, thought Charlie. Yet he made no sound. Charlie pulled McAdams's hands away from his face, revealing a bloody hole in each cheek where the bullet had passed right through while he had been taking aim himself. Frank pressed a field dressing on either side while Walter ripped off his perforated sleeve and carefully hooked it under McAdams's jaw and over his head to keep the dressings in place.

In the midst of all this frantic activity Charlie hardly noticed the two men at the front open fire towards the crest. They managed two rounds each before they arched backwards as if in a choreographed fall and crashed simultaneously to the ground. Frank ran over to check them out but the neat holes between their eyes told their own story. He looked at Charlie and shook his head. 'Both dead,' he said grimly.

Charlie looked around. Bodies littered the sangar and apart from himself only Frank, Walter and the wounded McAdams were left alive. The little group desperately needed reinforcements but they were nearly a quarter of a mile away, pinned down by incessant Boer fire. At least he was with the men in the battalion he most trusted. Charlie calculated that the attention of the Boers on the crest would be focused on keeping the reinforcements at bay and that their most immediate danger came from their flank. 'Position yourselves by the side wall, lads. We have to be ready for an attack. The Boers in the next sangar will know how badly they've hit us and may fancy their chances.' Frank and Walter went to help McAdams off the floor but he shrugged away their offer and with a grimace of pain struggled to his feet unaided. With his bayonet Charlie widened a tiny gap between the bottom two layers of stones just sufficient for him to observe the occupied sangar at minimal risk to himself. 'Your move, Boers.'

Amid the swirl of his gradual return to consciousness Piet made out the exhortations of a disembodied voice urging him to move. 'Come on man, we've got to get out of here,' it said. He felt his body being shaken. 'Come on', implored the voice with a mixture of agitation and urgency. 'It's too dangerous here.'

Piet squinted at the man. He didn't recognise him and as his thought processes gradually unscrambled he guessed this Burgher must be a straggler from another commando. The sound of rifle fire from different directions and distances formed a background to this man's unrelenting insistence. As he began to recall the circumstances of his current situation he suddenly became aware of the scorching heat of the sun. His head was still spinning, his mouth was parched and the taste of stale vomit lingered on his tongue. 'Water,' was all that he managed to utter. The Burgher took a water bottle from a dead soldier and trickled some into Piet's mouth before tipping more over his head. This served to revive him almost instantly and he snatched the bottle from the Burgher's hand and drank greedily, pausing only to swill and spit to purge the bilious acidity from his mouth.

'What's happening?' asked Piet, having quickly recovered his awareness of their surroundings.

'We're exposed here,' said the Burgher. 'British reinforcements have been trying to push forward but the concentration of our fire here is not as great as further along and they're starting to make ground.' He pointed to the body of a Burgher. 'I stayed behind to look after my brother. He was hit early on and I dragged him in here.' He wiped a solitary tear from his eye with the sleeve of his jacket. 'He died soon afterwards but by then everyone else had gone.' He waved his arm around the sangar. 'There's no one else left alive here,' he added unnecessarily.

Piet jolted back into reality. Where was Christiaan? 'Have you seen a boy, fourteen, and an old man with long grey hair and beard?' he asked anxiously, grabbing the Burgher by the lapels of his jacket with both hands.

The Burgher backed away, alarmed by Piets's sudden aggressive outburst.

'Well have you?' he insisted. 'The old man is Field Cornet Koos van Oppen. He's my father. The boy is my son.'

The Burgher relaxed and shook his head. He hadn't heard of any Field Cornet van Oppen or seen anyone matching the descriptions of Koos or Christiaan. 'It was dark when we took this place but there's been plenty of fighting further up. They're probably in the next sangar.'

Piet grabbed his Mauser and made a move to leave. The Burgher grabbed his arm. 'It's too dangerous to run to the next sangar,' he said. 'We need to withdraw to the crest. It'll be safer.' A stray bullet whistled past the emplacement as if to emphasise his point.

Piet realised he was right. He prayed that his father and son were safe but right now there was nothing he could do about it. He followed the Burgher in a crouch around to the unexposed left outer wall of the sangar and after a shout to let their comrades know they were coming, ran to the crest and dropped over into the cover beneath. From the reaction of the other Burghers deployed on this part of the crest his companion was clearly back among his own commando so Piet made his way over the rocks and scrub below the crest line until he was almost opposite the second sangar. He squeezed into the line. 'Any idea how many Burghers are in there?' he asked the man next to him, nodding towards the sangar. The Burgher threw him a curious look. 'I'm trying to find my son and my father,' Piet explained. 'I think they may be in there,' he added. 'At least I hope so.' The Burgher gave an understanding nod. He wasn't sure how many were in there but there had been a number of casualties. Piet was far from reassured by this vague information as he joined in the firing towards the pinned down reinforcements.

Koos was in a dilemma. There were just seventeen of them remaining out of the party he had originally led on to the darkness of the plateau all those hours ago. 'There's only a handful of them left but it's too dangerous to rush the position,' he said. 'On the other hand it's going to become too dangerous to stay here without making any further progress.'

There was a mutter among the other Burghers 'What are the options?' asked one.

'The best one is to retire to the crest line,' said Koos. 'At least there we'll be under cover.' He didn't need to add that this option also had its risks. They would have to run the gauntlet of the survivors in the next sangar but at least they would no longer be exposed to the eventual advance of the reinforcements that could not be resisted indefinitely and would pose a much greater hazard. 'We'll go in four groups,' he continued. 'The first three groups will be covered by the others.' One of the Burghers expressed his concern about the lack of protection for the last group. 'Those who have already reached the crest will have to cover us as best they can,' said Koos calmly. He had made it clear that he would be in the last and most vulnerable group.

As the first four prepared to go, he pulled Christiaan aside. 'You go with the second group.' Christiaan started to object but Koos stilled his protest. He knew the boy wanted to be in his group. 'The last group will be too dangerous. You're in the second group. That's an order.' He didn't add that his choice of the second group for Christiaan would give him the option to abandon the manoeuvre if the first ran into trouble.

'Go!' shouted Koos to the first group as he and the other Burghers fired over the shortened side wall.

After the volley Charlie took the opportunity to squint through the small hole he had opened up at the foot of the side wall. 'It looks like they're making a run for it but I can't see too clearly through here.'

Within a couple of minutes another volley crashed from the occupied sangar. As Frank and McAdams quickly returned fire, Walter sat with his back to the side wall and carefully held out his small shaving mirror at almost ground level. He ran the risk of attracting the Boers' attention but it offered a wider view than Charlie's spy hole. 'They seem to be going in small groups with the rest covering them,' he said, angling the mirror upwards. Walter had already calculated that the position of the sun ensured he would not be betrayed by a reflection. Another volley zipped overhead. They hadn't spotted the mirror. Charlie took the mirror and changed places with Walter in time to see the third group dashing for the crest.

'There can't be more than four or five in each group,' said Charlie. 'Only a few rifles fired then so they must be down to the last group with no one left in the sangar to cover their withdrawal.' He pondered the options. As the last group was preparing to go they could rush them. If they were successful they would retake the position but the consequences of failure could be catastrophic. They would risk attracting fire from the crest but on the other hand they would catch the Boers by surprise. They would never expect them to attack and might even be fooled into believing that their own sangar had been reinforced. On the other hand if they stayed where they were or tried to retake the other sangar after it had been abandoned they would be the target of every Mauser on this part of the crest, especially if the Boers realised how few of them were left. Above all they needed to buy time until reinforcements reached the forward positions. He put it to the others. Frank and Walter thought for a few seconds and agreed to attack. McAdams, his swollen face cradled in Walter's blood soaked tunic sleeve, simply clicked his bayonet on to his rifle. The others did likewise.

'Here's to us all,' said Charlie offering his hand. They all shook hands and prepared to charge.

Piet's heart was racing. One of the Burghers in the first group whom he had helped to drag over the crest had confirmed that Koos and Christiaan were in the sangar. His son would come with the second group and his father with the fourth and last. The first group had made it safely and he awaited the emergence of the second.

'Here they come,' shouted a Burgher nearby. They were running almost directly towards him. There were four men but no Christiaan. 'You said he was coming in the second group,' he screamed hysterically at the Burgher who had given him the news.

'Don't blame me,' replied the Burgher aggressively. 'The little bastard was told to go with them. It's not my fault if he's disobeyed orders.' Piet bristled and started to raise his fist but the hostile look on the Burgher's face quickly brought him back to his senses. Amid the urgent thud of boots and a flurry of limbs the second group stumbled and dropped over the crest.

A mere minute or two passed before the third group appeared but to Piet it seemed like an eternity. Four Burghers dashed from the sangar and he was horrified to see that Christiaan was not among them. As they crashed safely over the crest line he knew he was powerless to do anything but wait for the last group and pray that both his son and his father would be with it.

Koos slid down from the wall and stopped in his tracks when he looked round. He had been too preoccupied giving covering fire to notice that Christiaan had not already run to the safety of the crest but had not expected to see him still in the sangar. 'I told you to go with the second group,' he bellowed. Christiaan looked into his grandfather's eyes but said nothing. 'You would have been safe by now,' he continued. 'I thought you might have learned about obeying orders after seeing what happened to the men who listened to Nel instead of to me.' Christiaan thought that his grandfather was shaking with anger. He would never have guessed that it was a result of Koos's mounting fear for their safety.

Christiaan saw the disapproving glare in the eyes of the other three Burghers as well as those of his grandfather and hung his head. He wasn't afraid of going in the last group but was ashamed that his disobedience might now compromise the successful withdrawal to the crest. When he looked up again he froze, more in astonishment than fear. A wild-eyed soldier, his jaw taped up with a piece of torn khaki tunic, and with bloodied dressings padding the sides of his face, had appeared in the sangar. As the others turned to look at this apparition one was instantly skewered by McAdams's bayonet. Koos and the two remaining Burghers raised their Mausers as McAdams struggled in vain to free his bayonet embedded to the hilt in his victim's chest. McAdams released his grip on his rifle and as the Burgher slumped to the ground he gripped another's throat, contorting his face as he squeezed tighter.

Koos and the third Burgher fired simultaneously as Charlie, Frank and Walter entered the emplacement. Without releasing his grip both McAdams and his adversary fell dead to the ground together. Walter bayoneted the third burgher who still struggled to pull the steel blade from his chest until Walter squeezed he trigger. 'Get the old bastard!' screamed Walter, fearing that he would be shot at point blank range while trying to extricate his bayonet. As Koos swung his Mauser towards Walter, Frank instantly knew he would not have time to use the bayonet and shot the old man in the stomach. Koos reeled backwards against the inner wall and as he levelled his rifle for the last time, Frank followed up with a bayonet thrust into his heart.

'*Oupa!*' screamed Christiaan frantically. He raised his Mauser to avenge his grandfather but in the same moment that his finger tightened on the trigger, a crack he never heard was followed instantly by the bullet that tore away a piece of his skull, ripped through his brain and ended his short life.

The adrenaline rush was over and the reality of how close they had come to death swept over them. 'Thanks Frank,' gasped Walter. 'You saved my fucking life.'

'Thanks, Charlie,' said Frank, leaning against the wall in relief. 'You saved mine.'

Charlie wasn't listening. He was kneeling by the body of Christiaan. 'Oh my God. He's only a young boy.' Charlie had caught sight of him about to shoot Frank and had instinctively fired to save his friend.

'It was them or us,' said Walter.

'It was him or me,' said Frank. 'And out of the two of us I know who I'd prefer to die.'

'But he's so young,' said Charlie, struggling to find any justification for killing a mere child.

'Not too young to carry a rifle, though,' said Walter. 'Who knows how many of our lads this little bastard has killed so far.'

'Walter's right,' agreed Frank, placing a comforting hand on Charlie's shoulder. 'If they're in the front line with a weapon, they're old enough.'

'Check them for any documents or intelligence reports,' said Charlie as he sat with his head in his hands. Frank and Walter went through the Boers' pockets.

'Nothing,' said Frank.

'Same here,' said Walter, going over to Christiaan's body.

'The boy won't have any documents on him,' said Charlie with a hint of exasperation.

'Maybe. Maybe not,' said Walter, rummaging through Christiaan's clothing. 'You're right,' he said finally. His eye caught a glint on the boy's chest. He fingered the medal and turned it over to examine it before yanking the pinned ribbon from his shirt and slipping it into his pocket. 'I'll have this though.' He met Charlie's disapproving stare. 'Well *he's* not entitled to it is he? He probably took it from the body of one of our lads he killed.' He pulled the battered bugle from around Christiaan's neck and read the inscription. 'There you are,' he said triumphantly. 'The little bastard stole this from the Rifles.' He tossed it disdainfully over the sangar wall. 'It's no use to anyone now, though.'

The Burghers on the crest had been slow to react to the unexpected charge of the four soldiers and were powerless to assist in the brief fight inside the sangar. In the ensuing silence Piet was frantic with worry. There had only been five shots between nine men. Maybe at least some of the defeated had surrendered. 'Christiaan! Koos! Christiaan van Oppen!' he shouted through cupped hands, praying for a response. It came in the form of Christiaan's bugle hitting the ground outside the sangar, bouncing once and rolling to a halt. In a panic he cupped his hands again but his cry was drowned out by the low rumble of thunder from the thick black clouds that were rolling in behind the Burghers' positions.

As the first large drops of rain that invariably precede an African rainstorm started to fall, there was a blast of a different kind. The explosion of a shell on the corner of the ridge was quickly followed by five more as a field battery opened up from the British lines in the valley below. Grey puffs of smoke preceded bursts of shrapnel and case shot sprayed the crest and slopes of the ridge. The detonation of the artillery bombardment competed with the crash of thunder and the intermittent flashes of lightning as the rain lashed down with a rare ferocity, blotting out Piet's field of vision so that he could barely make out the shape of the sangar.

'Get down, you idiot!' the Burgher next to him yelled through the din. Piet felt a tug on his already sodden jacket and slipped back down into the greasy red mud that oozed between the rocks.

'You don't understand,' said Piet. 'My son and my father are in there.'

The Burgher looked at him sympathetically and instinctively ducked at the sound of a shrapnel burst nearby. Piet didn't move. 'There's nothing you can do,' said the Burgher, shouting to make himself heard over the combined din of the rainstorm and the artillery bombardment. 'My guess is that we'll be pulling out before long anyway. Our chance of victory has been and gone.' Another shell burst on the corner of the ridge, spewing earth and rocks into the air. 'We haven't gained any ground for hours and we've just lost possession of that sangar.' Not for the first time in his life Piet felt powerless and inadequate. The drenched Burgher shivered at the sudden drop in temperature that accompanied the rainstorm but Piet was unmoved, his blank expression confounding the turmoil of emotions running through his head as the rain cascaded over the brim of his hat down through his beard and on to his chest. 'I'm sorry,' said the Burgher simply.

The crimson blood from the wounds of the dead swirled among the pools of rainwater in the sangar and mingled with the rust red mud. Incongruously, Charlie was reminded of an artist's palette. McAdams was still locked in the grotesque pose of his final struggle with the Boer he had throttled, his eyes wide open and his face still bearing the determination it had displayed at the moment of his death. 'It's no use,' said Walter. 'I can't budge his hands. They're too tight around the Boer's neck.'

'He must have broken his neck,' said Charlie. 'I doubt even McAdams could have strangled someone to death so quickly.'

'What next, Charlie?' asked Frank.

'Sit tight for the moment. I think we've turned the tide by taking this sangar. At least the Boers have been pushed back off the plateau and the reinforcements should be able to use the rainstorm as cover.'

Frank gave up trying to find sufficient dry cover to have a smoke and as he stuffed the remains of the disintegrating cigarette into his soaked tunic pocket he perked up his head. Momentarily oblivious of the lashing rain, Charlie and Walter also strained their ears in an attempt to confirm the faint but tantalisingly familiar sound coming from their left rear amid the thrashing rain, intermittent growls of thunder and shell and shrapnel bursts on the ridge.

The skirl ebbed and flowed as it tried to assert itself over the other sounds on the plateau. Despite its faintness there could be no mistake. 'It's the Highlanders,' said Walter cautiously. 'It's the bloody Highlanders!' he exclaimed in joyous confirmation.

'They're attacking the corner of the ridge,' said Charlie. 'Then they'll roll up the Boer line on the crest.'

'If the bastards hang around long enough,' said Walter.

'I doubt it,' said Frank.

Charlie doubted it too. There was no question that the Highlanders would attack the crest at the point of the bayonet. The Boers were brave fighters but had a dread fear of cold steel. They also knew when it was time to withdraw. There would be no last stand. 'Let's join in,' he said, gripping his rifle and edging his way round the side of the sangar.

Through the rain and gloom Piet caught a flicker of movement by the side of the shadowed hump of the sangar. He screwed up his eyes, partly because of the rainwater that had soaked through his hat and dribbled down his brow and partly to improve the focus of his vision. He wiped his eyes with his hand but it made no difference. Anyway he was sure. Whoever was coming out of the sangar wasn't a Burgher. The careless discarding of Christiaan's bugle had already proven that the victorious occupants were British. Until that heart stopping moment Piet had clung to a desperate hope that they were still alive. There were three shapes. He raised his rifle and fired just as a more cautious Burgher shouted the challenge *'Wie's daar?'* in an attempt to verify the identities of the shadowy figures.

One figure dropped as the other two ran forward. There was no response to the challenge but three men didn't normally constitute a charge against an entrenched enemy and there was no general response from the Boer line. In Piet's mind the situation was clear and he was frustrated at being the only one to respond to the situation. 'Shoot, damn you!' he berated the Burgher by his side with a sharp nudge of the elbow. There was no response and Piet had the fleeting impression that the man was sleeping until he saw the shrapnel hole in the back of his head and the dark red stain washing its way around his neck to the ground.

The figures were coming closer and Piet could now distinguish the rifles and bayonets they were carrying. He fired again and a second man fell. 'What's the matter with you all?' he cried. 'Why don't you shoot?' His answer came as he caught the movement of a few Burghers to his right, then more, until the line on both sides began to melt away. The sound of the pipes and the occasional shot far to his right announced the breach of the Burghers' line by the British. He looked animatedly around him. Apart from the dead and wounded there was hardly a Burgher left on the crest as far as his line of vision extended and the clump and clatter beyond it announced a general withdrawal.

He saw the third man, now clearly a *rooinek* soldier, reach the crest line to his left and bayonet first one startled Burgher, then leap over and skewer another as he turned to flee. He felt a tug at his sleeve. 'Come on. There's no point staying around to be bayoneted.' It was Coetzee, one of the Burghers from the sangar he had helped over the crest.

Piet looked ahead and then back at Coetzee. 'My son. My father.' It was all he could manage to say.

'You need to save yourself now. There will be a truce tomorrow to recover the bodies and bury the dead.'

Bury the dead. Piet had realised there was no hope for Christiaan and Koos but this cold, unemotional statement flooded him with despair. He felt no compulsion to flee, not because of any desire to continue fighting and killing, but because his spirit had been drained. He simply had neither the will nor the energy to continue. He sat on a rock.

'Look, van Oppen,' shouted Coetzee. 'Your father and your son were brave. They stayed behind in the sangar so that the rest of us could get away.' He looked disdainfully at Piet. 'Don't dishonour their memory.'

His father and son would be honoured as heroes of the *Volk*, a man and a boy who sacrificed their lives for others. He would be denied even that recognition because he had happened to survive. A wave of guilt flooded over him. He was the least worthy of the three van Oppens but he was the only one to survive. He looked at the increasingly anxious Coetzee. 'Why?' he asked plaintively.

The sound of the pipes was nearer and Coetzee was in no mood to discuss matters. 'If it wasn't for your father I wouldn't bother,' he said as he grabbed Piet's jacket collar and dragged him away. In his haste Coetzee slipped on the wet rocks and the pair of them slid and tumbled down the hillside until they hit a small outcrop. Apart from a few grazes they were unhurt but they were covered from head to foot in red slime. 'Come on,' he urged. 'Most of the others are ahead of us.'

Piet stopped to see the crazed Tommy shooting and bayoneting stragglers to their right. Occasionally a Burgher would shoot at him but he seemed to lead a charmed life. This man may have killed my son or my father, he thought. Maybe both of them. He wiped his muddy hands on his sodden jacket and raised his Mauser. The Tommy was an easy target and was not observing his flanks as he rushed after fleeing Burghers. He's either very brave or very stupid, thought Piet, but soon he would be very dead. As he got the Tommy in his sights his rifle was pushed upwards.

'We haven't got time for that,' said Coetzee. 'Let's go.' This time Piet didn't hesitate as kilted Highlanders appeared along the crest and fired into the fleeing mass of Burghers. He and Coetzee ran, jumped, slipped and slid down the hillside. More cuts and grazes from rocks and thorns. Gasping, wheezing, choking. No time to stop, no time to reflect. The deluge continued, assisting rather than hampering their descent as they sped downwards on their backsides whenever they lost their footing and by increasingly obscuring them from the view of the Highlanders. A few bullets hit the ground around them but the fire from the crest was sporadic and none of the Burghers fleeing with them seemed to be hit.

At the foot of the hill Piet stopped briefly to catch his breath. Coetzee was equally exhausted but signalled for them to continue. 'It won't be safe to stop even for a minute until we've crossed the *spruit*,' he panted. They ran on past two hobbling Burghers who either had not had time to retrieve their boots or had been unable to find where they had left them.

They regained their breath during the easier trot over the flat ground of the valley until they reached the *spruit*. A flash flood generated by the rainstorm had turned the ankle deep crossing they had negotiated the previous night into a raging torrent and Burghers were struggling across with difficulty. 'I hope you can swim,' said Piet. Coetzee didn't reply. Piet looked at him. 'You can't, can you?' Coetzee shook his head. Piet reflected that if it weren't for Coetzee he would probably be dead. I owe him a favour, he thought. Here's my chance to return it.

Coetzee hesitated when it was their turn. For the first time since he had dragged Piet from the crest Coetzee was not on top of the situation. 'It's not the width or even the depth that's the problem,' said Piet. 'It's the speed of the current. Just hang on to me.'

Piet gripped Coetzee's arm as he waded into the rushing current, edging slowly across until the water reached their necks near the middle. 'Don't let go,' pleaded Coetzee nervously, tilting his mouth clear of the freezing cold water that spun and splashed around their faces.

'Don't worry,' said Piet. He took careful steps on tiptoe. He could have made it across without much difficulty on his own but Coetzee was proving a physical burden and inhibiting his progress in the swirling water. He took another careful step but his foot slipped on a stone on the bed of the swollen *spruit* and their heads momentarily submerged. When they resurfaced Coetzee gasped for air and his reflex reaction was to lunge at Piet. They both went under again as Piet fought to free Coetzee's hands from around his neck. Coetzee was bigger than him to begin with and his natural strength was augmented by terror and panic.

Piet had not managed to take in much air before he had been dragged under and his lungs were bursting. Coetzee was flailing around next to him and he felt a kick in the stomach before they resurfaced for the second time. Despite gagging and choking, he managed a deeper breath this time before he went under again. Coetzee's head had hardly broken the surface and he was now the one with insufficient air in his lungs. He's going to kill us both, thought Piet as the eerie underwater silence and darkness enclosed on him. Even in this predicament he was struck by the irony of it all. His son and father had been killed in battle and he would be drowned. They would be acclaimed as heroes of the *Republiek* and he would be forgotten. He couldn't even die properly.

Another frantic tug by Coetzee sent them spinning upside down until the motion was reversed as the sudden restoration of his buoyancy propelled Piet to the surface. He gasped and coughed as the air rushed into his lungs before he floundered across to the other bank of the *spruit*. He clambered out and crouched on all fours, panting and spitting. Most Burghers ignored him in their haste to return to the safety of their lines but two from his own commando turned back to offer their help.

Still panting and wheezing, Piet's expression begged the question he was unable to articulate. 'You did your best,' said one of the Burghers sympathetically as they helped him to his feet. Piet looked back at the roaring water. More Burghers were making their way across but there was no sign of Coetzee.

'It was a brave effort,' said the other. Piet looked at him in inquisitive silence. 'He was washed away,' the Burgher continued.

'Probably hit his head on a rock,' said the first with a shrug.

Hunched, bedraggled and shivering with cold, Piet rejoined the exodus and plodded silently towards the Burghers' lines.

Since the early hours of the morning the attention of everyone at Intombi had been drawn to the sound of battle from Caesar's Camp and Wagon Hill. Sarah had kept herself continuously occupied doing her own work and helping out others in an attempt to shut her mind to the awful possibilities. Charles's battalion formed the first line of defence on Caesar's Camp and with their positions being nearest to the hospital camp the incessant noise of rifle fire had been clearly audible since before dawn.

'You've been very distracted today, Sarah,' said Tom as she tucked him back under the bedclothes. 'You've got something on your mind. Do you want to talk about it?' She was becoming concerned again for Tom. The bed sore he had developed was now the size of a florin but there was little that could be done for him apart from keeping the ulcer clean and changing the dressing each day.

'It's just the thought of all the wounded who will be coming in soon.' This was partly true but her main concern was for Charles. She had no way of telling how many wounded would be brought into Intombi. Dozens? Hundreds? She feared that Charles might be among them, crippled like Tom or maimed or disfigured. She had seen so many young men whose lives had been ruined. Tom seemed satisfied with her answer. She liked to think that neither he nor anyone else, apart from Ada and perhaps Joseph, knew about her relationship with Charles. Ladysmith, though, was an enclosed community where nothing could remain a secret for very long and this was especially so in the claustrophobic lines of Intombi.

The tent flap opened and Ada walked over and gently touched Sarah's hand. 'The first ones are arriving now,' she said softly. Sarah had kept her fears to herself but Ada sensed the concern eating away at her that would not go away until she was sure Charles was all right.

'I have to go now, Tom,' said Sarah. Tom wished her good luck for the arduous night's work that lay ahead but Sarah would be keeping an eye on the stream of incoming wounded while preparing for surgery those indicated by Dr. Barlow as being the most urgent cases.

She and Ada hurried over to the tent designated as the casualty reception area. The storm had abated but the churned up mud caked their boots and spattered their skirts. They heard the cries and groans of the wounded before they rounded a stores tent and headed for the illuminated entrance. A group of dhoolie bearers had arrived ahead of them with their fragile loads and more would be trotting through the mud and darkness throughout the night. 'Those poor boys,' said Ada.

Sarah heard her name called as soon as she entered the tent. 'Start tagging them,' said Dr. Barlow. He pointed to a man with a chest wound. 'This one's a priority.' She started writing out a tag. 'This one's a below the knee amputation,' he said, indicating a sergeant with a lacerated calf and a broken tibia. Sarah winced. It wasn't even a compound fracture and in a civilian hospital the limb would have been saved but they simply didn't have enough time to treat non life-threatening wounds without risking the lives of more critical cases. The man would be crippled for life not because of the wound itself but because he was not badly wounded enough. Barlow felt the pulse of the next man and pulled up an eyelid. 'This one's dead,' he said matter-of-factly, moving to the next case.

These men were a mixture of Rifles, Light Horse and Engineers. There was none from Charles's battalion. Nobody she could ask about him. She looked over to where Ada was comforting a badly wounded young trooper of the Light Horse, a boy from the same regiment as the monster who had raped and murdered her own daughter. Tears ran down Ada's cheeks as she held his hand and stroked his face and hair. Sarah felt a stab of pity for this fine woman. The trooper's regimental collar badge alone must have evoked an abhorrent image and this time she was doubtless crying for her murdered daughter as well as for this wounded boy and her son on active service. Sarah had volunteered for service in a field or stationary hospital out of a sense of patriotic duty but her original idealism had faded in recent weeks and sights like this made her angry and frustrated. While the politicians played their games on a grand scale, the young men of Britain and her empire were dying and suffering under such appalling conditions and the lives of innocent people were being destroyed.

Before Barlow had completed checking the first batch of wounded the tent flap opened, announcing the arrival of another. 'Nurse Dyson, go and identify the worst cases while I finish off here.'

Sarah ran over as the men were laid out in a neat line. Her heart started to pound as she saw their insignia. They were from Charles's battalion. She was bursting to ask those who were conscious if they had seen Charles and if they knew whether or not he was all right but her immediate priority was to help these wounded men. She moved quickly down the line assessing their injuries. There was the usual mixture. Men with chest wounds who might survive, others with head or stomach wounds who almost certainly would not and those with shattered limbs who would invariably suffer amputation.

'Miss,' called a man with a bloodied and shattered arm as she moved on. She didn't really have time to stop. 'Miss,' he called again.

'Yes?' she responded.

'Have you seen Private Clements? Billy Clements. He's my pal.' She replied that she hadn't but would look out for him. 'Our section got hit by one of our own artillery shells,' he added disconsolately. 'I haven't seen him since.'

There would be many cases of soldiers looking for their friends in the confusion following a battle, thought Sarah. This boy's quest was no different from her own. He was in the same battalion and was coherent. She seized the opportunity. 'Have you seen Corporal Browell? Do you know if he's all right?'

His face lit up in recognition. 'Ah, Charlie Browell!'

This was more than she had dared hope for. 'Is he all right?' she asked anxiously.

'I don't know. I haven't seen him.'

'What do you mean you haven't seen him?' queried Sarah impatiently. 'You just indicated that you had.'

'Oh, everyone in the battalion knows Charlie Browell,' replied the soldier absently. 'Great fellow. They tried to stitch him up on a murder charge but he got off. He's famous, you know.'

Sarah's spirits sank. The young soldier was in shock and it wasn't fair to press him like this but she was desperate for any information on Charles. 'Don't you have any idea how he is?'

The soldier seemed lost in thought for a few seconds then looked up. 'He's in 'D' company, miss. They were in the front line and took a hell of a pasting, if you'll pardon my French.' Sarah's head dropped. 'I'm sorry, miss.'

This vital but unwelcome piece of news made her yearn to see him among the wounded. His company must have taken heavy casualties and at least then she would know for sure that he was still alive. Barlow arrived at her shoulder. 'Hopeless,' he said, indicating the unconscious man he had just seen. 'Give him some morphine so he can die painlessly.' He made a cursory examination of the mangled arm of Sarah's informant. 'Amputation,' he said as he moved to the next case.

Frank wandered around the darkened plateau with a lantern looking for Charlie and Walter as they had done when searching for him at Elandslaagte but there were no answers to his calls. He concentrated his search in a zigzag pattern between the crest and the sangars as he was unsure of his bearings and had been unable to locate the point from where they had charged the crest. He saw the faint specks of two lanterns about a hundred yards away and followed their light that led him to a sangar. As he walked around the side he could make out the shortened wall.

Three men were removing bodies. 'We've got a real case here,' said one of them as he entered the emplacement.

'How do you mean?' asked Frank.

'His hands were so tight round this Boer's throat we've had to cut them off.' In the light of the lantern he saw the raw stumps of McAdams's arms as his body was dropped on a stretcher and the severed hands still gripping the dead Boer's throat. The man gave a mocking laugh at the shocked expression on Frank's face in the lamplight. Frank unsheathed his bloodied bayonet and launched himself at the man, pressing the tip of the blade into his throat. The other two started to move but stopped when they realised Frank might just be crazy enough to kill him.

'He was a friend of mine,' said Frank. 'A friend and a brave man who fought on and died after being badly wounded.'

'I didn't mean anything by it,' croaked the man, fearing the slightest movement may puncture his windpipe with or without any further pressure from Frank.

'That's right,' said one of the others in a conciliatory tone. 'It's standard procedure. This type of thing doesn't happen very often but I've seen it a couple of times before.'

Frank relaxed his pressure on the bayonet and the man staggered backwards, rubbing his throat where the skin had been broken. 'I'm looking for Corporal Browell and Private Shawcross,' said Frank. 'Have you seen either of them?' They muttered in the negative.

'We've just been clearing the sangars so far,' said one. 'There must be more in front and behind. We haven't got that far yet.'

Frank picked up his lantern and continued his search.

Only the chirping sparrows flitting among the acacias broke the silence as the battalion stood to attention around two great rectangular holes in the earth. It was uncomfortably hot again and a bead of perspiration trickled down either side of Frank's temple. The violent storm of the previous afternoon had cleared during the evening and the desperate battle was history. So were the lives of the men whose cotton shrouded bodies were laid in neat rows in the mass graves on the plateau allotted for the battalion's dead.

Frank swallowed as his mind flooded with recollections of the three friends' lives together. They had been inseparable since childhood when the distortion of memory bequeathed an image of life as a succession of sunny summer days when they ran and played and stole apples from the trees in the vicar's garden. Now the lifelong bond that had seemed so inviolate had been broken on a South African hillside so far from the familiar homeliness of their Manchester.

Frank wrestled with the complexities of fate. If Walter had stayed at Cheetham and Betts, if only he hadn't got that girl pregnant, he would still be alive. Better a shotgun wedding than a shotgun, he thought ruefully but it was too late for 'what ifs'.

'Guard of honour,' shouted the sergeant-major after the chaplain had concluded the service and sprinkled a handful of the red earth into each pit. 'Present arms!' Frank gave a rueful smile. The guard of honour had been selected from the two companies that had sustained the bulk of the casualties and Walter had died owing money to at least three of them. He must be laughing his socks off up there, thought Frank.

Charlie said his own silent prayer for Walter, the character, the joker, the chancer, his friend. He had always felt that Walter was the most resilient and resourceful of the three and that if any one of them was going to be successful in life it would be him. But it wasn't to be.

The Medical Officer had tried in vain to persuade Charlie to rest on the day of the funeral and, when that failed, attempted to discourage him from being in the guard of honour. The M.O. had even appealed to Captain Young who had sent him packing. Charlie's forehead was still sore where the fragments of stone had sprayed into his face and gashed him when the bullet hit the sangar wall but his concussion had gone. He had hoped to be sent down to Intombi so that he might see Sarah but his wound had been neatly sutured up by the M.O. at the battalion's field dressing station. It had only dawned on him afterwards that this wound had probably saved his life as Walter had been killed only moments later.

'Aim,' shouted the sergeant-major. The rifles pointed skywards. 'Fire!' The noise of the volley sent the sparrows in a twittering panic in all directions. Twice more they fired before the digging parties started to shovel earth into the graves.

We don't even know which one is Walter, thought Charlie, or McAdams for that matter. They all looked so uniform and anonymous bound in those shrouds. He also said a silent prayer for McAdams, a tormented and misunderstood man but a brave and loyal soldier all the same. It was McAdams who had led the charge into the sangar despite being in unimaginable pain from his wound. Charlie had already been convinced that McAdams had felt he was living on borrowed time but now also wondered if the man had carried a kind of death wish ever since Colour Sergeant Reid had died. It wasn't so much that he had wanted to die but in hindsight it was almost as if he didn't care.

'Do you want me to write to Walter's parents on our behalf?' asked Charlie as the battalion was dismissed.

'I'll write,' said Frank firmly.

'Good', said Charlie. That was what he had hoped Frank would say. 'We'll both write.'

A clumping of shoes and squeals of excitement on the *stoep* reached the kitchen where Sannie van Oppen was supervising one of the domestics baking bread. The lace curtains flapped lazily by the open sash window and the aroma of freshly baked loaves drifted outside and hung in the hot summer air. She peered outside but from the window all she could see were the three girls clustered by the far corner rail of the verandah.

'What's going on?' she shouted but the girls either hadn't heard her or were pretending not to have. 'Katrien!' she called the eldest. 'What are you and the twins getting excited about?' It was no use. She would have to find out for herself. Wiping her floured hands on a towel she pushed the swing door open and walked down the verandah. A board creaked and sagged beneath her feet. Another job that needed doing. Since the men of the house had been on commando she had been consumed by the responsibility of running the farm on top of her normal workload in and around the house. She felt tired all the time and to cap it all at the age of thirty-eight she was four months pregnant with her sixth child. She hadn't yet told Piet in her letters. He had enough to worry about with Christiaan on commando.

A red and black butterfly fluttered across her path and settled on one of the azaleas beyond the rail of the *stoep*. They were everywhere at this time of year but it wouldn't have been the whimsical flights of butterflies that had captured the girls' attention in this way. 'Katrien!' she called again impatiently.

Katrien turned round. 'Ma, come quickly!' she shouted. She wore the full black dress covered by a white smock that was almost obligatory for the daughters of Burghers but at seventeen she was fast developing into a woman. They would soon be looking for a suitable husband for her. Sannie had already had her eye on Kobus Viljoen but the war had taken him. Perhaps one of his brothers.

Marie and Hendrina were jumping up and down excitedly by the rail as she quickened her stride. 'Look, ma,' said Katrien pointing to a horseman approaching slowly from the distance. 'It's pa!' Sannie continued wiping her hands absentmindedly while she absorbed the scene. She flicked a wisp of hair back over her head. The girls were consumed with joy at the unexpected return of their father but something was wrong. The girls ran to the steps of the verandah, jumped to the ground below and ran towards the lone horseman.

My God, thought Sannie as she tried to reason why Piet would be leading two other horses. 'Girls!' she shouted. 'Wait a moment.' It was too late. They had gone. Sannie dropped the towel and ran after them, then stopped as she felt a flicker of icy discomfort in her abdomen. With closed eyes she took a deep breath and followed at a brisk walk.

The girls' run slowed to a walk and then, as the hideous truth struck home, they stopped altogether staring silently at the forlorn figure of their father and then at the sackcloth bundle tied over each of the spare horses. Piet dismounted and hugged each of his daughters in turn. 'What happened, pa?' asked Katrien. Piet didn't answer as Sannie threw herself into his arms and they hugged each other silently for a full minute. Marie and Hendrina started to cry and Katrien stood at her father's shoulder waiting to hear him speak.

'Christiaan and your father,' Sannie said at last. She hardly dared utter the words she knew to be true. 'They're dead.'

'Yes,' Piet whispered hoarsely. It was the first time he had spoken in the five days since he had left the Burghers' camp outside Ladysmith.

'In battle?' asked Sannie. Piet nodded.

'Did they suffer?'

He shook his head. 'They were very brave. Everyone in the commando said so.'

She would cry and mourn for her Christiaan but right now she needed to be strong for Piet. Sannie touched her stomach. New life for old. She had news to tell Piet. Happier news. But there would be another time for that too. She called for two of the farmhands to tether the horses and unload their sad burdens, took Piet's hand and led him up the steps and inside the farmhouse followed by their weeping daughters. She loved this good and honest man in spite of his weaknesses and knew exactly what he was thinking. He was wishing he was dead and Christiaan was alive.

'You've come for a view of the action, have you, sir,' said Second Lieutenant Bennett over his shoulder. He introduced himself and handed Young the field glasses.

'I'm Captain Young and this is Sergeant Browell.' There was an embarrassed silence. 'Yes, the same Young and Browell from the court martial,' added Young, raising the glasses to his eyes. 'Is that a problem for you?'

'No, sir. Not at all,' replied Bennett. Charlie had baulked at Young's suggestion to go over to the Light Horse lines at the opposite end of the plateau on Wagon Hill to try to catch a glimpse of General Buller's second attempt to break through the Boer lines and relieve the town. Young had promptly amended his suggestion to an order.

'Good,' said Young. Charlie was uncomfortable at the thought of being among the Light Horsemen even though Young had assured him that the general feeling among the regiment was that Turnbull had been a bastard of the first order and had deserved to die for what he had done.

'Captain Turnbull was my squadron commander, sir,' said Bennett awkwardly. 'Nevertheless, I must say that justice was done. No one here wanted to see a man condemned for a crime he didn't commit.'

'There, Browell. What did I tell you?' said Young. On reflection Charlie felt foolish. The Light Horse was a distinguished regiment full of brave and honourable men who had fought with the same distinction on Wagon Hill as they had done side by side with his own battalion at Elandslaagte. Turnbull had never belonged here.

'I see you're a sergeant now, Browell,' said Bennett.

'Yes, sir.' There had been more gaps in the ranks of the NCOs after the battle on Caesar's Camp although Young had taken pains to assure Charlie that this promotion was more of an immediate reward for his gallantry and leadership. Frank had been pleased for him but Charlie felt sorry for Frank who had received no recognition. Under the circumstances he felt that Frank should at least have been appointed lance corporal.

'Over there,' said Young, pointing at a large round-topped hill in the distance and handing Charlie the field glasses. 'Spion Kop. Tell me what you see.'

'Lots of exploding shells on the summit, sir.'

'Yes, but are they ours or theirs?'

'That's been the scene all day, sir, but we can't tell for certain,' chipped in Bennett. 'We can only hope for the best.'

'The General Officer Commanding in Ladysmith is optimistic enough,' said Young. Full rations had been reinstated earlier in the day in anticipation of the relief force's success, partly to boost morale and partly to help restore the defenders' depleted strength that would probably be needed for more strenuous fighting when the breakthrough came.

'What's that cloud of dust, sir?' said Charlie.

Bennett took the field glasses. 'It must be caused by the movement of wagons and judging by the size of the cloud a lot of them. The Boers must be in retreat!'

Young peered through the glasses amid general jubilation among the other officers and NCOs who had interpreted the dust cloud in the same way. Young thanked Bennett and handed the glasses back to him. 'Let's go,' he said to Charlie.

'Is anything the matter, sir?' asked Charlie, perplexed by their hasty departure.

'There's no point arguing the toss with them while they're in such an elated mood but I also saw men marching ahead of the wagons.'

Charlie didn't follow. 'Sir?'

'Boers don't march, Browell. They ride horses. Those are our men taken prisoner by the Boers and the wagons are merely returning to their original *laagers*.'

'So there'll be no relief tomorrow, sir?' It was a statement rather than a question.

'Tomorrow we all go back on half rations.'

Ladysmith
February 1900

It was a recurring dream and the ephemeral subconscious pleasure it provided served only to heighten the sense of deprivation and disappointment when she awoke. Sarah swung her legs over her cot in the tent she shared with ten other nurses and volunteer assistants and rubbed her eyes.

She had been immersed in a hot bath, the water sprinkled with delicate essences whose fleeting trace odours she imagined she could still sense as she adjusted to the real world. The exquisitely perfumed soap with which she sensuously caressed her body and the glass of chilled champagne she sipped as she lay would be rare extravagances in real life anyway but represented a luxurious ideal which contrasted so vividly with the scarcity of essentials at Intombi.

She looked over at Ada who was still asleep but several of the other nurses had stirred in the darkness. Sarah lit the stub of a candle, hung its lantern on the pole by the entrance and stood looking at the star filled sky. It was only then that she realised what had disturbed her exquisite dream.

'General Buller's on the move again,' she said to a nurse who had joined her. The distant grumble of artillery announced the beginning of yet another attempt to relieve Ladysmith.

'I thought it was another thunderstorm at first.' The nurse rubbed her eyes and yawned. 'I'm sure he'll break through this time, Sarah.'

'Third time lucky, you mean?'

'I suppose so,' she said, unconvincingly.

'We'll see.' Sarah held her watch up to the flickering light of the lantern. 'Three twenty.' She was back on duty at six and the artillery barrage would continue until after dawn. There would be no point trying to get back to sleep now. The light of two more lanterns illuminated the tent as other nurses whose rest had been disturbed reluctantly hauled themselves out of bed and started to move about. She walked over to one of her ward tents outside which Joseph slept when the weather was dry. She expected to see him curled up in his usual spot tucked between the guy ropes and the outer canvas but only his crumpled blanket was there.

'*Sawubona*, Miss Sarah.'

Sarah jumped. 'Joseph. You startled me.'

'I'm sorry, Miss Sarah. I didn't mean to. I knew you would be awake so I went for your water.' He held up a large bowl filled from the Service Corps's kettles. Joseph had become a popular figure throughout the hospital camp. He was a willing worker and nothing was too much trouble for him. He also continued to risk his life running the mails and would always bring back small treats of sugar or sweetmeats whenever he made a delivery to Zachariah Dunkley. He waddled over to Sarah's tent and deposited the heavy bowl inside the entrance.

Sarah scooped two jugfuls into an enamel bowl on a trestle table in the middle of the tent and rubbed the hot water into her face and arms. Even carbolic soap was a forgotten luxury for personal hygiene, the dwindling supply having been reserved for use in the operating theatre tents and for washing the fever patients' bedding. She peered into the mirror hanging on the central supporting pole and in the light of its lantern saw a face she barely recognised. Her face had been burned red-brown and her hair had become dried and tangled by the sun and a lack of soap.

She had been off duty less than four hours but despite the fatigue of the increased workload and insufficient food Sarah knew that there would be no respite until the relief – the blessed, longed for relief – of the town. She had slept in her clothes and hurried directly over to her first ward tent. Like all the other nurses she had shortened her skirts to keep them out of the mud and dust but the lower part was still ingrained with the grime that soapless washing could never remove.

'Anything to report?' she asked the duty nurse. They had already lost the fever patient in the bed next to Tom before she had retired the previous evening but it would soon be filled with another. At least most of those wounded in the battle on Caesar's Camp and Wagon Hill were now convalescent.

'One more died in the night,' said the nurse. 'The Jack Tar,' she added simply. Sarah glanced down the tightly packed rows. There were no empty beds. 'We had two more admissions an hour ago,' said the nurse, reading her mind. 'Both enteric cases.'

Sarah took a lantern and went to the bed she last saw occupied by the sailor where a young infantryman with wispy brown hair now lay. He was feverish but restful so she moved towards the end of the opposite row where Tom also appeared to be sleeping peacefully. She bobbed down beside the new admission's bed and held the lantern above his head. She let out an involuntary gasp and clasped her hand over her mouth. She hadn't seen Charles since Christmas and at first was more distressed by his gaunt face and the fresh scar on his forehead than by his fevered condition. She had been desperate to see him again but their frequent exchange of letters had not prepared her for the sight that now met her eyes. After the initial shock she stroked his hot brow and wondered why she had been surprised. Rations had been reduced for the whole garrison and everyone had lost weight but this had clearly been less noticeable among people who saw each other daily. Charles hadn't mentioned his wound, slight though it was, and it occurred to her that he probably hadn't told her anything he feared might cause her undue anxiety. In his letters he had told her precious little about the battle except that they had driven the Boers off but his friend Walter had tragically been killed.

She tried to assess his chances. Overall they were fairly good. The hospital that was designed for three hundred patients now held two thousand, mostly enteric and dysentery cases. Despite the congestion and lack of supplies the survival rate, albeit with the possibility of chronic debility, was about seventy-five percent. She had to hang on to this hope.

'Is there anything wrong, Sarah?' It was the duty nurse.

'I know this man,' she said softly.

'We'll all do everything we can for him.'

'I know. Thank you.' Sarah took comfort from the fact that this nurse's own brother was convalescing from a bout of enteric.

Tom's arm twitched and he let out a low groan. 'I'll see to him,' said the nurse. She felt his brow. 'He's burning up. I'll fetch Dr. Barlow.'

'Still the same,' said Ada.

Sarah nodded. 'Thank you.' Her obligation of duty towards all of her patients prevented her from spending any more time with either Charles or Tom than was justified but Ada was able to pay closer attention to them when she was busy elsewhere.

Rations had been reduced again after General Buller's relief force had failed to breach the Boer positions at Vaal Krantz the week before and this meal was far sparser than was good for sick and convalescent men. 'You take care of Charlie and Tom,' said Ada. 'The other nurses and I will see to the rest.' Sarah gave her a weary smile of gratitude. She had hardly slept since Charles and Tom had both gone down with enteric and spent most of her meagre off duty hours by their bedsides.

'Time for your Chevril, my boys,' said Ada with forced cheeriness, carrying mugs of substitute beef tea to those who could feed themselves. The rumour Tom had heard the previous month had been correct. Cavalry horses were being slaughtered daily at a makeshift processing plant in a shed at the railway station. Minced horsemeat was served to the garrison and the extract had been christened Chevril, being the equine equivalent of the famous Bovril. Under normal circumstances even hardened soldiers would have turned their noses up at horsemeat but the garrison was close to starvation and there wasn't even enough horsemeat to fill their bellies.

Sarah sat carefully on the side of Charles's bed and dribbled diluted condensed milk into his mouth from a feeder cup. Fresh, clean water and milk were absolute requirements for an enteric patient to have any chance of recovery. He recognised her and tried to speak but no words came out. 'Don't stir yourself, my love,' whispered Sarah. 'Just drink your milk.' His face was flushed and he was hot and agitated. Sarah tried to calm him. 'Steady, Charles,' she said, her hand gently holding his.

There was no crisis with enteric as there was with some other fevers but the next two weeks would be critical. If he was still alive after then he would recover but there was a long way to go. She knew the progression of the disease. Now in the second week, the inflamed patches at the lower end of his intestine would be casting off, leaving open ulcers, and his spleen would be soft and enlarged. Milk and milk products were the only food he could digest. Anything more solid could trigger off the already significant risk of haemorrhage. She finished feeding him the milk but despite his fever he managed to indicate that it was not enough.

'More.' It was an effort to gasp just a single word. Sarah knew what he was going through. It wasn't just the insufficient nourishment. His mouth was dry and he had an almost insatiable thirst.

'There is no more, my love,' she whispered. He tried to reach her but sank back into the pillow, exhausted by even this small effort. 'Steady, Charles,' she soothed, stroking his hair. It was soaking and his pillow was saturated. She turned it knowing that it would be equally saturated within a matter of minutes, wiped his brow and made him as comfortable as possible. 'I must attend to Tom now, Charles. Rest easy.'

Because of the coincidence of their sickness Tom's symptoms were at the same stage as Charlie's. Beneath his shirt isolated pink spots had erupted across his chest and abdomen, scattered between the faint blue blotches that marked the progression of the disease. He had the same flushed face and was soaking with perspiration.

'Sarah,' he gasped as she tried to feed him his milk. 'Trust me to get sick in hospital.' It was an effort to speak and he had to take several breaths before he had the energy to swallow the milk. Sarah marvelled at him. By rights he should have died of his wounds two or three months before but he was a fighter. She hoped that Charles would fight as hard and that they would both emerge safely from their present ordeal.

'Eight shillings for a tin of condensed milk!' exclaimed Ada, who had gone into town to check on the house and try to find a few bits and pieces. 'Eight shillings! It's disgraceful!' Sarah had to agree that it was a ridiculous amount of money for such a basic commodity but there was precious little of anything left in Ladysmith now. The cheerful optimism of Christmas and New Year and the disappointments of the triple failure of the relief column to break through had served to deplete the reserves of luxuries and necessities alike. Fabled, though ever diminishing, quantities of champagne had been consumed by the cavalry officers when Buller moved against the Boer positions at Colenso, Spion Kop and Vaal Krantz. Now there was none left or if there was it was being well hidden.

'It's a pity,' said Sarah. 'We could have made good use of some.'

Ada pulled a large tin out of her bag. 'It's a scandal all right,' she said sheepishly. 'But I bought some anyway.'

Sarah squealed with delight. 'Oh, Ada, you shouldn't have.'

'I know, but I did. If it helps get your patients better then it will have been worth every penny.'

Sarah planted a kiss on Ada's once podgy cheek and noticed for the first time how much weight she had lost. 'Thank you, Ada,' she said. 'This will last a tent full of enteric patients a whole day once we've diluted it.'

'*Sanibona.*' They turned round at the sound of Joseph's voice and met the flashing white teeth of his famous grin. They returned his greeting. 'I am running the mail again tonight, *nkosikazi*,' he said to Ada. 'Miss Sarah says you have a letter for *Mnumzana* Dunkley.'

Ada rummaged in her bag and produced a tiny folded square of paper. Like others among the besieged she had become proficient at miniaturising her handwriting while maintaining its legibility. In the aftermath of the failed breakthrough at Vaal Krantz the Boers had been on heightened alert and the runners had been unable to breach their lines. This was the first mail run for ten days and she was anxious to hear from her husband, especially as his last letter contained the news that Ralph had been spotted with a Carbineer patrol. Her son was alive and well but there had been another battle since then.

Joseph pocketed the letter. When the time came he would wrap Ada's letter and the other one he had been commissioned to carry in separate pieces of paper and fold them inside his mouth. The Boers had got wise to the reed trick and anyone seen carrying a reed would be shot on sight.

'I believe the rate is one guinea,' said Ada, fumbling for her purse. 'Unless it's gone up again like everything else in this town,' she added with a chuckle. Humour in adversity was to be admired in any case but it struck Sarah immediately that this was the first time she had seen Ada laugh since the tragedy some two months before.

'No charge, *nkosikazi*,' said Joseph holding his hands palms outwards against his chest. This had become a regular ritual. Ada always offered to pay and Joseph always declined but Ada never took for granted the free passage of her mail. 'Is there anything I can do for you, Miss Sarah?'

Sarah held up the tin of condensed milk. 'A few more of these wouldn't go amiss.' she said, laughing at the thought. Joseph grinned back. '*Salani kahle,*' he said as he turned to leave. 'See you tomorrow.'

The stores corporal looked him up and down and stared back at the requisition in disbelief. 'Since when does the British army issue supplies to niggers?' He called over to a colleague. 'Here, Norman, what do you make of this?'

Norman studied the requisition, looking up at Joseph twice before handing it back to his colleague. 'I don't know, Wilf,' he said with a shrug. 'It looks genuine enough.'

'Where did you get this?' asked Wilf with no attempt to disguise his suspicion and hostility. Joseph went through the sequence of events, still bewildered that anyone could question an order issued by a British officer. The supplies officer at Intombi had had no hesitation in issuing Joseph with a requisition for six large tins of condensed milk for the fever patients and even commended him for his initiative and courage in making the suggestion in the first place. In Ladysmith he had a particular status but once through the siege lines he was truly back in the white man's world. He had come to the conclusion that once the siege was lifted his efforts would be quickly forgotten and when this white man's war was over he would revert to being an inconsequential kaffir.

'It is for the sick soldiers in Ladysmith,' repeated Joseph, unable to comprehend how this uniformed non-combatant who went to sleep every night with a full belly could deny his stricken comrades the basic nourishment they needed to survive.

'I'll give you sick soldiers,' snarled Wilf, thumping the table. He struck through the requisition with his pencil and dropped into his out tray. 'Now get out of here before I kick your arse you thieving little nigger.' He rose from his seat threateningly when Joseph made no move to leave the supplies tent.

'Anything the problem?' came a voice from behind Joseph. Wilf and Norman stood to attention and saluted. The tall young officer returned their salute and approached the table. '*Sawubona*, Joseph.'

Joseph beamed with delight at the familiar face he had not seen for so long. '*Sawubona*, Master Ralph.'

'I've heard many good things about you, Joseph,' said Ralph. 'My father has told me all about your mail runs and the evidence you gave at the court martial. You've conducted yourself very bravely and been of priceless service to my family. It's only because of you that my parents have managed to stay in touch with each other during the siege.'

'I have just come from your father at Estcourt,' said Joseph delightedly. He brandished the equally tiny square of paper on which Zachariah Dunkley had proudly announced Ralph's recent commission to Ada. 'I delivered your mother's letter to him and here is his reply. She will have it in the morning.' Joseph assured Ralph that his mother was well and waited patiently while he wrote a note to her on a scrap of paper. Joseph knew that nothing else in the world would mean as much to her as these few lines from her son.

'Now then,' said Ralph as Joseph pocketed the note. 'What seems to be the problem?' Wilf stumbled through the reasons why he believed the requisition was bogus and added his opinion that all niggers were born thieves. Even Joseph was taken aback by the explosive outburst that followed. It was as untypical of the normally urbane and unflappable Master Ralph as it was vaguely familiar. Ralph laid into the hapless store clerks without mercy. 'This young fellow has risked his life on many occasions to bring mail into and out of Ladysmith while you two have sat on your arses pushing bits of paper about.' He grabbed the requisition from the tray and thrust it in front of Wilf. 'Now get this fulfilled immediately!' He cracked his riding crop on the table to emphasise his anger and impatience then pulled another requisition from his pocket and slapped that on the table. 'And while you're at it you can bring me a new stirrup leather.' Joseph smirked as the clerks rushed off to fulfil the requisitions with all haste. Master Ralph wasn't prepared to suffer fools gladly and delighted in discomforting pompous and malevolently stupid people. He was just like his mother.

Joseph rested against the steep wall of a partially dried up streambed, panting for breath in the sultry night air. He had begun to wonder if it was such a good idea volunteering to carry a sackful of condensed milk back to Intombi. There were only six large tins in the sack but the burden was heavy over thirteen miles of rough ground and on reduced rations his strength had diminished along with his weight over the long weeks of the siege. He lay on the sack and gazed up at the sky. At least the moon was obscured by the cloud cover. It would probably start to rain before morning. He was very tired and quickly drifted into an exhausted sleep.

The snort of a horse beyond the opposite bank jolted him from his slumber and he was instantly alert. The mist and drizzle subdued the first light of dawn but he had to think fast. He could make a run for it or stay where he was and hope that he would not be discovered. If he ran he would have to abandon the milk. That would mean letting down Miss Sarah. If they caught him with the two letters folded in his mouth they would kill him anyway. He was too tired and too weak to be sure of running to safety. He decided he would have to take his chances here and squeezed into the concavity of the bank.

The soft plod of the horse's hooves approached the bank and stopped. There was only one of them. He heard the rider dismount. *'Werda?'* The unanswered challenge was repeated and Joseph heard the click of the rifle bolt as a cartridge slipped into the magazine. He could see nothing from his huddled position in the early morning gloom but heard the rider drop into the streambed to his right front. He carefully took out one of the condensed milk tins and adjusted his position. There was no sound as the rider cautiously rounded a bend and came into sight, progressing slowly down the middle of the streambed, only the faintest splash of his boots in the lazy trickle of water breaking the silence. He stopped close enough to touch but was looking directly ahead and hadn't seen Joseph in the recess of the bank. Joseph let his gaze wander slowly up the figure from his black boots, brown corduroy trousers and black jacket criss-crossed with bandoliers. He looked every part the Boer except for one thing. Beneath the brown felt hat was a face as black as Joseph's own. Joseph had heard about these *agterryers*, camp followers attached to small groups of Boers on commando. Their principal function was the performance of menial tasks but they were often armed like this one and lost no opportunity to prove their loyalty to their Boer masters. Joseph could expect no mercy from him.

Joseph clenched the tin and smashed it as hard as he could against the rider's knee, his legs buckling as he sank on his other knee with a yelp of pain. His face crumpled with the shock of the blow, he looked up just in time to see Joseph spring out of the recess and bowl him over. He was bigger than Joseph but the young Zulu had the advantage of surprise. He struck the heavy tin against the *agterryer's* head and a trickle of blood oozed from a gash on his temple. Joseph straddled the fallen figure and as he raised the tin for a second blow the rider shouted at Joseph first in Dutch and then in a language he didn't understand. The tin crashed down. '*Sotho! Sotho!*' he cried desperately in an effort to make himself understood while trying to buck Joseph off him. So he's a Basuto, thought Joseph as he struck his head a third time, spawning another trail of blood. It would make no difference if he were a Zulu. Right now he's my enemy and he'll kill me if I don't kill him. He felt weak and light-headed. In spite of the injuries he had inflicted on him, Joseph knew that if he didn't finish the Basuto off now it would only be a short time before his energy would be spent and he would be overpowered. Garnering his remaining strength for one final effort he gripped the tin in both hands and pounded the Basuto's head.

The struggle ceased. Joseph wondered if he might be shamming but it would have made no difference. He no longer had the strength to defend himself. He rose slowly from the Basuto's prone figure and tossed the dented tin into the sack, twisting it at the neck as he slung it over his shoulder. The drizzle had lingered but it was now fully light and he had to get as far away as possible before the *agterryer* was missed. The Basuto's legs twitched in a convulsive dance much as he imagined the witch doctors of his grandfathers' tales had done in the old days when they would smell out *abaThakathi* in ritual purges of sorcery among the clans. The Basuto was still alive – just – but he no longer posed a threat to him.

With aching limbs and throbbing head, Joseph clambered up the bank and grabbed the rein of the Basuto's horse. He raised his foot into the stirrup and swung himself over the saddle, gripping the sack over its neck. He kicked the horse into a steady canter and crouching low in the saddle headed for Ladysmith whose tin roofed buildings beckoned in the distance. Despite his fatigue he couldn't help being struck by the irony of a death struggle between two black men in a white man's war.

'This one's taken a few knocks,' said Sarah brightly as she emptied the tins from the sack in the ward tent. The unexpected supply of six tins of condensed milk was a wonderful surprise.

'Accident,' said Joseph with a shrug.

Sarah thanked Joseph effusively. 'I know the risks you've run to bring this for us,' she added. He was pleased that Miss Sarah appreciated his efforts. He just wished other people did. As he was strutting proudly down Murchison Street on his newly acquired horse, a remount officer had grabbed its bridle and commandeered the animal.

She instructed one of the orderlies to dilute the condensed milk while she walked over to the first ward tent to check on Charles, Tom and the other patients. The early morning drizzle was clearing and the emerging sun promised another stifling hot day. She flicked away a cluster of flies hovering around her head. It was a pointless gesture. They would not be deterred that easily. A gang of Indian gravediggers making the their way back from the camp cemetery, their spades balanced on their shoulders in a pathetic parody of military precision, passed a handcart containing three shrouded bodies being pulled in the opposite direction. The freshly dug holes in the ground would not stay empty for long.

Ada greeted her at the tent entrance. 'It looks like General Buller is trying the back road into Ladysmith this time,' she said, cocking her head in the direction of the artillery fire.

'We live in hope,' said Sarah flatly. Word had spread that the relief force was attempting to break through by a different route and was slowly progressing through the chain of hills hugging the banks of the Tugela River to the south of the town. The optimism of the besieged had waxed and waned with the sound of the artillery bombardments on the heights. Sometimes it sounded close and ferocious, on other occasions distant and feeble. 'Our priority is the care of our patients,' continued Sarah. 'The sick and wounded aren't going to get better just because General Buller marches into town. We'll be here for some weeks after any relief.'

'Come on, Sarah,' said Ada brightly. 'Keep positive. I'm sure General Buller will succeed this time.' Sarah gave a wry smile in response to Ada's encouragement. That was the difference between the two women. Ada was desperate for the relief of the town so that she would be reunited with her husband and son. The thought of that joyous day was the only thing that kept her going. Sarah was as anxious as anyone for the siege to be lifted but her loved one was already with her and her immediate personal concern was Charles's recovery.

Sarah had managed to snatch less than three hours sleep during the night. She was unable to share Ada's optimism about the relief but her spirits had been raised when there had still been no empty beds in either of her tents when she had last looked in during the early hours of the morning. As she walked down the first row another nurse smiled and gave her a thumbs up sign. It was the first time in nearly three weeks that they had had no deaths during the night.

For Charles and Tom this was a critical time. Tom was fighting the disease as he had fought against the wounds to which almost any other man would have succumbed long before but after two bad days and nights punctuated by bouts of delirium she had become increasingly concerned for Charles. He looked more peaceful now, his shallow breathing occasionally catching in his open mouth. She pressed her forefingers against his wrist. The pulse was fast but weak. A muscle in his arm twitched involuntarily and his leg jerked beneath the bedclothes. He mumbled an incoherent word. Then again, more clearly. 'Sarah.'

She leaned forward and whispered softly in his ear. 'I love you.' He nodded. This exhausted and emaciated figure was barely conscious but he was aware of her presence and she was heartened by his response to her words of love. Another two days, three at most, and he would be over the worst of it, she thought. Then he would spend a few weeks convalescing before he was either posted back to his unit or invalided home after the siege was lifted. Either way they would part company sooner or later but she could live with that providing their separation would be only temporary.

'Sarah.' She turned round at the sound of Tom's voice and was thankful that his mother was spared the sight of the crippled, hollow eyed wraith that met her eyes. He was fully conscious but very weak. 'Sarah, fetch my tin from under the bed please.' She pulled out the yellow tobacco tin and offered it to him. The picture on the lid of the robust, bearded sailor enjoying his pipe contrasted sharply with the sickly young Highlander who lay before her. 'No,' he said. 'You open it.' Sarah prised off the lid to reveal the pathetic contents that represented Tom's entire possessions on campaign. There was a locket that may have contained a photograph of a sweetheart but more likely of his mother, a folded letter, a few tunic buttons and badges, a silver sixpence and two pennies. 'I wrote the letter before I went down with fever but can't afford the cost of sending it. Please send it and the locket to my mother when the siege is over. The other bits and pieces are for you.'

'What are you talking about?' said Sarah. 'You can send the letter yourself when you're better.'

He made an attempt to shake his head. 'No, Sarah.' His voice was clear but weak. 'The game's up.'

Sarah had never before heard him utter a despondent word even during the days after he was first admitted to the town hall hospital with his appalling wounds when any thought of survival seemed hopeless. 'Don't talk like that, Tom. You've overcome worse than this. Another couple of days and you'll be well on your way to recovery.'

He clutched his lower stomach. 'There's something wrong.' Sarah reacted immediately. Below the navel his paralysis shielded him from pain but not from the injury or complications it signalled. She whipped back the bedclothes.

'Get Dr. Barlow!' she ordered a nurse preparing the patients' breakfasts. The sheets were smeared in blood where his lower bowel was haemorrhaging through his rectum. 'Hang on, Tom,' she said, cradling his head in her arms but the look on her face confirmed what he already knew. At least one, but probably more, of his ulcers had perforated and he was bleeding to death.

Barlow rushed in and examined Tom but there was nothing he could do. This was a daily occurrence at Intombi but a personal tragedy for Sarah. She had nursed this young boy for four months and had been determined that he would celebrate the lifting of the siege with her but instead of returning home to his mother in Elgin he would be laid to rest in the camp cemetery in the shade of the blue gum trees. His gaunt face looked into her eyes. 'You won't forget the letter and the locket, will you?' he said softly.

'No, Tom. I won't forget.' She held his head under her chin so that he wouldn't see her tears. By the time she had composed herself sufficiently to look down at him his eyes no longer met hers but stared glassily past her.

It was still hot even in the shade of the tent awning but Charlie didn't mind. It was the first time he had been out of bed in three weeks and the tent was hotter, stuffier and smellier. It was also a thoroughfare for scorpions, centipedes and large spiders of which only the convalescent patients seemed to be aware. The other patients were too ill to notice and the nursing staff appeared to have become accustomed to them. As a born and bred Natalian such creatures were nothing new to Sarah who teased him for his squeamishness.

'Any more please, Mrs. Dunkley?' he asked, scooping the last of the paste from the dish and licking the spoon several times. It was only army biscuit pulped with diluted condensed milk but it tasted good. The only problem was that there wasn't enough of it.

'You really are getting better,' said Ada. Charlie hoped so. The effects of the fever had accelerated the weight loss caused by poor diet and reduced rations and he had been shocked to see how thin he had become. He could stretch flaps of skin from almost anywhere on his body and limbs while his ribs and collarbones had become prominent. 'I'm afraid that's it until this evening when you can have another mug of Chevril.'

'Someone must be getting more than their fair share then,' said Charlie with a smile.

She avoided the temptation to tell him that a general order had just been issued reducing the garrison to quarter rations. 'I don't think so, Charles,' she replied lightly.

Charles. She was getting as bad as Sarah. He couldn't even remember his own parents calling him that. He would be the butt of all the jokes if the other lads in the company ever knew people called him Charles. Especially... He paused in his thoughts. He was about to say to himself, 'Especially Walter.'

'The artillery fire's particularly heavy today,' said Ada. 'It won't be long now.' She remained convinced that relief was only a matter of days away but most people had dismissed that as wishful thinking. Hopes had been raised and dashed too many times before.

He heard Sarah's voice giving instructions to an orderly. One advantage of recuperating at Intombi was that he could be close to the woman he loved but on the other hand she had to devote the majority of her time to those patients in most urgent need of care. There was no time to pamper convalescents. 'Enjoy your rest today,' she had told him. 'I'll have you rolling bandages and laying out dressings tomorrow.'

A muffled noise drifted down on the breeze from the edge of Caesar's Camp where Charlie's battalion was still deployed. Gripping the armrests of his chair Charlie forced himself slowly to his feet, his arms shaking with the effort. He and Ada shaded their eyes from the bright sunlight, straining to see what was happening but all they could make out was a cluster of tiny figures waving their arms. 'I wonder what that's all about,' said Charlie.

'Perhaps the relief column is coming,' said Ada. Sarah had told him that Ada had been confidently predicting its imminent arrival each day for the previous two weeks.

'Don't build up your hopes too soon, Mrs. Dunkley.' Charlie didn't want her to suffer the disappointment that had followed when her earlier expectations had been dashed.

Joseph ran towards them, gesticulating wildly. 'Riders,' he said breathlessly.

'Boers?' asked Charlie.

'I don't know.' Word had spread quickly through the hospital camp. Many people had emerged from the tents and everyone's attention had been drawn towards the small ridge below Caesar's. The riders galloped towards the hospital camp and more followed them over the brow of the ridge.

'It's not a patrol returning to Ladysmith,' said Charlie. 'Our horses aren't that fit or in such good condition.' Besides, the patrols could not venture far beyond Intombi and none had passed in the opposite direction that day. He peered again. The riders were wearing slouch hats. So did the Boers. There were no arms in the camp but the staff and patients were in no condition to defend themselves anyway. They would just have to wait.

As the riders approached the camp everyone watching was drawn irresistibly towards them with a mixture of curiosity and trepidation. Charlie's steps were slow and deliberate and Ada easily outpaced him in her eagerness, despite the combination of the heels of her boots and the rutted ground resulting in a curious waddle. By the time Charlie had reached the gathering crowd the first troops had reined in.

More people emerged to swell the crowd, the convalescents with laboured steps but overjoyed faces, as the sound of the cheering rang through the hospital camp. 'The Boers are in full flight,' shouted a lieutenant to a loud cheer. 'The siege is over.'

Ada pushed her way to the front and touched the leg of the young officer. 'Ralph,' she said, as if trying to convince herself it was really him. 'Thank God you're all right.'

He dismounted and hugged her. 'It's good to see you, mother. Father will be back shortly.'

Ada had shed so many tears of grief and sadness over the previous four months but now wept in silent thanks for the safe return of her son and the promise of an early reunification with her husband. 'I have to go now, mother,' said Ralph softly. 'I'm sure we'll see each other again over the next day or so.' Ada reluctantly released her hold allowing him to remount and all but one of the Carbineers rode off towards the town.

The lone trooper reined in beside Charlie as more mounted men from other units followed close behind, cheered on by the ecstatic throng of medical staff, patients and civilians as myriad dust clouds announced their headlong dash into Ladysmith. 'Do you know Nurse Sarah Dyson?'

'Yes. She's in one of the ward tents I think.'

'How is she?'

'Tired and hungry like the rest of us but otherwise fine.' Charlie was about to ask who was enquiring after her when the trooper introduced himself.

'Please tell her that her brother William has passed through and is all right.'

'Of course.'

'Thank you.' William's horse reared up its head and snorted as he dug his heels into its flanks and turned to catch up with his comrades.

'Good luck,' shouted Charlie with a wave of his hand but William had already disappeared beyond his own dust cloud.

Ladysmith
March 1900

It was as if nothing had happened. A thorough cleaning and two days of arduous labour in the gardens was all it had taken to return the Dunkley residence to its pre-siege appearance. Charlie sat on the porch, shaded from the relentless heat of the early afternoon sun and took one last drag from his cigarette. Exhaling a swirl of grey smoke, he ground the stub out in the ashtray by his feet and lay back in his chair. A small lizard on the canopy above him snatched a fly that had ventured too close and resumed its patient, motionless pose.

He heard her footsteps climbing the path and rose to greet her as she came into view. 'Hello, Sarah,' he said simply. She returned his greeting and he kissed her on the lips, lightly at first and then more passionately as she sat on the arms of his chair and put her arms around him. Although they were largely hidden from view from the road they curtailed their embrace spontaneously in mutual embarrassment at their public display of affection.

'Charles,' said Sarah in mock self-chastisement. 'We really should be more discreet.'

Charlie laughed and held her hand, rubbing his thumb across the bridge of her fingers. He looked into her eyes. 'It's lovely to see you again.' She nodded and squeezed his hand. 'Let's go inside,' he said leading her towards the open front door. He was enjoying his convalescence as the guest of the Dunkleys. Many of the recuperating men had been dispersed among the private homes of grateful citizens and Ada had insisted on taking in Charlie.

'Have you heard from Frank?' asked Sarah.

'He called in yesterday. The battalion will be moving out by the end of the month.' Sarah had expected this news sooner or later. Her consolation was that it would be at least another month before Charles was fit to join them. 'They're to be part of the force being assembled to recapture Dundee and clear the Boers completely out of Natal.' His ingrained sense of duty almost made him add that he wished he would be going with them but there was only one place he would rather be and that was with Sarah. There would be time enough in this war for him to discharge his responsibilities to queen and empire again.

The drawing room was as cluttered as it had ever been, the only change being the addition on the hearth of a gilt framed photograph of Grace with a piece of black ribbon across one corner. There was no sign of anyone else. 'Where are Mr. and Mrs. Dunkley?' asked Sarah.

'He had some business in Pietermaritzburg and she went with him.' Ada had hardly let her husband out of her sight since his return. 'They took the early morning train.'

This unremarkable piece of information reactivated their emotions and they fell into each other's embrace. Charlie felt the sweet softness of Sarah's lips against his before probing her mouth with his tongue. He felt her hands caressing the back of his neck as his grip on her waist loosened and he began to stroke her thighs.

She pushed herself closer to him and felt his swelling pressing through his pyjamas and flimsy dressing gown against her lower belly. Her nipples hardened and a warm moistness tingled between her legs. Her desire was as urgent as it was irresitible. 'Yes, Charles,' she whispered.

'Cook is in the kitchen,' said Charlie but this wasn't a deterrent to her. Cook would be too busy to notice and even if she did it would not matter. Within a few short weeks neither of them would still be in Ladysmith and that thought served only to spur her desire. He led her by the hand upstairs past Grace's bedroom, its original purity restored behind the permanently locked door, to his room that once used to be Sarah's. He shut the door behind them and she drew the curtains before they undressed themselves impatiently in their longing to be part of each other's body. His dressing gown and pyjamas almost fell off of their own accord and he stood naked and erect in front of her, helping to pull off her dress and skirts. She could barely wait to be fully undressed and she gripped and stroked his shaft, exposing the swollen extremity. She leaned forward and he gasped as she closed her mouth around it, sucking and licking, giving him a different, but no less pleasurable, sensation than he had known from their first lovemaking.

She loved to pleasure him by any means but she wanted to feel him inside her. She took him from her mouth and gently pushed him back on to the bed. Despite a marked improvement in his condition since the relief his prominent ribs continued to bear the signs of his illness and other privations of the siege. Still wearing her stockings and boots she straddled him and guided him into her soft, wet part. She caught her breath as he entered her, filling her with his firmness, and felt another tingle as he gripped her breasts and stroked her swollen nipples. She moved up and down on him and saw the pleasure she was giving him as he moved with her, thrusting upwards to get as deep inside her as he could.

'I love you, Charles,' she said as she leaned forward to kiss him, her tongue playing with his.

He ran his hands down her back. 'I love you, too, Sarah.' She moved back upright and raised herself until he was almost out of her before plunging back down. The sensation was overwhelming and they both moaned and gasped as she repeated her movements. Their breathing came in shorter, faster bursts until he let out a low, almost animalistic, groan and she suppressed a scream in a mutual explosion of ecstasy.

She leaned forward exhausted and propped her arms against the pillows while he ran his hands through her hair. They looked at each other and kissed again before she uncoupled herself and lay next to him, her head cradled in his arms. He stroked her face and kissed both eyelids. 'Will you marry me, Sarah?'

She ran her hand down an arm that was once muscular and in a couple of months would be once again. 'You can't imagine how much that would mean to me, Charles. I'd be proud to be your wife. Of course I will.' She paused. 'It won't be easy, though. We both know we'll soon be parted until the end of the war.' His recuperation was progressing well and he wouldn't be invalided back to England. He would at least see the war out in South Africa.

'I'll see if we can get married here. I'll speak to Captain Young.' He smiled. 'Frank can be my best man. He'll be thrilled by that.' He looked back into her brown eyes and kissed her lips. He didn't want any other woman but Sarah ever again.

He had been right. It was a white man's war and it had been a white man's siege. The defenders and citizens of Ladysmith had lined Murchison Street for almost two hours as the troops of the relief column marched past and in his official speech Lieutenant-General Sir George White had thanked God they had kept the flag flying. The multiracial euphoria of emerging victorious through shared dangers and hardships nevertheless dissipated with the crowds after the official victory parade as Ladysmith exited the world stage and prepared to return to its former obscurity.

Joseph had volunteered to work with the labour gangs under the direction of the Royal Engineers to repair and reinforce the defence works left behind by the retreating Boers among the outlying hills and to reposition them in a north facing semicircle. The increased mealie ration had not been sufficient to restore him to full strength just yet and he struggled to lift a heavy rock into a cart.

'Get a move on, kaffir, or I'll kick your arse again.' It was the civilian foreman whose ungrateful boot he had felt earlier that morning for having dropped a rock short of the edge of the cart and startled the mule attached to it. This impatient and intolerant man didn't know that he had risked his life running the mails and bringing milk for the sick soldiers or that his testimony at a court martial had helped to save an innocent man's life. He wouldn't care anyway. It was all in the past.

Even many of the townspeople had turned against him with unjustified accusations of profiteering when he was running the mails and even of stealing and hoarding vital supplies. There were rumours that the condensed milk he had brought through the lines and which nearly cost him his life was part of a cache of foodstuffs he had salted away and that he had demanded and received an extortionate payment for them.

He lifted the rock but was unable to reach the lip of the cart and it dropped to the ground. He anticipated the kick that came but was still sent sprawling into the dust. One day, thought Joseph. One day.

Manchester
November 1976

Sally found the song as poignant as it was beautiful. She didn't know if she really heard it everywhere or if it just seemed that way. 'If you leave me now,' they sang, 'you take away the biggest part of me.' She still loved Gerald even though he could be a selfish bastard at times. She didn't want to stand in his way but if he was to go to Canada she wanted to be with him. The song had jumped out at her as soon as she had switched on the ignition and she sat listening to it with the engine ticking over. She flicked on the wipers to sweep away the horse chestnut leaves that the overnight rain had adhered to the windscreen. There was a particularly stubborn one that had lodged right in the driver's line of vision and refused to budge. She sighed. She would have to get out and remove it by hand but not until the inane and irritating disc jockey interrupted the song and talked over the fadeout.

She drove off in the fitful rain past swathes of uniformed schoolchildren huddled up against the swirling wind. More leaves landed on her windscreen but were swept aside by the wipers before they were able to stake a claim. The basis of her article, with a tentative headline of 'Last Boer War VC veteran found in Manchester', had been drafted following the interview the previous day but had to be held over for this evening's issue of the *Echo*. Mike had received Wagstaffe's message late and the old gentleman had become so tired that she had had to cut the interview short before he had finished relating his engrossing story and of course there had been no photographs. She glanced at her watch. She would be there in less than fifteen minutes even with the school traffic and hopefully so would Mike.

She pulled up outside Mrs. Bray's house and decided to wait in the car for Mike. She pushed the button from Radio One to Piccadilly in time to hear the last minute or so of Chicago's love song. She reconsidered her proposed headline. The VC veteran hadn't been found in Manchester. He'd been there all the time. It was just that so few people seemed to know or care. That headline was crap and Wagstaffe wouldn't hesitate to tell her so. She would have to have a rethink.

She heard her name and a tap on the glass. She wound down the steamed up window. 'Hello Mike. Glad you could make it.'

'Don't you start,' he said, shifting the weight of his camera bag as he bobbed down to speak to her. 'I bet you've only just got here yourself.'

She broke into a smile. 'A couple of minutes. We're still on time.' Mike hadn't worked on the *Echo* for long but was a popular choice with most of the reporters for a shared assignment. He was both professional and good company and had a dry sense of humour. Many of the women at the *Echo* also thought he was rather good looking but his rock star long hair and moustache didn't appeal to Sally. Carol had recently admitted to a brief fling with him but the attraction had been purely physical and the affair had fizzled out because she had found him unbearably egocentric and shallow. There again, Sally had thought when she had told her, Carol was notoriously hard to please when it came to men. Those who weren't too clever weren't clever enough so she ended up feeling either threatened or unchallenged. It was little wonder she never stayed in the same relationship for long.

It was like a rerun of the previous day. Mrs. Bray answered the door in the same dark blue dress and yellow apron with her arms covered by the same yellow Marigold gloves. 'Come in,' she said enthusiastically. 'I'm sorry about yesterday but dad does get tired easily and the fall didn't help.' Carol introduced Mike and Mrs. Bray gave him a cautious look that suggested men with such long hair were not the usual sort of visitor to her home. 'Dad,' she announced as she entered the lounge. 'That nice young lady from the *Echo* is here to see you again and she's brought a photographer with her.'

He was sitting in the same armchair and was as immaculately dressed as the previous day. He tried to rise as Sally approached. She signalled with her hand that his gallant gesture of good manners was unnecessary and noticed for the first time the faint scar running across his scalp beneath the sparse hair. He looked about eighty but like many old people had delighted in declaring his true age. God willing, he had told her the previous day, he would celebrate his hundredth birthday the following April. 'Good morning, Mr. Hoyland. It's kind of you to let me talk to you again.' She pointed to Mike who was assembling the flash on his camera. 'Mike has come to take a couple of pictures.' She sat on the settee opposite and Mrs. Bray, minus her apron and gloves, joined her. No doubt she wants to be in the photographs, thought Sally. 'You started to tell me yesterday about your two friends,' she continued. 'One was killed and the other survived.'

Frank thought for a long minute, his memory reaching back to the siege of Ladysmith and the battles before and after it. 'Yes,' he said finally. 'Walter, Walter Shawcross. Now there was a character! Everyone thought he was a born survivor but he was killed in the big battle when the Boers attacked Caesar's Camp.' He paused in remembrance of the vicious hand to hand fighting in the sangar when McAdams was shot dead as he throttled a Boer and the subsequent charge when Walter was killed, Charlie was wounded and he won his Victoria Cross. 'It was such a long time ago,' he said. 'But I can remember every detail as though it happened yesterday.'

'And your friend who survived?'

'Charlie, Charlie Browell,' said Frank. 'The best pal anyone could ever have. He taught me to read and write, you know.'

'What happened to him?'

'Well, firstly he was unjustly accused of murder but at his court martial he was found not guilty and the real murderer committed suicide. Right there in the courtroom. Blew his brains out with a rifle.' Sally busily noted down every detail. 'Then he got sick,' continued Frank. 'Enteric. That's what it was called then but they call it typhoid these days. Men picked it up from contaminated water.' He paused again. 'A lot of them died.'

'But he survived?'

Frank chuckled. 'He not only survived. He even married the girl who nursed him back to health.'

Sally posed her next question as delicately as she could. 'Is he by any chance still alive?'

Frank shook his head. 'No,' he said sadly. 'We remained close friends until he passed away.' He turned to his daughter. 'How long ago was it, Margaret?'

'Thirteen years ago. Just before Christmas.'

'You knew him as well, Mrs. Bray?'

'Of course. He was my father-in-law.' Sally furrowed her brow uncomprehendingly. 'He was the father of my first husband,' she explained. 'My original married name was Browell.' Her demeanour became more solemn. My first husband George, Charlie Browell's son, was killed serving with the RAF in the Second World War. Lost on a bombing mission over Hamburg.' She paused in reflection. 'My second husband passed away three years ago.'

'I'm sorry,' said Sally. It was a feeble and almost worthless commiseration but she never knew what to say in circumstances like this. It was nearly as bad as saying nothing.

Mike was ready and Mrs. Bray perked up. She fetched Frank's medals, all mounted on a bar, for him to wear for the photographs as he had worn them with pride at the remembrance service two days previously and on so many other Remembrance Sundays before that. She offered them first to Sally. 'Would you like to take a closer look? You didn't have time yesterday.'

Sally took them eagerly. There were nine medals with the heads of five sovereigns represented. She correctly assumed that the first bronze cross with the purple ribbon was the Victoria Cross. She turned it over and read Frank's name and regiment on the reverse along with the date '6 Jan. 1900.' The next one bore Queen Victoria's head and clasps with the names Elandslaagte, Defence of Ladysmith and Belfast while the third had King Edward VII's head with the clasps South Africa 1901 and South Africa 1902. She lingered over these attractive silver medals, holding them delicately between her fingers.

'Those are the Queen's and King's South Africa medals. The clasps on the Queen's medal are for the major actions I was in,' said Frank. 'Elandslaagte was where I got this,' he added, inclining his head and pointing to the scar. 'When Charlie and Walter found me they thought I was dead at first. I was in hospital for a while and Sarah, Charlie's future wife, nursed me.' He chuckled. 'I often thought that if I hadn't been wounded they might never have married.'

'But didn't you say she nursed him through typhoid?'

'Yes, but if they hadn't met and fallen in love before that he would have been just one among hundreds of very sick patients.'

'The next three are First World War medals,' said Mrs. Bray, indicating a bronze star, a silver medal bearing the portrait of King George V and a bronze medal with a winged figure. 'The others are for his work as an air raid warden during the blitz and coronation medals for George VI and the present queen.' She pinned them on Frank's blazer and sat on the armrest of the chair as Mike flashed away.

Sally noticed a slightly faded black and white photograph in a frame on the sideboard. It showed two middle-aged couples, arms linked and laughing, on a day out by the seaside. The men had open necked white shirts with the collars outside their jackets and the women wore print dresses and cloche hats. She dated it to some time in the nineteen twenties.

'That's us,' said Frank, seeing that it had caught her attention. 'Charlie and me and our wives,' he added in confirmation. 'Blackpool. Nineteen twenty-four, I think.'

'A long time ago,' said Sally, calculating that her parents hadn't even been born then.

'A long time,' agreed Frank, reflectively.

'And you're the last survivor of the group,' added Sally sympathetically.

'Oh no,' said Frank, brightening up. 'Sarah's still alive.'

Mike was due on another assignment but Sally wasn't going to let him get away that easily. 'You're staying with me until we get a couple of photographs of this old dear,' she insisted. 'It's the least you can do after yesterday.' Mike demurred but knew how persuasive Sally could be and conceded defeat. 'Besides, can you imagine the impact on the Victoria Cross article by including a nurse's story? Wagstaffe will love us for this.'

Mrs. Bray had offered to take them to see Sarah at her ground floor flat in a dedicated senior citizens' complex. She assured them that it was only a short distance from her house and as it had stopped raining they strolled over. 'The warden looks after the old folk but I like to pop round once a day just to make sure Mrs. Browell is all right.'

Sally could hardly credit Mrs. Bray's story of Sarah's existence. Ninety-eight years old, hard of hearing and with failing eyesight, she fiercely protected her independence. She had consistently refused to go into a home or even to lodge with Frank at his daughter's house. Her only concession was on Christmas Day when she joined the family for lunch.

Mrs. Bray rang the doorbell and rapped on the frosted glass in the upper part of the door to the flat. After a few seconds they heard a shuffle from inside. 'Who's there?'

'It's Margaret,' shouted Mrs. Bray. 'I've brought a couple of visitors to see you.' There was a pause as the key turned slowly in old fingers and two heavy bolts were released. The door opened to reveal a stooped old woman clinging to a Zimmer frame. She lifted her head and looked at Sally and Mike.

'Are they from Social Services?' she asked suspiciously. 'I've told you I'm not budging from here.'

'No, they're from the *Echo*.' She introduced them. 'They're doing a story on Frank and would like to talk to you about your experiences in the Boer War.'

Through the thick lenses of her spectacles Sarah squinted at them again and back at Mrs. Bray. 'You'd all better come in then. Make sure they wipe their feet.' She shuffled behind her frame back into the living room and as they followed Sally felt an empathy with this proud and independent old lady. The place was spotless but the furnishings were sparse and mostly old. Displayed on the little sideboard and in a glass cabinet next to it was a scattering of mementoes and ornaments accumulated over the course of the twentieth century and quite possibly before. A watercolour of a high waterfall hung over the sideboard. It was clearly not a British scene and Sally assumed that if it existed at all it must be somewhere in South Africa. No doubt most of her furniture and some of her memories had had to be discarded when she had moved from the family home. Sally imagined the house where she had lived with her husband and brought up her children having become a lonely and unfriendly place where even ordinary features like the stairs or an outhouse would have become a hazard.

Sarah insisted on making a pot of tea and politely but firmly declined Mrs. Bray's offer of help as she plodded into the adjoining kitchenette. Sally imagined the same scenario having been played out countless times over the decade she had been living here. She looked around at the collection of framed photographs on the sideboard. Pictures of children from the sepia tints of the early part of the century to colour prints of modern school photographs testified to at least three generations she had spawned. A recent photograph of a young mother clutching a baby in christening clothes suggested a fourth. Her attention was particularly drawn to the striking clarity of an old photograph of an army sergeant with his slim young bride. The sharpness of the facial details made it look like a modern sepia shot of people dressed in old-fashioned clothes like those novelty photographs one could have taken at certain museums or amusement parks. Mrs. Bray noticed Sally's lingering interest and leaned over. 'That's Sarah and Charlie on their wedding day in South Africa,' she whispered. 'The original was in a bit of a state so we had it restored.'

Abandoning her frame, Sarah lost her grip on the tea tray as she attempted to lift it and it slipped from her hands on to the draining board, slopping tea into the saucers and spilling sugar from the glass bowl. Sally instinctively jumped up to help but immediately wondered if she'd committed a *faux pas*. Sarah was already emptying the spillage into the sink and wiping the saucers. Sally let her finish tidying up before motioning towards the tray. 'I may be a stubborn old woman but I'm not stupid,' said Sarah. 'If you'd be kind enough to carry the tray for me I'd be very grateful. It's a long time since I had more than one visitor so I'm not used to handling a trayful of crockery.'

For nearly an hour both Sally and Mike were captivated by Sarah's memories of the siege of Ladysmith and other events of a war fought three quarters of a century before. Sally was fascinated by her accent which mixed the rounded vowels of the north of England with the clipped enunciation of southern Africa. The resonance of her voice and the clarity of her diction belied her physical frailty as she recalled stories of privation and hardship, the devastation of the typhoid outbreak and the impossible conditions for the medical staff at the hospitals. There were tales of courage and tragedy. The man she fell in love with had to overcome a false murder charge and a potentially fatal bout of enteric fever before becoming her husband and her story of the crucial battle on Caesar's Camp interleaved neatly with Frank's version. 'If the Boers had won that battle, Ladysmith would have fallen,' she told them and challenged them to imagine the consequences on history in that event.

'There was a young Scotsman, a Highlander, whom I nursed and I became particularly attached to him,' she said. She paused in contemplation for some seconds before continuing, the silence exaggerating the tick of the clock on the sideboard. 'He was very badly wounded and paralysed but he was such a fighter that I was sure he would come through it all.' She pulled a handkerchief from the sleeve of her cardigan and dabbed the moist eyes under her spectacles. 'The fever finished him off, though, like it did for so many of those young men.'

She paused again. 'Tom. That was his name. I can't remember his surname.' She sighed and almost imperceptibly shook her head. 'It was all such a long time ago but even now I can still see his face.' She leaned from her chair to open a cupboard in the sideboard and pulled out a rusted yellow tobacco tin bearing a picture of a jaunty bearded sailor. She opened it with some difficulty but Sally resisted the urge to offer assistance. 'Tom gave me these buttons and badges just before he died. The group of medals are my late husband's.'

Sally picked up the mounted group. The Queen's and King's South Africa medals and the First World War medals were identical to those in Frank's group but the first one, where Frank had the Victoria Cross, was different. Suspended from a crimson ribbon with a central dark blue stripe, it bore the head of King Edward VII and the reverse read 'For Distinguished Conduct In The Field.' Sally's attention was drawn to another medal in the tin. 'That's a beautiful medal,' she said. 'May I take a closer look?'

Sarah nodded. 'Of course.'

Sally delicately picked up the silver medal bearing the young head of Queen Victoria and a clasp with the date '1879.' She turned it over where the reverse showed a lion drinking from a waterhole in front of a bush with the words 'South Africa' above. She was attracted by the striking gold ribbon with thin dark blue stripes as much as the beauty of the design of the medal itself. She read the name on the rim, 'H. van Oppen Strydom's Burghers', and asked Sarah where she had obtained it.

'My husband retrieved it from Walter Shawcross's body along with a gold pocket watch he passed on to our son, Margaret's first husband, and a few other odd bits and pieces he had accumulated,' said Sarah. She chuckled. 'It seems that Walter had a few creditors in the battalion and in spite of a minor wound and concussion Charles had the foresight to take possession of them before anyone else did.' Her demeanour became more serious. 'The watch was lost with George when he was shot down over Germany,' she said sadly, becoming lost in her own memories for a few moments. 'Walter was a bit of a character who never let anything get past him if he could help it,' she said finally. 'It seems he took that medal from a Boer's body shortly before he was killed himself.'

Sarah went on to tell them of the Dunkley family and the tragedy that befell them, of the drama of Charles's court martial and Turnbull's suicide. 'What about the blacks?' asked Sally. 'Did they take any part in the war?'

'Oh, yes,' said Sarah. 'Some of them acquitted themselves magnificently. It didn't do them much good, though.' She told them of the dedication and courage of the Indian *dhoolie* bearers but mostly about Joseph. 'He was always a bright one and very brave.' Sally scribbled feverishly as Sarah recounted stories of Joseph's mail runs. 'Many of them died in the war but the blacks never received any official recognition of their loyalty and the risks they took,' said Sarah. 'It was all quickly forgotten.'

'What happened to Joseph?' asked Sally. 'I suppose he just faded away into the background after the war.'

'Not a bit of it,' said Sarah. 'Joseph Ncube became politically active in Natal and was one of the earliest members of the ANC.'

'Joseph Ncube?' mused Sally. 'That name rings a bell.'

'He ran into a lot of trouble with successive National Party governments after the introduction of apartheid and spent much of his later life in jail. He was something of a mentor to Nelson Mandela. After Joseph died Mandela took over his mantle as a high profile prisoner of the regime.'

Sarah's pauses became longer, partly as she pondered over the memories unfurling in her mind of that long ago time but also because she was becoming visibly tired. 'I think we'd best leave it there,' said Mrs. Bray. 'She needs to rest.'

As Mike assembled his camera Mrs. Bray moved towards Sarah, determined to be in these photographs as well. Sally intercepted her and fired off a string of inconsequential questions that would not feature in the article while Mike took some pictures of Sarah alone.

As she thanked her and they prepared to leave, Sally felt Sarah's slight grip on her hand. 'It's a pleasure, my dear. It's not often I get visitors apart from Margaret. Most of my grandchildren and great grandchildren no longer live locally.' Holding on to Sally for support she gently led her towards the array of photographs on the sideboard and picked up her wedding picture. 'Circumstances were against us but we were both committed to each other. We came through it and spent over sixty happy years together.' She gazed fondly at the photograph before turning to face Sally. 'If you love a man enough never let him go, no matter what.'

At her desk Sally looked with satisfaction at the finished article in one of the early editions which appeared under the headline 'They kept the flag flying' with the sub-heading 'Oldest VC and nurse recall the siege of Ladysmith.' Breaking up the text were 'then and now' photographs of Frank and Sarah and a map of the Ladysmith area. At her request Mike had resisted his original impulse to excise Mrs. Bray from the shot he took of Frank after she had dug out and lent them contemporary photographs of Frank and Sarah in uniform. She had after all taken them to see Sarah.

What had originally been intended as a short article had filled an entire inside page thanks to Sarah's perspective complementing and supplementing Frank's account. Harry Wagstaffe came and sat on the edge of her desk. 'Nice job, Sally. The non-combatant angle provides a neat contrast with the VC story, especially as the two of them have family connections.' He tapped the page. 'Your article has already attracted national media interest. BBC and ITV news are both going to feature these old folk in their main bulletins tomorrow night.'

'I enjoyed doing the piece,' said Sally.

'It shows.' Wagstaffe slipped off the desk and scratched the back of his head. 'Come to my office at three o'clock on Friday afternoon. I think I can steer you towards a more rewarding career on the *Echo*.'

'No more talking dogs?'

'No more talking dogs,' agreed Wagstaffe with a smile.

The rain started to fall heavily as she crawled along in the darkness of the early evening exodus from the centre of Manchester and her windscreen wipers thrashed backwards and forwards in a vain attempt to clear her line of vision. She flipped the radio on, subconsciously expecting to hear Chicago. She was disappointed to hear another chart hit but was reassured when it faded out to be replaced by the familiar brass introduction and Peter Cetera's haunting vocals.

As she pulled up in front of the gate leading to the entrance of the converted large terraced house where her flat was situated she saw

Gerald's blue Rover parked ahead underneath a flickering street light. She jumped out of the car and after locking the door ran to the gate. She wasn't avoiding Gerald. She just needed to get out of the pouring rain.

Gerald was at the gate before her. 'Hello, Sally.'

'Hello.'

'About the other night,' Gerald began. 'I'm sorry.'

'So am I. It marked the end of a beautiful relationship.'

'I hope not.' Gerald held out his hand. In his upturned palm was Sally's engagement ring. 'I deserved what you did to me and I'm sorry.'

Sally was oblivious of the driving rain that had already drenched her hair and was running down her face. 'What are you trying to say?'

'This ring is yours and I want you to be mine. I still want us to be married.'

'What about the job in Toronto?'

He shrugged. 'It wouldn't be any fun without you.'

She looked at him, partially silhouetted in the dim street lighting, and felt the irresistible tug of her love for him. 'So are you saying that you want me to join you in Toronto or that you've decided not to go?'

'It's your choice. Whatever you decide.'

Sally hesitated for only a moment before taking the ring from Gerald's still outstretched hand and slipping it on to the third finger of her left hand. She felt herself sinking into his embrace and the warmth of his breath on her mouth as their lips met. 'You know I love you,' she said.

'I love you too. And I nearly lost you. I don't ever want to go through that feeling of emptiness again.'

She grabbed his hand and they hurried up the path to the shelter above the entrance to the flats. As she rummaged in her handbag for the keys he ran his fingers down the side of her wet face. His face was illuminated by the light from the hallway shining through the frosted glass panes in the upper panel of the door. She had no doubt that he was the right man for her and had been as delighted as she was surprised by his unexpected appearance. She opened the door and they shook the excess water from their coats. As they went hand in hand upstairs to her flat she knew that they would enjoy a hot bath together and afterwards make love. Then they would need to have a serious talk. He had said it was her choice, Toronto or Manchester, and she didn't doubt that he meant it. It may well hinge on what Harry Wagstaffe would have to say to her on Friday afternoon, she thought as she threw off her clothes and ran the bath, the roaring surge of the running water failing to drown out the relentless pelting of the rain against the window. Either way it would be her decision.

# ADDENDUM

## Victoria Cross

*Private Francis William Hoyland*

On 6 January 1900 during an attack on Caesar's Camp, Natal, South Africa, Private Hoyland was one of a party of men who held a sangar for over twelve hours against determined enemy attacks. After the rest of their comrades were killed the remaining four men attacked and seized another sangar held by the enemy. Private Hoyland with his corporal and the other surviving private then attacked the heavily defended enemy line on the crest of Caesar's Camp but the private was killed and the corporal wounded almost immediately, leaving Private Hoyland to charge the enemy's position alone. With a total disregard for his own safety he cleared a way through the line and under a heavy fire pursued and accounted for several of the enemy. His selfless courage not only saved a critical situation but also facilitated the clearance of the rest of the crest line by relief troops.

Award notified in the supplement to the London Gazette dated 26 July 1901.

## Distinguished Conduct Medal

*Corporal C. Browell*

Award notified in the supplement to the London Gazette 27 September 1901 and issued under Army Order 15/02 for the Defence of Ladysmith.

## Mentions in Despatches

Extract from Sir George White's despatch dated 23 March 1900.

Corporal C. Browell (promoted Sergeant); Privates. F. Hoyland, W.Shawcross (killed in action), H. McAdams (killed in action).